PRAISE FOR

MERCY

"Everything I want in a book by HelenKay Dimon—emotional, sexy and smart." —*New York Times* bestselling author Jill Shalvis

"From the first page I was hooked. Captivating, steamy, with an intriguing hero and heroine, *Mercy* is one of the best books I've read this year."
—*New York Times* bestselling author Vivian Arend

"Masterful. Edgy. Hot, hot, hot. Read this now."
—Alison Kent, bestselling author

PRAISE FOR THE NOVELS OF HELENKAY DIMON

"She's a delight." —*New York Times* bestselling author Christina Dodd

"Sharp writing and plenty of sexy romantic sizzle." —*Chicago Tribune*

"HelenKay Dimon is a genius." —*Joyfully Reviewed*

"So smart, sexy and fast-paced, I devour her stories."
—*New York Times* bestselling author Lori Foster

"The sex is steamy. The repartee is witty. There are some things in life you can just depend on, thank goodness." —*Dear Author*

"I didn't want to stop reading." —*Smart Bitches, Trashy Books*

"Dimon's fresh new series is enjoyable, and the plot will appeal to many different readers. By turns funny and romantic, the sexual tension between the main characters is portrayed perfectly." —*RT Book Reviews*

Titles by HelenKay Dimon

MERCY

ONLY

ONLY

HelenKay Dimon

HEAT | NEW YORK

THE BERKLEY PUBLISHING GROUP
Published by the Penguin Group
Penguin Group (USA) LLC
375 Hudson Street, New York, New York 10014

USA • Canada • UK • Ireland • Australia • New Zealand • India • South Africa • China

penguin.com

A Penguin Random House Company

This book is an original publication of The Berkley Publishing Group.

Copyright © 2014 by HelenKay Dimon.
Penguin supports copyright. Copyright fuels creativity, encourages diverse voices,
promotes free speech, and creates a vibrant culture. Thank you for buying an authorized
edition of this book and for complying with copyright laws by not reproducing, scanning,
or distributing any part of it in any form without permission. You are supporting writers
and allowing Penguin to continue to publish books for every reader.

HEAT and the HEAT design are trademarks of Penguin Group (USA)

Library of Congress Cataloging-in-Publication Data

Dimon, HelenKay.
Only / HelenKay Dimon.—Heat trade paperback edition.
p. cm.
ISBN 978-0-425-27078-3 (paperback)
I. Title.
PS3604.I467O55 2014
813'.6—dc23
2014012889

PUBLISHING HISTORY
Heat trade paperback edition / October 2014

PRINTED IN THE UNITED STATES OF AMERICA

10 9 8 7 6 5 4 3 2 1

Cover image of "sexy woman" © Leszek Glasner / Shutterstock.
Cover design by Diana Kolsky.
Text design by Kristin del Rosario.

To Kate Duffy,
for starting it all

ACKNOWLEDGMENTS

A quick but heartfelt thank-you to Bree, Viv, Lillie and Jill for giving this one an early read and reassuring me it worked.

While I'd love to take sole credit for this book, it's a group process. It starts with my agent, Laura Bradford, selling it, continues with my wonderful editor Leis Pederson's guidance and edits, and only works because of all the hard work everyone at Berkley puts into making the finished project. And did you see that cover? It's perfect. Thank you to all!

And much love to my husband, James, and my fantastic readers who make it possible for me to do what I love for a living. I appreciate you all.

ONE

Sebastian Jameson sat at his usual table at his regular time at the supper club where he always ate a late dinner during the week. Some would say he was in a rut. Bast preferred to view his schedule as a sign of consistency. After his wild ride of a marriage and equally brain-numbing divorce, he craved a little boredom.

His best friend, Jarrett Holt, owned Holton Woods, the private club at the end of a cul-de-sac in the Dupont Circle neighborhood of Washington, DC. They'd known each other for more than a decade. Up until a month ago, they often shared dinner at the reserved table with the high-backed red-velvet-lined booths to the left of the bar. Then Becca Ford burst back into Jarrett's life like something out of an action movie. Their guys' nights had been taken over ever since, probably with nonstop sex . . . the lucky fucker.

Between his stupid grin and the uncharacteristically upbeat personality, Becca had smoothed out many of Jarrett's rough edges from his long-ago days of running the streets and doing whatever he had to survive. The guy was downright respectable now. He dealt in power and information and his club sat at the center of all of it.

The place also ended up being a great source of business for

Bast. But that's not the main reason he hung out there. It was familiar. Comfortable. The dark interior and high-end finishes appealed to him. So did the women Jarrett hired to serve the members, all of whom were male.

Bast never touched, because that was against the rules, but a guy could admire the combination of sexy, young and smart. Most had advanced degrees. All wore slim black skirts and lacy black bras that peeked out from their unbuttoned white silk shirts. The smokin' uniforms got a man thinking about ripping through the flimsy material with his teeth.

As soon as the idea popped into his head, his gaze strayed to a rather fine ass a few feet away. Long wavy blond hair and those stockings with the seam running down the back of the leg.

Christ, Jarrett knew how to make men happy and earn a lot of money doing it. He became wealthy years ago by having women strip off their clothes in his clubs. Now, keeping the clothes on, teaching his servers—whom he referred to as private attendants—how to get men talking by showing just a hint of the raw sexiness underneath did the job. Bast approved of the change and the business strategy.

He also realized he'd stepped up to the edge of leering and pulled his attention away from those nearby legs. He wasn't a fucking animal, though spending less time with Jarrett and more time sitting there staring at the female attendants was starting to take a toll on the subject of his daydreaming.

The sound of high heels clicking against the hardwood floor had Bast's focus zipping back to the woman. He looked at her face. Round with smooth skin and big chocolate-brown eyes. And very familiar.

Kyra Royer. So fucking hot, too damn young . . . and totally off-limits.

She stepped up to the edge of his table and threw him a welcoming smile. "Good evening, Mr. Jameson."

All the attendants referred to the members by their last name. With respect and enough hotness to, in this case, have Bast fiddling to keep his glasses on his nose. "Kyra?"

"What can I do for you this evening?"

He meant to hold the eye contact. He really did, but that husky voice licked over his balls and the blood rushed right out of his head. His gaze went wandering. The top buttons of her shirt were undone, treating him to a fair amount of smooth skin and an up-close-and-killing-him view of her bra down to the front clasp.

He cleared his throat and forced words to form in his head again. "Put on a sweater."

"What?"

But she knew. That smile told him she knew exactly what she was doing to him. Something about the mix of the provocative outfit and the sweet face had him going under.

"What are you doing here?" he asked because she should be in college, or high school, or wherever young women he shouldn't be allowed to touch hung out.

"Working."

"Here?" He pushed up his glasses again, amazed the lenses hadn't fogged or shattered from the heat pouring off of him. "Since when?"

"Business school costs money."

"Ah, right. You're in graduate school." He'd blocked that part. After Kyra grew up looking like that, with those breasts and that face, he had to think of her as a kid to keep from wondering about what would happen if she wrapped those legs around him and pressed her heels into the small of his back.

She smiled as if she'd read his thoughts. "I start graduate school in the fall, which gets us back to the tuition issue and the explanation for my presence at the club."

"Do you need money?" Because he would write her a fucking

check right now. Whatever it took to remove her from a room full of drooling men. He knew the type because in the last five minutes he'd become one.

Even now he caught the glimpses of club members at nearby tables. Some pretended to continue their conversations while they stole quick peeks at her tight ass. Others all but crawled over and wrapped their arms around her thighs.

Slimy bastards.

He concentrated very hard on not morphing into one. "Kyra, do you need some help?"

"That depends. Are you still talking about money?"

Good fucking question. "Sure."

Her head tilted to the side. "And what exactly are you offering?"

Something screeched to a halt inside his mind. He figured it probably had to do with a sudden loss of brain cells. No way was she suggesting . . . Actually, he had no idea what she was suggesting.

Then there was the very real possibility he'd be killed in the next two seconds if he tried to dig deeper on this topic. "You do know your brother is standing about twenty feet away, right?"

She glanced over her shoulder and gave the brute in question a little wave. "Don't mind him. He likes to hover."

Wade Royer stood behind the bar and managed the club. He looked official and civilized but he once held the role of Jarrett's enforcer. Bast had spent time keeping both men out of jail as they turned respectable and fought to leave their old lives behind.

Back then Wade and Jarrett owned the streets in no small part thanks to Wade's fighting abilities. He was built like a tank but size didn't matter when you had sniper shooting abilities and no compunction about carving up men who you thought did your boss wrong.

Bast tried to imagine what Wade would do to the man who touched his baby sister. Tried and then blocked the bloody images. "Your brother is also an expert with a gun, so let's stick to my questions."

Kyra's smile only widened. "Okay."

"There's no way Jarrett hired you to work here."

The bright wattage slipped a bit. "He was worried about Wade."

Exactly. "About Wade killing someone."

She shook her head and her hair fell around her shoulders. "Jarrett wanted to help Wade get through a tough time."

"Excuse me?"

She sent a second look in the general direction of the bar before turning around again. "Wade had a bad breakup."

"Yeah, I know." No further explanation necessary on that topic. Bast had occupied an unwanted front seat to the mess for the last five weeks. "But I really don't see your brother as the crying-in-his-pudding type."

"He is human."

"Are you sure?" Wade's former live-in lover now worked for Bast. The heat between the men had surprised Bast since he viewed both of them as fighting machines. But their breakup had been of the nuclear variety. Bast still dealt with the fallout on a daily basis.

"So, back to us," she said as her voice dipped even lower.

Bast almost swallowed his tongue. "Us?"

"What do you want from me?" She clasped her hands in front of her. The attendants here didn't carry notepads. They memorized everything and never got a detail wrong.

The move also pressed her breasts closer together, which had his gaze bouncing again, sick prick that he was. "It's probably best I don't answer that."

"My brother won't kill you."

Wade contradicted her comment by slamming a glass against the ornate bar and focusing all his attention on Bast's table.

Bast sat up straighter. "Tell him that."

"You have a drink." She nodded at his half-empty Scotch glass. "Did you also want dinner?"

Bast wanted an explanation for her presence in his place of relative peace and a promise she would be gone from the building soon. A room full of horny old men was not the right job for her. These guys thought they could buy anything and if one of them tried to touch her, Bast vowed to throw off the glasses and start slamming bodies. "Is Jarrett here?"

"He's upstairs with Becca."

Bast blew out a long, hard breath. "Of course he is."

Kyra shot him a don't-be-stupid look. "Jarrett's in love."

"My friend has lost his fucking mind." Over a woman. It was a good thing, but Bast never thought he'd see the day.

"I think we're basically saying the same thing." Kyra let her arms drop to her sides. "Did you want a private room?"

A normal question from the staff at Holton Woods. The club offered rooms for business transactions. For almost whatever a guy needed, except the ultimate release because the women who worked the club were not to be touched—ever.

Still, hearing the words on her lips . . . Bast knew he was never going to survive this conversation.

"No." He adjusted his glasses and tried to blink away the mental images running through his brain. The one about laying her out on the table and giving the room a show was especially persistent. He vowed to revisit that fantasy later, when he was alone in his bedroom.

Her smile never even bobbled. "Then dinner?"

As if he could eat anything. "Yes."

"Do you need a menu or do you want your usual?" Her posture remained perfect and her voice clear, just as she was hired and trained to do.

"I still want to know why, with a business degree in front of you, you're working at a supper club." At *his* club.

"I told you."

Bast glanced at Wade and saw him staring back. "Your brother's delicate feelings. Sure."

Kyra's eyebrow lifted. "Is there a problem?"

About a hundred of them, starting with the fact Bast was thirty-four and had screwed a lot of women. Maybe too many. His ex-wife had literally written a handbook on having threesomes, and all that knowledge came from personal experience. Now most women came to him looking for a specific kind of sex—naughty and temporary. He didn't know what the hell Kyra was looking for.

Her eyebrow stayed up. "Do you want another assistant for the evening?"

A reasonable solution. Send her away and forget about the bra and the exposed skin and that ass. Then Bast saw the judge with the sex-with-his-clerks reputation two tables away wave his hand as if trying to get Kyra's attention.

No fucking way.

"I want your private services," Bast said before he could come up with a better sentence.

Her smile morphed into one of pure feminine power. "That can be arranged."

"So none of these losers comes near you."

"The club has very specific rules about members harassing the staff. I only started on the floor a few nights ago, but my understanding from weeks of training is Becca tightened the restrictions when she moved in with Jarrett and took over security."

Becca changed many things at the club, including Jarrett. Bast approved of them all. "I know. I reviewed the guidelines with her."

Funny how Becca forgot to mention Kyra was coming on board. If Bast had heard that, he would have stopped the idea before it took hold. Even now Kyra didn't move away from the table, which could only mean she had no idea what type of skin-on-skin images flashed through his head.

"I thought you weren't a lawyer," she said.

He did spend a good deal of time saying that, but truth was he was the managing partner of a law firm. Just not the traditional sort. "By training and according to all the nonsense certificates hanging on the wall of my office in frames, I absolutely am. But what I do is negotiate. Solve problems. If a case I'm working on goes to trial, I've failed."

She pressed up tighter against the edge of the table. "Would you like to negotiate now?"

"What?" His hand flexed against the napkin. Only inches separated her body and his fingers.

"With me."

"I . . ." Damn it, no way did he hear that right. "What?"

"You asked that already."

"The way the night's going I might ask it a third time."

The tip of her finger traveled along the edge of the table. "I told you one of the reasons I work here."

An alarm bell rang in his head and the flashing warning light almost blinded him. Still, he kept pushing the boundaries, playing the game. "What's the other?"

"You."

Son of a bitch. "Excuse me?"

"You're here three nights a week, sometimes more. Since you work all the time and we rarely mingle socially, despite having several friends in common, this seemed like the best way to get your attention."

She had to be kidding. "Oh, you have it. Trust me."

"Good."

He waited for common sense to kick in. When it didn't he dragged it out of hiding. "I'm old enough to be your father."

"Only if you became a dad at eleven."

Man, it sounded even worse when she did the math. "You know exactly how old I am?"

"Of course."

"Do you also know your brother, Jarrett and Becca—those people we have in common—would get together and beat me to death if I said hello to you the wrong way?" That very event could happen within the next ten minutes. All of them had weapons training, and Becca used to kill for a living. Bast didn't even want to know how far Wade and Jarrett had gone to get things done in their old jobs on the wrong side of the law.

Kyra winked. "Then it's a good thing they aren't here."

Okay, time to backtrack and laugh all this off. "I'm sure I'm misunderstanding you, but—"

"You aren't."

So much for laughing. Hell, Bast could barely breathe and his pants were strangling his dick. "This can't happen, Kyra. Nothing can happen between us."

"I notice none of your excuses for us remaining apart center on attraction."

"What does that even mean?" But he knew.

"Are you attracted to me?"

"I'm not blind." A complete fucking dumbass on the verge of doing something epically stupid, but not blind.

"Then we don't have a problem." Her smile promised sex.

The sudden thumping in his dick suggested his lower half was totally on board with the idea. "Right, we have many problems. There's club policy, my personal code, the fury of everyone we know and the possibility of my impending death at your brother's hands." He ticked off the list of cons, then searched his brain for more reasons to add.

"Go back." Her eyes narrowed. "Personal code?"

Bast noticed the biggest "con" of all headed straight for the table at what felt like a hundred miles an hour. Thinking about Wade had conjured him up. In what looked like two steps, Wade was at the table, right at his sister's side.

He angled his shoulders so he stood just slightly in front of Kyra. "Is there a problem over here?"

Kyra jumped in without skipping a beat. "Mr. Jameson didn't know I was working here."

Yeah about that. "You okay with the arrangement?" Bast asked Wade.

"With douchebags staring at my baby sister's chest? No." Wade kept his focus on Bast as he said it. He didn't look around or point to some of the more troublesome members.

Subtle. "Okay then."

Kyra waved the warning off. "Wade doesn't mean you."

With that Kyra proved she wasn't picking up on the cues. That was fine because Bast surely was.

Wade shrugged. "I didn't actually exclude him."

With a hand on his arm, Kyra motioned toward the other side of the room. "Wade, I believe you're wanted at the bar."

Silence vibrated around the three of them. Wade finally shifted and broke the standoff. "Okay, but move this along."

She nodded. "Sure."

A few more beats of silence passed before Wade nodded and turned away. He stopped to talk to Kyra. "There are other customers and I'm sure Bast has work to do."

Bast watched the other man leave and knew messing with this guy's sister would result in a trip to the emergency room. Yesterday, hell a half hour ago, Bast would have said no thanks to the risk. But Kyra stood there, being cryptic, but not really, and Bast's good intentions imploded.

"Do you?" she asked.

He had no idea what the question was, so he went with the one running in his head. "Want to die? No."

"You haven't told me what I can do for you this evening."

She had to know what she was doing to him. About how hard his dick was and how he couldn't stand up any time soon. "This isn't—"

"Right now I'm talking about the club, Mr. Jameson. Drinks, dinner, a private room. Some gambling. What do you need?"

The sexy smile and the way it lit up her face did him in. "Heart medicine."

"I'll order your regular meal." But she didn't leave. "But we still have the other issue to handle. The private one."

"Okay," he said because despite making a living at talking, he had no idea what else to say.

Her palm flattened against the table as she leaned in. Just for a second, but it was a definite lean combined with a deadly sexy voice. "Consider this my move."

She couldn't mean . . . "What?"

"Now you know what I am willing to do to see more of you. I tracked you down, took this job and stated my case. And I am happy to do whatever you want within certain rules."

He tried to say something but only a strangled sound came out.

She straightened. "The rest is up to you. You get to show me what, if anything, you plan to do to see more of me."

"I don't think—"

"Yes, Sebastian. Stop thinking." Then she was off, those sexy hips swishing as she went.

TWO

Kyra didn't know how she got through the rest of her shift after making her big play. Leaving Bast's table, her legs shook and her heartbeat thundered in her ears. Not that he even noticed the effect he had on her body. After their initial skirmish, he sat and ate and read paperwork for hours, hanging around until Jarrett came on the floor and joined him for a drink.

When Bast finally left the club, the trapped air rushed out of her lungs. Everything about him caused her insides to tighten and her mind to spin. She'd planned the moment—the confrontation—for weeks. Taking a job to chase after a man was not her usual style, but then no man had ever played duck-and-run with her quite like this one. And no matter how hard she tried, she couldn't get him out of her head.

While walking up to the table and laying out her case, she could see him mentally draft a list of reasons why he needed to maintain a hands-off policy. He'd been doing that for a year, walking out of a room when she walked in, his gaze lingering just long enough to give her hope. But the panic in his eyes tonight, complete with that sexy low voice, convinced her to move in now instead of waiting for him to get a clue.

She might be young in his eyes but she knew what she wanted, and for more than six months the "what" was Sebastian Jameson.

He'd certainly kept her mind off the rest of the crowd at work all night. Evading the guy whose entire smooth-talking repertoire consisted of smarmy winks and wandering hands got old fast once Bast walked out. At one point the guy promised her a job where she could be on her back most of the day. She somehow saved the eye rolling for her trips to the kitchen, but just barely.

Thinking about the lame line and the way she pretended not to hear it—both times the douche said it—had her smiling as she walked out of the club and headed for the small employee parking lot next door. A shadow fell in front of her right as she cleared the brick wall and turned the corner. Tension pounded her but quickly evaporated. She'd know that scent anywhere. Something smoky with a touch of citrus.

Bast frowned down at her. "What are you doing?"

At six-one, he managed to tower over her. Her spiky high heels brought her close to his height but she'd exchanged them and her stockings for flats and now the five-inch difference had her backbone straightening. So did his attitude. "Walking."

"Wade lets you dance around out here at night without an escort?"

That seemed like a little much. "Dance?"

"Fill in whatever word you want then answer the question."

Never mind that she stood inside a high-walled fence and locked well-lit pathway that ran directly from the side of the club to employee parking, or that even now Becca watched over them from her office and the bank of monitors she installed to ensure the staff's safety. "I'm a grown woman, Bast. I tried to explain that to you earlier."

"When you made your offer."

Despite the late hour, or early hour to be technically correct, car horns honked and tires screeched in the distance as DC nightlife roared with life only a few streets away. But all of the noise and mumbling faded as she stared into those intelligent green eyes. The Ivy League buttoned-up type never did it for her before Bast. With him, the clean-cut, wire-rimmed-glasses look had her wanting to strip his tie off and drill down to the naughty center underneath.

His light brown hair, all trim and perfect, begged for her fingers. And if the rumors around town were to be believed, this man knew his way around a woman and what to do to get one naked. Man, she hoped that part was true.

Not that she only wanted a turn in his bed, a quick in and out. No, when she looked at Bast the longing kicked in until her breath stammered in her chest. He made her wish she were someone else, someone like him with his stable upbringing and fancy job. Since all the degrees and polish in the world couldn't clean up her past, she'd settle for making a move and taking what she could get.

But first they had to scale whatever defensive walls he planned to throw up between them. "How did you slip inside the gate?"

Bast waved the comment off. "Jarrett gave me the code."

Not a surprise. They were as close as brothers and Bast practically spent every evening at the club. The idea of him enjoying some member benefits others didn't wasn't a surprise.

Still . . . "That really doesn't explain your presence right now. At the club. On the property." Waiting for her long after he slipped out of the building.

In the universe of good signs, she figured this had to be one, but bit down on the inside of her cheek to keep from smiling. Bast stood there, all commanding and sure, but she sensed inside he ran scared. She recognized twitchy panic when she saw it and he had a heaping dose of it.

"I'm parked at the far end," he said.

She had no idea how that was relevant to anything, so she circled back to her point. "You left the club more than an hour ago but you didn't actually leave the parking lot."

"I wanted to talk with you."

Fighting for calm and ignoring her jumping pulse, she leaned back until her shoulders hit the brick wall. Much more of this and she'd chew through her cheek.

Thinking this might take some time, she dropped her gym bag on the ground. "About?"

His frown moved into full-on scowl territory. "Are you kidding?"

But he moved in closer. One palm smacked against the wall by her head and his face hovered just inches from hers.

They were so close, with the darkness curling around them and his body cast in shadows from the security lights, but she could see that face. Make out every expression. She wanted to wrap her fingers in that crisp white shirt and pull him in and against her, but she waited. Knowing him, the commonsense lawyer side of him could take over at any time and mess this forward progress up.

She balled her hands into fists by her sides . . . and waited. "If this is the point where you mention my age and talk about my brother and how afraid you are of him—"

"Okay, that's enough of that. I am not afraid."

"—then let me stop you." She rushed on, pretending she hadn't stomped all over Bast's ego by accident. "Wade is not out here and I assure you I am of legal age."

"I know."

Well now . . . She dropped her head down. "For anything."

The words whispered across his cheek and he visibly swallowed. Even in the darkness the bobble of his Adam's apple stuck out. "I've done the calculations."

This guy had a thing for math. "Interesting."

"I'm not sure that's how I view the eleven-year difference."

She almost wished he couldn't add. "I make my own decisions. I go after what I want. What I want right now is you."

"For?"

"Oh, come on." She treated him to a "don't be an idiot" eye roll to keep from saying the words. "Now who's kidding?"

His second hand slapped against the wall, trapping and sur-rounding her. "Everything about this is wrong."

There, in the cocoon of his body, with his suit jacket hanging open and the heat pounding off his body into hers, everything felt pretty damn right to her. "I disagree."

"Are you looking for a threesome? Is that what this is about, you trying something new? Wanting some big thrill with the guy who has a reputation for liking sex with more than one woman at a time?"

The words crashed over her in an icy wave, washing away every sexy thought and replacing them with fury. "No."

"Maybe you want to try some toys or new positions. We could set up a camera . . ."

This time she did touch him. She put both hands against his chest and shoved. "What is wrong with you?"

He didn't move. "Don't act like you don't know what I'm talking about. People like to gossip about how dirty I am in the sack. Women volunteer to join me just to get a taste. I'm guessing that's what this is. You want your turn."

"You're jumping to conclusions."

"Do you blame me? That was a pretty heavy pass and you've never shown any interest before."

The man was clueless and right on the border of being an ass. "Clearly you haven't been paying attention."

If he heard her, he didn't let it show. His words tripped over each other as he talked right past her. "I can only guess you want a wild ride and are looking to me to get you there. Strip you naked, maybe call in a friend to make the night extra special. That's the expectation, right?"

Something in his voice broke through her flashing anger. His eyes had turned as dark as his mood, but a note lingered. An emotion tripping around the edges that sounded oddly like pain.

The realization sucked the anger, and some of the life, right out of her. "You're not even close."

"You have to know about my past."

It took three swallows for her to kick out a word. "Yes."

One of her hands dropped to her side and the other trailed down his firm chest, sliding along his tie, until he caught it in his. She noticed he didn't let go. Instead, his fingers slipped through hers.

"Exactly my point." The heat had left his voice but the husky vibration remained.

"Everyone knows. Your ex-wife wrote a book." Kyra almost hated to point out that fact, but it sat between them, so why not deal with it.

"Two." He trailed his thumb along the back of her hand.

Once, twice . . . all the blood left her head. "What?"

"My ex wrote a handbook on living a threesome lifestyle and then she wrote a novel where the couple happened to be in a threesome." He held up two fingers. "Two books. One that ended nasty and rough."

Kyra could barely hear him over the thumping of her heartbeat echoing in her brain. "Right."

"The latter is fiction. Most people miss that small but very important fact."

"The husband in the novel is a dick." Kyra regretted the comment as soon as it was out.

"That is the general consensus, yes," Bast said as he lifted their joined hands.

She knew from Jarrett this qualified as a sore subject for Bast, and the last five minutes highlighted that point. Jarrett insisted Bast treated his ex well and she crapped all over him, though the language Jarrett used was much more colorful.

Her fingertips brushed along Bast's chin. "The man described in the novel isn't you."

Somehow she got the comment out. Through the rush in her ears and the thundering in her chest, she found the right words. That guy, the one people whispered about, the one who shoved his wife around and made sexual demands that scared her wasn't real and couldn't be Bast.

Kyra didn't trust many people, but for some reason she trusted Bast to be decent. Maybe it stemmed from his friendship with Jarrett and Wade, or how he acted in the club. She didn't analyze her certainty. She just knew she wanted to show him not all women operated like his ex.

"Lena makes it clear in the acknowledgments the book is fiction and not a memoir, but I'm thinking readers skip those, at least that's what my emails and disappointed calls from my father suggest."

Father, yeah, there was a subject sure to suck any sexuality out of the moment. And that is not what Kyra had planned for the next few minutes.

Despite the detour, she needed to stop and make Bast understand one simple thing. "I didn't."

His eyes narrowed. "What?"

"Skip the acknowledgments."

His expression went blank. All emotion wiped clean and he stared at her with flat lips and dull eyes. "So, you really did read the whole book?"

There was no use dodging now, and she was determined they would be honest with each other, no matter how much moments like these hurt. "Yes."

"Right." He pushed off from the wall and stepped back. Two feet of warm summer heat pulsed between them. "Everyone else in town did, so why not you."

The shuttered expression, the emotional distance, dropping her hand. He was shutting down and she didn't know how to get them back to where they were a minute ago. "I know the difference between fact and fiction."

He shoved his hands in his pants pockets. "Did you read the handbook, too?"

"No." And that was the truth. She had zero interest in reading a manual about his sex life with his ex. About his sex life with anyone but her. "I assume that part, whatever is in the handbook, is real."

He shrugged. "In a sense."

She had no idea what that meant. "Then I was right not to read it."

He stopped putting more space between them. At her comment, he shifted, moving in closer as he leaned. "I'm not following you."

"I wanted to get to know you and not the version of who you were when you were married." Despite what he thought, she wasn't looking for a good time or to reenact one of the more descriptive chapters. She wanted him, with her, alone and uncontrolled until neither of them could walk.

Voices grew louder as a group of young males headed into the cul-de-sac. With every stumbling step they took, she held her breath, sure being interrupted would be just the excuse Bast needed to run. When the guys broke into drunken laughter and a chorus of some song that sounded vaguely familiar, she stiffened and waited.

Tripping and wailing, they hit the first driveway and looked around. Then the shoving started. One after the other shouted about the "right address" but when the security light of the first building on the street popped on, the guys turned and took off.

And Bast wondered why she wasn't interested in guys her age.

At least the light meant crisis averted. Now she had to figure out how to keep Bast engaged. She feared losing him now could mean losing any forward momentum.

But he didn't step back. "Maybe the guy in the marriage and the guy in the novel are the same guy."

No way did she believe that. He grumbled about the rumors of his sex life, but clearly missed the ones about him getting sick of a life he never wanted and getting out of the marriage rather than continuing with the fun. Kyra held on to those and hoped those strayed closer to the truth.

"Why did you leave your wife?" Inside Kyra winced at her clumsy delivery. The answer wasn't really her business, yet it meant everything.

Bast didn't squirm or get angry. He just stood there, calm and in control, just like the Bast she knew.

"How do you know she didn't leave me?" he asked.

"As you said before, we know a lot of the same people. They talk."

His control slipped a fraction as his eyes grew wide. "About my private life?" He threw up his hands. "That's just fucking fabulous."

To a guy like Bast, all proper and educated, having his sex life blared in headlines and people snickering as they passed around stories had to be a huge blow. She felt for him but she had no idea how to make it better. Not yet. Not while they were apart. But she did know what she wanted. "Also, so we're clear, I don't have any interest in threesomes or sharing you with anyone else."

He went still. "What if that's my thing?"

"Then I'm not your girl." Everything, all her plans and how much she ached to be with him, depended on his next response to keep the dreams alive and breathing.

"Kyra . . ." He adjusted his glasses even though they hadn't moved. "Look, we—"

"No. Don't feed me a line." She rushed to stop whatever awful thing he might say to kill her attraction. "And don't try to scare me off, because I don't think you're interested in threesomes either."

"That comment makes me wonder how much you know about men."

"Enough to keep one satisfied." She waited for the disappointment to skate across his face but his expression stayed the same.

If anything, the corner of his mouth lifted just a bit. "That's quite an answer."

No name-calling or prodding for information. It was a nice change. The guys she dated before expected her to be virginal yet somehow experienced. To deliver the perfect blowjob yet never have given one before. The sexual double-talk struck her as ridiculous and immature, and she expected more from Bast.

Fact was she grew up knowing while men focused on her body, she could use her mind to wallop them. Her father brought her on jobs back when she was in her early teens and put her in situations she pretended she could handle. Or he did until Wade found out she'd started in the family crime business and threatened to rip their dad apart.

While her upbringing wasn't one she ever would have chosen, she refused to shut down her sexual side now. She didn't have Bast's vast experience, but she'd been around enough to know what she did and didn't like. And how to make a grown man squirm.

Her fingertips traced the line of his jaw. "I could show you what I want from you."

"In the parking lot?"

"Just a taste." Whether she could stop there was the real question. Forget the street noise and club looming behind her. She'd been dreaming about kissing him, touching him, for so long she didn't know if she could stop once she started down that road.

"You actually think it will end there?" he asked, sounding stunned at the possibility.

Looked like she wasn't the only one doubting her control. If he could step inside her body and feel the tremor shaking through her, he'd know how much of the act consisted of bluster and spit.

"I've told you my terms. Made it clear the next move is yours." When his eyes narrowed and his feet started shuffling again, she wrapped a hand around the back of his neck. "But I'm thinking you may need an incentive."

"You are very wrong on that score."

At least he'd stopped denying. It would be nice if he threw the switch and started acting, but she'd take the lead if she had to. "You're the city's king of negotiation, right?"

He chuckled. "Not the title I'd use, but let's say yes."

She blocked the sexy smile playing on his lips and the whir of a siren through the neighborhood. "Here's my argument."

She didn't hesitate or wait for him to make a move. She swooped in, with both hands on his cheeks and her mouth falling over his. Kissing him long and deep, she let the aching she fought off each night seep into her cells and burst to life against him.

At first he stood still, his shoulders straight and his head slightly dipped from the force of her palms on his face. Then he shifted as his hands moved over her. Along her back and down her spine to tighten on her ass. A second later a hand clenched against her hip and brought her body tight against his.

The heat spiraled around her as the force of his need drove her hard against the wall behind her. Those fingers danced over her clothes, burning a path until she feared the material might catch fire. When she broke away to steal a breath, his mouth followed and covered hers again. His lips traveled and his tongue dipped inside her mouth to mate with hers.

Dizzy and short of breath, her world spun until all the blood left her head. His fingertips brushed the side of her face while something tugged at her skirt. The warm night breeze caressed her legs as her skirt slid higher on her thighs and a deep, almost rusty groan vibrated against her lips.

The haze cleared long enough for her to feel the trail of his fingers over her skin. She opened her legs a little wider and those knowing fingertips brushed against the thin fabric of her tiny panties. She was wet and ready, and the lace proved no barrier to his searching hand. A finger ran along the seam between her legs, pushing the cloth inside her. The rough friction against her sensitive flesh had her gulping in air.

She could smell her body readying for him and feel the hard steel of his erection against her stomach. A warning flashed in her head, something she needed to remember but couldn't grab onto.

Then as quickly as the kiss turned nuclear it, along with all the touching, stopped. Their rough breathing filled the air as the sounds of the city floated back to her. The cars and low mumble of voices in the distance. They stood in the open, shielded by a wall and fence but little else. Despite that, her control faltered and she almost grabbed him close again. Probably would have if he hadn't dropped his forehead to rest against hers.

His chest rose and fell as his words pushed out in staccato beats. "Jesus, I'm practically fucking you in a parking lot."

"Not quite." But so close and with all the passion she'd hoped he kept chained up inside him. "I guess that confirms the attraction goes both ways."

"Hell yeah it does." His breath rumbled as the words blew over her hair.

She laughed but the sound cut off as reality came rushing back and smacked right into her stomach with enough force to double her over. The club, the security. The cameras. Without meaning to, they were giving Becca a show.

Kyra tried to clear her throat but something stuck there. "We should . . ."

"What?"

If she told him about the unintended audience, he'd balk. Might even leave the state on a trumped-up work trip to stay away from her. She could not allow that. Not when they were so close.

Kyra pushed the potential surveillance video out of her mind. She'd deal with the ramifications and her new boss later. Right now she had to deal with the stunned man in front of her. "You okay?"

He kept his head balanced against hers and shifted his weight so his lower body lifted away from her, but not by much. "My hand is still inside you."

"Was." She already missed the warmth of his touch.

At her words his hand slid over her upper thigh. Another tug and he freed it from the tangle of her skirt and let it drop to his side. "Admittedly, your argument about us being together is persuasive."

"Good." In his frenzy to touch her, the material of her skirt had wrapped around her hips. Hitting him with an accidental elbow, she pulled and yanked until she brought the edge to a respectable length again, or at least one that didn't show off the tiny straps of her lace underwear.

"You're killing me here." He pulled back and watched every move, every shimmy. "I'm ten seconds from throwing you in the back of my car and putting my mouth all over you."

She heard the clunk as her lungs shut down. A list of very sexy possibilities ran through her head. She could go for it like her lower half begged her to do or she could build the excitement. Her body screamed for the first choice but she knew that would lead to quick and dirty sex, the type that happened once, and she wanted way more than one time with him.

Inhaling as much air as possible and hoping the oxygen would feed her brain cells, she brushed her hands against her skirt one last time and straightened her shoulders. "I should go."

"What?" He practically yelled the word in her face.

For some reason his rapid blinking and shocked tone told her she'd made the right decision to step away now in favor of something bigger later. "Good night."

She tried to pivot around him on shaky legs but he caught her arm and held her close. For a second he didn't say anything. Just stared and frowned and generally telegraphed an I'm-not-happy vibe.

"You're leaving now?"

The word "no" popped into her head but she pushed it out. "Yes."

This was the right answer. He needed time and she needed a few inches of space. Stretching their time together into more than one night meant making him understand wanting him and falling into his bed when he blinked the right way were two different things. A slight distinction, maybe, but one that mattered to her.

"Is this some sort of game?" His fingers tightened on her arm, not to the point of pain but firm enough to hold her attention. "If so, you should know I fucking hate games. I had enough during my marriage to last a lifetime."

Kyra pulled his fingers off one at a time. "Honestly, Bast. I've made this pretty easy for you."

"I don't think you're easy."

Not what she meant, but she'd take it as a compliment and move on. "A woman wants a man to work for it. Just a little."

He shot her the same look he might have given if she'd grown a second head out of her armpit. "That's nothing more than a waste of our time."

With one last deep breath she took her stand. "It's your turn."

"To what? What are we even talking about?"

The poor thing, with his dropped eyebrows and frown, looked truly confused. As if women usually just stripped off their clothing and climbed on top of him when he flashed that crooked smile. If they did, she didn't want to know.

Through the attraction zipping between them and the lingering memory of that heart-stopping kiss, she knew he'd only move forward if she doubled back. "Getting what you want will mean more if I don't just fall in your lap."

He treated her to a second round of staring without talking. Finally, he let out a huffing breath. "So that we're clear, you will eventually crawl into my lap if I ask you to, right?"

Lap, chair, bed, kitchen floor. She'd dreamed about every scenario. "I will do whatever you want—and I mean whatever—so long as we're together one-on-one. No one else."

After a brief hesitation, he lifted his hand. He didn't pull it back. It just hovered there between their bodies. "If the goal was to gain my undivided attention, I promise you have it."

About time he noticed her as something other than Wade's baby sister or a petty thief's daughter. Still, it wasn't nearly enough. "I want to be your only."

"I thought I followed you until right there . . ."

The whole clueless-guy thing didn't really suit him. She saw the gate come down and the heat leave his eyes and decided she liked the commitment fear even less than the cluelessness. "You're a really smart guy, Bast. I have every faith you'll figure it out."

His arm dropped without reaching out or touching her. "Why not work out the particulars now?"

Because one more minute and she'd be on top of him with her wet panties around her ankles. "Soon."

Before he could argue or circle back and remind her of their age difference, she took a step. Her legs wobbled and her stomach flipped, but she forced her feet to move. His gaze burned into her back as she moved, but she kept going because she didn't need another look. She already knew the truth: she was his.

THREE

Bast spent the next day in his office and on the phone, but the memory of Kyra's hot mouth and the taste of her on his fingers picked at his concentration. Twelve hours of analyzing documents and attending meetings couldn't extinguish his sudden pounding need for her.

He shifted in his chair and thought about routine things like mergers gone wrong and clients in trouble, but her face kept popping into his mind. Before now he viewed her as sexy but untouchable. Having trailed his hands all over her, all he could think about was what it would feel like to plunge inside her. And unless he'd lost his ability to read a woman or understand a conversation, she was offering him exactly that.

No wonder his concentration was so fucked up.

The sirens squealing on K Street eight floors below his corner office grabbed his attention. This area of DC played home to lobbyists and think tanks. He looked out the scaling windows and saw the red brake lights from lines of traffic. The prestigious business address put him in the middle of the action and impressed clients as much as the pricey artwork on the walls in the reception area. He found that part of the game to be necessary bullshit, much like the big office with the leather couch and chairs.

The dark furniture, the walls lined with bookcases and that fancy Oriental rug his ex-wife had insisted he purchase all fit with his image as a powerbroker in a town knee-deep with them. He had an advantage. He'd grown up privileged, attended the right schools and married his college sweetheart.

He played the game right up until he committed the cardinal sin of getting a divorce. Then his proper father launched an all-out propaganda war that cost Bast his fancy high-end law firm job, though many in town thought the fight said something about the size of Bast's balls. He capitalized on the support and spun it into a lucrative career.

Now he worked in an office he helped build and managed as a partner. One that thrived thanks to his billable hours and ability to wrangle his way through any situation. Even though he was a lawyer, he stayed out of the courtroom. Instead, he negotiated deals on behalf of his clients that he never dreamed he'd see.

Like his best friend, Jarrett, Bast dealt in information, most of it confidential and some of it top-secret. The type that would impress his old man, if they ever bothered to talk to each other.

Despite all the trappings and healthy bank accounts he'd stock-piled, all Bast could focus on at the moment was the raggedy blue bag with the ripped seams sitting next to his antique desk. Kyra dropped it last night on the walkway when she wrapped her arms around him. Now he had an excuse to seek her out on his terms.

He'd fought the temptation all night. Convinced his brain that his body was out of line and she was off-limits. Maybe he could blame the lack of sleep, but by morning he'd outlined an impressive "pro" list that included everything from "she approached him" to "he wanted to say yes." The mere idea of taking Kyra up on the offer was dumb and self-destructive, two things he normally avoided, despite what his father might think. Being with her couldn't lead anywhere and might alienate people he cared about, but he had to believe he could handle all those negatives.

The door opened after one firm knock. "You wanted to see me?"

Bast glanced up in time to see Elijah Sterling, the newest member of the staff, walk in and shut the door behind him. Tall and lean, he radiated confidence even though he spent most of the day alone in an office. His Japanese mother had gifted him with his coal-black hair. An operation gone wrong from his time working for the Central Intelligence Agency gave him the faint scar along his jawline.

Coming off an attempt on his life and a violent disassembling of his undercover team that left only two alive—he and Becca— Eli was raw. Giving him a job and putting him in charge of surveillance and information gathering for the firm qualified as a risk, but Bast recognized a man who needed a true purpose. He'd seen it in Jarrett's eyes a decade before and hoped Eli's transition from trained killer to civilian would go half as well.

But the information Bast had to deliver threatened any progress. "We had a call from Natalie Udall."

Elijah didn't flinch. Didn't show any reaction. Just stood with his arms folded in front of him. "That sounds bad."

Bast drummed his fingers against the desk. When the tapping started clicking in his head, he stopped. He didn't have many nervous reactions because he didn't really get nervous about much, but tapping meant his mind was racing and he needed it to stop for second.

He motioned across the table. "Take a seat."

This time Elijah exhaled. "So, it's really bad then."

"She's leaving the company." For some reason the word sounded better than "CIA" in Bast's head.

The chair creaked as Eli sat down. "Okay."

"She's basically being run out." Which was a nice way of saying she could be in the type of danger that ended with two bullets to the brain and a phony obituary talking about a sudden heart attack.

Eli picked at the seam on the armrest where the leather and wood met. "How does that impact me?"

Bast watched Eli's fingers move. Looked like they both had a problem with wandering minds. "I think you know."

"Because she took care of Todd?"

The word choice impressed Bast. Natalie had run Elijah's team, at that time called Spectrum Industries and posing as a legitimate satellite company, even though it was an illegal op. The CIA didn't have the authority to investigate U.S. citizens without a foreign threat. When the team leader, Todd Rivers, went bad, he tried to cover his tracks by wiping out Spectrum agents and shifting the blame to Becca. Natalie put an end to Todd and made it possible, with Bast's negotiating assistance, for Becca and Eli to escape a life of being tracked and hunted.

Now it looked like the CIA higher-ups wanted to clean up the mess by dumping it at Natalie's feet. If true, she'd become a burnable asset and that meant her life didn't mean shit to her bosses.

"Natalie did make it possible for you and Becca to get away." Not that Elijah needed that reminder, but Bast offered it anyway. "Apparently there are some who think people with your talents shouldn't just be able to just quit the CIA."

Elijah smiled. It was a rare sight and only lasted a second. "Go figure."

"Well, you did pretend to be dead a few months ago." All while hiding out in the living quarters above Jarrett's club and investigating why life had blown up.

Bast still couldn't believe Jarrett had stepped up to help after Becca and Elijah's team had Jarrett arrested on trumped-up drug charges. But that happened more than nine months ago and was all resolved now. Jarrett had clearly forgiven Becca for double-crossing him, proving love was more than blind. It might just be stupid.

"I keep wondering why I bothered to stop pretending," Elijah said.

"To work here with me, of course."

Elijah snorted. "Right."

"Anyway, Natalie is coming in to see me in a few days." Bast watched for any signs of anger or panic but Eli had been well-trained to hide those, along with every other emotion bouncing around inside of him. That detachment saved his life many times but Bast knew it cost Eli something, too.

Eli leaned forward with his elbows balanced on his knees. "Why are you telling me all of this?"

"You know how this works. As we hammer out a deal for Natalie, other problems will come up. Your safety could be at issue because someone might want to blow your deal apart."

Elijah tapped his fingertips together. "I can handle myself."

The man had sniper skills and once commented on killing a guy with a pen, so Bast didn't doubt the statement that from other men would be nothing more than a burst of empty ego. "No question, but I want us to be extra careful."

Eli's expression morphed from blank to questioning. His head tilted as he frowned. "Why do I think you're leaving out some important facts here?"

Bast now knew what a bug felt like under a microscope. It wasn't as if he could just spill what happened with Kyra and what might happen soon with Kyra and how that might add her to the list of people who needed protecting.

He fought to keep from shifting around in his chair. He was the boss after all. "Once I see Natalie I'll have a better idea what we're dealing with. Until then, stick close."

"You think they'll come after you?"

The guy was missing the main point of this little meeting. "No, Eli. After you."

Eli slumped back in the chair. "Nothing about Natalie and her bunch scares me. I fought them once and won."

"They tried to kill you, you crawled to Jarrett for help and he shot you. That was before you spent months hiding on his second floor."

"Your point?"

Bast did a mental pivot and tried again. "There are other people involved."

Eli's mouth fell into a flat line. "You mean Wade?"

There it was. Eli's great weakness. Not that he'd ever admit it. "Yes, and Becca and Jarrett. All of them. Anyone related to the original deal that freed you and Becca from CIA service."

"You may have missed the big news, but Wade and I aren't exactly on speaking terms."

No, they were too busy being locked in a battle of wills. They'd lived together, slept together, in Wade's apartment in Jarrett's building for all those months. Then they broke up and the ground still shook over the fallout. "I'm aware."

"Someone else will need to worry about him." Eli's expression didn't change but pain flashed in his eyes.

Bast shook his head. "You're not as hard to read as you think."

"Meaning?"

Bast wanted to put Wade and Elijah in a room and let them work it out, but neither man would cede an inch. "I'll ignore that question for now since you could probably kill me with a stapler if I gave you a truthful answer."

"With my finger, actually." Elijah blew out a long breath as he stared at the ceiling. When he met Bast's gaze again, his mask of indifference was firmly back in place. "Maybe Jarrett could convince Becca and Wade to hang around the club and limit their activities to the building."

"It might come to that. I just wanted you to know something big and pretty terrifying could be coming. Again."

"Fair enough." With a nod, Elijah stood up. No fanfare or questions about what to do next. He wasn't the typical employee. He instinctively knew what was needed and willingly put in long hours to get there.

Bast waited until Eli's hand hit the doorknob to exit the office. "Eli?"

He glanced over his shoulder. "Yeah?"

"I'm going to the club soon. You're welcome to join me for dinner. Maybe we could give Jarrett a head's-up while we're there." Bast made the food offer at least once a week. Matchmaking wasn't his thing but if throwing Wade and Eli together worked to break through the impasse, Bast was all for it.

Eli's frown came back. "You're eating this early?"

That was the problem with having a smart former undercover agent on the payroll. They saw through the bullshit to the agenda underneath.

"I need to drop something off." And that was all Bast planned on sharing on that score. Life was convoluted enough without having to explain to Eli about wanting to have sex with his former lover's baby sister. Yeah, their social circle was a bit too tight. "Yes or no, Eli?"

He shrugged. "If you're paying, I'm in."

"Happy to know you can be bought."

Eli's sly smile came and went again. "When I want to be."

Kyra rushed around her studio apartment, first in bare feet then on her knees. Throwing one shoe over her shoulder, then another, she crawled along the slim strip of hardwood between the bed and the closet, ignoring the way the floor dug into her skin and searching for her weirdly comfortable spiky black heels.

First her missing stockings and now this. She only had so many work outfits for the club and what she had to wear on duty was pretty specific. Becca and Jarrett supplied the store account to get the right clothing and provided a credit card for the more personal parts of her required outfit each night, but the shoes were a carryover from her life before the club. Becca approved them, which worked for Kyra since they had these special cushy pads inside. Now she had to find them.

Last night she'd taken the pumps off at the club and put on her flats and . . . damn.

She sat back on her heels as she remembered dropping the bag in the parking lot. She let it go so she could grab onto Bast instead. She refused to question her priorities but this did cause a logistics problem.

Scrambling to her feet, she got up and slid the mirrored closet door open. She scanned the floor looking through the piles of shoes for something suitably sexy that she could stand in for hours on end. She didn't have the opening shift at the club, but it was Friday, which meant she closed tonight. It also meant being on her feet until she thought they'd fall off.

She snapped up a pair of open-toe sling-backs she hadn't work-tested yet. "I can't worry about that now."

She turned around to hunt for her backup stockings and plowed right into Gena McBride, her neighbor from across the hall. Gena stood almost six feet tall with short black hair in a bob and a skirt she dyed herself but looked like it could hang on the rack in any high-end store.

Kyra thought of her friend as this Amazonian goddess with an art degree. She'd been out of school for a year and earned enough freelancing to live in a matching studio in the building, only two blocks from the center of the George Washington University campus. No bad for the free-spirited, no-ties type.

Kyra didn't have many female friends. Growing up with a

father who made a living on the wrong side of the law and kept her insulated from all but his closest deputies messed with her bonding skills. Then there was the problem where she made what she thought was a great friend freshman year of undergrad who turned out to be a plant from her father, watching and reporting back to him from the life he did not approve of for her.

"I'm sorry but I'm late." Kyra reached around Gena and tugged on the drawer, opening it just wide enough to slip out the unopened hosiery package.

"You're making me dizzy." Gena lifted her hands in the air and plunked down on the bed and out of the way. And since the apartment consisted of a bed, a double chair, a kitchenette and little else, being in the way was pretty easy if more than one person was involved.

Gena leaned back with her palms against the mattress. "Are you really not going to tell me what happened last night?"

Kyra ruthlessly valued her privacy but recently opened up to Gena. Five months of tiptoeing around a friendship could do that. They didn't yet have a revolving-door policy, but close. Gena had a key and some idea about Kyra's love life plans.

Kyra wrinkled up her nose as she debated how much to divulge now. She trusted Gena but this thing with Bast, whatever it was, was so new and not defined. Hell, it might not even get off the ground, but not for lack of trying on her part. "I got one step closer."

"Really?" Gena's mouth dropped open. "To this Sebastian guy?"

Not the biggest vote of confidence, but Kyra ignored that. "He goes by Bast."

"One step meaning you kissed him or one step meaning you can accurately report on whether the rumors about him are true?"

Kyra stopped spinning around, looking for another gym bag, and stared at her friend. Kyra saw concern and something else lingering behind those big blue eyes. "Not you, too."

"I own a computer and know how to use it." Gena tapped her forehead as she talked. "You gave me his name a few weeks ago and I looked him up. Not like it was hard. The guy is all over the Internet. There are interviews with his wife."

"Ex," Kyra said, jumping in before Gena finished her sentence. "That's an important distinction."

"My point is, the guy is notorious."

Taking an extra second she didn't have, Kyra dropped the stuff weighing down her arms and sat down next to Gena. "How much do you think is real?"

"Is that your plan? To find out?"

That sounded like Bast talking. Kyra didn't like the theory no matter who said it. "I'm not looking to be a chapter in the next book."

"Then what do you want?" Gena reached over and picked up Kyra's hand.

"Him. Every inch of him."

The unconditional affection was one of the things Kyra loved about her friend. Her mother had died before Kyra hit elementary school and her father believed in ruling by intimidation, so openness was pretty foreign to her. Gena touched and hugged everyone. Something Kyra took a while to get used to and which still caused her to involuntarily tense at times.

Gena stilled. "Wait a second."

Kyra's fingers went numb from the force of Gena's squeezing. "Uh, ow."

"This is real?"

Kyra tugged her hand out of the vise grip and shook it to get the blood flowing again. "What's wrong with you?"

"I thought this was some fancy crush. That you wanted to check him out because you were curious but he didn't actually mean anything to you." Gena got up and paced to the small chest of drawers across from the end of the bed.

Something weird happened in the last two seconds and Kyra wasn't sure what. "Wrong."

Gena looked at her hands then the floor. Everywhere but up. "Kyra, I . . ."

"Say it."

"I'm worried about you." Gena faced Kyra now. "This guy seems like the type who will have some fun then move on fast."

So, that's what friendly concern felt like. Kyra didn't hate the sensation though Gena could work on her delivery a bit. "I hope not."

"You're thinking long term? God, Kyra. I had no idea this was more than a crush on a powerful guy you happened to know."

When Gena continued to look as if she'd swallowed rotten fish, Kyra stood up and went to her. "Hey, you really are worried about me, aren't you? Don't be. I know the downside. I've thought this through."

"Of course."

Reality was she'd been taking care of herself for a long time. Wade had stepped up and rescued her from what would have been a rough life, likely pawned off on one of her dad's underlings and running the streets looking for marks. Wade insisted on helping pay for college and she worked to save the rest, even taking time off to stockpile some cash. Wade's only requirement was that she stay away from their father. Wade just had no idea how hard that was.

For the first time that she could remember, Kyra reached out and touched Gena's shoulder. "Trust me. I have this under control."

Gena's pained expression didn't ease. "Just be careful."

FOUR

Bast put his briefcase down in the booth at his usual table and gave Elijah the okay to order whatever he wanted. Bast had one more piece of business before he could go in search of Kyra. He almost hoped she didn't work tonight because being off meant more touching, and right now he couldn't think of much else.

Then Becca motioned for him to meet her across the dining room. She leaned against the doorframe leading to the back office hallway. As usual in the club, she wore a sleek formfitting dress, this time dark blue. It hugged every curve and stopped right above her knee. The thing probably drove Jarrett to total distraction. Her brown hair flowed in waves over her breasts and that face had more than one man in the room risking Jarrett's wrath to take a peek.

What none of the men here knew was her background as a CIA field agent. She'd been trained to infiltrate, and collect and decipher information. To do whatever she had to do to get the job done, including killing, which was one of her specialty areas. Next to Eli, she was the most dangerous person in the room, and that was saying something since high-ranking government officials with the president's ear sat scattered around the room at private tables.

The Becca Bast knew preferred cargo pants and T-shirts to fancy dresses but she knew how to play the game and fit in. They'd had a rocky start since she once sent Jarrett to jail, and that shoved Bast's trust of her past the breaking point, but he'd grown to like her. She stepped up and fought for Jarrett instead of leaving him about a month ago. She put his safety before her own, and Jarrett loved her so much he couldn't see straight. That last reason was good enough for Bast to give her a second chance.

He slipped in next to her and surveyed the room. "I'm not used to the early crowd."

"It's almost seven."

He winked at her. "Like I said, early."

A smile lit up her face. "Thanks for stopping by on such short notice."

She'd called as he left the office. Her request for a meeting worked perfectly for cover with his plans to track down Kyra. "I'd planned to eat here tonight anyway."

Becca nodded in the general direction of Bast's regular table. "I see you brought Elijah."

"Is that a problem?" Bast knew all about Elijah and Becca's rough history. He'd heard them yell at each other more than once, but that hadn't happened in weeks.

"Not for me, though I think he still hates me." Her smile didn't falter as she said it. "I'm impressed with how you cleaned him up. The dress pants and blazer are nice touches. He no longer looks ready to kill someone every second. That's progress of a sort."

"If you say so."

Word was Becca and Elijah butted heads even when they worked together at the CIA. Then there was a day more than a month ago when Bast walked in to find them locked in battle, with Elijah pulling a gun on Jarrett and Becca pulling a few weapons of her own. The whole scene still made Bast chuckle, but only because

Jarrett defused it and no one actually got shot. Which was nothing short of a miracle.

Bast watched now as Elijah tried not to look over at the bar and the man behind it. Eli paged through a folder and glanced at his phone. Did everything to look disinterested in his surroundings, which Bast knew not to be true.

After a short time working together, Bast realized Eli constantly soaked in information. Probably part of his training but a really helpful gift. Bast doubted Eli could turn that off just because he sat in the club.

It was a real shame none of those skills Elijah collected had to do with being a people pleaser. "I've discovered Eli is not a big fan of humans in general."

"Except Wade."

Bast's gaze shot over to the man in question, the same man sneaking peeks in Elijah's direction. The two men went to great lengths not to notice each other. Never mind that each had stopped cold when their gazes met a few minutes ago. No way had that attraction died.

Bast exhaled. "Right, except Wade. Not that Elijah admits to his feelings on that score."

"The lovesick staring gives him away." Becca leaned forward and looked around Bast at Wade. "Both of them. They're making me nuts with this."

"Is this why you called me here? Are you matchmaking?" Not really his expertise, but if she wanted to try, Bast figured he could help. If only to stop the pathetic displays of masculine stupidity.

"Actually, I wanted to talk about club security," she said.

Now that subject sat well within Bast's comfort zone. "Did something happen?"

"This is more of a coverage question."

He listened but his gaze kept sweeping the room for any sign of the sexy blonde who had his nuts in a grinder. "Go ahead."

"You know how I wanted to make sure the staff was protected as much as possible from the wandering hands of members and any potential problems leaving the club at night." Becca had insisted on greater protections for the women who worked at the club, the same ones who already thought Jarrett did a good job watching over them. Making them an even bigger priority won the immediate loyalty of all. Becca then insisted Jarrett cough up the funds to do whatever she wanted.

Bast doubted the convincing was all that hard. "Sure."

"We increased security and added the locked walkway to the employee parking lot to prevent run-ins with drunks stumbling out of nearby bars." She turned so she faced Bast. "See, the thing I forgot to share with you is how I installed all of these extra cameras. Some you wouldn't even notice if you were looking at them because they're hidden. One of those tricks from my old job."

He was smart enough to listen to the alarm bells ringing in his head and treaded carefully. "Okay."

"I'm wondering if, as a result of these cameras, I have a problem."

"How so?"

"Liability."

Not what he expected her to say. Then again, he wasn't totally sure where she was going with this. Becca didn't rush into anything and talked all of her plans over with him and Jarrett first. So, whatever she was poking around here involved something else and Bast didn't know what. "You lost me."

"Well, there's no warning to people that they're being taped." She crossed her arms over her chest and leaned a shoulder against the wall. "So, let's say a member with access to the staff parking lot stops one of our female attendants and kisses her. Shoves her up against the wall and basically climbs all over her."

Son of a bitch. "Listen, I think—"

"Nuh-uh." Becca waved a finger in front of his face. "Interrupting me right now is not a good idea."

It was the way she said it that had his jaw snapping shut. "Go ahead."

"You know the type of touching I mean. Complete with putting his hands up her skirt and only stopping a short step away from carrying her to his car and screwing her there."

This time he didn't wait. She might carry a gun, but he had limits on how much of his personal life he wanted batted around. "I know what you think you saw."

"I saw you stick your tongue down Kyra's throat as your hands disappeared in her underwear." When he started to talk, Becca cut him off with a slice of her hand through the air. "I can only assume from that behavior that you've forgotten I used to kill for a living and that Wade will rip through you like paper."

"Trust me I am aware of all those possibilities." And was kind of sick of hearing and thinking about them.

"Then what's with the sudden bout of idiocy?"

The nasty words rushed up on him. The biting retort about the choices she'd made in her love life and how much she'd fucked up her relationship with Jarrett before she set it right.

But he skipped the personal jab and reined in the anger threatening to explode inside him. Because that's what he did. That's how he operated. He maintained his control and generally won his arguments. "Frankly, this isn't your business."

"I disagree."

"We're not debating the point."

"Interesting approach." Becca eyed him up. "The tough talk. Not how I thought you'd handle this."

"What did you think I'd say?"

Her stance relaxed a bit. "Denial, whining. It's amazing what some men do when cornered."

"None of that is my style." This time he cut Becca off before she started talking again. "And Kyra is a grown-up."

"One I happen to like very much."

"Me, too."

Becca snorted. "Obviously."

The conversation had passed the point of annoying him. "I mean as a friend."

"You tongue all your female friends?"

He decided to ignore that since it was a legitimate shot in light of the parking lot kiss. "Admittedly, what happened shouldn't have happened in public, or at least not in direct line of a camera. For that I apologize. But when it comes to my love life, to whatever role Kyra plays in it, this conversation is over."

"Maybe I disagree."

"Unlike my ex, I do not kiss and tell. Ever."

"Don't mess with her, Bast." Becca's shoulders fell as she rested a hand on his arm. "If you play around and string Kyra along, even Jarrett is going to come down on your head."

"Did you tell him what you saw?" Not that it mattered. Bast didn't need to run his love life by Jarrett for permission, but he did want to be the one to tell his best friend before any gossip reached him.

Problem was Bast didn't even know if there was something to talk about yet. Becca rammed into the middle of what amounted to one kiss. A fucking spectacular kiss, but that was all. Bast could still turn this around and walk away.

Not that he intended to do that. Not after a long night thinking about Kyra.

"Jarrett's been busy dealing with a member who's on the verge of bankruptcy and wants to throw around what little money he has here instead of on his family." Becca rolled her eyes as she said it. She worked with Jarrett and Wade and managed many of the business's aspects now, but she'd been clear that she found many of the members to be hypocritical windbags.

Bast didn't disagree.

"People make bad decisions all the time. That's what pays my fees." If people started acting smarter, he'd have to find a new career, and he had zero interest in that.

"Which brings us back to the Kyra situation."

Not in Bast's mind. He glanced around, making sure Wade and Eli stayed locked in a non-staring contest rather than noticing him. "Like I said, that subject is closed."

Becca squeezed Bast's arm then let go. "I admire the fact you're sticking up to me. It's a little stupid since I could kill you in about two seconds, but you haven't cut me any slack from the beginning. I've always liked that about you. That and your loyalty to Jarrett."

With that Bast could feel the tension leave the room. The tightness winding around them eased and they returned to the relaxed conversation he'd grown to enjoy with her. "Is that all it took to win you over?"

"Who says you have?"

For the first time in a few minutes, he felt like smiling. "I think you're softening. It's the glasses, right?"

"More like the big brain."

"Thank you."

"Your don't-mess-with-my-sex-life position gives me hope you're not playing games with Kyra."

He sobered. "I'm not."

"Whether you are or not, Wade is going to kill you."

Bast looked over in time to see some man approach Wade at the bar. The guy looked familiar and Wade sure seemed happy to see him. Or as happy as Wade ever looked. "Absolutely, yes. I'm sure that's going to happen."

"Thanks to your swift negotiating skills I'm alive and not on the run. I'm here with Jarrett at the club and in his bed instead of in witness protection somewhere. I get that you helped save me from a life in hiding and appreciate all of your work. If I didn't, you wouldn't be breathing right now."

This was the Becca Bast had come to know. The woman Jarrett loved—smart, independent and fierce. "It's always good to reach an understanding."

"But now I'm wondering if what everyone says about you is correct."

He almost hated to ask. "And that is?"

"That you're almost always the smartest man in the room."

Overeducated people ran all around DC. Those first few times with those early clients, he'd been in the right place at the right time with the right degree to take advantage of career opportunities. Since then he learned how to stay in the fray and be there to clean up the mess. And DC's powerful did like to make a mess.

"That's a vast overstatement." Bast had heard the comment often enough and always ignored it.

"For your sake, let's hope not." She winked at him then disappeared into the private hallway.

FIVE

Breaking in a new pair of stockings qualified as one of Kyra's less favorite things. She stood in front of her wood-paneled locker at the club and smoothed her hands up her calf to her knee, straightening the seam up the back of her leg. With her right foot balanced on the bench, she pushed the hem of her skirt high on her thighs and slipped her thumb under the elastic band at the top.

"If I had known you were wearing those last night, I would have stripped them off you with my teeth."

At the sound of Bast's voice, she spun around and shoved her skirt down at the same time. "What are you doing back here?"

"I believe you said the next move was mine."

The words turned her body into a trembling mess. Her temperature spiked even as a tremor shook her. Every nerve ending sparked to life right when she needed to concentrate on getting through a shift.

With her already running a few minutes late, his timing needed work, but then again, she suspected this was a calculated move. One to make sure she knew who was in charge. "Now?"

"Belonging to me means all the time. On my schedule. In any way I want."

It was a good thing she had both feet on the floor because the room bobbled a bit. If he hoped to shake her up or scare her, he failed. His comment started a revving deep inside her that she longed to satisfy.

Gathering her control, she peeked around the corner into the next locker bay. Running late meant she was alone or had been until five seconds ago. "Becca will strangle you if she finds you in here."

Bast pushed off from the door and walked toward her. "Becca and I have come to an understanding."

"About?"

"Her place in my sex life." Bast stopped right in front of Kyra. Didn't reach out or touch but stood there with his presence filling every open inch of the room. "For the record, she does not have one."

The man talked in sentences she couldn't always decipher. This time she thought she knew. "And you had some sort of discussion with her that made that clear?"

"I'll explain later."

But he wasn't the only intelligent one in the room. She didn't claim his killer IQ, but street smarts had helped her survive this far. "I'm guessing she saw us on the security cameras and confronted you."

His head pushed back. "You knew she could see us?"

"I forgot about the added layers of protection until after." Kyra put a hand on his arm and let her fingers rest against the expensive fabric of his suit jacket. She guessed the gesture looked loving but she'd really planted her body there in case he bolted after her admission. "What exactly did she say to you? No threats, I hope."

"I can handle her."

Kyra assumed that meant threats. "Tell me."

"The usual 'I'll spill your blood and hide the body' stuff."

Instead of running, he slipped his hands around her waist and pulled her in tight against him.

This close Kyra could see the bright green of his eyes and smell the soap on his skin. "Are you upset?"

"About?"

"Becca knowing."

One of his hands slid over Kyra's skirt to cup her ass. "I'd rather talk about your choice of undergarments."

She was two seconds from stripping them off. "Someone could walk in."

"I'm a problem solver, so let me fix that issue before it consumes you."

The second he backed away, a rush of air hit her skin and punched her lungs. She didn't know she'd been holding her breath until she ended up with empty arms. She wanted to call him back but the sound of squeaky wheels broke her concentration.

As she watched, he rolled over the towel cart and tucked the metal edge under the door handle. Also did a quick look around the shower area in the back.

"Yeah, jamming the door won't bring attention to you being in here. Not suspect at all." But the man was on a mission and since getting to her seemed to be the end goal she did not argue. If he wanted to take the risk, she would stand right by his side . . . or wrap her body around his and ride it out.

His gaze zipped back to hers. "Want me to leave?"

"No."

"Good." He took off his black jacket and draped it over one of the benches. "Then stop talking."

The man still had the tie and shirt on, every inch of skin stayed covered, but being one layer closer made her breath hitch. She'd probably have a heart attack when he finally stripped down to nothing.

"This is how it will be between us." His hands came around

her and settled on her lower back with his mouth dancing around the edges of hers.

"With you in charge?"

"You won't be able to hide from me," he whispered between delicate kisses.

"And you want secrecy." Her fingernails dug into his crisp white shirt until she hit the muscles of his forearms.

"Compliance and discretion, yes."

"I'm not balking at those terms."

His lips went to her neck, lightly grazing until every nerve ending inside her tingled. She tried to pull him in and bring his mouth back to hers but he seduced her with firm hands and soft caresses.

"But you're still talking." His hot mouth moved behind her ear. "I would rather have your mouth on mine."

She started to agree but he shifted and his lips covered hers. This kiss rivaled then surpassed the one from last night. Hot and deep, flaming through her and driving out every other thought. With his hands on her ass, he pulled her lower body tight against him as his mouth branded her.

Her balance teetered and her skin heated. Through the waves of aching need pummeling her, she held on, gripping his broad shoulders as she balanced on tiptoes. The kiss continued with his head moving from side to side and no inch of her mouth going untasted.

But he didn't stop there. Her skirt slid up the back of her legs and she broke off the kiss. Safe in the circle of his arms, she stared at his flushed face. Ran a fingertip over that sexy mouth.

He walked his fingers down the back of her thighs as he slipped to the bench and sat down almost beneath her. "Are you wearing underwear, Kyra?"

"Yes." She didn't recognize the breathy sound as her voice.

Brushing his hands up this time, he lifted her slim skirt. Clothing rustled as the material slid against her stockings. He bunched the hem in his fist and gathered the bulk near her waist. The move left her lower body open to his gaze and his appreciation of her body on full display.

He smiled as he ran the fingertips of his free hand over the front of her black bikini bottoms. "Pretty."

"I thought of you when I picked them out tonight." Which was the truth. She'd hit the end of the week and the choices came down to practical or sexy. Picturing him, she went with the black and planned on spending a little time this evening imagining him peeling them down her legs.

"Take them off."

She shook her head, sure she missed something. "What?"

His thumb slipped to her entrance and danced across the thin material. "I think you heard me."

She struggled to catch her breath. To hold on to a thought for more than a second. "I'm working."

"And I want to sit out there in my booth knowing you're walking around bare."

"Bast, you can't mean . . ."

"You won't wear anything when you stay at my house."

She planned on holding him to that promise . . . just not here. "That's in private."

"I've made myself clear."

With any other man she'd think this amounted to a test to check her resolve. Not Bast. He touched her and watched her and meant every word. He was letting her know his expectations and leaving it to her to figure out if she could handle them.

Well, she had something to prove as well. "You do it."

He glanced up at her and shot her the kind of smile that made a woman feel wanted and powerful.

"That's a very good start." His palm slipped up high on her thigh and his fingers eased under the edge of the elastic. With a tug, he had the material over her ass and caught in the wedge between her legs.

As the silk rolled down, her vision blurred. She tried to say something—anything—and the words caught in her throat.

"Open up." He leaned in and placed a sweet kiss on the slim line of hair that covered her. "I can smell you."

Her heart pounded hard enough to muffle the sound of his voice in her ears. Yet somehow she obeyed. Shaky and on the verge of falling into his lap, she moved one foot to the side.

The material slipped down but she barely felt it. Once he pressed a palm to her, she had to use all her energy to stay on her feet. Brushing back and forth, he caught her skin on fire. Her hips lifted forward as if begging his fingers to plunge inside.

He glanced up again. "Do you need to come before you go out on the floor?"

The words slammed into her. She knew he would be like this, sexy and open, bawdy and so damn hot her brain would fry. Saying no to him, holding any sort of line, was going to be so hard when all she wanted to do was surrender.

But a room full of obnoxious men sat not far away and she had to be careful. "I can't—"

"I'm pretty sure you can." One of his fingers, long and lean, slipped inside her. "You feel like you need to come."

Her hips rocked in time with the gentle back and forth inside her. "I'm already running late."

"You're wet." His other hand rubbed her against her ass, pulling her forward. "Can you work in this state? Right on the edge."

Before she could say anything, his tongue swept over her. The combination of mouth and fingers took her mind to another place. She forgot about the mumble of the crowd and Becca's wrath. The club, her shift, none of it mattered in that second. Not when he licked her, dipping his tongue in deeper and blazing a trail through her wetness.

"Ah, so that's what you need." He took off his glasses and put them on the bench beside him as the whispered words rumbled against her clit.

Her head dropped forward and her hands slid into his hair. One knee gave way as her bones turned to mush. If he hadn't been touching her, holding her, she might have melted into a puddle at his feet. Instead, she felt him turn her. Without any help from her, he raised her leg and moved until she straddled the bench and his legs.

The new position left her totally open to him and he took advantage. His mouth worked on her as his fingers held her open. His tongue rotated around her clit and she grabbed onto his shoulders to keep from ending up on the floor.

The friction of fingertips and sleek tongue had her hips bucking and her breath hiccupping in her chest. She wanted him to plunge in deeper, to ride him. To feel him inside her. But he kept rubbing her sensitive flesh until her body tightened around his fingers. The constant torment had waves of heat crashing over her and her body moving without any direction from her head.

She tried to beg for more but the last of her air rushed out of her. Those inner muscles clenched and her blood pulsed. The orgasm hit her as she balanced her weight against him. She wanted to sit down, hold him—something—but he didn't let her. He kept her on her feet with his fingers planted inside her.

After what felt like an hour, the sensations eased and her eyes opened again. She still stood in the middle of the locker room . . . with her panties on the floor.

She looked down in time to see him move his hand. Her wetness glistened on his fingers. She almost lost it when he touched the tip to his lips.

"Very nice." The corner of his mouth lifted as he looked up at her. "Feel better now? If so, you should tell me so I know for next time."

And to think he worried about being older. This man would be able to keep up with her just fine.

"Yes, thank you."

"So polite." He chuckled as he stood up. After smoothing down her skirt, he kept his hands on her hips, holding her steady. "And thank you, but next time you'll scream my name."

Her nerve endings jumped as if begging for more and the room smelled like sex. The bulge in Bast's dress pants didn't leave a lot to the imagination either.

She nodded in the general direction of his pants. "Do you want me to take care of you?"

"Not this time." He reached for his glasses and put them back on.

She glanced again at the tiny scrap of black material by her foot. Thought about the hours ahead of her and how hard it would be to push the memory of this moment out of her head during that time. "What if the other club members can tell I'm naked under the skirt?"

He walked over to the sink and washed his hands and made a scene of drying them. When he turned around, he held a tissue for her. "Only I'll know."

That sounded like wishful thinking to her. And *she* would know, which could mess up her concentration. Some idiot could end up with ice in his drink by accident and then the world would end because these guys insisted on perfect service. Always.

Not that she regretted any second or the smug look of satisfaction on Bast's face. She put that there and she would keep it there.

She took the tissue and balled it in her fist. "Does this mean you're really taking me up on my offer?"

"What do you think?" He put his hands in his pockets, which only highlighted his impressive erection.

Rather than evade, she stared at it, letting him know she intended to be as active as him during the sex. "You want me."

"That's no secret."

The attention proved intoxicating. Having him focus on her turned out to be an even bigger rush than she expected, but she had to know he understood her terms. "You get that I insist on being your only?"

"I heard your requirements."

She wasn't totally convinced they'd agreed on anything but she refused to ruin the moment figuring out his verbal gymnastics. "Is that what you came to tell me tonight? That we're on."

This time he broke into a full laugh. "No. I didn't come for any of this, but I did enjoy that last part."

It seemed indelicate to give herself a cheer, so she refrained. "Okay."

He picked up his jacket and shrugged his way into it. With a few steps, he stopped at her underwear. Without any fanfare, he picked up the black silk and slipped it in his pocket. "I have your bag. I wanted to get it back to you. Seeing you was the bonus."

She stood there like an idiot, not moving or speaking until he raised an eyebrow. "Oh . . . yeah. Right. The bag. I wondered where it got to."

With his hand out, he stood in front of her. "Give me your keys and I'll put it in your car."

Never mind the fact she had to bite her lip to keep from chanting his name a few minutes ago, or how he stuffed her panties in his jacket. The conversation was so normal. So mundane. Something people dating might talk about and it threw her off.

"Kyra, you're going to trust me to enter your body, I think you can trust me with your keys."

"Right." Still she couldn't figure out how to move.

He snapped his fingers. "Hello?"

The clicking sound broke through thoughts barraging her brain. "It's not that."

Not that she could tell him where her thoughts had wandered. She'd barely gotten him on board for an offer of unlimited sex. One whiff of the word "relationship" and he would bolt. No way did she want that.

"Then what's wrong?" he asked.

But she could give him something to think about while she walked around the club half naked. If she was going to feel uncomfortable and on display, so was he. "I want you outside of this building. Over me. Inside of me."

Heat flashed in his eyes. "Soon."

She opened her locker and dug around her purse for her keys. The move seemed to take forever but she knew it was more like seconds. Turning, she returned to him. The keys jangled when she reached over and dropped the chain into his jacket pocket.

"I thought you'd want to spend more time with me . . . what was the word you used?" Refusing to move back, she straightened his tie, taking her time with the task and making sure her body rubbed against his. "Bare."

"Oh, you will be naked." That sexy voice had plunged even deeper.

"Good." The word didn't come close to expressing how she felt or the nerves jumping around in her stomach.

"Oh, I'm betting it's going to be great." His satisfied expression didn't change. "Slip me your phone numbers at some point tonight."

If she waited one more minute before going out on the floor she'd likely get fired. Worse, Becca could come hunting for her.

Despite the risks, Kyra couldn't drag her mind away from Bast and to where it should be. "Will you call me tonight?"

"We'll see each other tomorrow."

Close enough plus the delay would give her time to look perfect. "What do we do about Becca?"

"You worry about pleasing me and I'll take care of everything else." He cupped the back of her head in his palm and treated her to a lingering kiss.

Just when Kyra lifted her hands to join in, he broke away. He went to the door and removed his impromptu lock. After a quick glance both ways down the hallway, he stepped out.

She didn't want it to end, so she called him back. "One request."

He looked at her over his shoulder. "Yes?"

"When you finally get naked for me, wear the glasses."

His smile promised the scenario would be happening very soon. "They turn you on?"

"Everything about you does."

"Good to know." He winked at her and left.

It took her another few minutes to adjust her stockings again.

SIX

Elijah sat in the club booth and counted to twenty for the second time. Then he tried a third round. The mindless activity didn't do anything to ease the twitch in his neck or his pants. Seeing Wade had the same effect it always did. The churning started, then the rush of heat. It had been that way from the beginning and the epic fight that ended with Wade kicking Eli not only out of his bed but out of the building hadn't cooled Eli's need one bit.

Watching Wade flirt with the blond with the swimmer's build and expensive suit forced a different kind of heat through Eli's veins. So did the way Wade smiled before the guy returned to his table across the room.

Eli knew the other man. Recognized him from a photo he saw in one of Wade's nightstand drawers in the condo above the club. Eli hated the live version of the man.

But Wade's smile brought back memories. Eli remembered months ago waking up from his wounds, including the one Jarrett inflicted when Eli showed up on his doorstep after almost being killed in an attack made to look like an accident. Wade had stood guard over Eli's bedside. He was the six-three enforcer with shoulders as wide as a doorframe, or so it seemed.

Back then the military haircut and scruff around Wade's chin had Elijah wishing for something other than an escape from the building. And when he'd brushed the back of his hand against Wade's fly and got a look of smoky interest in return, it was fucking game on until Wade called an end to everything.

They'd lived and slept together upstairs for months while Eli recuperated and after. As he began investigating who was systematically eliminating his CIA Spectrum front and why, the rage inside him had simmered. Most of it was directed at Becca, and finding her back in Jarrett's protection set Eli off. His hate spewed and Wade walked in at the wrong time.

It all ended after that. Wade refused to listen back then and they'd been apart ever since. Eli could count almost down to the hour since he'd last run his hands over Wade or been inside him. Wade put up the wall. All the calls and texts did nothing to knock it down.

And now this fucking blond popped out of nowhere.

Elijah couldn't sit still another second. He walked up to the bar and stood right in front of Wade to force a confrontation. Up close, Eli saw the ease on Wade's face. The comfort, as if their time apart had been good for him while it scratched and scraped at Eli.

Wade used his towel to dry out a glass. "Elijah. It looks like you're getting along well with Bast."

"The job is fine." The last thing Eli wanted was mundane bullshit chatter, but since some old guy with a bad comb-over sat at the bar two chairs down and didn't seem to be moving on, Elijah had little choice.

Without asking, Wade put a glass in front of Eli and poured a beer. The right one. His favorite.

"Not exactly like your last job," Wade said.

"Bast prefers if I don't kill people on company time."

That comment got the intruder moving. He grabbed his glass and headed for a booth filled with three other men in gray suits.

"Sounds like Bast. Lawyers are funny that way." Wade actually smiled as he looked at the retreating man's back. "You scared that guy away."

"He shouldn't eavesdrop."

"That's a favorite pastime at the club."

Enough mindless talk. Eli had a point and jumped to it. "You were talking with Shawn a few minutes ago. When did he start sniffing around again?"

Elijah knew exactly who the blond was and what he once meant to Wade. They were together for months before Eli arrived at the building.

"Excuse me?" Wade's smile was long gone now.

"You heard me."

Wade slammed the glass against the counter with a loud whack. The rattle of silverware and rumble of conversation in the club's dining room covered it, but did not hide the scowl. "It was your tone that ticked me off."

"If the problem wasn't the subject, then answer me." Elijah did a quick look around before lowering his voice even further.

"Maybe you forget but I'm not a fan of being ordered around."

A rule that didn't apply to the bedroom where Wade had ceded control to Eli but he didn't point that out. "I thought you had a rule against screwing club members."

"I'm trying to figure out what makes you think you get a say in who I talk to." With the towel draped over one shoulder, Wade balanced his palms on the edge of the bar and leaned in. "You gave up that right when you made it clear sleeping with me was nothing more than a way to pass the time and not something that meant anything to you."

"I never said that." Elijah had no idea what he'd said back then.

In his fury, words had spilled out of him until even Becca went silent. That was when he noticed Wade in the doorway and knew he'd blown it.

"I was standing right there. You said I was easy, a diversion, and one you could walk away from." Wade shoved away from the bar and stood up again. "So I gave you your wish."

What Eli wanted was the stubborn man standing in front of him. Before Wade sex amounted to a release or a job requirement. Eli had been with men and women and it all blurred together into one forgettable pile.

No matter how hard Wade had pushed, Eli refused to tag his sexuality with any sort of label because that never mattered to him. And he'd spent years running away from that and the judgment and all the other crap heaped on him by his father. If Eli had known back then a few simple words meant so much to Wade, Eli would have said them. Would have said anything.

"You missed the part where I was in the middle of a fight with Becca when you walked in," Elijah pointed out.

"You're forgetting the part where I've moved on. We're done."

The blow landed right in Eli's gut. He felt the devastating thud of the killing blow and forced his body to stay upright. "You think kicking me out of your bed changed anything between us?"

"Everything." Wade's word came out rough, grating. "Every damn thing."

"Don't fuck him." The words shot out of Eli louder than he wanted, enough to have a few heads turn in their direction.

Wade's eyes bulged. "Who the hell—"

"Do not fuck Shawn." Eli hesitated between each word, forcing them out through clenched teeth. The anger raging inside him boiled and sprayed until it washed through him and drowned out everything else.

"You no longer get to have a say in who I see and who I sleep with."

The fury in Wade's voice matched Eli's. They traded whispered rage, neither one giving any ground.

Eli wanted to reach across the bar and shake Wade. Shake him, then draw him in for a kiss that would knock the shitty words right off his tongue. "You're angry with me, fine. Then talk to me. Yell at me so we can get past it."

Whatever Wade was going to say died when he opened and closed his mouth, once then twice. Each time he moved back until he stood away from the bar with his back tight up against the shelves of bottles behind him. "We said all we needed to say to each other."

"You got pissed and went on a rampage."

"Said the guy with the anger management problem."

"I'm working on that." Watching Bast work every day helped with that. The man stayed steady while the world crumbled around him. Eli liked the style.

"Now you do that? When it's too late to help us?" Wade grabbed the counter behind him and held on until his knuckles turned white. "You're lucky I'm working and can't take you apart."

Eli held his arms out, taunting and ready to go. "If that's what it takes for us to move past this, do it. I won't even fight back."

"This conversation is over."

He'd already lost ground and pissed Wade off. Knowing he couldn't lose any more, Elijah went for it. He snapped the top off of all those words bottled up inside him. At least Wade finally provided a reaction, which was more than he'd done so far.

"Does the ongoing punishment make you feel better? That's what this is, right?" Elijah did a quick glance around and saw Bast staring at him but ignored the boss's interest. "You want me to pay for not saying the right words when I was pissed off at someone else—not you, but the woman who had pulled a gun on me and held a knife at my throat."

"Your fight with Becca had nothing to do with me but you pulled me in by mentioning our relationship." Wade executed the perfect exaggerated pause and held up his hand. "Oh, that's right. We weren't in a relationship. That's what you told her, right? We were just engaged in mindless forgettable fucking."

"I warned you before that day how she set me off." Elijah inhaled, searching for a final hold on his temper and finding the tether frayed. "Or were you looking for a reason to move on? To get rid of me? Maybe you were the one who wasn't into it but it's easier to blame the end on me."

Wade's jaw snapped closed with enough force for Eli to hear the click. But he didn't back down. Not now. Not after he finally got Wade to at least say something.

For a second, Wade stood there, staring as his chest rose and fell on heavy breaths. When he did speak, his voice carried a slap. "You are so far out of line."

"You going to kick me out again?"

A red wash covered Wade's face as he pointed at Eli. "You don't belong to the club, so I can throw your ass on the street if I want to. It's only out of respect for Bast—a loyal member—that you're still standing here. Jarrett is willing to bend the rules to make Bast happy and I'll go along with it for now, but do not push it."

As if saying his name conjured him up, Bast appeared at Wade's side. "Is there a problem here? People are starting to stare." He walked with his usual confidence and his voice sounded as calm and unruffled as ever.

Whatever club policy might be about dealing with members, Wade didn't back down. "Tell your guest we have rules here."

With his hands folded on the bar in front of him, Bast kept his attention centered on Wade. "I'm pretty sure Elijah knows that."

"He's not acting like it."

For the first time, Bast glanced at Elijah. "What exactly happened?"

But Wade jumped in, his anger still raging. "The same thing that always happens with Eli, he pushes the boundaries too far and things go to hell."

"Okay." Bast cleared his throat. "Could you be more specific?"

Eli had had enough of being ignored and of Wade's wrath and of wanting something he clearly could no longer have. "Wade doesn't want me on the property."

"That's not his decision," Bast said with the same steady calm exterior he used when negotiating with clients.

"My fight isn't with you, Bast." Some of the tension spinning around Wade eased.

"That's pretty clear."

Wade took the towel off his shoulder and threw it on the bar. "I'm not dealing with this situation right now."

"Or ever, apparently," Eli mumbled under his breath.

"I have someone I *want* to talk with." Wade pushed on the hip-height swinging door that protected his area from the rest of the room and stepped from behind the bar. He glanced at Shawn and then back to Eli again.

The second kick, this one a gesture instead of words, hit Elijah's gut just as hard. "And you say I'm the one who's pushing."

"We're done here." Wade treated Elijah to an expression that matched his words then walked over to Shawn's table.

Bast wasn't clear about what just happened, but he sure as hell knew it wasn't good. The raised voices and pointing and general feeling the club was one second away from breaking into violence gave that away. Wade kept his cool on the job. Eli had perfected an icy exterior. Seeing them both go off proved to be quite a show.

Not sure if he should defuse or investigate, Bast turned to Elijah, who had not moved from his spot in front of the bar. "Want to tell me what's going on with you two?"

"Nothing."

"Give me a break." For a trained killer Elijah looked like he was on the verge of shutting down and Bast didn't like it at all. He'd take Elijah's smart mouth and poor timing over the quiet seething any day. "Adults don't stomp off like that and Wade is not one to stage a public screaming match. And you look like hell."

"I've about had it with being told what's wrong with me."

"Then tell me what happened and I'll shut up." Bast looked over Elijah's shoulder and saw Jarrett standing in the doorway to the dining room with Becca. With a shake of his head, Bast telegraphed for Jarrett to stay back a second. "It's either tell me or tell Jarrett, and I know how you two get along."

"See that guy?" Elijah didn't turn. He nodded in the direction Wade traveled.

"The blond Wade's talking to? Yeah." Bast had seen the guy before. Used to see him a lot and always with Wade but usually after club hours. He worked at some big-time security firm. The type Bast pegged as a private military firm, sending people to war-torn areas to do no one wanted to know what. The guy wasn't a club member, as far as Bast knew.

Elijah downed his beer in two gulps. "It's Shawn."

"Is that name supposed to mean something to me?" But Bast was starting to suspect he knew where this was going.

"The guy Wade slept with before me."

"Wade sure does have a type."

That got Eli's attention. His head snapped around until he faced Bast. "What does that mean?"

"Look at him. You two have the same build." And theoretically they both could kill on command. Wade clearly liked his bedmates deadly.

"I'm Japanese and he looks like he walked out of a Viking poster." Eli spun his glass around on the bar, making it clank as the heavy bottom hit the wood. "I want to fucking punch the guy in the mouth, then we'll see if he smiles at Wade."

"That would definitely be a violation of club rules."

Bast watched as this Shawn guy took Wade's phone and typed, probably his number. When Bast looked back at Eli, thinking to distract him, he realized it was too late. The scene had Eli's attention.

Steadying the glass, Eli stood up and straightened his jacket. "I think I'll save us both the worry of being disciplined by Jarrett and skip dinner."

"Don't let Wade run you off. It's what he wants."

"He's made that clear."

Bast usually liked Wade. They'd worked together to watch over Jarrett—a man not really in need of babysitting—when Becca ran back into town and to his side. But this felt like a game targeting Eli, and Bast didn't play games.

Hoping to put a halt to wherever Eli's dark mood might take him, Bast tried reason. "Wade is looking to inflict some pain."

"I'm done with that." Elijah pushed off and was gone.

He walked through the crowded room, around the tables to the far side and away from Wade. His laser focus stayed locked on the door. Bast realized Elijah missed Wade watching the exit.

SEVEN

Elijah's big exit left Bast standing alone at the bar. He glanced over at Jarrett, who stared right back as he shook his head, likely at the testosterone display they'd just witnessed. For a second Bast saw the intimidating man others feared. From the black hair to the black suit, Jarrett could best be described as six feet of dark, commanding presence. He radiated confidence and operated with a practiced charm Bast knew Jarrett saw as an annoying business necessity.

Bast also knew he could be anywhere and need anything and Jarrett would drop whatever he was doing, shift all, to make it happen. They'd been friends for years. Through the Becca betrayal and Bast's marriage implosion, they commiserated together. Bast didn't have a brother, or even a sister, but he couldn't imagine the loyalty felt any different than his to Jarrett.

Before Bast could walk over and engage in a play-by-play over Wade's messed-up love life, Bast noticed Kyra slip out of the kitchen. She appeared by his side a few seconds later. Like some other people in the room, she'd watched Elijah stalk toward the far door. With his height and stern expression, he always attracted attention. He also had a look his former CIA boss Natalie described as irresistible to both men and women. Bast thought that went a bit far, but she insisted it was both a benefit and a deterrent for Elijah in his job because he couldn't blend into the crowd the way others could.

Kyra leaned against the bar in the same spot Eli just had abandoned. "Is your friend okay?"

"Not really." But Bast suddenly had something else on his mind. "How are you feeling?"

She frowned at him. "Fine, why?"

"Not too exposed?" He let his gaze travel over every curve. "What with the skirt right against your—"

"Keep your voice down."

"Be happy I'm not asking for you to prove you're still naked under that sexy skirt." Though it was damn tempting to drag her back in the locker room and have her show him.

"Don't try to derail me." Her voice stayed firm but her cheeks turned pink. "That guy who just walked out works for you, right?"

Bast just assumed she knew Elijah, but . . . "That's Elijah Sterling."

"Did you fire him or something?'

Bast didn't understand how she couldn't know the identity of the other guy in her brother's recent nasty breakup. The fight between the men wasn't exactly a secret among their small circle of friends. The specifics, maybe, but Wade had stumbled around for weeks after Eli left. Even if he wanted to say his time with Elijah meant nothing, there was no way Wade could sell that. The breakup had him reeling and he still hadn't recovered, as evidenced by the yelling tonight.

The whole mess and Wade's mood in the weeks since had been hard to ignore, or so Bast thought. "You don't know who Eli is?"

"Didn't I establish that when I asked who he was?"

"I thought maybe you'd heard his name before."

She turned to Bast. "In passing, maybe from Jarrett or Becca, but I'm thinking you believe I should know him. Feel free to fill me in."

The full force of her attention and knowing what she hid under that skirt made it hard for Bast to concentrate on anything but getting his hands on her again. "He knows Wade."

"Everyone who comes in here knows Wade. He's the unofficial bouncer."

Her brother and his messed-up love life qualified as the last thing Bast wanted to discuss with her. How to get her back to his place and what time she got off tomorrow, yes. "Elijah had some words with Wade. They've been fighting."

"That sounds odd."

Looking at her hair and the way it fell over her full breasts had Bast struggling to keep up with the conversation. "I'm not sure how else to say it."

"You're being weirdly cryptic."

"I missed whatever happened between them tonight. You'll have to ask Wade for details." Because Bast was ready to move on to a new topic. Preferably one that involved getting her out of that bra.

"I don't get it. . . .unless, are you saying—"

"Why is Elijah pacing my sidewalk out front and mumbling to himself?" Jarrett cut in with his voice booming from behind Kyra.

Bast had no idea how long his friend stood there. Kyra had him walking around dazed like some lovesick little boy.

Bast decided not to share that fact. "Eli had a rough night."

"Ah, I see." Jarrett's gaze went to Wade then back to Kyra again. "You should get to work before we have a backup and the members start complaining. I've had enough of that this week."

"Because of me?" Kyra asked.

Jarrett shook his head. "Of course not."

"Then I'll keep that streak alive and go."

"Wait." Lost in watching her, Bast almost forgot one of his supposed reasons for heading over here so early tonight. He turned her hand over and dropped the keychain in them. "These are yours."

"Uh, right." Kyra didn't give either male eye contact.

Bast thought her subterfuge needed work. He turned to explain to Jarrett. "She dropped her keys."

Jarrett's eyes narrowed. "Where?"

"By the door," Kyra said as the haze around her seemed to clear.

"Be more careful, Kyra. I don't exactly trust some of the guys in my club."

"Just some?" Becca slid her hand through Jarrett's arm when she joined the group and leveled her stare at Kyra. "And your shift has started."

With the bosses on the floor, the staff seemed to pick up speed. Bast noticed the scurrying, including Kyra. She left the group without a word and headed for a table in the middle of the room. Her smile in place, Kyra rounded the diners Bast knew to be commercial developers. Three focused on a file in front of them. One zeroed in on Kyra.

Jarrett put a hand on top of Becca's. "I love when you get bossy."

Bast had to pull his attention away from Kyra, and it took more control than he expected. "Okay you two. Let's keep that stuff for the upper floors."

"I find it hard to believe anything we do could shock you." Becca's head dropped to the side and her hair fell off her shoulder and across her chest. "But I'm willing to try."

"You'll scare him." Jarrett laughed, something he did more often now that Becca had come back and their relationship shifted to fast-forward.

Becca snorted. "I doubt that."

The light mood appealed to Bast and he tried to stay involved in the conversation. Tried and failed. The young developer shifted his hand and it would have landed on Kyra's ass if she hadn't done an impressive pivot and shuffle around the table. It looked natural and not like a defensive move, but Bast knew better.

Jarrett cleared his throat. "Are you staring?"

Fighting off a flinch, Bast turned back to his friends. His gaze clashed with his best friend's. Jarrett looked amused. Becca wore a "you blew it" expression.

Bast ignored both. "At what?"

Shifting, Jarrett leaned against the bar and looked in Kyra's direction. "Well, if I had to define it, I'd say at a woman who is far too young for you."

No way Bast could argue with that point. But he could preserve his privacy. If whatever he had with Kyra lasted more than a night or two, the time would come to tell Jarrett. Not today.

Keeping his cool, Bast called on his considerable skills at staying unruffled under pressure. "I'm just standing here."

"Uh-huh." Becca's voice managed to go flat and drip with sarcasm at the same time.

When in doubt, go with a half-truth. That had never been Bast's mantra, but he adopted it for this situation. "I thought the guy over there was making a move on Kyra. Last thing you all need tonight is Wade going ballistic."

Becca's smile was of the so-sweet-a-person-could-get-sick variety. "It's nice of you to want to protect her, but that's my job. That guy lifts a hand and I'll shoot it off."

The lawyer side of Bast rose up. "You mean theoretically."

"No, I don't."

"Which is why she's in charge of the staff and working with Wade on security." Jarrett leaned over and placed a kiss on Becca's forehead. When he turned to Bast again, the stupid grin still hadn't faded. "Speaking of Wade, want to give me a hint about the fight. I only caught the end."

They'd circled around to a topic Bast could handle without waiting for Becca to launch into a verbal strike. The fact that Kyra left the table with the handsy guy and now talked with a member old enough to be her grandfather also helped Bast concentrate. "I brought Elijah. He talked to Wade. They fought rather than doing what they both clearly want to do."

"Punch?" Jarrett sounded as if he liked the idea.

As far as Bast was concerned, Jarrett was off by several body parts. "That's not even close to what I was thinking."

Jarrett nodded. "Ah, yes. That."

"I agree with Bast," Becca said. "I wish those two would just go upstairs and get all naked and nasty and be done with this skulking."

Jarrett's eyebrow lifted. "Wow."

She scoffed. "Oh please. I can't be the only one who believes those two are volcanic together in bed."

Bast suspected Elijah wanted to get back to that time. But this Shawn guy sat over there working it hard. From this vantage point it looked like Wade tried to move away and the blond said something to bring him back.

"Could be Wade moved on," Bast pointed out.

Jarrett's gaze followed Bast's. "So, that's what caused this."

Shifting, Becca moved into the line of sight, bringing both men's attention back to her and breaking their view of Wade's flirting. "I don't buy it. Wade is into Elijah. Wades hates it, but he is."

"That doesn't mean he can't screw someone else." Bast knew that trick from experience. He saw the frustration in Wade's eyes. Saw and recognized it.

"This conversation has probably taken a turn into not-our-business territory." Jarrett leaned across the bar and grabbed a small bottle of seltzer water and a glass.

"True, but life would be easier for all of us if Wade and Elijah stopped circling each other like mad dogs in heat."

Jarrett glanced over his shoulder at Becca before standing upright again. "That's a lovely image."

"I don't believe in mincing words." Becca looked at Bast as she said it. "What was Kyra's take on all this?"

The woman sure knew how to go in for the kill. In Bast's view, the CIA messed up in trying to eliminate Becca. With her in weapon mode, no one would be safe.

But Bast didn't blink. "Kyra didn't seem to know about Wade and Elijah."

Becca started with a low whistle and ended with, "So many secrets."

Nice try, but Bast still refused to blink. "That's how we all make our money."

"Join us for dinner." Jarrett poured his drink, using a head nod toward the owner's table to do the rest of the work for him.

Becca waved him off. "Actually, you two go ahead. I like when you have boy time."

"Let me do a check-in with Wade first and get his sorry ass back to the bar." After a quick follow-up kiss, Jarett took off in Wade's direction.

Bast waited until Jarrett stepped out of hearing range. "You didn't tell him about me and Kyra."

"So you two are a thing now?"

"I didn't say that." He was sorry he said anything.

"That was fast. You fought it off for, what, all of two seconds."

"You know what I meant."

Becca shrugged. "This is your mess. You clean it up."

"I'm happy we understand each other."

"Do we?"

Clearly she didn't plan to let this go. Not a surprise. Bast didn't think he'd be that lucky. "Maybe not."

Becca twisted the lid back and forth on the bottle Jarrett left on the bar. "Since you trapped Kyra in the locker room a half hour ago, I'm guessing you made up your mind to chase her."

A man didn't have any damn privacy these days. "Is there any-where you don't have cameras in this place?"

The screech of metal against glass from the bottle filled the air. "I'm not telling."

Becca could twist things and threaten him and scowl all she wanted. Respecting her didn't mean she got a say in his personal decisions. "We're still not talking about my sex life."

She returned the empty bottle to the bar, letting it click as the glass tapped against the wood. Every move seemed exaggerated, as if perfectly calculated to take longer than necessary and draw all the attention back to her.

Bast knew that was a really bad sign.

Her hand wrapped around the edge of the bar. "I'll give you forty-eight hours to come clean to Jarrett."

Yeah, she could throw out whatever timeline she wanted. Bast planned to ignore that, too. "It's no more his business than it is yours."

Becca leaned in and whispered against Bast's cheek. "Then chase Kyra on someone else's property."

EIGHT

Elijah heard one of the large front double doors to the club open behind him but didn't look up. The doorman hadn't moved from the circle of light at the bottom of the town house steps a few feet away, which meant someone other than a member had come outside.

Only a few people would dare to follow him in this mood and signal the doorman to stay put, and Elijah knew which one this was. Didn't even have to close his eyes and call on his senses to pinpoint the identity. The soft click of spiky heels and the subtle scent of perfume gave her away.

"George, could you give us a few minutes. You can wait closer to the door." Only Becca could issue a command in that husky voice and have it play like a request.

"Yes, ma'am." The doorman's shoes thudded against the steps as he retreated.

Elijah envied the guy for getting to leave. Elijah wanted to but held his position on the sidewalk, backing up only to take them out of easy eavesdropping range of the doorman.

In these last days of summer the night hadn't cooled off from the sticky humid day. The slight wind was as refreshing as standing in front of a hair dryer. The longer they stood there the more the heat caused his blazer to stick to his shirt, which clung to his back.

She didn't show any sign of being affected by the warmth. A breeze caught her hair and whipped it back over her shoulders as she smiled. "You running from me?"

"Trying not to make a scene."

Her smile grew even wider. "Too late."

Seeing her in the sexy dress stunned him for a second. It hugged her body and highlighted everything a man would want highlighted. Not him. She, being a "she," was not his type, but he could appreciate a beautiful woman when he saw one. Unfortunately he no longer wanted one. Thanks to Wade.

When Elijah had seen her dressed up on the job the clothes operated more as a uniform. All for show to get to a required end on an op. He suspected the smile on her face now and the ease with which she held herself stemmed from happiness. From something real.

He felt a kick of jealousy and wanted to shove away and leave. But he couldn't exactly knock her over. Not and live to talk about it. Not that he would anyway. The days of them being at war were over and he didn't go after people who didn't deserve it. She'd earned his respect, though he was not ready to admit that to her yet.

But that didn't mean he wanted a confrontation, not when he was still raw from seeing Wade. The hollowed-out sensation refused to go away and now Becca took up staring. Yeah, Elijah knew he should have hit the outside and kept moving until he got back to his shithole of a studio apartment. Waiting here for forgiveness that would never come had been a mistake and now he'd pay with an unwanted conversation.

She crossed her arms in front of her. "I don't think I've ever seen you pace."

Elijah didn't even realize he was and forced his legs to still. "Burning off some energy."

"You used to do that by punching people."

He guessed it would be wrong to call those the good old days, so he kept that inside. "Bast frowns on that."

After years in the field doing anything to get the job done and survive, Elijah's view of civilized behavior needed work. He'd been trying to learn acceptable responses that didn't involve a gun or knife, if only to keep from having to go on the run again. He owed Bast and Jarrett that much.

"Bast is a killjoy." Becca laughed as she said it.

According to Bast, she did that a lot now. Bast credited her with drawing Jarrett back into humanity again. Elijah wanted to follow her lead and at least pretend to be normal, but he had no idea what the hell that was. Never did. His father's yelling and talk of an almighty wrath fit with the world Elijah knew before. He preferred to find another one now.

"My boss has other qualities," Elijah said.

"Like, offering second chances and providing a paycheck?"

Along with being decent and hardworking, as well as an example of how to dress and act in an office. All of that. "Yeah, those."

Despite all the security lights and guards, darkness wound around them. A few men went in and out of the club but no one bothered them. Most steered clear, taking a wide circle to keep away from them. Word of Becca being Jarrett's woman had spread fast and the club members treated her with extreme deference.

"Working with Bast brings you to the club." She didn't blink. Didn't move. She stood long and lean with her gaze fixed on Elijah.

Now he knew how her marks felt on the old jobs. She wove a spell and looked at you with those big eyes and you froze. Eli recognized her lethal nature, but this was something else. A strong woman on a mission and he sensed he'd crossed some line by coming into her territory.

"Are you trying to tell me to stay away from the club?" Because he fucking would. He needed an excuse to make him since he couldn't break the magnetic pull on his own. Anything was better than having priority seating to Wade's new relationship.

"No."

"You sure?" Something moved in her eyes and Eli worried it might be pity. The thought made his frustration spike and a ball of anxiety roll in his stomach. "You own the place. It's your right to say who gets inside."

"Jarrett owns the club."

"Don't act like that guy wouldn't turn over everything he owns to you and sign a contract in blood to make you happy." Jarrett had flipped his life upside down and taken every risk to ensure her safety. And he did all that for a woman he at the time believed had betrayed him.

Bast called it love. Elijah called it stupid. Either way, it saved them all.

Information came to Jarrett in his job that made him a target. Todd Rivers, the man who once led their black-ops team, recognized it and capitalized on it. He turned a simple surveillance into a sting. He planted false evidence and moved in when Becca threatened to pull the plug on the operation.

In the end Jarrett went to jail, the team disbanded and then Todd quietly removed anyone who could question his choices, leaving Becca the suspect as the likely killer. After months in hiding, not knowing when the next gunman would show up, they were all on edge. Jarrett had stepped up and offered a deal to make the danger go away. Elijah still wasn't clear what intel had changed hands, but Bast managed to negotiate for all of their lives. It was the kind of debt that took a lifetime to extinguish.

Becca dropped her arms to her sides. "Jarrett traded information to the CIA for us."

That's not how Elijah remembered the scene unfolding. "For you. I was a collateral beneficiary."

"Jarrett talks tough but he wouldn't have saved you if he didn't want to."

Since Eli had a bullet wound in his shoulder courtesy of Jarrett, Eli didn't exactly agree. "He saved me because he knew not saving me would upset Wade. At least back then."

"At first, but I think you've grown on him."

Eli didn't see a reason to argue with that obvious lie. "Right."

"You've grown on me, too."

Now that was bullshit. "When you realized I was still alive you tried to kill me."

"At the time you deserved it."

She wasn't totally wrong about that since he had just aimed a gun at Jarrett. But the friction between them stretched back for years. "And we hated each other when we worked together."

"I didn't hate you."

"Then it was just me hating you," he said, only half meaning it.

He'd resented her being put on his team. She'd been new yet the administration wanted her involved in everything. She was the one who went in undercover at the club despite Eli's protests about her not being ready.

The old Becca would have punched him in the balls. This one laughed. Maybe this was the new, improved and in-love version.

"Do you still?" Becca asked.

"No. That stopped when I realized everything you did to save the operation and how Todd and others at the CIA tried to make you the ultimate target." Elijah wasn't feeding her a line. He meant it. "You're actually pretty damn tough."

"I could take you."

Dress or not, if he blinked the wrong way, he'd bet she'd try. "Want to go a few rounds?"

"Is that what you need right now?" Her voice changed. It turned soft and concerned.

Pity hovered right there and Eli wanted to shoot it down fast. "I'm fine."

She took another step, basically cornering him by standing in front of him. "Tell him."

"What?" But Elijah knew. She'd been circling around this topic since she came outside.

She put a hand on Eli's arm. "Tell Wade you messed up."

The urge to deny and run coursed through Eli. The flight instinct smacked into him hard. Just turn around and go. Ignore her like he'd done in the past when they fought over a strategy. But his legs wouldn't move. His heart pounded against his rib cage and he inhaled long and deep to get his body back under control.

"I did that already." He didn't whisper but his voice dropped low.

"Did you also tell Wade you love him?"

The word battered Eli and he fought it off. "Come on."

"You do." She frowned at him. "Stop shaking your head at me."

"This is not—"

"Elijah, you've got to take a risk if you want him back."

He'd apologized. Come close to begging. What the hell else could he do? "Is that what you did with Jarrett?"

"Yes, but we're not talking about me. We're trying to get you back into Wade's bed."

The words called up an image, and on cue the hollowness swept back through Elijah. "Not going to happen."

"Maybe it will once you admit to yourself you love him." She sure had an agenda and kept hammering it.

"Did you take night school classes in psychology or something?" If so, he would stay miles away from her from now on.

"I should because all the men around here are tragic in the way they handle their love lives."

"Thanks."

"Let me be clear." She pointed at the impressive front doors to the club and stopped talking for a small wave to the doorman standing guard. "You are welcome here any time. I'll talk to Jarrett about setting up some sort of ongoing visitor arrangement."

An interesting gesture but seeing Wade move on would rip him apart eventually. He worked on the phrasing to make Becca understand but still save the small piece of his ego that hadn't been shredded. "Being here is not a great thing for me."

"How else are you going to win Wade back?"

"Maybe I don't want to." Now there was a big fat fucking lie.

"Like I said, you guys are tragic."

Standing out here arguing with her, actually talking about his love life, was the tragic part. It showed how desperate he truly had become. "Throwing myself in his face isn't going to work."

"How do you know?"

"Do you have any idea how many times I've called and texted him?" Elijah tried to stop the words but they kept rolling out of him. "How many times early on I came to the club door and tried to get him to let me in?"

Her wince showed she got it. "Wade sure does win the stubborn prize."

"He's moved on. So will I." It hurt to say the words.

"I know the two of us have had trouble with trust, but I need you to hear me when I say this, Eli." This time she grabbed his forearm and dug in with her nails. "Wade is not done."

"Did you see the blond inside tonight?"

"I saw Wade making sure *you* saw the blond."

Elijah wanted to believe it. It was how badly he *needed* to believe it that scared the hell out of him. "Look, I appreciate the pep talk."

"Eli, for once in your life don't shut people out."

"I don't know what that means." Sounded like more psycho-babble to him.

She gave his arm one final squeeze and let go. "Well, when you do you may be able to win Wade back."

Kyra followed her usual late-night after-work routine. Shower, find a T-shirt, throw her body across the bed. Done. Exhausted from a night on her feet and still aching from shoes that worked for a dinner date but not racing around tables serving, she lay there and stared up at her boring white ceiling. She kept meaning to paint the place but renting made her lazy and who wanted to ask a faceless management company for permission.

Right now she couldn't pick up a phone if she wanted to. Rolling over far enough on the mattress to slip under the covers proved impossible. She blamed Bast. Seeing him for hours and catching him staring at her as she worked, kept her senses on high alert.

She used up all her energy trying not to stare at him or give their upcoming plans away. So did the no-underwear thing. Their sexy little secret tormented her all night. In a good way. He exercised control and her stomach tumbled. Outside of the bedroom, obeying grated against her, but inside, it struck her as deliciously naughty.

As the minutes ticked by the darkness outside her window drew her in. She closed her eyes, deciding sleep ranked higher on the necessary scale than fumbling for covers. She'd barely sunk into the mattress when the knocking started inside her head. In her daze it seemed to echo through the room and thunder in her brain. She threw an arm over her eyes and the noise stopped.

When the banging started again, followed by the soft whisper of her name, she jackknifed out of bed. Sprinting on tiptoes, she got to the door. Not that it took long when the whole apartment measured something like five hundred square feet.

She stretched to look out the too-high peephole, then her ankles fell and her heels hit the hardwood again. This had to be a dream. One starring a brown-haired, glasses-wearing hottie. She smoothed a hand over her hair. Next came tugging on the edge of her sleep shirt, which brought the deep V-neck dipping down to her stomach.

As soon as she started the fidgeting, she stopped. His fingers had been inside her. His mouth all over her. There was no part of her body she wanted to hide from him.

Throwing the lock and bolt, she opened the door. Playing it cool proved to be beyond her grasp. Not when every nerve jumped to life inside of her. "Bast?"

The corners of his mouth lifted. "Nice shirt."

Of course he would say that since one boob almost popped out when she stepped back. "What are you doing here?"

"I think you know." He put a hand against the door, not pushing but making it clear he didn't plan to stand out in the hallway forever. "Is there anything you want to ask me?"

So many things but some would send him running. "How about, how do you look so good after a twenty-hour workday?"

Like, she wanted to take his glasses off and run her fingers through his hair. Over all of him, actually.

"Ask me to come in."

There was no need to say it twice. She stood back and ushered him in without saying a word. When she turned back around and watched him standing in the middle of her small place her mind went blank. The dark suit and wide shoulders looked out of place with her abandoned clothes and towel draped over the treadmill by the window. The same one she used as an expensive and heavy extra closet.

The way he stood over the bed, trailing his gaze across the comforter, made her sorry she'd bothered with underwear after the shower.

Since she was not the giggly schoolgirl type and he made it clear that wasn't his thing anyway, she tried to stay calm and think her way through this. The heartbeat banging through her with the force of a gong was a lost cause. She didn't attempt to bring it back down to the normal range.

She inhaled as she forced her body to stay still. No shifting her weight or tugging on the bottom of her shirt, even though it barely cleared her underwear. "Where did you get my address?"

"Hmm?" He turned around to face her with eyes that appeared cloudy.

"God, you don't own the building or something freaky like that, do you? That would be weird."

"No." The heat in his eyes suggested he had things on his mind other than real estate. "I checked your registration when I put the bag in your car."

That didn't sound all that much better. "I'm trying to figure out if that's still creepy. I'm thinking maybe. What about you?"

"I went back and forth on an answer."

"What did you decide?"

He slipped his suit jacket off his shoulders and added it to her pile of forgotten clothes on the top of her chest of drawers. "To lecture you about keeping something with your home address in your car."

This time she held on to the bottom of the T-shirt to keep from making wild hand gestures. "Where else would I keep the registration?"

"On you." Next came his tie. Those sexy lean fingers went to work and the knot slipped. He pulled and the rustle of material against material streaked through the room.

"I could forget it then get pulled over and get stuck with a ticket."

His gaze never left hers as he unbuttoned the top two buttons of his white dress shirt. "That's better than leading a crazed lunatic back to your house."

"Speaking of lunatic, go back to the part where you checked my registration."

He unfastened the buttons on his sleeves and rolled up the material. "It seemed like the quickest way to get the address and not raise suspicion, but the point is that I shouldn't have been able to find your home address so easily."

She had no idea how he managed to deliver a lecture and a striptease at the same time and be so damn hot doing both. "Now you sound grumpy."

"I wonder why." In one step he was in front of her with his hands low on her hips. "Do you always open the door wearing that kind of outfit?"

At this touch, the tee stretched across her breasts and moved up even higher. That left her bare thighs pressing against those dress pants.

Her concentration took a nosedive along with her breathing. Keeping up the mundane conversation and trying to state her case grew more difficult with every piece of clothing he peeled off.

"I checked the peephole first," she said, hoping the sentence made sense.

"Smart."

She rubbed her finger over the strip of skin peeking out from under his shirt. "I am, you know."

"Book smart and street smart." He nuzzled his nose against her hair. "A deadly sexy combination."

This guy was about to get very lucky. "You figured that out?"

"I read people for a living." His palms slid down to her ass and tugged her in until his erection fit in the snug notch between her legs. "I have one more question."

Anything. "Yes?"

"How long will it take to get that shirt off?" He trailed a line of kisses across her cheek to her mouth. He sucked her top lip between his own then whispered. "Technically, it is tomorrow."

Despite the warm night, goose bumps spread down her legs and a shiver ran through her. "You really are a lawyer. Working all the angles."

He licked her lips. "Do you want me to leave?"

She would wrap her body around his to stop that if she had to. "No."

"Then the day of the week doesn't really matter." He walked backward, bringing them closer to the bed.

"We might be more comfortable at your place." Doubt nibbled at the edge of her mind. Between his privileged upbringing and all those expensive private schools, she doubted he'd ever been in a studio. "There's not a lot of room here."

"There's a bed."

Well, he couldn't be clearer than that. "Then why aren't we in it?"

One of his hands slipped under the elastic band of her panties and slid over bare skin. "Kyra, first we need—"

"Is this the 'you're young and this is just sex' speech? Because you can save it. I understand the parameters." He should focus on touching her, like the way he was kneading her ass and rubbing his lower half against hers.

"I was actually checking to make sure you were on the pill and understood condoms were mandatory, which is what people having sex talk about before they get naked."

Another shot at her age. She'd assumed him being here meant he was over that. Apparently not. "Yes to both, or was that your way of asking me if I'm a virgin? Because I'm not. Sorry if that disappoints you."

For a few years when she was too young to handle it or even understand why she made the decisions she did, she used sex as a way of expressing her power. She couldn't control her father or her life. She wanted college and he threatened to stop her from going. Running through a few faceless boys, none of them memorable and all of them long gone, qualified as acting out. The boys didn't talk out of fear of her father. She hid her choices because her father wouldn't spare her his wrath if he found out.

Then he went to prison and that proved to be her ticket out. A few months in she realized letting some hyperventilating fast-talker in her pants didn't work for her. Making the choice based on what she wanted and needed amounted to real empowerment. She deserved better and made sure anyone who touched her passed her mental test from then on.

Bast cleared his throat as his hands tightened on her. "Not even a little. Maybe you couldn't tell but I'm not into naïve ingénues."

"Really? That's new. I assume all men want the virgin type. Something about being the first to go there seemed to make the guys in undergrad pretty damn thrilled." It had been a constant topic of gossip, especially in the first two years, and she'd heard similar comments while working. Maybe graduate school would be better.

"Then I'll assume you've been with idiot boys who don't appreciate how fucking great it is when a woman enjoys sex, knows what makes her feel good and goes after it."

"You do?"

"I am not a boy, Kyra." Before she could say anything, he leveled a dark look at her. "But let's go back to your topic."

"Which was?"

His other hand cupped her breast through the thin cotton shirt. "I don't want there to be any confusion. This is about sex. Between us and only for us. Hot, sweaty, want-more sex. That's it. That's what I can give you."

The words sounded final and somewhere inside she flinched. "Are you worried I'll lose my mind and propose?"

"You'll only do that if you want this to end."

Well, that was final. "I got it."

"I'm not sure what 'this' is yet, in terms of how long it will last, but it's about sex. I like you and I definitely want you, but this is supposed to be private and for fun. When it stops working for one or both of us, it ends and we leave like grown-ups."

For a second his attitude chilled her. The this-is-not-a-relationship warning rang in her ears. She waited for him to whip out a contract and make her sign it. But then she searched that gaze and remembered all the rumors floating around town thanks to his ex-wife. Maybe the guy had a reason to be cautious.

"We agree, Bast." Except that he kept forgetting her one mandate. "So long as you understand that while we're together I'm not sharing you."

"Yes, I got that requirement loud and clear." His fingers traveled over her breasts, lingering and learning. "Just the two of us."

The last hurdle fell. She could almost hear it crash and shatter.

"I'm a big girl, Bast. I know what I want." His hands all over her as he pushed deep inside, for a start. "You."

As if he heard her thoughts, he leaned in and kissed her as his thumb flicked over her nipple. Slowly, with few words and insistent touches, he primed her body for what was to come.

Then he lifted his head and stared down at her. "Take off the shirt."

NINE

As soon as the edge of Kyra's T-shirt slipped over her breasts, Bast had them in his hands again. The smooth skin rubbed against his palms. He had no idea about her level of experience, but he didn't intend to hold back. Not when he'd been aching to do this for longer than he should admit. She may have come to him with a proposition but that didn't mean he hadn't noticed her before that.

He bent forward and took her stiff nipple in his mouth. Sucking and licking, he enjoyed one then the other. He pressed them together and watched them plump over his palms, the whole time thinking how good it was going to be to fuck them. Not now, but soon.

There were so many things he wanted to do with her. So many positions. Last night he'd dreamed about her on her hands and knees, and now he could live it.

First thing after lifting his head, he saw her flushed face. Whatever she'd been thinking and feeling must have been good. She had her arms around him and her hands gripping his shoulders. She probably hoped he'd go slow, give her time to ease in because . . .

She jumped on him, almost knocking him backward. He held on to his balance as her arms tightened around his neck and those killer legs wrapped around his upper thighs. One minute she stood there looking stunned and the next she hugged him so close not a breath of air could pass between them.

She pressed every part of her body against his and did not stay still for one second. No, she angled her hips and rubbed up and down. Forget all the fears about her wanting him as a novelty. This was the knowing touch of a woman who craved something.

And the kiss. The force of it ricocheted through him. Hot and demanding, her lips crossed over his until his breath hammered in his ears. After searing him, practically marking him, she nibbled at the corner of his mouth then swept her tongue inside to tangle with his. Fingers speared through his hair and massaged his neck.

It was a full-body assault and he loved every minute of it.

This woman knew how to kiss and lure and seduce. She also knew what she wanted—happily, him—and went after it. That sexual awareness was so fucking hot his head almost blew off.

He wasn't lying when he said he didn't have any interest in virgins or ingénues. Some other guy could take those on. He wanted a woman who refused to accept shame about what she wanted. He knew from experience if a woman felt comfortable with her body and needs the sex threw sparks.

She tugged at the edges of his shirt and another button gave way under the pressure. "You have too much clothing on."

He'd been thinking the exact same thing. All he wanted to wear was a condom and her but getting there was the issue. "I have to let go of you to take things off and right now I don't want to."

The smile she shot him could power a small city. "Let me help."

Before he could say anything her legs loosened and her body slid down his. She didn't jump off or pull away. No, she glided down, letting the friction burn through them and every hard part of him press against her soft ones.

When his sanity returned, she had his shirt unbuttoned and

was sitting on the bed in front of him with her fingers on his belt. Those fingers moved in a blur as she got the zipper down and shoved the pants to the top of his legs.

No subtle disrobing here. This was a taking.

He knew right then, despite the years yawning between them, he should have made a move on her long ago. Still, tonight was supposed to be about getting to know her, exploring her body.

"Wait, I . . ." He reached to pull her up but stopped when she freed his cock from his boxer briefs and slid her hand over him. "Okay, yeah, that works."

"Mmm." She lowered her head and licked the tip.

Then the head disappeared in her sweet mouth. She pumped him. Swallowed him. Those lips suckled him as her other hand massaged his balls. What little doubt he had over starting this eased away and a different type of tension settled in.

His muscles grew heavy and his hips started driving toward her without any message from his brain. His body shifted into freefall. The feel of a mouth on his cock, all hot and tight, ranked as one of his favorite things, and hers wiped out the memory of others.

Having her peek up at him as he ran his fingers through her hair to hold her head steady almost did him in. "I love looking down and seeing your face. Watching your hands over me and your tongue lick my—"

"Yes." She took him to the back of her throat, right down to the base.

He almost lost it right there. "Sweet Jesus."

She let his cock fall almost away from her lips before licking the head again. "Get used to this feeling."

A groan rumbled in his chest but he fought to bury it. "This is going to be so fucking good."

"I've waited long enough."

He brushed the hair away from her face and watched his cock

disappear in her sweet mouth again. "We've been on fast-forward since you made your move at the club."

"I've watched you for so much longer. Work and hang out with Jarrett. Listened to you laugh." She slid her hand up his length. "But seeing you up close is new."

"That's because I don't take my cock out in public."

"You should." Her tongue swirled over his head. "It's impressive."

The mix of her hands and mouth had need slamming through his body. He had to get inside her before his control finally snapped. "You won't think so when I come in your mouth before I even get my shirt off."

"Wrong."

Her laughter vibrated against him and the blood drained from his brain. "Next time, because the idea of you deep-throating me and sucking me dry is the fantasy that won't leave my head until it's done. And then we'll practice it many more times after that."

She eased back and looked up at him but her hand kept working, sliding up and down, growing faster with each pass. "You're talking about the future but what's going to happen this time?"

"Lie back." He didn't give her a choice. With a nudge he pushed her back until she eased down on the mattress. "When we're having sex, I'm in charge."

"What if I want to take the lead?" She threw her arms over her head.

The way her round breasts jiggled made him rip his shirt off and throw it on the floor. The pants and underwear followed with his opened belt jangling as they dropped.

"You can suck me off or climb on top of me any time but right now I want something else." He held his firm cock in his hand as he put a knee on the bed between her legs. He barely remembered to slip the glasses off and drop them on the closest table.

She frowned. "Hey, I like those."

"With what I plan to do to you, we'll crush them."

"The condoms are in the top drawer." She nodded in the direction of the chest behind him.

Not wanting to waste time, he practically sprinted to the piece of furniture and yanked the drawer out. Shoving piles of soft lacy panties he vowed to investigate later to one side, he found the box. He didn't know how many packets he grabbed but he threw them, letting them scatter across the bed.

She balanced up on her elbows and stared at him. "Impatient?"

"You have no idea."

She let her legs fall open. "I think I do."

All that stood between him and what he wanted was a thin strip of silk. It didn't matter because with the adrenaline pumping through him he could rip steel.

On his knees, he crawled back up her body and stopped between her legs. Pushing them wider, he opened her up to his touch. A fingertip traced the elastic of her panties. Slid over the material, right at the heart of her. Back and forth until her scent hit the air and a telltale dampness singed his fingers.

When her hips rose off the bed, he knew she needed more. "Now who's impatient?"

"Sebastian, please."

Saying his full name . . . it was so hot his brain shut off and his body took over.

Sliding down until his elbows rested by her inner thighs, he lowered his head and licked a trail where his finger just tested. Grabbing the material in his teeth, he tugged it to the side and slid his tongue inside her.

His head ached from the pull of his hair through her fingers. The more he licked, the more she thrashed. And when he found her clit and sucked on it, her thighs tightened against his shoulders.

"More." Her body clamped down as if trying to drag him deeper inside.

Instead of obeying, he blew a warm breath over her and sat up. "Soon."

"What are you—" Her voice cut off when he sat back on his heels and bent her legs until her heels balanced against his shoulders. "I'm not going to survive this."

"I promise you will."

His fingers scissored inside of her, preparing her and whipping her into a wild frenzy. With the other hand he reached for the nearest condom packet and tore it open. As she watched, he pumped his hand up and down his length, letting her know how much he wanted her.

"Yes," she said, more as a breath than a word.

When he rolled the condom on, he did it nice and slow, letting her see every inch. She twisted the comforter in her hands as her hips moved in time with the pumping of his fingers in and out of her. Every time he pulled out, she clenched her inner muscles against him.

He didn't think she could take much more before she came. Hell, he couldn't either.

"I'm going to fuck you now."

Her head shifted from one side to the other on the pillow. "God, yes."

"One long plunge." His fingers mimicked his words.

She lifted her back off the bed and grabbed one of his forearms. "Do it."

"Put your hands above your head." He fought off a smile when she immediately complied, stretching them high and grabbing onto the bottom of the headboard. "I want to see your breasts—"

"Tits. You don't have to clean up the language for me."

Nice. "Yes, tits, bounce as I fuck you."

"I love dirty talk in bed."

"I'm happy to comply."

"Not now. Move."

Her husky voice licked against his balls. "The begging. Also good."

He couldn't tease her one more second. Didn't want to. And there was no reason to wait. He rubbed his tip over her, letting the head of his cock slip just inside. He made it through two jolting passes before the mix of her raspy breathing and the sight of her body swallowing his cock did him in. As promised, he pressed forward, giving her every inch in one long push.

Her gasp filled the room as he pulled back and plunged in a second time. This position let him go deep and control the thrusting. The steady rhythm started a pounding in his head that matched the throbbing in his cock. He played with her breasts and caressed her flat stomach, all while a breath-stopping churning built inside him.

When she lowered one of her arms to grab onto his hand as it moved over her, he wanted to order her fingers back to the headboard. He didn't have the breath or the will to stop.

His hands moved to her legs. He slid his palms over her calves as her heels dug into his collarbone. The slight thump of pain registered then fell away. He'd welcome the bruises if it meant seeing this response. Her skin flushed pink with excitement. Her head pressed back into the mattress. Those nails digging into his arm.

She was right on the edge and he needed to push her off. He pressed deeper, faster. The bed rocked and a floorboard somewhere near him creaked.

The building inside him threatened to explode. He exhaled, holding back his orgasm until she found hers. Not able to wait, his hand slipped between their bodies. Filling her while rubbing her clit had her toes curling against his skin. He knew he'd found the right spot when her eyes popped open and she threw him a wild stare.

"Now, Kyra."

One last push had her body tightening to the point of shattering. Her feet pressed harder against him and her hands tightened on the underside of her headboard until the knuckles turned red. Her chest rose and fell on rapid beats as she slid over the comforter.

When she gulped in large breaths of air and the tension eased out of her, he let go. His hands went to the back of her thighs as he pushed faster and faster. He shifted his hips in a circle, letting her feel every inch. And when she tightened her body against him, he lost it.

The orgasm rammed into him, knocking the air out of his lungs. He gasped and said her name as his body emptied and his muscles went weak. Every ounce of energy ran out of him and he lowered her legs then collapsed between them.

He didn't move. Just lay there, every now and then moving his head to kiss her breasts. He had to be too heavy for her and needed to get up. A quick look at the clock at her bedside told him the seven o'clock conference call would come very soon. He had to go home and shower and change, all before heading back to the office without even a small bit of sleep.

All he wanted to do was close his eyes and go to sleep where he was, still partially lodged inside her. His brain had to reboot first and that didn't seem to be happening.

"I should have let you screw me in the car." She made the announcement as she skimmed her hand through his hair. "There was no reason for us to wait."

The comment was so out of context, he laughed. When she didn't say anything else, he lifted his head and gazed up that impressive body at her.

Reaching over, he grabbed his glasses. With them on it would be easier to pick up on her expressions. "Uh, what?"

"In the parking lot at the club." Her hand fell to his shoulder. "I was trying to build the excitement."

"Mission accomplished."

She smiled. "I meant I probably didn't have to hold off in order to get this response. You seemed ready to pop."

There was an understatement. "Once you made your offer, I can assure you I've thought of nothing else."

"Good."

He eased out of her and immediately wanted back inside. "Except, right now I have to leave."

Her hand slid down his arm and landed palm up on the comforter. "Are you kidding?"

Her tone suggested he should be. Too bad reality crept in and smacked him. "No."

"You're going?" She poked a finger into his chest. "Just like that?"

Behind the tough words, pain flashed in her eyes. She didn't say it but he could almost see the questions about him race through her head. He was one of "those" guys. He fucked and then bolted without ever looking back.

None of that was true.

"Look." He slid further up her body. Balancing on his elbow so he could loom over her and look her in the eye. "I know this seems like a dick move."

"Gee, you think?"

He trailed the backs of his finger over her cheek. "I have to go home and get washed up before heading into work."

She glanced at the clock. "What time do you get in?"

"Early."

Skepticism still spun around her. "Define that."

"Before six."

Her eyes bugged as if the thought horrified her. "I'll barely get up that early for morning classes when school is in session. In summer, six is definitely still sleep time."

"I can't imagine that." For kicks he slept in on the weekends until six-thirty.

"Not big on sleep, are you?"

"I only need a few hours and this time the exhaustion was so worth it."

The doubt left her face. She lifted her head and kissed him, quick but firm. "Sweet talker."

"I hate to have sex and run, but—"

"Yet you are."

A fist of unexpected and wanted guilt punched him in the gut. "Kyra—"

"We could call it hit-and-run sex."

They'd made a deal, had an understanding. He's the one who blew it by jumping his own timeline. "I thought we understood each other. I'm not the guy who got what he wanted and now is moving on. This really is about work."

She shoved him away and sat up. "Stop, I get it. You have a big, important job."

Despite the words, he sensed they teetered on the edge of something pretty bad. "I didn't expect to come over this morning. Hell, I haven't slept for something like twenty-four hours."

She froze in the act of reaching for her tee. "Why did you come?"

"Once I touched you, put my fingers inside you, I wanted more. All of it."

"Well then." She took a long shuddering breath. "You should go before I forget my good intentions and have my wicked way with you. Don't want to mess up your billable hours or have a client end up in jail because you're sleeping at your desk."

With those words the tension that had been revving up a second ago fizzled out. Crisis averted . . . he hoped. Next time he'd pick his words more carefully. And work on his timing.

He should have stopped there and let it go, but . . . "We're good?"

"For now."

"Remember every move you planned to use on me and we'll practice them at my house tomorrow." He slid off the bed and grabbed for his pants off the floor.

"We'll see."

"I'm ignoring your attempt at a dismissal." It took two fumbling tries to get his zipper up and the belt redone. "What time do you work?"

"I'll switch shifts."

He had his shirt on and tried to focus enough to rebutton it. "Are you sure?"

"If you can go without sleep for me, I can shift my schedule around for you."

"I plan on doing many things for and to you." The list ran through his head and he almost unzipped his pants again. "There are positions I'm ready to try. A whirlpool tub I think you'll like."

"Maybe I should nap today."

Damn, she made him smile. "Definitely rest up because I will never be too tired to pin you to a bed and slide inside you."

He could see it now. Hell, he didn't even have to dream it. The memory of how she felt and smelled, the sounds she made as she came, all played in his head.

She stood up, holding her T-shirt in front of her. "On that note, you should go before we both forget our lives outside of this room and crawl back into bed."

Recognizing she was right, he planted a quick kiss on her sexy mouth. Locating the rest of his clothes took another minute. He felt her gaze on him. She watched it all, even him putting on his jacket and heading for the door.

Seeing her standing there tempted him to call in sick for the first time in . . . forever. "I'll call you in a few hours—"

"After nine, please."

"—so we can figure out a time and the logistics for getting you to my house."

She rolled her eyes. Looked as if she'd been saving that up during most of the conversation. "I have this thing called a car."

"And I have these things called manners."

"Sometimes those can get in the way." She dipped the shirt and gave him a shot of her breasts. Also sent him an eyebrow wiggle. "But I'll be waiting."

He couldn't believe how long it took him to drag his gaze away from her chest and give her eye contact again. "That sounds far hotter than it should."

But no way was he leaving her half naked and hanging out in the hall as he walked out. To keep that from happening and cut down on the temptation, he took the shirt out of her hands and slipped it over her head. But not before touching every inch of exposed skin before the material covered her. Then he kissed her again, loving the way she melted into him.

When he broke it off, she reached around him to open the door and push him into the hallway. "You're in charge."

"Yes, Kyra. I am."

Kyra's legs still shook as she watched him walk down the hall and away from her place. Confidence radiated off him and showed in every sure step. The way he looked back and winked had her insides doing a little dance. She was so lost in the memory of him and look of him that she didn't hear the door open across the hall.

"That was quick," Gena whispered as she joined in watching Bast turn the corner toward the elevator bank.

The sound made Kyra jump. "I didn't know you were out here."

With her hair in a barely-holding-on ponytail and wearing lounge pants, Gena looked as if she just staggered out of bed. "Obviously."

Sure he was gone, Kyra eyed her friend. "And the word you were looking for is 'spectacular,' not 'quick.'"

Gena laughed. More like giggled. "I can tell by the goofy expression."

Not wanting to put her private life on display, not after promising discretion, Kyra motioned for Gena to come inside and close the door behind her.

Despite the hour and the fact her bones had turned to jelly, Kyra smiled as she slumped down on the edge of her bed. "Why are you up so early?"

Gena hovered by the door, as if coming closer might put her too close to the just-finished action. "I was pulling an all-nighter and heard voices."

"In other words, you were nosy and listening with a glass to the wall."

Gena grew more serious. "I heard a hot male voice, so sort of."

Kyra refused to let her good mood be derailed by whatever was going on inside Gena's head. Kyra liked her, had even grown to trust her, but Gena spent a lot of time overthinking. She didn't jump in and never talked about men in terms of a raw physical attraction. Describing her relationships, they all sounded measured and, Kyra feared, a bit boring.

She wanted Gena to break out and experience something—anything—that made her gasp. Every woman should enjoy a good gasp now and then.

The thought brought her mind zipping right back to Bast. "The smooth way he talks is not even the sexiest part about him."

Gena shrugged. "The part I saw retreating looked pretty good."

At least she noticed. Kyra viewed that as progress. "You have no idea."

Gena leaned back against the wall and shuffled her feet. Then she stared at her hands. A second later she peeked up again. "What about the leaving?"

Something stilled inside Kyra. "What?"

"Are we dealing with the type of guy who leaves skid marks getting out after the sex is done?"

Even though the same worry shot across her senses when Bast talked of having to leave, Kyra's fury started to simmer. It was one thing for her to question and another for Gena to try to put doubts in her head.

Rather than yell and let her anger spew, Kyra tried to explain. "He has to go to work today. Something about a big meeting."

"Okay."

The anger bubbled. "Just say it."

"Nothing." When silence fell over the room, Gena started fidgeting again. The talking started right after. "It's that he seemed to be in a rush to go."

"Why are you trying to make this into something bad?" Kyra fought the urge to take a rough verbal shot. It was a defense mechanism—hurt people before they hurt her—and one Kyra had tamped down on for years, trying to stamp it out of her personality completely. It wouldn't be cool to unload and Gena didn't deserve to become a target.

But Kyra had to make her understand how jumping to the negative ruined everything. "I really like him and it's working out, at least for now, so I want you to be happy for me."

"It's his type. The rich, connected guy who can call up any woman he wants." Gena pushed off from the door and stood across from Kyra. "I'm worried."

Every syllable hit Kyra in the wrong way because she shared the same doubts. "That he's out of my league?"

Gena's mouth flattened. "I didn't say that."

"Almost."

"Are you sure I'm the one thinking that and not you?"

Well, that hit too close to home. Kyra had fought for so long to peek out from under her father's awful shadow. The same petty criminal who viewed himself as a crime boss. He'd challenged Jarrett years ago for the run of the streets and lost it and Wade.

After being beaten down and spending some time in prison, her father somehow rose again. He ran a crew and collected on bad debts from his various loans. She had no idea what else he did but guessed none of it was legal.

The only reason she had any breathing room from him now was she played the game. Without telling Wade, she stayed in contact and didn't close the door. Her father actually thought she'd come back and work for him, when she knew college was a way of breaking out and vowed that would never happen.

None of her father's actions connected directly to her but she still carried the guilt. The man buried two wives without shedding even one tear and was courting another, much younger version as he flashed his money and threatened anyone who challenged him. He'd shunned Wade long ago and claimed there was a bounty on his head, for what she could never figure out.

Her father tried to marry her off to associates and drag her into his schemes. And she couldn't hide much of the sordid history from Bast. She wasn't sure about which facts he knew, but he'd dealt with her father back in the Jarrett days.

Bast with his fancy degrees and important family. Her with a family tree filled with decay.

Pushing all the doubt and worry aside, she said the words she repeated in her mind all the time. The ones meant to convince her as well as anyone who would listen. "We're different. I think that's good."

Gena's frown continued to deepen. "Just because he's got money doesn't make him better than you."

"I know." The response was automatic and most days she believed it, but some days the insecurities rose up and kicked her ass.

"Does he?"

"Yes." Kyra believed that. She had to believe that.

There was a brief beat of silence before Gena delivered a wobbly smile. "Then it sounds like everything is good."

Kyra didn't know if that was true, but at least she'd made significant relationship progress. Her word, not his. He appeared allergic to the very idea of a relationship. "I'm supposed to go to his place tomorrow night."

"Now that's impressive." Gena traced her fingertip along the edge of the dresser. "If he didn't trust you with the silverware, you wouldn't have gotten an invite."

"I didn't think of it that way." And she wasn't sure she wanted to.

"You should." Gena dropped her hand and headed for the door. "We'll celebrate after we both get a few hours of sleep."

Kyra realized the knocking was the sound of her tapping foot and stopped. "Believe it or not, I know what I'm doing."

After holding at the door, Gena glanced over her shoulder. "You're not the one I'm wondering about."

TEN

The next day had gone to hell before eight in the morning. More than ten hours later Bast had corrected all the misdirection and cleaned up the fallout from every client explosion. It was as if the good people of DC had lost their minds. So much complaining, and one businessman after another who wanted out of problems without writing a big check. Talk about not understanding how the power game was played in this town.

The worst news came a half hour ago. Natalie insisted on coming in today instead of tomorrow as scheduled. He half expected her to show up in his doorway demanding his attention. That's the way she operated. She didn't give people the opportunity to say no. She hovered and swooped when you weren't looking. Bast admired the strategy.

If a man acted the same way, he'd be praised for his strategy. Natalie took a lot of flak for being tough and smart. For all the forward strides, the CIA remained a boys' club, run by powerful men and some who wished they were, hampered by archaic thinking. Things were changing but not fast enough for Natalie to get the credit she deserved.

Bast knew because he'd negotiated the deal for Elijah and Becca with Natalie in the room. She asked the right questions and pushed for concessions at the right time before talking about letting two valued agents—her words—go. She played every move as Bast would have done. Didn't concede much and stayed focused.

Her male superiors underestimated her and talked around her. Bast didn't make that mistake. He recognized her power and refused to attend any meeting without her being present and signing off on the deal. But that didn't mean he wanted to see her now.

No, he mapped it all out. He'd head over to Kyra's place in about an hour. Tuck her in his car and get her to his home and into bed, then keep her there. No clothes. No limits. No talk of anything except what he intended to do to her.

A simple plan.

Natalie ruined all of that. She talked about an emergency that heightened her concern for her safety. For a woman like Natalie to divulge even that much meant the walls were about to come down around her. Bast had a soft spot for her. One that took some time to develop, but it existed. Which meant all the things he wanted to do to Kyra had to wait.

After asking his assistant to hold his calls and shutting his door and locking it against the buzz of activity in the office halls and the conference room a few doors down, Bast lifted the receiver and punched in Kyra's cell number.

She picked up on the second ring. "Are you downstairs already?"

Wrong conclusion. He really had to work on the shitty treatment she accepted from guys in the past. "When I pick you up, I'll park the car and come to the door."

"Not the honk-the-horn type?"

"Not for about fifteen years." The scratchy sound on the line registered. When he realized she sounded breathless his mind went to a dirty place. "What exactly are you doing?"

Her long exhale echoed in his ear. "How can you tell I'm doing anything?"

"My hearing is fine and your breathing is all harsh and hot."

"Smart-ass."

The labored breathing continued but he also heard the smile in her voice. She had to know the breathy thing would do something to him. He wouldn't be surprised if she saw his number and got all flustered just to torture him. If so, point to Kyra because all he could think about now was her body stretched out across her bed with him over her.

He decided to share. "You sound like you did when you begged me to fuck you faster."

A beat of silence filled the line. "Are you really at work?"

Yeah, the sex talk on work time surprised him, too. He only intended to call and talk scheduling. Now his mind wandered to a much hotter place.

"In my big office with the door closed." He leaned back in his chair and brushed a hand up and down his leg as the sudden need to keep moving hit him.

"Well, aren't you naughty?" The breathiness fell away and that husky fuck-me-now tone took its place.

He loved that sound. "I plan to be very soon."

"What time are you coming over?"

He could hear her moving around. Her voice cut from soft to loud as if she kept shifting the cell in her hand. The temptation to stall by asking her what she was doing came and went. He needed to spell this out. "That's the problem. I can't."

"Why?"

"Scheduling issue."

"Okay." Her voice boomed through the phone. So did her anger.

"Wow." His chair squeaked as he rolled closer to the edge of his desk and leaned on his elbows. "It's amazing how that one

word managed to telegraph 'you're an ass' and 'I'm going to cas-
trate you' at the same time."

"Picked up on that, did you?" The sharp whack of her voice
made her point.

"I have a work emergency." He kept the response simple and
clear. She should understand and—

"Uh-huh."

Son of a bitch.

Frustration smacked into him with an edge of anger right behind.
People might not like him or want to deal with him, but they trusted
him. He didn't fuck around when negotiating and never screwed
anyone by playing a bait and switch. Yet the woman he wanted to
strip naked and keep that way doubted him.

"You think I'm lying." Every time he thought it his temperature rose a degree.

"Are you?"

That time he heard another sound in her voice. Maybe hurt.
He wasn't sure but now he wondered about the men who came
before him. Maybe younger guys threw her lousy pickup lines.
The dumbasses. The whole playing-games part of being with someone turned Bast off. He said what he meant and expected to be
treated the same way.

Tiptoeing through this minefield would be tough because he
could guess the thoughts spinning through her mind. He went with
the response least likely to get him kicked in the balls later. "No."

"That's succinct."

"Do you need me to have my law partner write you a note
verifying my absence? He's out of town but maybe he could fax it in."
When she didn't say anything, not even a "no thanks" to his sarcasm,
Bast stomped down his rising anger and tried again. "Well?"

"I'm still thinking." But some of the heat left her voice.

"This is one of those cases that impacts a lot of people."

"Including me, apparently." She huffed as the moving sounds started again.

"Listen to me." His hand tightened on the phone as he focused on the streaks of color in the painting directly across from him on the wall. "We will push the dinner back one night. That's all I'm talking about."

This kind of thing happened when people met up to have sex. Schedules got messed up and changes had to be made. No big deal . . . yet part of him sensed it was.

"That means I have to change shifts again."

She didn't say "duh" but he sensed it. He also hated putting her through a game of musical shifts. That amounted to a big mess, annoying for her and the other attendants at the club. No one liked the person who kept moving schedules around and ensured nothing ever stayed settled. Bast knew that from the in-fighting that occurred every year at the firm as they attempted to work out office coverage over the holidays. The posturing made him sorry to be managing partner.

"Okay, the shift thing sucks. I get that." He closed his eyes and cursed Natalie. If her life literally wasn't on the line, he'd push her off and go through with his plans.

"Imagine how I feel."

"I want to spend the whole night with you." Since he fucked up the leaving part so badly last time, he needed things to go right or this arrangement could end before he had the chance to explore more of her. And he could go a lifetime without seeing a repeat of the expression she shot him early this morning as he reached for his shirt to go. The one that didn't match their casual understanding.

"What are the chances of you canceling again tomorrow?"

"Zero." No hesitation. That was the goddamn answer. "We'll have dinner at my place tomorrow and—"

"Don't talk about sex when I want to gut punch you."

"You do?"

She barked out a rough laugh. "For a guy who's supposed to be such a big-time ladies' man, you're being a bonehead."

"This won't be the last time, so you might want to get used to it." But it was time to get them back on the sex track. "But maybe there is a way I can make you feel better."

"That sounds like a lame line."

"Trust me."

"A little warning here, there are any number of things you could say next that will ruin your admittedly slow forward progress in our relationship."

He decided to ignore the word "relationship" and smile anyway. "Like?"

"I'm not a woman you bribe."

He had no intention of doing that. Exact opposite. His idea would be fun for both of them. "What about seduce?"

"I'm listening again."

The catch in her voice let him know she was on the hook. "What were you doing when I called?"

"Honestly?"

He thumped his fingers against his desk. The steady beat gave him focus as he fought for control. "That is always how I want you to answer my questions."

"Okay, Mr. Lawyer Man."

The way she shot back and verbally sparred with him turned him on almost as much as those legs. She opened her mouth and his temperature spiked and his dick got hard. The thing where she didn't take any shit made him wild to have her. She carried her body and held her ground with a confidence well beyond how he remembered being when he was twenty-something.

"I'm serious." At this point he was more curious than serious.

"I was on the treadmill."

Not really the answer he expected. "What?"

"The thing by the window was not, as you may have thought from the stack of shirts, a clothes rack." She mumbled something unintelligible under her breath. "I cleaned it off for once and used it. Well, technically, I used it for eight minutes, then I saw your number on my cell. Thanks for the diversion even though the subject of this call kind of sucks."

That was a lot of words. Almost amounted to babbling. He tried to wade through it all. "Why would you have a treadmill and not use it?"

"Laziness, maybe? I have no idea."

"Yet you look like that." One of the benefits of being younger and possessing a speedy metabolism, he guessed. If he went days without exercise, his brain got clouded and his gut expanded. "Must be nice."

"What?"

"Nothing." He'd be damned if he knew what she was trying to tell him, or not tell him. "I guess I'm wondering why you turned it on all of a sudden today."

She sighed. Even miles away and over a phone line he knew what the noise meant. Something about men being slow and clueless, and him being their idiot king.

"Because I plan to get naked and slide all over you tonight and pretended one day of exercise would tighten up the not-so-tight parts." This time she snorted. "Scratch that. I *planned* to do that. I may as well go eat a brownie now."

He ignored the shot because it was crap. The rest could only be described as unbelievable. She had to be fucking kidding. He looked at her ass and could barely form words. He entered her and his brain malfunctioned. And she was over there worrying about calories. The whole idea she didn't see what he saw made him lose his mind.

Trying not to yell because he was already hanging on the edge of never having sex with her again due to the cancellation, he stated his case. "So that we're clear here, you do not need to change your body in any way for me."

"Decent guys always say things like that."

"This one means it." She just didn't give an inch. Women rarely made it this hard on him. He had to admit he didn't hate the change of pace with Kyra. Being challenged suited him. "I think my reaction to seeing you naked should tell you I love everything about how you look."

"Okay, you're forgiven for being a dumbass earlier."

If she said one word about a diet, he would drag her over to the club and sit her down for a lecture, then let all of their friends have a turn. "I'm also serious. Do not change one thing for me, except maybe your insistence on wearing underwear. You can knock that off."

"I'll take that request under advisement."

Time to get back to the other reason for his call. The one that rose up after he heard her voice. "So, what are you wearing now?"

Her laughter filled the line. "Dirty old man."

"Damn straight." No way would he back down now. "Tell me."

"An exercise bra and bicycle shorts. In other words, an outfit I would never wear outside my apartment."

Funny but he wanted to see her in it. Look and then peel it off piece by piece. "You shouldn't be wearing it now either."

"You mean . . ." The breathless quality returned but this sounded different. Deeper . . . sexier.

"Are you all sweaty?" In his mind she was. Sweaty and half naked and two seconds away from getting on her knees in front of him.

"Let me run my hand over my chest and see . . . Well, look at that. I'm wet."

The inflection in her voice. The soft draw that let him know her thoughts mirrored his own. He loved that she played the game with him. "You should take the clothes off so you don't get sick."

"It's summer."

"It can happen. I've read studies."

"You like stories?" She let out a soft sigh. "Tell me one."

He had a vision in his head and followed that. "I only know dirty ones."

"Maybe I should lie down for this."

Sweet damn, he wished he was in her apartment. He'd have her on her stomach in two seconds. Pushing back against him, begging for his cock to enter her, in five.

He'd have to settle for getting her naked and wet. "But you need to take those clothes off first so you don't get the sheets all sweaty."

"I have to put the phone down to take off the bra."

All good answers. "Put it on speaker." Because he wanted to hear every move and she was going to need her hands free.

So was he.

Dropping his cell on the desk, he hit a button and let the sound of her rough breathing fill the room. With his hands free, one went to his lap.

"I can wait." But he really couldn't. He craved that gruff rumble in the back of her throat. She didn't scream when she came—not yet—but that damn noise set his blood on fire.

"Done."

"Are your breasts—"

"Tits." She sounded so naughty, so tempting, when she used the word.

"Very good. Are your tits all wet with sweat? Rub them and see." He closed his eyes and pictured her smooth skin. The way they fit his palms. "Hold them in your hands."

She let out a little groan. "They feel good."

"Massage them to make sure." He rubbed a hand over his crotch. "Swirl your fingers over the nipples."

"So good."

"Harder." He heard her mumble something but he needed her gasping. "I don't think you're giving them enough attention."

"I am." Her breath hiccupped.

It was as if she wanted to torture him. "If I were there, I'd push your breasts together and suck on those nipples until you screamed."

"Come over."

"I can't but it doesn't matter because you're touching them for me." The temptation to get in the car and race over there rocked through him. "Imagine my hands under yours, right against your bare skin."

"I love your hands."

He wanted her brain misfiring as she fought for words and shifted on the bed. "Squeeze them together."

She groaned. "You should see them."

"I remember." He could feel them without even touching them. "I remember every delicious part of you. How your skin turns pink and your hips come off the mattress as you get excited."

"It's happening now." The words slurred together.

He had to move to the next step or risk losing it right there. "Now your pants. Your underwear . . . are you wearing any?"

Hints of shuffling filled the line. "White cotton."

Sounded sexy to him. On her, he'd take her in anything. "They're probably wet and tight."

"So uncomfortable."

His hand clamped down on the armrest of his chair. "Shove them down. All the way off. Clothes will get in your way."

"Why?"

Man, she did dirty well. The questioning tone and mock

innocence. She played the role and revved him up. And if he didn't have her again soon, he'd rip walls apart in frustration.

"You know why, Kyra. Don't be naughty."

The deep laugh echoed through the phone. "But I love being naughty."

"Answer me. Are they off?" He pressed his palm against his pants and rubbed the ridge of his erection. "You need to be naked."

"I am." She made a sound that suggested she stretched out and loved the sensation of it.

"Should I believe you?" Fuck, with his eyes closed he could see her, even smell her.

"You should come see me." She cut off to treat him to a series of soft moans. "My tits are so sensitive. So ready for you."

He was never going to survive his time with her.

"Lie back on the bed and open your legs." Those incredible legs and soft thighs. "Nice and wide."

"Okay."

The way she obeyed played with his head. He slid his hand over his pants and let the friction of material on material build the pressure inside him. "In my dirty story the woman liked to touch herself. Do you like that, Kyra?"

"Yes."

"Say my name." Because he loved hearing it on her lips.

"Sebastian."

The way she said it, as if on a whisper . . . fucking damn. "Are you already touching yourself? Are your fingers inside you?"

"On my inner thighs."

The heel of his hand rubbed in circles over his fly. "You are so close. Just slide your hands until the tips of your fingers touch your pussy."

"There's a naughty word."

And he wanted to hear her say it. "Tell me where your fingers are."

"Oh, no." She sounded like she was scolding him. "I can't say that."

She was born for this game. Destined to drive him to wild distraction. One minute she pitched her voice and sounded confused and embarrassed and the next she hit him with heated disobedience calculated to disarm. The dual act had his insides clenching.

"Tell me, Kyra. I want to hear the word." He outlined his erection as he imagined her hands on him. "Where are your fingers?"

"In my pussy."

He felt the word rattle inside him. "How many fingers?"

She gasped as her breathing quickened and grew louder. "One."

"That's not enough, is it?"

"Hmm, no." The half moan sounded like pleasure.

"Rub a fingertip over your clit. In circles, round and round." Just as he would do if he were there.

"It feels so good." She drew out the last word.

"Now slide the middle finger of your other hand inside your pussy. The whole way in. But don't forget to give that clit the attention it needs." He could hear the rustle of the comforter and the beginnings of that adorable throat rumble. "Are you doing it, Kyra?" When she didn't answer, he kept pushing. "Raise your hips so your finger can go nice and deep. Pump it in and out while you rub your clit."

"This is . . ."

"Do you need more?" His erection pressed against the back of his zipper and he lowered it with careful ticks before he had an accident he couldn't hide. "I think you do. I think you need to come."

"Sebastian." Her breath cut off at the end of his name.

"Add a second finger to the one pumping inside you." He had his cock in his hand now, rubbing up and down and dreaming about entering her and how good she would feel against him.

"It's too tight."

"You can stretch. Your pussy stretched around my cock, it can hug two fingers." She was so fucking tight. The clench of her body around his tip almost had him coming before he slipped fully inside her. "Are you doing it, Kyra?"

The bed creaked and she sighed.

She was close. Hell, he was close. The sounds of the traffic floors below reached him and the life of the office outside his door filtered through the walls. He'd demanded his time with her be private and this barely qualified. And there was no one to blame but him for the violation.

Still, hearing her and imagining her body around his took him to a mental place that was anything but professional. "Plunge your fingers in faster."

He needed her to come.

"I can't—"

"You can. I've seen you reach your peak. It is so fucking sexy."

"Tell me." It sounded more like a sigh than words.

"Your head snaps back and your pussy clenches." A glorious sight and one he wanted her to repeat soon. "Is it clenching now?"

The shifting. The sexy sounds from her throat. They all came through before her answer. "Yes."

"Clamp down on your fingers. Do it hard and hold." He tightened his hand over his cock and pulled harder. "Are you right on the edge?"

"Yes."

Imagining her, thinking about her body sprawled out and her legs wide open, his hips started to move. They slipped forward in time with his hand. "Flick your finger over your clit faster and faster. Pretend it's my tongue licking over your slick wetness. My cock fucking you."

Her harsh breathing and the thump of the bedpost were his only answers.

"Clench one more time." She teetered on the edge. He could feel it. "There you go, baby. Keep pushing and tightening."

A half-strangled sound escaped her and wiped out every other noise. Having watched it all, he knew she was coming. The orgasm washed through her as he listened. He heard rustling and thudding and then only breathing, rugged and fast. She would blow out air and gulp it back in.

He put his elbow on the desk and imagined being there in her room for every expressive moment. Her heels digging into the mattress and head thrown back. The way she arched her back and pushed out her breasts. How slick she got and how hard her pussy pulsed.

He loved it all.

That fast the fire swept through him. He dropped his fist to the base of his cock and pulled one last time as his head fell forward. He barely grabbed the tissues in time. His cock twitched and jumped. He sucked in a breath. Come filled the tissue and dribbled onto his palm. He missed the suit pants, but only by pure luck.

When his head cleared enough to listen, he realized everything had stopped and the other side of the line had gone quiet. "Kyra?"

"Damn." Her voice was filled with awe.

"You can say that again."

"Your groan—"

"I groaned?" He had no memory of anything but her sexy sounds.

"Did you come, too?"

There was no reason to lie and he'd promised her he wouldn't. "In my hand like an untested teen."

The lack of control shocked him. Not just the part about using his office, the idea he let his mind go there and couldn't hold the reins on his body's reaction.

She giggled. Actually giggled. "It's kind of flattering."

He would never understand women. "It was all you."

"And what you heard from over here was all you."

Man, he loved the thought of that. "This couldn't have been the first time you did that to yourself."

"True, but I don't usually do it naked across the bed in the middle of the afternoon."

"That's a shame." Because he'd be able to call up the mental picture whenever he wanted now. She could be at work or in class, and in his head she'd be on that bed touching herself. The vision worked for him.

"And I've never had a director before."

He made a mental note to have her do it again. Soon. "Think of how it will feel when I'm there with you, watching you touch yourself."

She blew out a long breath. "I'm going to have a heart attack."

Damn, he wished he could see her face and the flush on her skin. "Then you will never know the joys of my whirlpool."

There was a weird clicking sound, almost as if she were hitting her tongue against the back of her teeth. "I know it's cliché that women like bubble baths and all that, but I have a confession."

Since she sounded weirdly shy, he had to know. "Go ahead."

"I've never been in one."

That seemed like a pretty fundamental experience to him. "How is that possible?"

"Didn't have one growing up. It wouldn't have gone with the dinners of cheese and crackers. And if I tried to put a bathtub in my apartment now, I'd have to lose the bed."

"I oppose that option."

The giggle turned into a deep throaty laugh. "I thought you might."

Every now and then he forgot about her upbringing. The idiot dad who thought he was a player but didn't bother with feeding his kids. The guy kept both kids on a tight leash and put them in the family business—basically, loan sharking and stealing—early. Wade wasn't his biological kid but the father insisted he owned them both.

Despite the odds, they both broke out. Kyra relied on her quickness and toughness to find another way. She'd earned a better life.

No reason not to start with a tub full of bubbles. "Then you can enjoy my tub."

"I'll try it."

He wasn't there to see the shoulder shrug but could almost hear it. "Did I mention there's a separate sprayer?"

"Do I want to know what that means?"

"I'll show you one of the many uses for the strong jet spray tomorrow. How I can use it on you and get you squirming." Just thinking about the water hitting her sensitive pussy made him fidget in his seat. "Think about that while I'm working tonight."

"I doubt I'll think about anything else."

ELEVEN

An hour later all Kyra had to do was call up the memory of Bast's deep voice and her skin flushed with heat. Touching her body while she listened to his words turned into a wild ride. Which turned into a shower and a mental countdown until tomorrow night.

If he canceled again, she would head over to that fancy office and make a scene. Better yet, she'd go over and drag his sorry ass out of there and to the nearest bed. She had no idea what his ex-wife was like, except for her unfortunate love of tattling, or any of the others in the parade of women Bast had dated. Could be he liked the type who took his nonsense without complaint and let him do whatever he wanted. The ones who hung on every word and sucked up whatever precious few minutes he deigned to give them.

Screw. That.

In this relationship—and that's what it was no matter how he referred to it—she insisted on being equal. He could boss her around in bed because that was so hot her blood sizzled, but she was not a sex toy or a mere convenience. The sooner he realized that, the smoother the whatever-it-was-they-had would go.

But the idea of seeing him in his office did have some appeal. Maybe she could wear a coat and nothing underneath . . . just to test his control. As far as she was concerned, the man could stand a little less. The whole cool, detached smart guy thing with the sexy glasses totally worked for her, but now she knew he possessed another side. A guy who lost it in bed, didn't hold back. She wanted to explore more of that guy.

Tightening her belt across her stomach, she pulled the lapels of the short robe closer together. The heat on her skin died down, leaving her with a slight chill. It was the perfect excuse to sit on her bed, eat soup and watch bad television. Not the night she had planned, but an okay alternative.

She walked over to the kitchenette lining the wall. Not having a full stove turned her into a microwaving expert. She doubted Bast would be impressed with her cooking skills. Hell, he probably had a cook or some other weird rich-person thing.

And that fast, a wave of insecurity washed over her. She balanced her hands against the edge of the counter and fought it off. She refused to feel inferior. She'd spent her whole life pushing back on that useless emotion and shoved one more time.

She'd almost wrestled the negative thoughts down when the knocking started. Not a gentle tap. No, this was an insistent banging. The noise had her jumping from one side of the small studio to the other to check the door.

Up on tiptoes, she peered into the hallway hoping to see Bast but knowing she wouldn't. The hovering presence outside took on an eerie vibe. That's what happened when a person stood right on top of the door.

The knocking started again. "Open up."

The angry voice matched the scowl she could just make out through the distorted lens. All of it reminded her of the days before she broke away and found a life of her own.

"Now, girl." Her father's demands hadn't changed. He used the same command he'd used since she was six.

Him being here, in her private space, shook her confidence and had her mind racing. So did the bodyguard bouncer type hanging around out there with him.

Almost without thinking, certainly without entertaining the possibility of saying no, she unlocked and opened the door. Her father's furious gaze raked over her. The guy with him took more time on the visual tour. Both of them had her wanting to tug down the bottom of the robe and hide behind the door.

"What took so long?" her father barked out.

The gruff voice had the same effect as always. At least the same since she became an adult. She stood up even straighter, refusing to snivel and hide. "What's going on?"

Ignoring her, her father motioned to his man. "You stay out here."

Before she could say anything, her father pushed his way in and slammed the door shut behind him with the toe of his foot. He walked around, checking out every inch. Touching this book and that plate. He stopped at the window and pulled back the curtain to the streets of the Foggy Bottom neighborhood below.

"What are you doing here?" She crossed her arms over her chest and held her ground near the door.

"You know why."

Her mind zipped to Bast and her protective instincts rose. "I don't—"

She broke off when her father turned around. Fury pulsed off him and almost smacked her across the room. Richard Royer stood just under six feet. He wasn't blessed with Wade's size or strength but they could both pull off a death stare that made her want to crawl under a bed and stay there. Her father shot it at her now with full force.

"You've been keeping some interesting company." He dropped

down into her oversized chair with his arm across the back top of the cushions. "Secret company."

This couldn't be about Bast. If her father knew, if he mentioned Bast, she'd have to walk away from him. Anything to keep him clean of her father's stench. Of his awful reach.

The idea of her time with Bast being over before it started had her fighting to keep from doubling over.

"What are you talking about?" The question was her way of stalling. Possibilities ran through her head as she tried to figure out where she messed up.

The days passed as they always did. She checked in with her father, provided scattered bits of information on her life, enough to keep him satisfied, and stayed as far away from him in person as possible. Appease and survive. That had been her motto since she turned eighteen. Before that survival at any cost had been the only game.

Wade believed she'd broken all ties with the man who always acted like being her birth father meant having ownership over her, whether that meant battering her as a potential future unwilling bride to some slick piece of garbage he did business with, or having her play lookout on a job. But she knew one did not simply disappoint Richard Royer and go on to find a normal life. Her father hounded and destroyed. He figured out what mattered and tried to take it away.

That was his way of handling someone. Wade escaped but only because of his size and his luck in having the power of Jarrett looming behind him. Her father had tried to move in, insisting that by adopting Wade all those years before and giving him a new last name, he'd earned rights over his stepson. Jarrett and Wade had pushed back and kept pushing back.

They stepped in and issued demands about her father's organization leaving her alone, too. But things were different with her. Wade was the disappointment he inherited when he married their mother, then drove her to an early grave. She was his blood.

"You continue to test me." Her father pointed to the edge of the bed. "Sit."

She thought about refusing but knew that would only result in him grabbing her arm and putting her there. Tucking the robe under her, she sat down. "Why?"

"Jarrett Holt."

The name skidded through her. She'd expected one thing and heard another, and her brain rushed to catch up. "What about him?"

"You're working his club." Her father leaned forward with his elbows on his knees. "Are you fucking him?"

Her thoughts screeched to a halt. Forget trying to reason or form a new argument. "No."

"That's a shame."

And that summed up her father's belief in the value of women. He used them for sex and as pawns, and neither wife—her mom or Wade's—lived long enough to contest the treatment. "Jarrett has a girlfriend."

"How is that relevant to my question?"

"Jarrett is loyal to her." Kyra tried to imagine how Becca would react to her father. To Kyra's mind, Becca was this tall, beautiful strong woman. That didn't mean she couldn't be broken.

"You know the rules." Kyra's father peeked up at her. Gray touched the edges of his black hair and the veins stuck out on the back of his hands. He'd lived a rough life and seemed to age at rapid speed, adding years each time she saw him. "If you move in on a mark, you contact me."

"I'm going to school. I'm not working Jarrett."

"Bah." He waved her off and stood up. "It's a smart cover. The degree will put you in bigger circles than managing that clothing store in Georgetown did."

"The job was fine." It grated to defend a job where she hated the people and the work, but no way was she giving her father one inch.

He shook his head as he started to pace. "Like that school, it was a waste of good time and money."

Never mind that it was her time and her money. This man had never paid for a thing for her. After her mother died, he barely provided the basic necessities. He got away with as little as he could to keep child services off his tail.

"Holt has access to important people." Her father nodded his head, as if he became more enthralled with his argument the longer he talked. "Getting in there, wearing that tight skirt, will put you in touch with them. It's smart."

"That's not what's happening."

"Take credit, girl." He went to her small fridge under the counter and shoved some of the bottles around. "For once you're using your gifts the right way."

The temptation to agree just to get rid of him proved great. The easy way out. Lie and duck. But that solution went nowhere. "I am not working a con on Jarrett."

He slammed the door hard enough for the jars inside to clink together. "You will do what you're told."

A scream rattled in her throat. "I'm in school now."

"No one cares about that."

She did. An education gave her a start. Let her put a few inches between the life she'd known and the one she wanted.

He snorted. "Don't make me bring you back home."

The threat started a terrified twisting in her stomach. She was an adult and had resources and it couldn't happen but the thought of it brought all the youthful worries rushing back. "I am not playing Jarrett. It's a job. A good job. It pays the rent."

So did the loans and the series of jobs she'd taken to earn cash. Undergraduate school took forever because she kept stopping to stockpile some money. She let her father believe she kept leaving because of poor grades. Truth was she left to maintain her independence, to not have to beg Wade for money or rely on her father for anything. The strings to him were the type she'd never be able to snap.

"We are not arguing about this." Her father stopped in front of her.

"I agree."

He towered over her like he always did, intimidating and menacing while his ego sucked all of the oxygen out of the room. "You finish the setup and I'll work on how we can use this to our advantage."

"No."

"It's done," he said, talking over her as if she'd never spoken. "What are you wearing?"

"What?" She looked down, relieved the material pulled tight and hugged her body. She hated anything that made her more vulnerable in front of him. "My robe."

"You'll need something sexier if you plan to make this con work." He headed for the door and opened it, stopping only to issue one last warning. "Be ready for my call."

When the door shut, Kyra slipped down to sit on the side of the bed. A frigid air filled her apartment. Her father had that talent. To freeze everything in his path. Hollow and aching, she sat there with her hands open on her lap.

She didn't hear the door open. Nothing registered until Gena crouched in front of her.

"Are you okay?" she asked.

"No." Because that was the truth. The chill wouldn't leave Kyra's bones and her head throbbed.

"Who was that?"

"My father."

After a brief hesitation Gena spoke again. "And the other guy?"

"I don't even want to know. Probably the latest version of his mindless muscle."

"I don't understand." Gena sat next to Kyra on the bed. "Did he just stop by for a quick visit?"

"To issue threats, actually."

Gena's head snapped back. "What?"

The stunned sound of her friend's voice woke Kyra up. She glanced over and saw the pale skin and stunned stare. For a second Kyra wondered if she wore the same expression.

"He's not a nice man." In the world of understatements, Kyra considered that a doozy.

"He's your dad." Gena said it as a statement, drawing out each word.

"Not the take-you-to-school, father-daughter-dance type." Kyra didn't even know how to explain it. Gena came from a regular family in a regular town somewhere in the Midwest. Someone like Richard Royer probably moved in very different circles. "He's more like the 'do what I tell you or someone will get hurt' type."

"Are you exaggerating?"

"Not even a little." Kyra thought she undersold it. The man she knew growing up, the one who went to prison and came out more paranoid, liked to hurt people any way he could. "He thinks he's a mafia-like figure but he doesn't have that much power."

"Then he can't be that bad."

"Don't be fooled. He wallows in filth and does awful things." She had to get up. Move. Maybe making the soup would help.

"But he looks . . ."

"Normal?" With the graying hair and khaki pants he resembled other men his age. It was the gun and the scar along his check that suggested otherwise. "Yeah, he's worked on that over the years. He fits in better since getting out of prison."

"Prison?"

Kyra's hand shook as she reached for the can of soup. Setting it down without slamming it against the counter took all her

concentration. "It was the one time he couldn't get one of his min-
ions to take the fall, and the charges stuck. Thanks to those nine-
teen months I was able to get into college and settled without him
being able to stop it."

"I don't get it."

"You don't want to." With a deep inhale, Kyra abandoned the
can and turned back around to face Gena. "And he treats me well
compared to how he treats my brother, Wade."

"You never talk about your family."

"I make sure to keep my father as far out of my life as possible.
I talk to him to ensure he doesn't come looking for me and messing in my life."

"Like he just did." Gena stared at the door as if waiting for
him to burst back in. "Why was he here?"

Such a good question. Kyra had a list of answers, each one
scarier than the one before. She went with the global excuse.
"Because he's tired of being left out of my life."

She frowned. "He said that?"

"It was implied."

"So, now what?"

The possibilities there were even worse. She'd have to warn Jarrett and tell Wade the truth about how much she talked with her
father. When it came to Bast, she'd have to hope their privacy pact
kept him insulated and safe. Any inkling that wasn't the case and
she'd leave. No matter how much it killed her.

"I work around him." She thought she had but clearly that had
blown apart. Figuring out why became her immediate goal.

It was possible her father had people checking on her. Wouldn't
be the first time. It was equally believable her father stumbled into
the information. Happened to have the right guy at the right place
and gathered the intel. That was more likely since the club, up until

now, had been off limits and not in the part of town where her father worked his schemes.

"Will that work?" Gena ran her palms up and down her legs. The material from her sweatpants scratched under her nails. "Will he just go away?"

Kyra skipped over that question because the only honest answer sucked—no. "If you see him or his goon around here again, stay away from them."

"Your father is that dangerous?"

That was the easiest question of the night. "Yes, he is."

TWELVE

Bast knew from experience he had to hold the line on Natalie Udall. She dealt in secrets and traded in information. She'd been trained to evade and pick at a topic until she uncovered the intel she needed.

On top of all that, she generally insisted on getting her way. So did he, which led to the distinct possibility of an impasse whenever they met. Since she showed up forty minutes early and refused to wait in the reception area, another showdown appeared to be looming.

He leaned back in his leather desk chair and eyed the formidable opponent across from him. And after spending so much time with her, negotiating and then celebrating the deal afterward, that's still how he saw her. Transitioning to attorney-client hadn't officially happened yet, though it would in a second, so long as they didn't get locked into a power struggle.

To prevent that from the first sentence, Bast started with a challenge. "I'm not a fan of having my schedule dictated to me by clients. Don't do it again."

She exhaled as she crossed one leg over the other and stared him down. "I'm not a client."

Technically, she wasn't wrong. "Then why are you here?"

"I don't want to be."

"I picked that up from the anger in your tone." It bounced off her and filled up the room until it threatened to choke off everything else.

"I'd rather be back in my office, but instead I'm here discussing a purely hypothetical situation with you."

A parameter he expected and didn't fight . . . for now. "Of course."

"One that's also confidential."

He held out a hand and motioned across his large office. "Look where you are. I deal in confidence."

"Your skills are of great interest to me right now."

He noticed she didn't specifically comment on needing help. Knowing her, she never would. "I'm taking from that convoluted sentence you intend to retain my services."

Thirty-something and striking with blond hair and big brown eyes that worked in deadly sexy combination, she downplayed her looks with conservative suits like the navy one she wore today. Everything about her said restrained and in command. He knew under the tight, pulled-back hair and severe frown was a smart and determined woman. One who possessed more than a touch of humanity and let it show back when they negotiated Becca's release from service.

Natalie's unblinking stare held now. Silence overtook the room and Bast vowed to sit there and not say a thing until he picked Kyra up tomorrow night if that's the stand Natalie needed to see before she spoke up.

The quiet lasted for a solid three minutes. No movement. No talking. Nothing but the soft tick of the clock on the wall and steady hum of the air conditioning. Sounds he never heard during regular work time.

At three minutes seven seconds she brought her hands together in front of her and started talking without any fanfare or reference. "I was told my clearance has been downgraded and would be revoked as soon as I sign a separation-from-service agreement. Of course, if I don't sign, the clearance will be revoked anyway."

"Which automatically terminates your position. That's a tidy circle." A typical CIA trick and a lousy one.

"You're not surprised."

"Are you?" Bast admired her. She'd taken a risk when she argued for Becca and Elijah to walk away clean, which required tough talk and balls of steel. The men in positions above her made it clear they viewed her as overstepping. "Do you have a copy of whatever they gave you?"

"I can't remove it from the office."

Bast hated the cloak-and-dagger bullshit in this town, and the folks at the CIA threw out the secrecy card in every sentence. This was just one example of the constant overreaching. True she had restrictions on her employment, but it wasn't as if she signed a blood oath to work for the CIA and faced a death squad at retirement. Some folks at the CIA acted as if the tiny print included those provisions.

But there was no need to run through that with Natalie because she once used the tricks now being turned on her. Karma was a fucking bitch. "We're dealing with the usual MO where you're supposed to sign it without legal input or having someone walk through it with you?"

"Of course."

"That's convenient for them."

She rested an elbow on the armrest and her foot started swinging. "At least I didn't find myself the unwitting victim of a car accident or mugging."

She threw the comment out there like it didn't matter. From the tension around her mouth to the sudden uncharacteristic fidgeting, he knew it did. Her body language telegraphed her concerns. Since she could potentially be taken out, he didn't blame her. She'd been at the CIA long enough to know it could happen. Had seen it happen.

The scenario played in Bast's head. The accident would occur and her files would be passed to someone else. If she were lucky, her exit would look as if it happened on the job and she'd get a star on the wall at Langley. In either case, some underling would pack up her desk and she'd be forgotten.

"You think, despite the document, they're not going to let you leave the easy way." He skipped asking it as a question because he knew it was fact. The woman had seen too much. Someone might think she was too savvy to be out there with all that knowledge in her head.

Good thing he possessed an impressive memory. He didn't bother with taking notes because they'd only be taken away later. Working on cases involving powerful people with a top-secret clearance both inside and out of clandestine agencies required the lawyer be cleared and certain case requirements be met. Bast knew the drill.

But there were so many questions in this case. "I'm wondering what exactly you're being set up to take the fall for."

"Well, Todd did have an accident." She didn't sound even slightly upset about the man's death. Probably had something to do with him being a traitor and attempting to sell secrets to the highest international bidder.

The official line talked about an "explosion following a gas leak" and the victim was some random Todd Rivers who worked in a boring job and most certainly *did not* work for the CIA. Those closest to the case knew the truth about Todd's death. Knew and stayed quiet.

"I assumed that order came from above you," Bast said, parsing his words to keep from violating her oath or his.

"There was no order. It was a gas leak." Her expression never changed but a hint of her Southern accent crept back into her voice.

He took that as confirmation. "Understood."

"Apparently my lack of loyalty and my betraying behavior went well beyond cleaning house." She blew out a long breath. "Negotiating the agreement with you for Elijah and Becca upset some of the old-school higher-ups."

It's what she didn't say that caught Bast's attention. He leaned forward, never breaking eye contact. "But this is really about Jarrett isn't it?"

The staring contest continued until her gaze danced to the right and lingered for a second on the bookshelves. When it returned to his face again it radiated with a new intensity. "The information Jarrett could have provided that did not change hands, yes."

"How does the CIA know that information even exists?" Bast knew because he collected it and worked up a bundle that served as Jarrett's safety net.

The CIA came after him once and if it happened again, Jarrett had intel on foreign threats to trade. He tried to trade it to buy Becca's freedom but Bast and Natalie made a different deal. One that didn't leave Jarrett vulnerable or cart Becca away from him in witness protection.

"If you don't think the agency continues to stake out the club and come up with ways to plant someone in there, you're not as smart as I need you to be." The whip of her voice was more like the Natalie he knew.

"The last person the agency planted ended up giving up her job and staying with Jarrett. I'm half expecting a surprise wedding between those two soon."

"Lord." Natalie rolled her eyes, but a touch of a smile appeared before she could swallow it back. "Ignoring Becca for a second, there are other ways to plant someone close to Jarrett. Maybe some guy who becomes his friend and confidant."

"Are we talking about the same Jarrett Holt?" The idea bordered on laughable. "He's not exactly open to making new friends."

"There are some people in the agency who still believe Jarrett is a direct line to significant information. They authorized an operation once to put people in here and look for intel, and they could do it again."

The words sent something dark spilling through Bast. This went past the ego blow of having his agreement threatened. Jarrett was his best friend and the idea of Jarrett being in danger was a constant red warning light flashing in Bast's brain.

"The plan backfired." First it worked and landed Jarrett in jail, but Bast breezed over that part. "Hell, thanks to Todd's double-dealing, the CIA had to disband an entire black-ops team."

Her foot kept swinging but she'd returned to her impromptu staring contest. "I am aware of that since I was the point person for most of it."

That was likely the closest she'd ever come to admitting she took Todd down because he not only crossed the agency and his country, but he crossed her.

"So, with you out of the way someone plans to set Jarrett up again?" Bast asked.

"I think they know he's holding material back that could hurt a lot of important people."

The first good news Bast had heard during the conversation. "That was the hope."

Her eyes narrowed. "You want people going after Jarrett? Fill me in on how that's a good thing."

"The bug was planted in the right ears of the right people as a scare tactic." Careful wording kept him from implicating his own ass. "Jarrett deals in secrecy on a level that rivals your operatives' skills but his is all the more powerful because it comes directly from the ground. But he will continue to hold those secrets until and unless the people he cares about are threatened."

She nodded. "In other words, one move and all of the nasty information, all of it backed up with evidence, becomes public knowledge."

That had always been the play. Bast put the pieces together. Jarrett played chicken. "It's a tense but necessary balance."

"But someone has to pay for an expensive op gone wrong. For the loss of potential CIA intel, even though it came from a rogue and illegal operation." Which brought them back around to the reason she ran over here and her need to retain him.

"Bottom line here, Natalie. You think the CIA will end your employment by ending you, then go after Jarrett and anyone else connected with this, regardless of the risk since there could be—and is—a safeguard in place." When she didn't respond, Bast kept going. "Even if that extreme case is not true, you have more fundamental issues. You're out of a job and some people are looking to make you an example."

"I was told I'll be lucky not to be subjected to criminal charges."

"I see the agency still runs by the same old rules, stupid as they may be." It issued threat after threat. Bast found the tactic tiresome but beatable. "What do you need from me?"

"This could be dangerous."

"You're giving me a protective warning?" There was a surprise. They'd always met as equals, neither needing protection but both ready to do battle. "Interesting."

"We have a history."

"We do." Talk about a delicate balance. She leveled accusations. They fought. They spent a lot of time together.

She reached into her blazer pocket and took out a folded piece of paper. Pushing it across the desk, she began outlining. "I want out, my pension even though I'm not vested, some guarantee of safety, a buyout and a way to make a living elsewhere. There's some other stuff on there."

Without opening it, he could see the markings of the blue pen and what looked like a list. "Fair enough."

Her head dropped and she watched her hands. "You need to understand that while we negotiate there will be a group of people sitting somewhere in a room running scenarios about whether it's easier to kill me."

"I know." He was not new to this horrible game.

Her head shot back up. "And whether they can ignore the agreements for Elijah and Becca or need to take them out as well."

Bast saw the comment coming and braced against the flinch. "Loose ends."

"We know Todd was about to sell information that could have hurt a lot of powerful people, businessmen and congressmen. Some might decide maybe it would be easier if no one knew." She shook her head. "I get that Jarrett has leverage but is it enough to save all of us?"

It would be. Bast would make it happen. "Why did you ever work for this agency?"

"I believed."

"In what?"

Her chin lifted. "There are a lot of people there doing good work. Necessary work."

"But it only takes one dirty one to cause a tragedy."

This time she did smile but it never reached her eyes. "Then I guess you better do your job well."

"Looks like you're officially a client."

Kyra listened to the mumble of activity seeping through the walls from the club. Raised voices and hints of music. The familiar sounds should have been soothing but she looked across Jarrett's massive desk and debated running off without opening her mouth.

Racing over here seemed like a good idea a half hour ago. Sneak in the back hall, talk with Jarrett, go home. Simple. Then she sat in the chair across from him and her mind went haywire.

They'd known each other for years. He functioned as a second brother to her, bossy and so sure he knew what she should do about *everything*. Many people viewed him as this Teflon millionaire who dabbled in the dark side, just on the edge of criminal life, but managed to look respectable on the outside. She knew him as the guy who helped her with math when she was a teen and sat with her for hours to pick the right graduate program.

But he was frowning now. "It's your night off, so why am I seeing you here?"

"There's something important I have to tell you, but you can't tell other people or try to fix this or anything. Basically, I need you to not be you."

"Excuse me?"

"You just need to have the information." If her life imploded and her father moved in, she needed Jarrett to know from the start she attempted to make it all right. "So, the plan is for you to listen and then wait before acting on what you hear."

"There's no way I'm agreeing to those terms since I don't even understand what we're talking about."

She shifted in the chair, missing her robe and her evening of soup eating, and dove in for the kill. "I know it sounds weird, but I need you to help me but to do it my way."

"It?"

"Please just go along."

"You're not fighting fair." He exhaled as he balanced his head against the back of his big chair. "You know I'm intrigued and know I will say whatever I need to say to figure out what's happening."

"You can't fix this. You can only be warned." She ran her fingers up and down the armrest, comforted by the feel of the smooth wood under her fingertips.

His gaze followed the small movement. "You have my attention."

Even though he technically didn't agree, she knew he would honor her request unless he thought she was in danger. The nerves stopped firing inside her. She relaxed for the first time since her father walked out of her apartment.

"Now I'm wondering what's so important that I need to know whatever this is at ten o'clock on your night off," Jarrett said.

"My father came to see me." As bomb dropping went, that was a pretty big one. She winced as she said it and waited for the yelling to start. Saying her father's name in either Jarrett's or Wade's presence guaranteed yelling.

Instead of nuclear fallout, Jarrett's jaw clenched and his words came out strained as if he had a stranglehold on his control. "Now I see why you wanted the guarantee."

"And you gave it."

"I'm listening, so keep going."

When she realized the annoying tapping sound echoing in the room came from her fingers against the chair, she grabbed onto the armrest and dug her nails in. "He knows I work here."

Jarrett's frown morphed into a feral smile. "Happy to hear it."

"Good God, why?"

"Maybe that will keep him away from you for good this time."

A lightness hit her out of nowhere. She would have bet nothing could amuse her after that unexpected familial visit. "You think you're that scary?"

In a way, maybe Jarrett was. He had a reputation and a criminal past. She got that. Wade also told stories, many of them scrubbed clean for her hearing but all centered on Jarrett issuing an order of some type years ago that stopped her father. But last she checked, a bullet to the head from her father's gun could stop even the formidable Jarrett Holt.

"Actually, yes. And if I'm not, Wade is. It will only take one of us to stop your father." The tension snapping across his shoulders suggested Jarrett relished the idea.

For the first time in a long time she caught a glimpse of the power behind Jarrett's suit. He always had time for her and treated her with patience and respect but the stern expression said he could use his bare hands to fight, if needed.

"My father pretends Wade is dead." A horrible fact that when added to all the other horrible facts made her hate her father even more.

Jarrett scoffed. "Because Wade's gay?"

She doubted her father knew that piece of information. No doubt he'd see that as some sort of personal or family betrayal, because her father was that twisted. If he did know the truth he'd likely do more than disown Wade, and she could never allow that.

"No, because he's disloyal."

For a second Jarrett stayed quiet and the noises from the club poured through again. "Aren't you in the same category since you also left the family business?"

The question went to the heart of her secret. One she did not plan on sharing today. "You mean stealing."

"Among other things. Your father has been surprisingly enterprising since getting out of prison."

A cold chill blew through her. "You've been keeping an eye on him?"

"Somewhat."

She knew that meant Jarrett could tell you what her father had for dinner last night. "Is that safe?"

"For me? Yes. Him? We'll see." Jarrett's gaze searched her face as he flipped his pen end over end on the desk. "So, what did your father say to you?"

"He acted as if I took this job to help him gather information for his activities."

"Not a surprise." Jarrett dropped the pen. "If that's the concern, you don't need to worry."

"You're not?"

"About Richard Royer? Not since I was about sixteen and too dumb to know your father consisted of equal parts hot air and stupid." Jarrett's smile came back. "Honestly, I have no idea how you and Wade turned out normal."

"Are we?" The tightness that had the room in its grip a second ago eased. Kyra had no idea what she said or what Jarrett inferred but whatever battle he was mentally preparing for, it looked as if he decided he'd won.

"I'll take care of this right now." He reached for his cell.

She had her hand out before he hit a button. "No."

One eyebrow lifted. Jarrett was not a man accustomed to being denied anything. "Excuse me?"

"I told you I don't need you to muscle in and threaten people." She closed one eye and waited for him to lecture her on her delivery. He was her boss now, in addition to being a family friend.

Instead, he shrugged. "But I'm good at it."

"You're respectable now." She didn't even know what that meant but she'd heard both Wade and Bast say it, so she dragged it out and tried it.

Jarrett made a face. "That's a terrible rumor."

She refused to be sidetracked by his calm or his jokes. This was too important, and her father too crazy, to ignore. "I'm trying to figure out who is feeding my father information so I can stop the trail from your club back to him."

"Could be anyone. Knowing your father and his limited resources, he probably found out by accident."

Jarrett had a point. She had thought it herself. Her father's crew had always been second rate. He didn't inspire loyalty and tended to gather men who could be bought but not convinced to care. "Leave it to him to stumble over something that messes up my life."

"That's consistent with what I know about him." Jarrett held on to his cell. "Tell me again why I'm not resolving this for you?"

"You can't."

"You underestimate me." His voice dipped to the deadly low range.

Last thing she needed was for him to see this as a challenge of some sort. "I mean I don't want you to. I'm going to ignore him for now."

"Wrong strategy." Jarrett typed in his password. "We can tell—"

She reached across and tried to take the phone but his reflexes had her grabbing air. "You are not going to tell Wade."

Jarrett didn't dial. His phone hung from his fingers but that's as close as he got. "When did I agree to that?"

"Wade would kill my father, then we'd have a huge mess."

Jarrett glanced at the ceiling as if he were considering the cleanup. "No offense, but I'm not convinced your dad being gone would be a loss to humanity."

Father. She never referred to him as dad because that felt loving and sweet. Her relationship with her father left her reeling and raw. Forget that she'd never had dolls or the regular little-girl things. That stuff didn't matter compared with the fact she knew, deep in her soul, he would sell her out for nothing more than a hearty lunch.

That kind of man attacked when cornered so she needed Jarrett to back off. "We'll see what my father does. If he makes a move and comes to me with some idiotic plan, and I'm not totally convinced he will since he's afraid of you, then we'll know what he wants from you."

"That scenario sounds as if you're putting your body in the middle." When she nodded, Jarrett's jaw-clenching thing came back. "The answer is no."

"I'm an adult." Some days she got tired of saying that. The men in her life should know and give her some breathing room. "I'm telling you this because I want you to know and be prepared. And if my father does something stupid, I wanted you to know I was never trying to scam you."

Jarrett's mouth dropped open. He shook his head in what looked like shock before saying anything. "Christ, Kyra. I know that."

Relief zipped through her. If she'd been standing, her knees would have buckled. The circle of people in her life remained tight and closed and she rarely opened to include one more. Jarrett was one of the few. "I'm trusting you to keep my confidence."

Jarrett's thumb swiped across the cell's screen again. "Speaking of which, we need to call Bast and—"

"No." She knew Jarrett hated being interrupted and she'd done it twice, maybe more, since sitting down, but the word came out on a near-shout before she could stop it. The point was to keep Bast out of the middle. He wanted uncomplicated and she planned to give him that. Uncomplicated and sex.

"Do you have a problem with Bast?" Jarrett sounded far too intrigued now.

There was no way to answer that one without stumbling and stuttering and otherwise giving the whole deal away. "Lawyers? Come, on. Why add them to the mix? No Bast. No Wade. No interference."

Jarrett swore under his breath. Then he did it again. "I'm not saying yes to any of this."

"But you won't betray me."

This time he pointed the phone at her. "The first sign of trouble and the next time he contacts you, you come right to me. You understand?"

"It's going to be fine."

"Kyra, you promise right now or I call Wade." Jarrett shook the cell.

"I don't want this to blow up."

Jarrett's arm dropped to the desk. He tossed the cell on top of the legal pad to his left. "Your father is known for fucking up everything he touches."

"I need everyone safe and your business protected." She was almost pleading now but she didn't care. The truth poured out of her and she couldn't call it back.

"I'll take care of my club."

He made his vow. Now she'd make hers. "And I'll take care of the people I care about."

THIRTEEN

Bast spent the night working on Natalie's case, going back over every document he used for Becca's agreement with the CIA and the few redacted ones given to Natalie. He waited to take notes but now he had legal pads full of them. Connecting the dots and setting out a strategy took hours in the office and more at home.

The next afternoon, he was out of meetings and ready to start making calls. Or he was until his assistant made her unexpected announcement.

He let go of the intercom button and stood up. Out of habit, he rebuttoned his suit jacket as his office door opened.

Then she came in and closed the door behind her. *The* she. The one who haunted his few hours of sleep and whose name lingered in his mind as he dressed. The same she who shouldn't be in his office. But there she was in a sexy black skirt, similar to the one she wore to work at the club, and a slim black short-sleeve sweater that hugged every curve.

She managed to come off as business appropriate and hot as hell. Blonde hair flowed over her shoulders and he could almost smell the fruity scent of her shampoo from ten feet away.

He blinked twice but she didn't disappear. "Kyra?"

"Surprised?" With the flat tone and blank expression, she didn't give anything away.

"You could say that." She took two steps and he noticed those bare legs. Her skin looked smooth and shiny, as if she put lotion on it.

Damn, he'd be thinking about that all afternoon.

His instincts yelled at him to go to her, but he refrained. If he dropped to his knees every time she showed up, he'd spend his whole fucking life there. He was an adult and needed to act like one. Especially here, in his office, where an entire staff looked to him for cues on appropriate behavior.

"We have a problem." Her tone didn't change as she held her body tall and stiff.

That snapped him out of the seductive stupor. "What happened?"

"Really?"

Wade, Jarrett, the job, her work. The list of endless possibilities flipped through his mind but he couldn't help until he knew the exact issue. "Tell me what's wrong."

She walked over, stopping opposite from him on the other side of his desk and balanced the tips of her fingers and those sexy red nails against the desk. "You."

The look, the voice—it combined to pull his attention away from the topic . . . until she dropped the word and stopped talking. "I don't understand."

"It's almost two and you haven't called." Her head tipped to the side and her hair fell over her breasts.

Anger swept over him in a heated rush. "Are you serious? That's what has you ticked off?"

He had a job and responsibilities. They had an understanding. They agreed on privacy and she walked into his office. That had to be a violation of something.

"Very."

He dropped to a rough whisper to keep from yelling and bringing security running. "Jesus, Kyra. I'm at work here."

"I get that . . ." Her eyes narrowed. "Wait a second. You're upset I showed up without permission?"

Somewhere in the back of his head an alarm bell rang but he ignored it. He was too busy reeling from the surprise in her voice. "We aren't playing house."

Her face fell. Tension pulled on every muscle and her mouth dropped. "Excuse me?"

Trying to rein in his control, he concentrated on lowering the pen to his desk and doing a mental countdown from twenty. None of it helped. Truth was this could not happen, not today when everyone they knew would arrive within the hour.

Rather than unload and risk lecturing, he pulled back hard and searched for calm. "We had a deal."

"Am I supposed to pretend I don't know you?"

"Come on." The snap of her voice set his temper running wild again. He slammed the pen against the desk. "That's totally different from refraining from walking in here off the street in the middle of the day and demanding attention."

"I'm demanding what?"

The deadly cool tone had him changing strategies. Yeah, he'd gone too far. Time to pull back. "I didn't mean it that way."

"You said it." Her hands went to her hips. "For the record, I came here to tell you I feel taken for granted."

The comment struck from out of nowhere. It seemed so out of context. "What are you talking about?"

"You promised to call this morning. When you didn't, I called you and never heard back."

The simple explanation, despite it being delivered at a near roar, took some of the sting out of his anger. This was about a call.

Something they should be able to work out in two seconds and move on. "I got stuck in meetings."

"You run the place, Bast."

Clearly she didn't think this was so simple. "Which is why I can't always break away."

She nodded in the direction of his cell. "How long does a text take? The phone is right there, two inches from your hand."

He looked down, saw the cell. Glanced at the office phone with its ten lines. Maybe he did stumble his way through this. They had plans and in his mind it was all set . . . but he had said something about calling.

He wiped a hand over his chin as he exhaled. "Okay, let's back up."

"Did you want to go back to the part where you're an ass?" The furious scowl suggested she could give him a list of his failings if he wanted it.

"What did I do . . ." When she balled her hands into fists at her side, he rushed to cut through the potential screaming. "Okay, I mean other than the missed call."

Which still didn't seem like an unforgiveable crime to him. He kept a punishing work schedule. Not much slipped, but when things did they tended to be in his private life, not the office life.

"How about the look of rabid terror at seeing me in your office?"

He fought to keep his expression neutral. "Okay, that's an overstatement."

"And referring to you as an ass might be an understatement."

Her reaction to the dropped call struck him as overblown but he didn't dare say it. "Admittedly, I should have called."

She took one more step and came right up against the edge of his desk. "That's the only point you're taking from this conversation?"

Defuse. That was his only thought. Their voices kept rising and the energy racing around the room had them in its grip. "You're the one who came to my office."

"You came to my work and cornered me in the locker room."

"That was different." Even he didn't buy that explanation. It rang hollow in his ears.

"Because you're so important?"

"I didn't say that." The room went quiet after his vibrating shout.

With the conversation spinning out of control, he tried to mentally step back and assess. The whole thing blew into something irrational. Her anger raged and breathed and covered everything.

"I think we need to review what's happening here." After a deep breath, her body relaxed and her voice dropped back to normal range. "We are in a relationship."

The word sliced across his nerves. "I wouldn't say—"

She held up a hand and shot him a you-are-right-on-the-edge frown. "Don't go crazy anticommitment on me here. Maybe it's just sexual to you, but we agreed to see each other, only each other. That carries with it a requirement to treat each other with respect."

They'd finally found common ground. He could work with that. "I agree."

"And you are failing."

The conversation pivot had him stumbling again. "It was one call."

"A canceled evening and a missed call. Do you know how many things you told me you'd do since we started this?" She held up two fingers and counted off. "Exactly two—an evening together and a call. The way I see it you're zero for two."

Spelled out like that, it didn't sound so irrational. He'd plowed ahead with his life, knowing she'd be there tonight. It never dawned on him to prioritize better. For a smart guy he'd been pretty damn dumb.

Her anger kept rolling, aiming right for his head. "Are you embarrassed about being with me? Rethinking us getting together?"

"No." The idea of seeing her tonight was the only thing holding the day together. "None of that."

"I am not a dirty little secret." Her voice cracked on the last word.

Guilt rushed over him, wiping out everything else. "I never said you were."

"You're acting like it."

She was right.

Forget their deal and the call. This went deeper. He owed her time and needed her to know she counted for more than booty call points. "Lock the door."

She sputtered. "You think you can boss me around after acting like a dumbass?"

"Do it." He motioned for her to follow his order. "I told you we would be together tonight, and we will."

"And I'm supposed to wait around until you call me like some shallow sex toy. Is that the plan here?" She kept firing harsh words, but she also locked the door and returned to her position in front of the desk.

"No."

She went to his head so fast it threw off his balance. She got him riled. No one pushed him to the edge like she did. She didn't just accept what he offered. She demanded more. With his need for control and issues in the past, her attitude should be a no-go. Instead, it revved him up and drained him of the will to fight her off.

"Your other women may have said that was fine—"

"Don't do that." There was the line he did not cross. "We're not talking about other women I've dated."

"Maybe we should because it seems like they let you get away with being a gigantic ass." She leaned in. "So we're clear, I will not accept that bullshit."

The woman kept shoving and testing until a headache boomed in his brain. "I don't really tolerate people calling me names and you've done it numerous times in the last five minutes."

"And?"

Clearly she was not impressed with his comment. "Just pointing it out."

Some of the air seemed to seep out of her then. Her shoulders fell and the anger pulling at her mouth eased. "You deserved it each time."

"I did." No question about it. He fucked up.

Now he had to un-fuck it.

She crossed her arms in front of her and made a clicking sound with her tongue. "What's happening?"

"Come here."

She froze. "Why?"

But there was no confusion in her voice. She knew what he wanted. The mood in the room shifted and the anger fell away. The buzz of energy morphed into a different type of heat. The kind he could handle.

He crooked a finger at her. "I said, come here."

"What do you want?" she asked as she walked around the side of the desk.

"To apologize."

She came to a slamming halt. Her hand went to the desk as if her balance faltered. "Is this some lawyer strategy? Because you don't strike me as a guy who apologizes much."

She wasn't wrong. Not that he planned to tell her that. Not when they stood on the edge of a cliff he still didn't quite understand. "I do when I mess up."

"What do you think you did wrong?" She slid her fingers along the smooth edge of the wood. "I mean, I know, but I worry you don't and are just throwing out words to charm me. Or, worse, shut me up."

Time to spell it out and take responsibility. "My sins include taking for granted you'd be there when I found time to call this afternoon instead of calling you first thing—well, your first thing and my late morning—to confirm."

The rest of the strain left her face. "Okay, that was nice."

"Impressed?"

She made a *hmpf* sound. "Well, it was pretty."

"You're pretty."

Not done with the noises and gestures, she rolled her eyes. "That's not going to work."

He was banking on the fact it would.

He pushed his chair back from the desk and patted his lap. With a hand on her thigh, he guided her to the space in front of him until she leaned against the desk. "Are you sure?"

She grabbed onto the edge behind her. "I shouldn't let you win this battle. You already border on impossible."

"I was thinking we both could win." He eased up her skirt until it rested high on her thighs and she could straddle his legs. "Are you wearing panties?"

One hand skimmed up her inner thigh.

She clenched her legs together, trapping his hand against her skin before he reached anything good. "Dark purple lace."

"Let me see."

"I thought you didn't want me in your office."

"Kyra, do it now."

"Fine." Shimmying her hips, she drew the skirt up even higher.

Her legs and intoxicating smell hit him with a punch. She was so damn sexy, fierce and unyielding. She owned her sensuality and didn't back down from a fight. It was a miracle he could get through the day right now without driving to her place and getting her into bed. He chalked the blood lust up to the newness of them being together.

Whatever it was, he wanted more. "Kyra, show me."

She opened her legs and he let his hand drop to her knee. The material made a rustling sound as it brushed over her bare skin. She stopped when the edge of her underwear peeked out.

"You've been a bad boy."

His finger slid along the crotch of the tiny scrap of material. "I intend to be."

"I thought you had these important meetings and calls."

After a quick look at the clock and time check, he reached around her for the intercom button. "Roberta? Go ahead and take a break."

Kyra frowned at him. "That was subtle. For a man who's so worried about people knowing his secrets, you kind of suck at subterfuge."

"I still haven't seen those panties."

She put a hand on his shoulder and pushed his chair back. "I have something better."

He laughed. "I doubt that."

"Let me cure your skepticism." With the added space between his knees and the desk, she slid down. Kept going until she hit her knees in front of him.

She ran her hands up and down his legs. The friction heated his skin but the way she stared at his zipper had him.

He cleared his throat. "Okay, I was wrong. This is pretty damn good."

Her fingers went to work on his belt. Slipping the leather out. Unbuttoning the pants. Before she slipped the zipper down, she leaned forward and rubbed her cheek against the fly. His erection jumped to life. He twitched and grew until the material strangled him.

"You're all bunched up." She slid her hands inside his waistband and opened him to her.

Then her mouth was on him. Her hand tightened on the base of his cock as her finger swept over the head. She sucked and squeezed.

Looking down, he saw her head bob as she worked her mouth up and down on him. Soft hair spilled over his lap. Lips wrapped around his cock. The storm of sensations had him forgetting where he was and all his rules about keeping his distance from her. When she stood in front of him, his resolve faltered. When she touched him, he couldn't remember why he needed to hold her away from him.

His head dropped back against his chair and his fingers clenched in her hair. The sound of her mouth over him mixed with the creak of the chair and shuffle of clothing against the leather. He got lost in the feel of her lips and hand. The knowing pull that had his mind shutting down and his body swamped with need. It all built until he closed his eyes and let the pressure grab him.

His hips pumped and her fingers tightened. A small breath escaped his throat as he came in her mouth. Holding him and sucking him, she dragged him over the edge. He filled her mouth and she took it all.

Everything about her turned him on.

When the pulsing stopped, he looked down and saw her staring up at him. His fingers slipped through her hair. He tried for gentle, because in that moment that's how he felt. "I'm sorry I was an ass."

He meant it. He got a lot of things right but his failed marriage showed him how completely capable he was of destroying things, too. He didn't want to destroy Kyra.

She kissed the tip of his cock and smiled when it twitched in response. Then she was on her feet and tugging her skirt back down. "You're forgiven."

"Good, we can—"

"One thing." She leaned down until her lips hovered over his. "You've messed up twice. Let's not try for three."

She pulled back before he could kiss her. "I can't promise I'll be perfect from here on."

"Try, but I'll settle for not-annoying over perfect."

"I will not take you for granted." He watched her tuck her shirt in and smooth down her skirt. "But I was wrong about the office. You're welcome here any time."

She shot him a how-are-you-so-clueless look. "Men are so predictable. Wrap your mouth around their cocks and they shut up."

He couldn't argue with that. "True."

She skated around his legs and made it to the other side of the desk before he could catch her. "Do yourself a favor."

He braced his body for a new blow. "Meaning?"

"Regardless of your busy important schedule, figure out a way to call or text me within the hour and finalize tonight."

"I can do that now."

"Nope." She shook her head. "Let's see if you really do know how to use a phone and can remember to use it."

As she unlocked the door and slipped into the hallway, he set his cell alarm with a reminder.

FOURTEEN

With the latest news from Natalie and the unexpected arrival in his office a half hour ago, Bast called an emergency meeting. Just before four he stood at the head of his conference room table and looked down both sides. Jarrett and Becca on one. Wade and Natalie on the other. Elijah stood with his back to the glass double doors and looked ready to crash through them to escape.

Bast pulled out the chair and dropped into it. "I know you need to be at the club for dinner prep, but this couldn't wait."

"That can't be good." Becca liked to jump right to the point.

This time Bast appreciated the no-nonsense approach. It fit with her sleek black dress and intense stare. "We have a problem."

Natalie shifted in her seat. The move, subtle and consisting of no more than placing a hand on the table, caused all gazes to shift to her. "He means *I* do."

"Why are the rest of us here?" Wade asked. He'd never been a big Natalie fan but the way he steadily avoided looking at Elijah suggested he'd pick her over him right now.

"Natalie is about to be terminated." Bast tapped his hand against the closed file in front of him. This one contained Natalie's official notice with citings to regulations and comments about "regrets" about her behavior.

Becca's attention shot back to her former CIA boss. "Since when does the CIA give notice?"

Natalie didn't have to move this time. All eyes stayed locked on her. "As of this morning my clearance was revoked and I was placed on administrative leave."

Whether former agency employees or not, they all knew what that meant. The clock had started ticking. The CIA declared her unemployable in the covert realm and now she'd either get to walk away or meet with an accident. "We're working out a separation agreement."

The room buzzed with energy now. All of the people around the table had either been trained to hide emotion or came from the criminal world where that skill served to keep them alive. No one panicked or demanded explanations. They sat and listened and assessed while saying as little as possible.

"Let me cut through the legal and spy talk." Jarrett put a hand on the back of Becca's chair. "You think someone is going to make Natalie disappear."

Eli piped up from the other side of the room. "Or hit her with a bus."

"Well." Wade shook his head. "I see you still have a problem with tact."

"Why tiptoe? These people blew up Becca's place and tried to fill me with bullets." Elijah stepped closer to the table, hanging back at the opposite end from Bast. "Natalie argued for our continued breathing and now she's in the firing line."

Natalie opened her mouth but Bast jumped in first. "Eli is right."

"Not something you hear every day." Jarrett said the comment under his breath.

Eli stared down the table. "It's not hard to do the math and figure out Natalie is in trouble and our deals could be in danger."

"I agree." This wasn't a time to parse words or be careful about agency protocol. The CIA planned to fuck her, at the very least by taking away a job she worked hard at and deserved. Now he had to figure out how bad the personal attack would be and prepare for collateral damage.

Jarrett sobered. His face became even more drawn. "Now what?"

They still remained calm. Bast picked up some fidgeting and a hint of worry zipping through the room. He guessed most of that came from Jarrett wanting to pack Becca away and leave town.

Bast didn't blame the guy but they hadn't reached emergency status yet. "I will handle everything but I need you all to make my life easier."

Jarrett jumped in before Bast finished the sentence. "How?"

"You and Becca stay low, and preferably at the club, and tighten security."

Wade snorted. "They rarely go outside anyway."

That led Bast to his next point. "And, Wade, you need to be locked in as well."

Wade's eyes narrowed. "I never worked for the CIA."

"Neither did Jarrett and yet you both got arrested the last time the CIA came calling." Bast angled his chair to stare at Natalie. "You will have a bodyguard."

"No."

The reaction was not a surprise. That didn't make it any more welcome. Bast had a file full of photographs showing how Becca and Eli's old team members died. Accidents and a random theft-gone-wrong. All of it bullshit.

That meant she got a shadow, regardless of how much she whined about it. "It's happening."

"Do you mean Eli?" Jarrett sounded amused by the idea.

Eli swore under his breath. "No fucking way."

"For once, I agree," Natalie said at the same time.

The round robin could go on forever. Though letting the conversation circle and dive sounded better than fighting Natalie. Bast guessed that was about to happen on a large scale. "No, Gabe MacIntosh."

Jarrett hummed. "Interesting choice."

It struck Bast that way. A former Army special-ops guy turned contractor-for-hire with sniper skills that rivaled Eli's was the perfect man for this assignment. With his diplomacy skills, Gabe could handle anything . . . including Natalie's sharp personality.

"Why is it interesting?" Becca asked.

"Gabe's a man's man, live-in-the-woods type." Jarrett held his hands far apart. "And huge. He makes Wade look small."

Natalie glanced at Wade. All six-foot-three of him. Then back to Bast. "No way. I'm a trained operative. The precaution is not necessary."

Eli shrugged. "That's what I said before two goons shot me."

"Probably the same goons who tossed a bomb in my kitchen," Becca added.

It wasn't often Eli and Becca joined forces in support of something. Bast appreciated it happening now. "Right. Natalie is with Gabe and Eli will move in with me."

The comment caught Elijah sneaking a look at Wade. Eli's head snapped back and he scowled at Bast. "What?"

One problem at a time. Bast focused on the most obvious one. "Natalie, you will have a shadow or you can find another negotiator. Last thing I need is someone shooting at you before you can sign an agreement."

Becca leaned against Jarrett's shoulder. "Your friend's bedside manner needs work."

Bast heard that. Then again, he supposed that was the point since she didn't bother whispering. "That's doctors."

"Wait." Wade leaned back in his chair. "Go back to the part where Eli becomes your roommate."

"He lives in a shithole." Which qualified as an understatement as far as Bast was concerned. "It would be easy for someone to take him out and make it look like a robbery gone bad."

He paid the man good money but Elijah chose to live in a pay-by-the-week hotel in a sketchy neighborhood. Bast knew because he brought Eli on and checked his employment file after the office manager confided that she'd seen him sleeping in his car in the parking garage under the law firm's building.

Wade sat up again and for the first time since the meeting started faced Eli head-on. "Where is this place?"

Eli waved him off. "It doesn't matter."

Not one to be ignored, Wade leaned forward, a mass of intensity and frustration, and tried again. "I'm thinking it does."

Eli's expression turned feral. "You suddenly care?"

"Okay, stop." That was enough of that. Now was not the time for these two to work through or fight about their messed-up relationship. Bast could only deal with so many impossible situations at a time. "There's a basement condo at my town house. Eli will move out of the crack den and stay with me."

"Now *I* want to know where you're living," Becca said.

"No you don't." Jarrett rested his hand over Becca's and shook his head. "We could make this easier and Eli could move into the crash pad at the club."

"Absolutely not." The fury in Eli's voice ratcheted up with each comment.

Silence flashed through the room after the yell. Other than the rocking of some of the chairs and flipping of the corner of Bast's file, time ticked in quiet.

Finally Natalie broke the stalemate. "Well, that was adamant."

Becca snorted. "I wonder why."

Jarrett being Jarrett, he cut through the bullshit. "Why do you need Eli with you?"

Not that Bast wanted to discuss this topic. "I don't."

"Liar." Becca pointed at Bast. "You think you need protection."

Eli's eyebrow lifted. "Why didn't you just say that?"

Because Eli would step up. After only a few weeks of working together, Bast discovered that trait. Eli might be surly and difficult but he worked his ass off. He came in early and would stay all night. To catch up on the firm's files, he studied and learned protocol. He didn't need lectures on confidentiality because the man had been trained to hold on to a secret through interrogation and torture.

"Bast isn't good at asking for, or accepting, help."

The softness in Jarrett's voice didn't fool Bast. Jarett had added up the pieces about the potential need for security at the house. Bast sensed a confrontation in his future. "I'm fine. It's just a precaution and would be better for Eli if he were with me."

"I can keep watch from outside of the house. Guard the perimeter, check the car and those things." Eli stood with his hand in front of him. The stiff shoulders and dark hair gave him a menacing affect. "If you need a real bodyguard, I'll do that."

Exactly what Bast expected. Eli figured out he was needed and stepped up. The guy was rock solid. It was a shame he didn't recognize that.

"You have a job and starting tomorrow you get a better apartment." Bast knew he should move Eli in right away, just to be sure, but nothing was stopping him from seeing Kyra tonight. Bast didn't want spectators for that, so he could postpone Eli's arrival by one day.

Jarrett rested his elbow on the table and shook his head. "I don't like any of this."

On that, Bast agreed. "Everybody be smart and this will be fine."

He needed time to get this done. This wasn't his first negotiation with the agency. It likely wouldn't be his last. But this one dealt with people he cared about, which made it all the more important.

· · ·

Elijah sat with his elbow on his desk and tried to ferret out the information he just learned. This wasn't just about Natalie. The tentacles reached everywhere. Kept growing.

The air in the room changed. Subtle and not noticeable to most people, but he'd survived more than one situation by being able to read the signs around him. His Japanese mother had called the ability *mono no aware*, literally "a sensitivity to things," and it kicked in now.

Forget a panic button. He was the guy who got the call when someone else pushed it. Now, he'd handle this. He reached for the gun velcroed under the desk. In the same second his fingers touched it, he heard the familiar voice.

"Nice office." Wade walked in and shut the door behind him.

The windowless room stretched, maybe, eight by eight. There was enough room for a desk and a cabinet. A paralegal used to sit in there. Now Eli looked at the bare beige walls. He should have been crawling out of his skin from boredom. That hadn't happened. He admired Bast, liked him even, and if that meant putting his body in front of Bast's to take a bullet or stop an explosion, Eli would.

And now he stared into the eyes of the other man on the planet who mattered and the anger festering inside him exploded. "What are you doing in here?"

Wade leaned back against the wall. "You know I'm not a threat. Take your hand off the gun."

He knew about the hidden weapon. Of course he would know. Whether Wade believed it or not, he was the one person in the world who "got" him . . . at least Eli used to think that was true.

He held his hands out, turned them over, then put them on the desk. "There."

Wade nodded as he stepped further into the small room to stand directly across from Eli. Only three feet of desktop separated them. "We're going to have to find a way to deal with each other."

"Why?" Eli would rather stay away. The scene at the club and talk about Shawn proved the feelings for Wade hadn't died. Not on Eli's part.

"We know the same people. You work for Bast."

"That's been the case for the last month and you managed to ignore me just fine." Hadn't returned a call or a text. Pushed off any attempts to talk.

"It's easier."

"On you, maybe." It had been a fucking bitch for Eli. Between the memories and the desperate need to crawl back in bed with Wade, Eli had lost all sense of perspective.

He wasn't a guy who needed anything. His family had kicked him out the minute he questioned the sermons. His father traveled from camp to camp, engaging in his form of preaching while dragging his family behind him. His world centered on hate and when telling a makeshift congregation how to live their lives wasn't sufficient, he branched out to demonstrations. He'd picket anything. Despised everything that didn't fit with his idea of how people should act.

Finding his son with another boy had been an unforgivable crime. One against God and against humanity. Eli had been alone ever since. Even though he worked on a team in the CIA, he functioned as an island.

Until Wade.

"You understand you caused this, right? Your denial. Your dismissal of whatever we had together," Wade said.

"Denial?"

Wade kept moving. He circled the side of the desk and leaned against the wall to Eli's left. "Come on, Elijah. Don't act like I'm an idiot."

"What are you talking about?" But Eli knew because every argument with Wade circled back to this.

He shook his head. "You insist you like women and that I was the aberration."

"I didn't say that." Eli knew better than that. Didn't believe that. He'd used sex on jobs, but sex with Wade had been different. Right. "The real problem is you're only happy if I accept your label."

"Is it that hard to accept who you are?"

Eli fought it every damn day. If he sat and analyzed, let himself think for even a second what his life had become, he'd go insane. "And what is that? A killer. If you're putting a good spin on it, I'm now part bodyguard and part investigator."

Wade stared at the ceiling for a few seconds. When he lowered his head again, his eyes held a certain starkness. "Sexually."

"In other words, everything would be fine between us if I told you I was gay." There, he said it.

The word meant nothing to him other than a memory of the last time he saw his mother. Even then, his father used other words and repeated them until they rang in Eli's memory. His mind rebelled from saying the word and the hatred behind it.

No faggots here. Faggots go to hell.

"We had deeper problems than you being gay, which you are." Wade didn't add the word "idiot" but it sounded like he wanted to.

If that's what he needed, Eli would give it to him. It was too late and far too little, but if he could put one issue between them to rest, he would. "Fine."

Wade's eyes widened as he came away from the wall. "What?"

"Does that make you happy? I'm gay." The word felt raw in his throat. Actually scraped and burned, but he said it. The label meant nothing to him, but it meant something to Wade. So there it was.

"What are you doing right now?" Wade put a hand on the back of Eli's chair and pushed until he had no choice but to look up.

Engaging in honesty for a change. "Trying to give you what you want."

"This is about you accepting yourself."

"You want to know what I accept?" Eli shoved the chair the rest of the way back. Heard it thud against the wall as he stood up. "I blew it. I get that you meant something. That you're the only person who's ever stayed in my head until I thought I'd go insane from wanting to kick you the fuck out."

The anger drained from Wade's face. "Elijah—"

"I also can state without question that nothing lasts." Not able to face Wade head-on this close, seeing the shoulders and the scruff around his chin, Eli reached for his chair.

Wade grabbed Eli and forced him back around. "Don't do that. Don't turn this around and make this into my issue."

"I'm not." With Wade's fingers wrapped around his arm, Eli couldn't move. Not that he held too tight. The wash of memories paralyzed him.

"Sure as hell feels like it."

"What the hell do you want from me?" Eli shrugged out of the hold. The chair spun as he hit it with his leg and then almost lost his footing before he pressed his back against the wall behind his desk. "I've admitted I messed up. I've tried to explain why my anger blew. I'm working on controlling my anger."

"I'm wondering why you're doing all of that now." Wade closed in. One palm hit the wall next to Eli's head. "Is this because you saw Shawn?"

"You know what? Fuck away. Enjoy him." Eli tried to spin away, go anywhere but here.

Wade put a hand against his chest and slammed Eli back into the wall. "Easy."

Nothing about this qualified as easy. "As you've reminded me, I don't get a say in what you do."

"You want me to feel guilty."

"You'll be happier with Shawn anyway." Saying those words ripped Eli in two. Shredded him to the bone.

"I'm not buying it. You're saying the right words and standing there looking half pathetic and half homicidal, but you know how to play people." Wade leaned in until his breath brushed over Eli. "You were trained to be the best at it."

Heat pumped through Eli. He tried to fight off the rumbling inside him, the need building and clawing to get out. "My training centered on ways to kill people."

"You forget I've seen you in action. This strikes me as another long con and I'm the victim."

"Yeah, Wade. You're the victim."

"Right there. That's what I mean." Wade's other hand found the wall, trapping Eli between his arms. "Just stop."

"We're not in the bar. This is my office." Eli knew he should shove Wade away. Put space between them and laugh this off. But he couldn't move. Not when he wanted to be this close to the man.

"It's Bast's office."

Eli dropped his head back against the wall and closed his eyes. "I'm done fighting with you."

"Good."

His eyes popped open. "What?"

Wade was right there. His face hovering and his mouth . . . Their lips met and Eli heard a thud as Wade's body weight crushed them into the wall.

Strong hands touched Eli's face and a knee worked its way between his legs. Rough and hot, Wade's mouth moved over his in a kiss that conquered and demanded. A steady humming sound filled Eli's head as he grabbed at Wade's shirt. Fingers dug into the material as his other hand traveled down his back.

Their mouths crossed over each other. Tongues battled. Clothing rustled as Wade rubbed his lower half against Eli's. When Eli skimmed his hands up Wade's back and hugged him close, Wade broke away. He stepped back as heavy breaths pumped out of him.

Eli saw the heated skin and eyes filled with confusion and guessed his look mirrored Wade's. With a hand on his stomach, Eli tried to bring his breathing back under control and searched his mind for the right thing to say.

When nothing came to him, Elijah went with what was likely the exact wrong thing. "What was that?"

Wade shook his head as his gaze skipped over the room, never landing on Eli. "Left over."

The words shot out like a kick to the stomach. "Just working me out of your system?"

"I guess that's it." Wade stumbled back. Wiped a hand through his hair. Still didn't give eye contact.

If he wanted to say *we're done*, he was doing a hell of a job.

"Right." Eli rubbed a hand over the spot that ached. One of them, anyway. A flu-like weakness had swept through his body and he knew he'd go down soon. "Have fun with Shawn."

"I will." Wade grabbed for the door then was gone.

FIFTEEN

Bast followed Kyra up the staircase from his garage to the first floor. She left her hair loose and long, hanging down her back. Hoping to inflict a little slow-motion torture, she swung her hips from side to side and felt her dark purple dress slip up the back of her thighs.

On the third step she heard him swear under his breath.

Mission accomplished.

"You okay back there, Sebastian?" She loved his full first name. The way it rolled off the tongue. How good it sounded when she whispered it in bed.

"I will be now that we made it up those damn steps without me tackling you." When they reached the landing, he reached around her and typed in the alarm code.

She shot him a smile over her shoulder. "Problem?"

"As if you didn't know."

The cool breeze from the air-conditioning hit her as he opened the door and guided her into the house. The touch of his hand against her lower back had her insides tightening. She thought about shoving him up against the wall and jumping on him, but the sight in front of her held her enthralled.

They stepped into a mostly white room with what looked like closets along the far wall and a counter with shelves above. There were hooks for coats and sneakers lined up in a row. She assumed the door with the locks led to the outside and the open one emptied into a dark hallway. Everything was neat and tidy. Really kind of perfect, just like Bast.

"The mudroom."

At the sound of his voice she stopped gawking and looked at him. "What?"

"This is the mudroom." He opened one of the doors in front of her to uncover an oversized washing machine.

Well, of course it was. "Your laundry room is bigger than my entire place."

When he didn't say anything, she glanced over. The suit-and-glasses combination felled her every time. The way his hair brushed over his forehead. Those shoulders. So sexy and smart, and when he smiled she melted. Actually felt her bones disintegrate.

That couldn't be normal.

"I have to admit I don't spend a lot of time in here." He touched a button on his cell and the lights in the hallway came on.

That was a sexy trick. The kind of thing to turn a girl's head. Well, this one's anyway. She loved the idea of conveniences that made life easier. Maybe one day she'd have one or two. Right now she had a burned-out lightbulb over her bathroom mirror that she was too lazy to change. Someone should create a phone app for that.

"Because you have people who clean your clothes." She did have a hard time imagining him standing in there folding his underwear.

"Yeah."

"Really?" Well, damn. She was joking. "Is that person here now?"

"She doesn't live here."

"On a different topic." Because she refused to dwell on his wealth and the wide gap between them. "It's nice to know you can learn."

"Do I want to know what that means?"

He steered her into the hall and toward the front of the house. They passed the open staircase on the left and walked into a room with books lining the shelves and a huge desk set up near the window. Her high heels clicked against the hardwood, then she stepped onto plush carpeting.

She stopped in front of the fireplace and fingered the framed photos stretching along the mantel. "You called twice this afternoon."

"I also scheduled an emergency meeting earlier than I normally would and moved another until tomorrow to make sure I'd be free tonight and we could meet." He leaned against the side of the blue leather couch and crossed his arms in front of him.

"Which is why you are going to get very lucky tonight." She looked through the open doorway to the room beyond. One space ran into the other. The next one had a sectional sofa the size of a truck and two wall-mounted televisions to match. "This is one house?"

"A town house."

"I'm familiar with the term." She felt his eyes on her as she moved around the room and gazed out the front windows, through the trees to the paved patio out front. "My point was you live in a stinking big house."

"I'm not sure how to respond to that."

She heard the flatness of his voice and went to him. Stood so the pointy toes of her uncomfortable shoes touched his dressy ones. "You tell me you work hard and it's just a thing. Things don't matter."

"All that is true." He opened his legs and dropped his arms. Didn't pull her in but seemed more approachable than he did a second ago. "Do you want to see the rest of the place?"

Well, if he wasn't going to make a move, she would.

"You mean your bedroom?" Resting her hands on his shoulders, she stepped in close until his body cocooned hers and his fingers went to her hips.

He shot her one of those panty-dropping sexy smiles. "I'm a little classier than that. I can show you the dining room first."

"That's very hot."

"Yes, you are." His hand brushed over her hips then down to cup her ass. "The dress is—"

"All I'm wearing." The strangling sound from his throat had her biting back a smile. "Was that a *guh* I heard?"

"Pretty much."

Wrapping her arms around his neck, she leaned in until her chest rested against his. "I'm not wearing anything other than a spray of perfume under this."

He stood up fast enough to pick her feet off the floor. In the next beat, his mouth found her neck and he started walking her backward toward the staircase. "Maybe we will go look at the bedroom."

Intense panic hit her out of nowhere. Her fingers tightened as she worked up the nerve to ask. "Did you live here with your ex-wife?"

In the middle of maneuvering her into the entry hall. His mouth, his hands, his feet. Everything stopped moving. "A hint here. Bringing up Lena is a sure way to kill the mood."

Kyra pulled back and searched his face. His expression, so heated and sexy a second ago, had closed up. "I didn't ask for her phone number."

"That's a good thing."

Kyra slipped the whole way out of his arms but kept the contact by wrapping her fingers around his forearms. "Good grief, you're clueless."

He blinked a few times. "Wait, you think I'm—"

She tapped a finger against his forehead. "Do you really not know what I'm asking?"

"When did you ask a question?"

She fixed him with an eye roll then because he clearly deserved it. "Are you going to screw me in the bed where you slept with your wife?"

The tension drained from his face and his shoulders fell back down to a normal level. "Ah, now I see."

"I would hope, since I just spelled it out for you."

When Kyra tried to pull away, he caught her around the waist and tugged her back against him. "Lena never lived here. I bought this place after the divorce."

"Let me guess, this was after you gave her the house you lived in while you were married." Kyra dropped a quick kiss on his mouth because if true, then he really wasn't a dick.

"Have you been reading my divorce papers?"

"No." She assumed from his reaction her guess was an accurate one. "And for the record that sounds like a horrible way to spend time."

"You should have tried living it."

Kyra broke his hold around her waist and headed for the bottom step of the towering staircase. "Nah, women aren't my thing."

"Can we stop talking about my ex now?" He stopped just below her, with his hand on the big wooden knob at the base of the railing.

"Please." Kyra looked up and saw where the top of the staircase turned and what looked like fancy paintings on the walls. She could only imagine what goodies he kept squirreled away up there. "I believe you said something about a whirlpool."

"I also promised you dinner."

She took his hand as she took another step. "That's cute, but I guarantee you I'm a sure thing tonight, food or not."

"I'm not a complete animal." But he followed her until they'd both gone three steps, him one below her.

"Uh-huh." She tugged on the zipper running down her side and starting under her left arm, lowering it just an inch. "I'm guessing that big fancy tub is up here."

At the zipping sound, his gaze went to her breasts then to her hand. "You're making it hard for me to act with decorum."

She pulled it down another inch, letting the teeth click as she went up another step. "Why would you want to do that?"

"I can be chivalrous. You know, not invite a woman over and guide her right upstairs to the bed." He ruined the Boy Scout speech by putting his palms outside her knees and drawing her dress up to mid-thigh.

"Hmm."

He stood just below her as his fingers skimmed up the back of one leg then touched her ass. "What are you thinking?"

"We seem to have a misunderstanding."

His finger slipped closer to the spot she craved his touch. Ran over her, never pushing inside. Somehow she kept her balance. Grabbing for the railing helped.

Then his finger trailed over her again, ignoring the invitation when she opened her legs even farther. "How so?"

"The one thing I don't need is you being all proper." Fumbling and fighting her racing pulse, she got the zipper the whole way down.

"What do you want me to be?" He pressed a kiss against her stomach through the dress. The next one touched skin as he found the opening of her zipper.

"Dirty."

"Oh, I can do dirty." He dragged his tongue over her skin, up her side, and didn't stop until he kissed the underside of her breast.

Air hiccupped in her lungs and got trapped there. "Then we'd better find that tub."

He took another step until they shared the same step. "Bed first."

His legs straddled hers and she would have fallen backward if he hadn't wrapped his arms around her and balanced her body against his. He kissed her then. Deep and so smoking hot her feet left the ground. She covered him, clung to him, as his mouth traveled over hers and her breath expired.

When she tipped her head back, desire clouded her gaze. Need wrapped around her and the heat of his body seeped into hers.

God, she wanted him. "Get us there."

The rest of the trip up the stairs blurred. Walls flipped by her. She saw a chest . . . in the hallway. The idea they were wide enough to hold furniture barely registered as he turned the corner and kept going until he reached the room at the end of the hall.

He hit the switch with his elbow and soft white lights flooded the bedroom in a soft glow. She took in the huge space—was that a couch?—right before the room spun and her back hit the bed. Her dress bunched up high on her hips and twisted the top of her dress until a breast peeked out.

Then he loomed over her with his face right above hers. He'd somehow lost his jacket but his white shirt stood out in the low light. "Hello."

His deep voice washed over her. She reached up to touch his cheek because not touching him proved impossible. A slight brush of stubble scratched her fingertips. Thinking about him all scruffy had her insides winding nice and tight.

She touched the tip of his glasses. "Any chance you can keep these on while you slide all over me?"

"I can see all of you just fine without them."

That was cute. Adorable, really. Like this wasn't about her objectifying him. "Yeah, I was thinking more for me than you."

"Explain that."

"I'm intrigued by how sexy you are in them." She hooked her

leg around one of his and brought him in even tighter. "If you're afraid of smashing them or having them fall off, I can fix that."

"Do tell."

She gave his chest a gentle shove and pushed her body against his. They rolled until his back hit the mattress. In perfect rhythm her legs shifted and she straddled his hips. His erection pushed against her and the satisfied look in his eyes said he approved of her solution.

Taking his hands in hers, she pinned his arms to the bed. "I want to ride you."

"Do it soon."

She lowered her upper body over his, letting her hair swing down and over his chest. "We have to get you undressed first."

"I can be naked and inside you in two seconds."

"I think we can manage a bit more finesse than that." But not if she didn't get moving. The bulge under her thigh told her he was ready to go. Hell, so was she.

"I'm all yours."

That was so sweet she took the time to treat him to a lingering kiss that had his head lifting off the bed when she tried to break it off. With a hand on his chest, she pressed him back down and went to work on his tie. She'd just slipped it off when she felt his hand on her hip.

She shook her head. "Nuh-uh. I want your arms on the bed."

The smile he shot her generated enough energy to power the house. "Yes, ma'am."

Well, wasn't that sexy.

She opened his shirt, button by button, placing a kiss on each inch of skin she revealed. Watching his chest rise and fall and seeing his open palms against the bed nearly did her in. He radiated confidence but he forfeited the lead to her, giving her control over his body. And she loved every second of it.

"You should be naked." He didn't move. Just made the comment as he watched her hands travel over him.

"You're right." Taking her time, drawing it out, she shifted her hips and scooted around as she dragged her dress up on her hips, then over her stomach to her shoulders and off.

His gaze wandered all over her, stopping on her breasts then dropping to the space between her legs. "You really were naked under there."

"My gift to you."

"I'm hoping it's the gift that keeps on giving." There was nothing subtle about the heated look or the way his fingers flexed.

"Now you want me to strip?"

"All the fucking time."

She half expected to see steam rise off the mattress. The friction of his pants against her bare skin and burning stare combined to light her nerve endings on fire. "Let's get you out of these pants and inside me."

When she unbuckled his belt and slid down his zipper, his head came off the mattress. His hands didn't move but his body trembled. It was as if his muscles ached to take over.

Not happening. She shook her head. "Not yet."

He groaned and flopped back down. "Faster."

Of course that made her slow down even more. She slipped her hands under his hips and worked the pants and briefs over his ass and down. With every inch she uncovered, she stopped to place a kiss on his skin. His stomach. The base of his cock. The top of his thighs. By the time she reached his knees his body shook.

"You're killing me," he ground out.

She smiled against his calf then finished the delicious unveiling. "That's the idea."

Making sure to give him a show, she moved down the bed and bent over in front of him. Pulling his shoes and socks off, she treated him to a long look at her breasts. Even stopped to touch them while he watched.

The noise he made sounded a lot like a growl. "Oh, come on."

She glanced up and saw he'd raised his body up on his elbows. She knew her time for running the show was almost up. "Condoms?"

"Nightstand." He motioned with his head.

She stood at the end of the bed and gave him her best you're-not-listening glare. "Lie back down."

He didn't move. "Are you going to climb back on top of me if I do?"

The man insisted on negotiating everything. It's as if he couldn't help himself. "Only if you're a good boy."

He wiggled his eyebrows. "I thought you wanted me to be dirty."

"That would make you a *very* good boy."

He dropped back so fast she was surprised he didn't bounce against the mattress. To reward him, she took long strides around the bed and bent over, giving him a nice shot of her ass.

"You are so damn beautiful." His gaze traveled down to her legs. "Every last inch of you."

She took a minute to return the favor and look him over. From the broad chest to the flat stomach to the muscled legs. For a man who spent most of his days behind a desk he took care of himself.

And she couldn't ignore the very impressive part of him. "I can see your appreciation."

He lifted his hips off the mattress. "I've pretty much been in this state since you made your offer in the club."

"That must have made work difficult." She plucked a packet out of the drawer and dropped it on his chest.

"Why do you think I kept tracking you down and running my hands up your skirt?"

She crawled on top of him, throwing a leg over him and going slow as she brushed her skin over his. "Every time I put on underwear I think of you."

She ran her hands over his arms until her fingers threaded through his. In this position, her hair drifted over him and her mouth met his. The kiss blew through her, grabbed her and took hold. She felt him in every cell and wanted him with every part of her.

When she lifted her head, his expression was almost pained and his breathing unsteady. "Two things."

She had to smile at the shake in his voice. "Go ahead."

"Stop wearing underwear when you're near me." He lifted his head and gave her a hard fast kiss. "And put me inside you. Now."

"What if I'm not ready?" She so was. Wet and hot and churning inside.

"Touch yourself."

His gruff voice sent her heartbeat racing. "You *are* very dirty tonight."

"With you, all the time." He nuzzled her neck. "I want to watch."

She rolled the condom over him, loving the way his eyes closed and his body flinched when she took advantage and squeezed her hand around him. "You are so ready."

"Yes, now it's your turn." His voice cracked.

Lifting up on her knees, she crawled up higher on his body, making sure he had a great view for the show. Straddling his stomach, she opened her legs nice and wide and slid a finger through her wetness. Back and forth, over and over, until her hips jerked.

His skin flushed and his hands balled into fists next to his head. "Slip it inside."

She didn't pretend to be confused. Two fingers slid around her clit before one plunged deep inside. Her body moved in time with the pumping and her head fell back. The touch felt so freeing.

"Fuck. That's it."

She opened her eyes in time to see him come off the mattress and put his arms around her. With a spin, she landed on her back and he pulled her arms over her head. Fingers slid through hers as his cock skimmed along her wetness.

"I can't wait." The words came out of him on heavy pants.

She couldn't deny him. Didn't want to. "Do it."

When he still waited, she slipped her legs around him and dug a heel into his back. The man had the ultimate green light and he did not waste it. He rubbed against her, then entered her in one long stroke. She'd barely adjusted to his size when he slipped out and plunged in again.

She grabbed onto his shoulders. Her body accepted his as he pushed in and out. The bed moved under the force of the thrusts. Their bodies rocked back and forth on the comforter. He kissed her neck, squeezed her fingers and angled his hips until her vision blurred.

The extended foreplay took its toll. The orgasm hit her before she was ready. Energy rolled through her and she flushed with heat. Just as her breath caught, she felt him stiffen on top of her. His head dropped to the space between her neck and shoulder and his pace quickened. She inhaled one last time and clenched her muscles tight, and her body let go.

Her last thought was that this night was worth the wait.

SIXTEEN

Elijah picked up his cell then put it on the desk again. Tomorrow he'd move in to Bast's downstairs apartment. He'd take a step that meant moving on. While living in the cheap hotel, not having furniture or possessions of his own, he could pretend it was temporary. That he'd somehow get back into Wade's bed.

That was before fucking Shawn showed up again.

The fucking asshole.

But that kiss. Eli closed his eyes and remembered every second.

He wiped his hand over his mouth. Could still taste Wade. Feel the heat pour off him as their bodies touched. A flood of memories sent his mind racing back to the days before. The sex. The comfort of living together. The simple things, like eating breakfast or watching a movie.

They'd been in this bubble where Eli couldn't leave the condo and Wade ventured out only to work. The enforced closeness made their relationship move in double time. And that's what it had been. A relationship.

They argued a lot at the end, almost always about Becca. Over

Eli's worries about her being in the building and being a traitor. Those fights colored everything. Eventually destroyed it all.

Eli spun his phone around, letting it thud against the wood as it turned. When it stopped he swiped his finger over the screen and entered the lock code. Finding Wade's number only took a second since he was right there in his favorites. One call, maybe a pathetic hookup for old time's sake, like with that kiss. Something to hold on to the bond.

But Wade had made it clear it was Shawn's turn now. He admitted he'd go there next. That the kiss meant good-bye.

With a groan, Eli swept the phone off the desk and heard it crack against the floor. Now he'd need a new phone. He'd already been given a new life and a chance not to be on the run. It should have been enough.

It wasn't.

It didn't take long for Bast to realize Kyra left the bed and he had to go searching. The delay in satisfaction made him grumpy. The warm bed upstairs called. The time he had her on her hands and knees, a palm pressing her back down as he entered her, kept running through his mind. Taking a second run at that position appealed to him.

The memory led to his dick getting hard. Made him wonder why the hell he bothered pulling on his briefs to go downstairs. When he found her, he'd likely take her. He had a condom in his hand just in case. Which, the more he thought about it, had a creepy vibe.

He got to the bottom of the steps and rounded the banister to head toward the kitchen. A flash of movement caught his attention and he stepped into his library instead.

For a second he just stood in the doorway and watched her. She

hummed as she reached for a book on a high shelf. The stretch had
his dress shirt riding up and flashing her impressive ass. God, her
body fucking killed him. So tight and the fluid way she moved had
his cock in a permanent ready-to-go state.

As if she sensed him, she turned and pushed her hair back over
her shoulder. "Did I wake you?"

That smile, so warm and full of life. He wondered how he kept
away from her for as long as he did. He wasn't the scouting-for-
younger-women type. He preferred women who knew the score.
Enjoyed sex and a good time.

But with Kyra he didn't get easy and smooth. She demanded
time and attention. She refused to be forgotten or left in a corner
or used only for sex. They'd reached an understanding and she'd
somehow pushed him while still following the spirit of the thing.

He should be panicked and ready to bolt. Instead, every minute
with her made him want another. The sensation scared the hell out
of him, but he wasn't ready to back away. Not this soon.

"You didn't." He stepped farther into the room and closer to
her. "What are you doing down here?"

"Checking out your library."

The whole scene struck him as ridiculous. Her wearing his
mostly unbuttoned shirt and him in his underwear.

When he laughed, she hugged the book tighter to her chest.
"What?"

"Sounded like a euphemism."

"For sex? I think you're obsessed." She set the hardcover on the
shelf and leaned against his desk with her hands balanced on
either side of her thighs.

The way she stretched her long legs out in front of her. Those
dark red toenails . . . she had to know what the lounging did to
him. "With you? Definitely."

"I got that from the groaning and shouting an hour ago."

"That was you." The sounds she made as she came would stay in his head for weeks. So earthy and guttural. So damn hot.

"Yes, it was."

She shifted and the edge of the shirt slipped up, revealing the very top of her thighs, and his gaze zoomed right there. "You're still not wearing underwear."

She flashed him. "Didn't bring any."

"Good." He walked over to the book she abandoned and put the condom down to study the spine. Seemed her taste ran to the classics. "You can borrow anything in here."

"This is amazing. Growing up I didn't really have books."

He couldn't imagine that. His parents filled the house with books and educational videos. They sent him to special classes and all the best schools. When a grade dropped to a B in a class, he got stuck in hours of tutoring with specialists. The Jamesons were all about proper. Even after they divorced, his mother kept up his father's strict standards. She eased up the reins now and then but once Bast lost her the expectations from his father for his only son rose even higher.

Then Bast got divorced. But not quietly, as his dad insisted. That led to the end of any father-son bond other than the one his old man turned on and off for show.

"I'm assuming there wasn't a lot of extra money to go around," Bast said, trying to be as diplomatic as possible.

"Have you heard about what life with my father was like?"

"Unfortunately, yes." He watched her foot swing back and forth and guessed this wasn't an easy topic for her.

Jarrett had filled Bast in long ago about Wade's home life. Bast had stepped in more than once to keep Wade out of trouble and watched over Kyra from a distance. But that didn't mean he knew every detail. He wasn't sure he wanted to.

"He didn't spend money on books. On anything for us, really." She stared at the shelves as her gaze traveled over the books' spines.

"I remember discovering the library at school. My breath jammed up in my throat and I wanted to race around the shelves touching each one."

"I'm trying to imagine you as a little kid." She was so fierce and headstrong. Maybe she picked it up as a means of survival.

Bast knew from Jarrett that she wouldn't take money from Wade for school. She worked, she got loans. She took time off to collect what she needed and didn't ask for help. He admired her independence, that she never complained about getting a raw deal in the parent department, even though she certainly had.

"I was all long legs, constantly tripping over things. And bad teeth." She laughed. "So crooked and messed up because I never went to a dentist. It cost me, with Wade's help, a fortune to fix them a few years ago."

His dad qualified as difficult but Bast never worried about the basics. Never had to scrape together money for textbooks or to pay to fill cavities. "I'd like to kick your father's ass."

"Prison didn't change him. I doubt anything could."

That sounded like they still had a relationship, and that couldn't be right. Wade broke off all contact and insisted she do the same when her father tried to pull her into his scams. "You still see him?"

"I'm speaking in global terms." She waved him off. "But I remember the librarian, this fabulous older woman named Mrs. Pillard. She'd set aside books for me to read and I'd sit there through lunch, when the doors were locked and no one was supposed to be in there, and cuddle up in a corner of the stacks."

The lifeline was something but she deserved more. "When did you eat?"

"Food didn't matter."

The urge to protect her surged through him. She didn't need him fighting her battles but he wanted to step in with fists up. "Maybe I should kick your father in the teeth instead."

"You grew up with books." She stood up and went wandering. Her fingers trailed along the edge of the desk and over the computer monitor. She fiddled with the pens lined up by the blotter.

She moved with such grace she mesmerized him. "Yeah. Lots of books and expectations."

"Were you a bad boy as a kid?" She smiled as she said it.

"A typical one, I guess. The school was strict."

Her head popped up. "What does that mean?"

"I went away to boarding school. Came home on holidays and when my dad needed me for a work event." The bitterness filled his mouth. He was gone when his father dumped his mother for a younger version. Gone when his mother died two years later from breast cancer.

"I know it sounds weird, but going away and not being in my father's house was my childhood fantasy."

"Compared to your home life, I bet it was."

She went to the fireplace and studied each photo on the mantel. "You didn't like it."

"Not really a fan of being shuffled around and forgotten." He shifted around to face her. He'd answer just about any question to keep her talking. To get to keep watching her.

"You're a nester."

Not really a word he associated with his life or personality. "Is that a good thing?"

"You like home and hearth. You're connected to friends and work and when you're not with either, you want to be here. Where it's comfortable."

"Good guess." The assessment nailed it. He didn't hang out in bars or look for women in clubs. He worked and ate with one of his partners, or with Jarrett and hung around the house. When he dated, it was short-term and usually with a woman he already knew.

No surprises. No uncontrolled reactions. Nothing that made his blood simmer until he met Kyra.

"An informed one, maybe." Her gaze bounced from one corner of the room to the other. "You're not that hard to read. For example, I bet this is your favorite room."

"Why do you say that?"

"You're in every inch of it. The house is organized and impressive but the desk looks like a real person works here. The stack of newspapers and magazines on the side." She sent him a heated look. "I like that you go old-school for your news, by the way. It's sexy."

Christ, her mouth kicked up and her eyes grew warm and his dick went into countdown mode. "Then I won't cancel the subscriptions."

"The photos with Jarrett and . . . other people. Not sure who." She leaned in closer as if studying them then stood up again and pointed to frames on the wall above the mantel. "These look personal. Like, I'm wondering if you took the photos rather than purchased them. Knickknacks you've collected. Books with turned-down pages, which means you've read them rather than just stockpiled them because they looked good in the room."

The inventory bordered on spooky. She got every fact right. "Impressive."

"It's homey." She rushed her hand over the top of the leather couch. "The house is big and expensive, located in a hoity part of town, but still comfortable."

"Hoity?"

"You have a driveway with a garage. Normal people, even those who live in Georgetown, do not have a driveway in DC."

"You have an interesting definition of hoity." Though he had to admit he picked this place over two others because of the garage. Paid too much for the house, too.

"It looks like the guy next door has a driver. And I'm pretty sure I saw a woman in a traditional maid's uniform open the door across the street." She walked to the front of the room and pulled back the heavy curtain he closed each night for privacy. "I almost feel like you should have snuck me in through the servant's entrance . . . I'm assuming you have one of those."

The words piled up until they tripped an alarm in his brain. He spent most of his life ducking from the type of women who wanted to land a rich guy with a pedigree of sorts. Kyra seemed to want the exact opposite and merely tolerated his financial status as an unwanted characteristic that came along with him.

So, he had to ask. "Does the money bug you?"

She shrugged. "It adds a barrier."

Not the clearest answer but he got the point. Now he wanted her to understand his position on the topic.

"Not for me. The 'who are your parents' and 'what school did you go to' thing is not on my radar." Two topics many DC types, married and not, put a lot of stake in.

"No, I guess not. Jarrett doesn't act like a crazy rich dude either. I think you're the same. Grounded despite all the flashy stuff."

Bast decided to take that as a compliment. "Jarrett has a lot more money than I do."

"Really?" She whistled. "Damn."

Bast could have stopped there. Should have . . . "And thank you."

"For what?"

"Seeing through the bullshit to the man beneath." Not everyone could. He'd learned that the hard way.

With that sexy smile and seductive walk, she came back to him. His shirt hung off her shoulder and barely hugged her breasts.

She wrapped her arms around his neck. "The man beneath is pretty hot."

"We should see." His hands slipped under the shirt to touch the bare skin of her waist.

"What?"

"How hot I am when I'm underneath you."

She ran her fingernails at the edge of his hair, right by his ear. "Wow, that was quite the segue."

In a short period of time he'd learned that she liked to touch him. It was like a subconscious gesture. One he loved and had already come to count on.

He massaged her back. "Well, I do make my living using words."

"I can totally tell."

"I'm prepared to say some really dirty ones to get that shirt off of you." He let go of her only long enough to grab the condom off the bookshelf.

She snatched it out of his fingers and held it up in front of him. "Do you keep these all over the house in case of sex emergencies?"

Since she sounded more amused than angry, he told her straight. "I brought it down with me."

One eyebrow lifted. "I'm not sure that's a better answer."

"I know." He looked around the room for the best place to lay her out. "I also know that you wanted to be on top earlier and I took over."

She managed a pathetic frown. Very dramatic. "I did want that."

"I stopped you. I'm sorry about that." So damn sorry.

"Are you suggesting we break in the couch?"

He nodded toward the desk. "The chair."

"I like where your head is."

He walked backward, dodging the edge of the desk and stopping when his ass hit the side of the chair. He used his foot to hook the corner and spin it around. Just as he started to drop, she stopped him.

"Not yet." Her fingers trailed down his chest.

"But soon, right?" Her hand stopped at the waistband of his briefs. "Well, damn. For a second I forgot I was wearing these."

"Let's get them off."

He shoved them off and sat down in record time. "Done."

"Wow, that was quick."

"Not my favorite word in these situations, but I can ignore it."

"I don't have any complaints about your speed in bed."

"Right back atcha." He patted his thighs. "Your turn."

Rather than sinking down, her fingers went to the buttons of the shirt. She undid the few holding the material together and dropped it to the floor behind her with a whoosh. "Are you ready for me?"

He would have answered if his tongue hadn't gotten jammed in his throat. He went with a nod.

The gesture worked because she slid down, balancing her knees on his outer thighs and bringing the heat of her body close to his. Her smooth skin had him staring and wondering how he'd ever attracted someone like her. He traced his fingertips over her collarbone. Somehow he'd missed how damn sexy that part of a woman could be.

She reached for his hand and took the condom out of his fist. Never mind he'd forgotten he grabbed it. With the packet between her teeth, her hand slipped lower. Fingers wrapped around his cock and the slow pump up and down had his body primed. Within seconds she had the condom out and rolled over him.

"I can't believe what you do to me." He didn't question the awe in his voice because he felt it down to his toes.

She brushed her lips over his forehead and down his nose. Across his cheeks. "Tell me."

"I forget everything." He felt her smile against his throat. "I don't care about anything but getting inside of you."

She sat up, bracing her palms against the back of the chair and rocking it back a fraction. "Can you feel how wet I am?"

For emphasis, she curled her hips under and brought the tip of his cock right to her entrance. With his hand in hers, she guided his fingers to her and dragged one through her wetness. She swiveled her lower body, so his caress traveled.

"Beautiful." And by that he meant everything about her. Inside and out.

He stretched two fingers inside her. Twisting his hand, he made her gasp.

"Sebastian." She rode up and down on his fingers, tightening around him and drawing him in closer.

She was ready. Past ready. Energy pulsed around her. Adrenaline shot through him. The timing would never be better.

Using one hand on her hip to steady her, he guided his cock inside her with the other. Like every other time, she swallowed him, her body taking him in, adjusting while he watched. The sight of her opening, the feel of being inside her, wove a spell around him. He couldn't reason or build a wall. She'd broken past his defenses and for a few minutes while she raised her body over his, he didn't care about the lack of control.

Her palm cupped his cheek. "Sebastian, I want you to move."

The haze cleared his head and he realized she held her body still above him, waiting for him. He didn't wait. Shifting his hips up and down, he filled her then retreated. In this position, he could go deep and feel her tightness all around him.

That lasted for a few passes only. Then she eased her body down. Took him down to the base and had them both gulping in air. She bent forward, pushing him farther, though he didn't understand how that was possible.

With her hands on his shoulders, she leaned in and kissed him. Then she pulled back until her lips tickled his. "Now it's my turn to ride."

SEVENTEEN

Kyra didn't intend to go to Bast's office the next afternoon. It was Saturday and he should have been home like a normal person, but he'd gone in. Since she managed to leave her wallet in his car in her rush to get in his house and on him last night, she had to go there first instead of heading straight home from his place. And she needed to go home because her father kept leaving messages and promising another surprise visit. Having him live on the fringes of her life, just waiting to go off, kept her from ever feeling calm.

The timing had her in the same dress and without underwear for the second day in a row. Not her finest moment but her options were limited. Okay, maybe she could have had him drop the wallet by her apartment, or done that thing where they secretly passed it between them at the club that night. But the covert bullshit seemed silly to her today. Not after last night.

Not on a day where so few people should be hanging around the office. Or so she thought until she'd stepped off the elevator and walked into activity in the reception area. Now she sat in his office, waiting for him to finish a conference call in the other room. Good thing she texted rather than just dropping in or they could have had a replay of her last office visit. Not good.

She heard his voice in the hall. Then his footsteps. By the time he walked in the office and shut the door behind him, her body had revved up and excitement pinged around inside her at the thought of seeing him.

He didn't disappoint.

The man looked hot in a suit. The casual office attire worked on him, too. Blacks pants and red polo. The contrast brightened his skin. Also made her want to strip him down.

He leaned down to give her a quick kiss before dumping a file on his desk. It was so natural and sweet . . . her brain almost imploded. The door was open and this was his office. She could only hope the open display of affection meant his insistence on secrecy might be fading.

He slid into the big chair across from her and smiled. "I'm starting to think you have a thing for the leave-behind."

He looked so good but sometimes she had no idea what he was talking about. "Is that guy talk?"

"It's a standard guy trick." He stacked the file he just brought in on top of a stack of others. "You leave something to have an excuse to see the person again. A reason to call back or come over a second time without officially asking for a second date or running the risk of looking overeager."

This sounded a bit like tips for the lovelorn. "Have you used this inventive trick? And by 'inventive' I mean it's really not."

"Sure." He drew out the word. "All the time when I was eighteen."

This side of him, playful and charming, appealed to her on a fundamental level. "Did it work?"

"Absolutely. I saw a lot of action at my all-boys boarding school."

She laughed at his put-upon, woe-is-me expression. "Poor Sebastian."

"Yes, exactly."

She glanced around the office. Saw the phone lines lit up and heard noise in the hallway. Activity buzzed around them, but not as much as the other day when she came in. A few people walked by but the mad rush had died down.

"I can't believe you're working on the weekend. That you dragged other people in with you."

"I'm not making anyone work today. The other people here have caseloads and they handle them. I supervise, not micromanage."

That felt a bit like a lecture. "This appears to be a sensitive topic for you."

"Sorry. When you're in charge you worry you mess up that line." He leaned back with his elbows on the armrests. "And, honestly, I work every day."

So matter of fact. He said the comment like it made sense. "All work and no play makes Bast a boring boy."

"Am I?"

She thought about what he could do in bed . . . in the shower . . . in his desk chair. "No."

"I thought if I put in a few hours today then we could try that whirlpool tonight."

She got a glimpse of that infamous tub last night. So deep and huge that it looked like a family of four could live in it. "You keep promising but you've yet to deliver on this heavenly sprayer thing."

"I'll take that as a challenge."

"The use of water in our sexual games has me intrigued." He worked wonders with everything else and she bet water would be no different.

"Excuse me." The female voice floated through the room.

Kyra jumped at the invasion.

The blood drained from Bast's face. "Lena? What are you doing here?"

"I left a message."

He stood up. His hand went to his stomach as if he meant to button a jacket he wasn't wearing. "With whom?"

"I'm sorry." Lena let out a sharp intake of breath. "I didn't mean to interrupt a client meeting."

Not exactly how Kyra viewed herself. Then again, she got the distinct impression the woman was fishing.

"She's not a client." Bast might be secretive but he wasn't outright lying about her.

Kyra counted that answer as progress. Seeing his ex-wife look all at home in his office was not.

"Hi, I'm Lena McNamara." The woman held out her hand. "Do you work here?"

A nice touch but definitely fishing.

"I'm Kyra." She reached out her hand but cut off her comment before giving her last name because she wasn't sure how much Bast wanted to spill.

As soon as Kyra let go, an unexpected mix of anger and jealousy washed over her. This was the woman who made Bast's private life a public spectacle. She also slept by his side for years. Just thinking about it gave the jealousy spinning around inside Kyra the fighting edge.

Kyra had struggled to push out images of Bast and Lena together before. It would be impossible now. Seeing photos of Lena online was one thing. Those were from charity events and parties, usually with Bast all handsome in a tux and Lena with her hair pulled back and in a fancy dress. Everything looked so done-up and stuffy— neither style of which she associated with Bast.

But the live version of Lena was another story. She had shoulder-length brown hair and these big green eyes. Kyra knew the other woman to be in her early thirties but the petite figure and sweet round face made her look years younger. The dark blue jeans and slim sweater probably cost more than a month's rent for Kyra, but they fit Lena's overall look. She came off as sleek yet approachable.

She was pretty when Kyra wanted her to be a troll. Friendly when Kyra wanted to write her off as an awful bitch. But she did seem to have a boundary problem. A grumbling she'd heard from Jarrett a time or two.

And the way Lena looked at her ex-husband, with a sparkle in her eyes and a loving smile. No way was this woman over Bast.

"You should knock before you come in." Bast came around the desk and put a hand on Lena's arm. A kiss on the cheek came next.

Somehow Kyra kept her butt in the chair. She wanted to stand up and punch Bast while simultaneously shoving his ex out of the door. Yeah, no irrational anger there.

"The door was open and the conversation sounded like it might be . . . personal." When Bast didn't say anything to that, Lena's gaze bounced to Kyra then back to Bast. "Okay. Look, I just wanted to drop this off."

She slipped a thin manila folder from under her arm. Kyra hadn't seen it until right that second. Now she noticed the file and the expensive watch . . . and the diamond wedding band. What the hell was that about? Kyra knew Lena hadn't remarried. Everyone knew. She'd become a celebrity of sorts when her threesome manual came out. The follow-up novel made her a bestseller and now she gave talks on everything from writing to sexual freedom.

Bast looked at the envelope but didn't take it. "What is it?"

"The deed."

"I thought we agreed we'd keep the property."

"You mean you gave in to my request." Lena pressed a palm against Bast's chest with sweet familiarity married people often shared. "I appreciate it, but I owed you this."

Bast frowned as he took the envelope. "Thanks."

"You're right. It was a good deal." Lena made the pronounce-
ment, then stood there.

At first Kyra stared at the other woman, unwilling to make the
situation any easier or cut through the building tension in any way.
Then, as the moments ticked by, Kyra felt a kick of sympathy for
Lena. She clearly wanted to talk but seemed to be in some sort of
emotional and physical lockdown.

"Was there something else?" Bast asked.

Lena nibbled on her bottom lip. "I was going to see if you
wanted to get some lunch, but it looks like you're busy."

"I am."

"Right." She went up on tiptoes and kissed Bast's cheek, lingering
for a bit longer than necessary. When she stepped back, she turned to
Kyra with a strange sadness in her eyes. "It was nice meeting you."

Kyra didn't know what to say so she went with nothing. The
forced smile would have to do.

"I'll walk you to the door." Bast put a hand on Lena's elbow
and turned her toward the door. Before walking out of the office,
he pinned Kyra with a warning glare. "Wait here."

"Like I'd leave now." Not when she planned to ask Bast about
a thousand questions about his ex, including if Bast knew she was
still in love with him.

Minutes ticked by and footsteps sounded again. Kyra turned
around in time to see a man's tall, lean frame turn into the room.
He had his head down and was reading from a piece of paper.

"Bast, I need—" He lifted his head and slammed to a stop
when he saw her. "Oh, shit. Sorry."

She remembered the face. Handsome Asian with enviable thick
black hair. The same guy who stomped his way out of the club a
few nights ago. "That's okay. Elijah, right? I saw you the other day
and heard Jarrett and Bast mention you."

The man stood frozen. "Uh, yeah."

Not the warmest welcome she'd ever gotten from a man. He kind of had that about-to-be-struck-by-a-truck look. "I'm Kyra Royer."

He nodded as his arms dropped to his side and the paper hung from his fingertips. "Wade's sister."

Interesting. Not a question. Then there was the paleness and the scowl. The guy looked ready to vomit. She half wondered if she should call 911. "Are you okay?"

"Why?"

"You should see your face." Many people feared Wade. He was big with a well-earned reputation, but this was something else. Not fear. A totally different emotion and one she couldn't nail down.

"What does that mean?"

"You mentioned my brother's name and you . . . I don't know. Let's say it wasn't a great expression."

The guy's skin went from pale to green. "Wade and I don't get along."

That was not the first time she'd heard that. Members of her father's crew hated Wade. Most considered him a traitor for throwing in with Jarrett, then eventually leaving the business. Others had been on the wrong end of Wade's anger and felt the spike of temper.

"Jarrett says Wade is an acquired taste." Only Jarrett could get away with that kind of comment.

Elijah didn't seem impressed at all. He practically ran from the room. Or he would have if he hadn't run smack into Bast.

Bast held out a hand to steady the guy. "Eli, what do you need?"

"Nothing." Elijah did a spin and a pivot and raised a hand in a weird wave right before he disappeared around the corner. "I should go."

Kyra couldn't help but stare after the man. "What was that about?"

"Which unexpected office guest are you referring to?" This time Bast shut and locked the door when he came inside.

Good call. "Excellent. Let's start with Elijah and work our way back to your ex."

"Lucky me."

Kyra ignored that. "I said my name and . . ."

Bast nodded. "Elijah looked hunted."

"Yeah, is something wrong with him?" Bast just smiled. Something about the look got the wheels turning in her brain. Wade and Elijah and . . . "Wait, how does your employee know Wade?"

"Biblically."

"I don't know what that means."

Bast retook his seat behind the big desk. "I think you do."

The fight at the club made sense now. So did Elijah's reaction and Wade's weirdness. "That's the guy Wade had the huge breakup with?"

"Yep."

"Wade has good taste." Bast wasn't smiling now, so Kyra rushed to explain. "I mean, from an objective man-that-guy-is-hot perspective."

"I'm going to pretend you didn't say that so I don't have to irrationally fire him." Bast tapped his fingertips together. "Did Elijah strike you as being over your brother?"

"Apparently the breakup was terrible. Wade moped around and refused to talk about it." He sneered any time Becca or Jarrett said anything about a date or men or . . . well, anything.

"I know. I saw some of it firsthand, but don't let the yelling and emotional angst fool you. Those two still have a thing for each other."

"Hate?"

"Some would say the opposite."

She didn't need a law degree for that one. The guy she just met showed a broken quality as soon as she mentioned her brother's name. Whatever happened between them had been of the full-destruction variety, but the feelings still lingered.

Man, love sucked sometimes.

And as soon as her mind went there, she cut the line of thinking off. Love was a forbidden topic. She had sex with Bast. That's it.

Rather than dwell on her mixed-up love life, she concentrated on Wade's. "If they're so miserable apart, why doesn't Elijah move back in?"

"Wade won't let him."

And Wade wasn't one to rethink his decisions. Generally, if you were out, that was it. "Oh, huh. Should he?"

"I like Eli."

"I'll take that as a yes." And now to the topic Kyra tried to put off but it kept circling her brain. "So, Lena is pretty."

"Yes, she is."

A part of Kyra liked that he admitted it. He didn't call the ex names or play the hate game. Still, it wouldn't hurt the woman to be a little less attractive.

"And I notice you don't get angry when she walks in and out of your office. Apparently that nasty reaction is saved for me, your sex secret." That one stung. She needed prior approval and Lena waltzed in and out without Bast raising his voice.

"I apologized for that outburst."

In his mind that likely meant the issue was over. She loved how men compartmentalized. "True . . . I guess."

Bast exhaled as if the conversation bored him and he wanted it over. "We owned some rental properties. One just sold."

That sounded a tad too cozy. "Haven't you been divorced for a few years?"

"Yes." His chair made a creaking noise as he sat forward and folded his hands on the desk in front of him.

"But you own property together."

"The market wasn't great. Rather than lose money, we held on to some."

That felt like legalese to Kyra. Like he was using half words or something. "Whatever she brought has to do with one?"

"The last one."

"Now tell me what you're not saying."

His eyebrows lifted. Both of them. "Excuse me?"

"When your words get clipped and your answers get short, I know you're telling only part of a story."

"You can tell that after we've been seeing each other for less than a week?"

Interesting how he slipped in the shot without taking a breath. He also conveniently left out their history before. "We've known each other for a lot longer. Your legal speak is legendary. Now, stop stalling."

"She wanted her money out of the property, we're doing that."

"Really? Because you seemed surprised she signed the deed." Kyra might not have a law degree but she knew shock when she heard it. She also knew him well enough to pick up the inflection in his voice.

"She needed money, so I paid her for her interest in the property."

"Without making her sign it over to you." The puzzle pieces fell together. He tried to make it all sound like a normal transaction, but Kyra knew this was something else. Lena came with her hand out and he gave her money. "That says something about the type of man you are."

"A sucker?"

"Since the woman wrote a book that tanked your dating reputation, I would think you'd be on less friendly terms." Kyra expected anger or at least frustration. Instead, she got comfortable friendship. Well, from his side. Lena's side still had a flashing *I Want You* sign on.

"The split was amicable."

Kyra wondered if he'd ever searched for his name on the Internet because, wow. "How can you say that?"

"I lived through it."

"She wrote a book—"

"Two." He held up the fingers to emphasize the point.

Kyra slumped back in her chair. "Is this a guilt thing?"

"No."

"You're sure?"

"Look, I don't talk about this—ever—but the reality is I changed the rules." The comment hung there. Bast dropped it then stayed quiet. It took almost two minutes of silence for him to keep going. "The threesome thing, that was part of our marriage from the second year on. She wanted to try it, I was game. It grew into something bigger, took over our entire sex life, and I pulled the plug, but I was the one who changed."

It sounded to Kyra like they both had. Bast soaked up all the blame and apparently Lena let him. Their dynamic was a mess.

"Aren't you allowed to change in a relationship?" Kyra asked.

"She was my neighbor growing up. We knew each other before I got shipped off to boarding school. She was a lifeline when my mom died."

A case of puppy love morphing into lifetime love, or that had been the plan. Again, jealousy kicked Kyra. Not hard but enough to start a gnawing in her belly. The woman she just met shared a life with Bast. No woman since then had done so.

That made Kyra wonder. "You still love her."

"Not how you think." He blew out a breath as he struggled to say the words. "I love her and will always love her in a nostalgic type of way. I am not *in love* with her. I haven't been for a very long time."

That all sounded healthy on his part, but it overlooked one key fact. "She would take you back in a second."

"My tastes have changed."

Kyra noticed Bast didn't deny it. He clearly read the body language, all the signs Lena threw out there. Read and discounted.

Hope sparked back to life inside Kyra. "What do you want now?"

"A younger blonde with amazing legs and a mouth that drives me insane."

The man could sweet talk almost as well as he could dirty talk. "I do like to kiss."

He crooked a finger at her. "Then come over here and do it. Then you need to get out of here so I can work."

"How could I say no to that proposal?"

Warmth filled his eyes again. "I like it when you say yes."

She really worried she'd never be able to say no to this man.

Elijah waited until almost five to move his bags into Bast's basement apartment on Saturday. All two of them. It took exactly five seconds to drop them on the kitchen table and look around.

Despite being half underground, the space was bright. It consisted of a small kitchen, a family room and a bedroom in the back. It didn't come close to Wade's place but it was still better than every other place Eli had ever lived.

Even while in the CIA, Eli kept his expenses low and stockpiled his cash. That meant living in a series of studio apartments. Since he'd never been in a relationship that lasted more than a few weeks—other than Wade—there was no reason for space.

"Here you go." Bast slipped a set of keys off his chain. "Unless you have any questions about parking or security codes, I'll be—"

"How long have you been sleeping with Wade's sister?"

Bast's body snapped straight. "What?"

Eli had held the question, waiting for the right time. From Bast's open mouth and unusual silence, Eli knew he'd picked correctly.

"The two of you. Sex." When Bast continued to stare Eli realized he'd stumbled into the middle of something. "What, is it a secret?"

"Fuck, yes."

"Oh. Huh, I didn't get that." Because what the hell else did you say when you confronted your boss about having sex with your ex's baby sister.

"How in the world did you figure it out?"

There was no way Bast couldn't know. He was a smart guy . . . and he looked like he'd been hit by a bus. Eli guessed it was willful blindness or something. "Really?"

"Yes." Bast didn't lose it often but looked right on the verge. "Did she say something? Did you overhear a conversation?"

Elijah had a feeling this part was not going to go over well. "You have a tell."

"Excuse me?"

"You get a look when a woman comes into the room and you've had sex with her." The dumb smile was pathetic really, but Elijah kept seeing it. Connecting the dots wasn't all that hard. He'd been trained for harder stuff than Bast's clandestine sex life.

But Bast was too busy shaking his head to listen. "That's not true."

Eli decided to tick the list off on his fingers. "The list includes your ex—"

"Well, that's obvious."

"—Natalie and Kyra." The middle name still had Eli wanting to choke up bile. "Not that female attorney from yesterday who would clearly like to climb all over you, or your partner's assistant, who would stand in line as well."

If possible, Bast's mouth dropped open even farther. Much more of this and his jaw would be on the floor. "Are you kidding me with this?"

"Imagine how I felt when I realized Natalie was on your list of sex partners." A shiver of revulsion moved through Elijah. "I mean, really?"

"She's blond and pretty and that Southern accent . . ."

"Please don't." Even if Eli was into chicks that would never happen. "No way do I want to know more."

"It took place after we negotiated your deal and before she was a client."

Elijah figured that covered the ethical angles. Bast would know better than Eli would. "I'm not judging."

"Yeah, you are."

About the sex part he kind of was. "I am because Natalie was my boss and . . . damn, man. She could be shitty."

Bast sat down hard on a kitchen chair. "I'm a bit more disturbed that you can tell about Kyra."

"No offense but it's obvious."

Bast rubbed a hand over his forehead. "You're not making this moment easier on me."

"Just saying the truth." And one that didn't take a genius to see. "You get this stupid grin."

"That's just fucking fantastic."

Elijah wouldn't go that far. "But the Kyra thing?"

"Yeah, I know." Bast held up a hand. "Wade's going to kill me."

That wasn't quite what Eli was going to say. Wade would hate any man who touched his baby sister, but Bast was a better pick than most. "Only if you keep hiding it."

Bast looked up. "You think he'd be able to handle the idea of his baby sister having sex?"

"With you? No. With any other guy? Not that either." Okay, maybe Wade wouldn't take any scenario all that well. "But it seems to me he does better with the facts than he does with people trying to hide things from him."

"You're talking from experience?"

It seemed to Eli that someone should learn from his missteps. "I'm suggesting trying to keep Kyra a secret is a mistake."

"It's about privacy."

Yeah, Elijah wasn't so sure. "Is it?"

"Of course."

Eli grew less sure hearing the confusion in Bast's voice. "I guess you know what you're doing."

Bast exhaled. "I'm starting to wonder."

EIGHTEEN

Kyra made it until Sunday night before insisting she try the whirlpool tub. The thing took up an entire corner of Bast's spacious marble bathroom. Getting in it had proved daunting. Something about stripping down and walking around with all the shiny white surfaces and oversized mirrors everywhere made a woman a tad self-conscious about her ass . . . and every other part of her that might be jiggling.

But that was ten minutes ago. Now she laid with her back against Bast's naked chest and ran her toes under the water cascading out of the silver tray at the opposite end of the tub. This was no simple spigot. It was flat and fancy, like everything else in this house, and the water ran down and into the steady bubbling like a sexy little fountain.

The bath gel smelled like the beach and despite being all stone the room stayed warm and cozy from the combination of steam, heated floors and hot male behind her. The same male who had his arms around her as he spent valuable minutes exploring her breasts. He massaged them then pinched the tips.

His erection pushed against her and his legs cocooned her

around the hips. She felt precious and sensuous and so at home.
This level of luxury—any luxury, really—was beyond her realm of
understanding, but Bast handed it to her like she deserved it. He
brought her into his house and seemed to revel in her enjoyment
and wide-eyed wonder.

She leaned her head against his shoulder. "This is the best
invention ever."

"Thought you'd like the tub."

She relaxed into his body and enjoyed the move of his hands
over her skin. "So relaxing."

"Happy to hear it but I'm not sure I want you going to sleep."

Her eyes popped open. "You did say something about a sprayer.
We might want to get to that soon."

"Always so impatient when it comes to pleasure."

She held up her hand and turned it around, studying the bumps
and dimples. "My fingers are all shriveled."

"Want to get out?"

A soft melody played in the background. She looked up and realized the small television over the tub had been set to a music station.
Another unnecessary toy she could really grow to appreciate.

"Don't be ridiculous. Why would I want to move?"

"You do enjoy getting all wet and soapy." His hands disappeared under the water again.

"As much as you enjoy massaging my . . . oh, now it's my thighs."

Pushing her knees open, his palms trailed over the tops of her
legs and up to her stomach, then back down again. "You were
very dirty."

Lethargy had set in but at the rub of his hands every nerve ending in her body jumped to life. He'd taken her in the shower on
Saturday. Right there with her palms flattened against the wall.

Looked like it was time to christen the rest of the room. "One
of us is."

He chuckled, in a sound so rich and warm. "Admit it, you love that about me."

The word skidded across her senses. For him this was about sex. For her it had always centered on more and it kept growing. She'd been attracted to men before. Dated them. Slept with them. Connected with them on some level. But this was the first time her mind and body dove into a freefall over a guy.

"What I know is you're never going to get me in that fancy shower again now that I've tried the whirlpool, which is a shame because that thing is magical." She stared at the glass door and shower instrument panel that looked more confusing than panels for industrial machinery. "Who has jets coming out of the wall, and dripping like rainfall from the ceiling?"

"A man who likes a good pounding."

She curled her arm over her shoulder and around his neck. "Consider yourself lucky I'm going to have sex with you despite that lame line."

"Very soon." He leaned in and kissed her, lingering and deepening as a hand brushed over her stomach. "But first you need to try the sprayer."

He bent forward, taking her with him, and grabbed the silver sprayer. The hose made a clinking sound as he pulled it forward.

"You've been promising for a week now." With a press of a button, warm jets of water pelted her skin. "Oh, that's nice."

He ran it over her knee where it stuck up out of the water. "Oh, I think we can do better than nice."

Before she could catch her breath, he lifted his body and brought hers to the surface. Her lower body broke the water line as he positioned her feet on the edge of the tub. Being exposed to the bathroom's cooler air chilled her skin.

"I don't . . ." Then the spray hit the sensitive skin at the top of her thighs. "Sweet mercy."

"Just relax." With one hand he opened her legs wide and with the other he aimed the sprayer against her, trailing along the outside, never dipping in.

The drumming sensation against her had her squirming. Heat pounded through her even as goose bumps spread over her skin. She wanted to get closer and pull him inside her. "I can't stand it."

"Press your back harder against my chest."

The shift had her hips lifting higher. Closer to the force of the spray. "Sebastian . . . oh my God."

"Right there." He outlined her. Brought the spray closer then pulled back and again. "Not in."

"Why?"

"This is better for you."

She had no idea what that meant but her skin was too busy tingling for her to care. "Yes."

"You like that." He whispered the words by her ear.

Each syllable vibrated through her until her entire body trembled. "Forget the shower. The sprayer is magic."

Her chest heaved and she grabbed onto his forearms for leverage. Even sitting down, the room started to spin. Her body kept clenching and her hips moved without direction from her brain.

With the gentlest of touches, his lips brushed over her temple. "Don't fight it."

"I can't stop moving." It wasn't an exaggeration. Her nerves jumped and her muscles twitched. She felt frayed and right on the edge, begging to be tumbled over.

"I'll anchor you."

"No, I want . . ." He drew the spray right over her, then went back to the outside, rimming her opening. "Do that again."

"Ready?" A finger slid inside her.

The pressure. The pulse of the spray. "No."

"You can take it."

"I'm going to lose it." Her lower body ached from the need to release. She clamped down on his finger and tried to pull him in deeper. To find release.

"And I get to watch." He swore under his breath. "I love watching you come."

Her fingernails dug into his skin. "You're next."

"Maybe we'll just do this again and again." He moved the spray around, touching the top of her thighs and washing over the finger inside her.

Sensations bombarded her until it all became too much. She ground her head into his shoulder and raised her hips. "I'm going to pass out."

"I'd rather see you come."

As if hearing it gave her permission, her body let go. Energy raced through her, stealing her breath and snapping her muscles until they strained. "Yes."

"Now."

Then she came. Hard and loud. Water splashed over the sides of the tub and her body bucked against his. Her mind went blank but she felt his hands sliding over her, his fingers inside her. She surrendered to the rush as the breaths pumped hard through her body. Then she sank down and let him catch her.

More than an hour later, dry and tucked into his king-sized bed, Bast wrapped an arm around Kyra's shoulders as she snuggled naked into his side. Every muscle in his body screamed for a few hours of sleep. From the whirlpool to the mat in the middle of the bathroom floor to bending her over the end of the bed, the last hour had been a blur of unbelievable sex. Busy, heart-stopping and draining.

Totally exhilarating.

For a man who'd experienced a lot of good sex in his time, the last week shot off the charts. There was something about her that went beyond how incredible she looked in and out of clothes. She had all the trappings any sane man would find attractive—a sleek body, long blond hair and a face that lit up when she smiled. She was beautiful by any objective scale.

But he'd had pretty before. He'd enjoyed a steady diet of two women at a time when Lena hit her want-to-try-females stride at full speed. Women who knew the score. At first, the novelty worked for him. He had a good time and made sure the women did, too. Then the boredom with a lifestyle he didn't want on a permanent basis sunk in.

He'd spent the majority of his marriage craving quiet and couple time. The normal time discussing the day and gossiping about friends and family like married people did. Having dinner. Whispering in the dark in bed.

He'd mourned for the marriage he thought he'd have and ended the one he did.

Through it all, he appreciated women of all types and sizes. Smart women, funny women, pretty women. He'd been lucky to know many of each. Kyra combined and covered every category. She appeared more repelled than excited by his wealth, she exhausted him in bed, excited him in conversation. The part where she refused to back down when she wanted something drove him wild.

That all those exciting, amazing parts came wrapped in a twenty-something package still stunned him. From the second after she made that pass in the club he knew they'd be together. But not like this. He'd expected good sex and some awkward after-the-deed conversation, followed by a brief discussion about moving on. He got a woman he wanted to keep close.

The need for her blindsided him. Shook him and had him stumbling.

Her hand swept over his chest and stopped on his stomach. "You're lucky I didn't drown in there."

So much for thinking he wore her out and sent her into a deep sleep. "You believe I would have let you slip under the water?"

She squeezed his biceps. "Nah, you're pretty strong for an old guy."

"Oh, that's nice."

"You hadn't mentioned our age difference in days, so I thought I'd remind you."

She had the power to disarm him. Throw him right off balance. "I'm managing to keep up."

"Please, your stamina matches mine in the sex department." When the quiet stretched, she stopped skimming her hand over his stomach and looked up at him. "What?"

"With my history, that's not the kind of thing I hear very often." People tended to whisper behind his back but not talk straight on with him about sex. But Kyra discounted his history, except to the extent she insisted the multiple partner part be over. "Honestly, women usually avoid the topic."

"It's not a secret."

"Very true." His mind went to Lena and his frustration over her decision to drag their private life into the open.

He pushed the thoughts away as soon as they came because thinking about your ex while in bed with another woman, even in a nonsexual way, struck him as pretty sick.

"Your background is part of you, so why ignore it." Kyra's intense gaze locked with his. "You never ask about my dating past before you or judge . . . or do you do that silently?"

"I don't." Except to be happy that whatever and whoever came before him gave her such a healthy attitude toward liking sex.

"Well, then it seems to me I should be grateful you had all that practice and got so good at it before I came along. I'd hate to break in a novice." She sounded so serious but a bit of mischief twinkled in her eye.

He had to laugh. "Glad to know you're satisfied."

"That's not up for debate." She traced a finger over his lips. "But I'm thinking your reputation is overblown."

Typical of Kyra, he expected her to say one thing and she said another. "Is it now?"

"You've been with all these women—"

"Maybe we should find a new topic." They hadn't hit a snag. He didn't see a reason to find one.

"That's interesting." Her foot traveled up his bare calf. "Does it make you uncomfortable that we're talking about this?"

The combination of her hand low on his stomach and her thigh sliding over his made his concentration slip. "Doesn't it upset you?"

"No, and that's my point."

"You're going to have to use more words because I'm lost." And he was ten seconds away from rolling her under him and spreading those amazing legs nice and wide. Talking would consist of grunts and begging after that.

"Tell me the truth." She shifted, moving her body up higher on his. The sheet around her tugged loose and she flashed him a healthy view of her breasts. "Is it possible, maybe just a little, that you hide behind your reputation to keep from getting seriously involved with another woman."

Thoughts of breasts and sex blinked out of his mind. A strange ball formed in his stomach. One that felt a bit like anxiety, which made no sense since little made him nervous.

Refusing to give in to the odd reaction, he moved his arm under his neck and lifted his head to get a better look at her. "How did you come up with that?"

"I know about the threesomes. Hell, everyone does."

One day he'd forgive Lena for making it so that every fucking non-work conversation in his life came back to this topic. But not today. "People know what they've read and assume the rest."

Kyra smiled. "Well, counselor, did they happen?"

"Yes."

"Throughout your marriage?"

That was enough past-relationship sharing. "Your point is?"

"Except for me, you attract a certain type of woman now. Ones who want a thrill or to take a turn." Her head tilted to the side as she ran the back of her fingers over his cheek and down to his chin. "Just seems to me that's easier for you."

His jaw clenched and he had to exhale to keep from letting the anger spinning inside him seep into his voice. Not anger at her, but at the reoccurring sensation of being viewed through one lens. "I'm not a circus sideshow."

"Have I ever treated you that way?"

"No." The answer was automatic. She hadn't. She'd dealt with his sexual past early and head-on.

"So, there are women out there who want you for you." She ducked her head and kissed his throat. "I know because I'm one of them."

The fury jamming up inside of him ran out again. She offered a rare gift—acceptance. She didn't judge or condone. She didn't seek out a thrill ride or an experience she could gossip about to her friends.

He got why he was with her. He had no idea what she saw in him.

"You could have anyone yet you picked a guy with emotional baggage and a very public history. And let's not forget my dad, who made statements to the press about me being at fault for my divorce."

"There's also your freaky need for secrets and the ex-wife who pops up out of nowhere." Kyra closed one eye and shot him a confused look. "Why do you tolerate the latter again?"

He noticed she ignored the question about her attraction to

him but let the conversation get sidetracked to make a point. The same point he'd been making to Jarrett every time he asked why Lena kept coming around. "It's not that bad."

"Uh-huh. So, the answer is?"

That would teach him to let a conversation go sideways. "I got down on one knee and proposed to her. I stood at the end of an aisle and took vows. That has to mean something."

"True."

Kyra didn't sound convinced so he said the rest. "Basically, I don't want an angry post-divorce where I hate Lena and we fight. We loved each other once and it seems to me we can treat each other with respect now."

That was the truth. Bast let the marriage get away from him. He didn't speak up or put the brakes on their sex life until they wanted different things and couldn't find a common ground. He owned that.

But asking another woman to deal with his guilt over Lena and his need to make sure she stayed okay was a different story. Bast couldn't tell from Kyra's staring what the response would be. She didn't frown but she didn't smile either.

He tried to explain it another way. "Kyra, look—"

"I think that's pretty great."

He lifted his head to get a better look at her because she couldn't just accept this and move on like she had with the rest . . . right? "What?"

"I think she takes advantage of you." When he started to respond to that, Kyra held a finger to his lips. "But that's about her. The way you treat her tells me the most important thing I need to know about you."

"Which is?" He mumbled the question around her finger.

"You're not a dick."

The comment, so simple and straightforward lifted a crushing weight off his chest. One he didn't know stood there until his breath started flowing again. "I'm guessing most women would hate it. The ongoing conversations with Lena could be seen as threatening in some way, though I don't mean it that way."

"Well, I don't want to have lunch with your ex and go clothes shopping, but I get you wanting to maintain a good relationship. She's an important part of your past." Kyra bent her leg and waved her foot around in the air behind her. "In many ways DC is like a gossipy small town but you have history with her, some of it good. I want you to hold on to the good parts."

He searched his mind for the right words. To say the right thing. When that failed, he went with simple.

He pressed a soft kiss to her lips and let his forehead rest against hers for a second. "Thanks."

"You're welcome." Kyra lifted her head and put a bit of space between their mouths. "And when it comes to emotional baggage and messed-up fathers, I have you beat by a mile. So there."

Bast welcomed the lighter mood. Was also happy to take the conversation off him and put it on someone else. "You could be right on that."

"We all have things, Bast. We carry them, they weigh us down and sometimes they suck us under. The goal is to know when to drop and when to reach for a hand."

If he let himself feel more for her, he could really . . .

He cut off the thought before it took hold. This was about sex. Really great sex. Not anything else because God knew saddling her with his bullshit when she already had so much of her own wasn't fair.

"How did you get so wise?" he asked, half joking but he really did wonder.

"I watch a lot of television." Her fingers trailed along his collarbone and she rested her head on his shoulder.

"I'm serious. You're young—"

She groaned. "I thought we got over that hurdle."

"Let me finish." In some way they had gotten around this, but time was still a reality. Not that numbers were his point. "You're young but that's about years and not maturity or life experience. You act older. Wiser. Definitely smarter than me most of the time."

"I didn't have the luxury of being a kid when it came to my father. He wanted me in the family business."

That was a nice way of putting it. Bast decided to clarify. "Stealing."

"*That* I could handle. It was the part where he was happy I wasn't ugly or chubby so he could use me to lure men."

Bast now knew what people meant when they said their blood ran cold. His insides iced over as he lifted her off him to look right at her and gauge her reaction. "What?"

The answer didn't come immediately. She waited. Stayed quiet as the gaze from those big sexy eyes roamed his face.

Some of the spark left her and her skin dulled. "That was his brilliant plan. Set up guys and blackmail them and when my looks started to fade, which he thought would happen about now, arrange a relationship between me and some random criminal guy with more power who my dad needed for something."

"Did that happen?"

"I didn't let it get that far."

But her father put her in that position. Left unsaid was that for some period of time, she played that horrible game. It made Bast sick for her.

"Wade should have killed him." Bast debated calling the man now and filling him in. The result would be pure vengeance but part of Bast wanted that for her.

"My dear brother doesn't know the sex-as-a-weapon part of my father's plan." Her eyes went wide and she stopped blinking. "And he never will. Wade would go after my father and I can't have that. I want Wade safe and out of prison."

"But you're telling me about what happened." Bast dragged out the words, trying to figure out why being her confidant felt so good.

"I trust you."

Warmth spread through him, weird and pumping so strong. He hadn't felt the sensation for a long time but welcomed it now. "You can, you know."

She smiled then and that foot kept flipping in the air behind her. "Because you're a big-time lawyer?"

She was joking but he was serious.

Wanting to touch her, to have her understand, swamped any concerns about sending the wrong message. It was probably too damn late for that anyway. He held her face in his hands and brought her in closer. "Because I care about you. I don't want anything to happen to you."

Turning her head, she kissed his palm. "I'm pretty tough."

"We all need someone sometimes." Bast remembered saying that to Jarrett years ago and now he had Becca. Interesting how life cycled and changed.

"Do you need anyone?"

Part of him wanted to say no, but he knew deep down that wasn't true. A guy didn't yearn for a comfortable, happy home with a wife who loved him, and wanted only him, and not believe. "Yes."

Her focus never slipped. "Do you need me?"

That was too easy. "Yes."

With a hand behind his neck, she brought his mouth closer to hers. "Then take me."

"Again?"

"I'm rested up and ready to go." As if to make her point, her fingers slipped down his waist to his cock. She gave him a little squeeze. "I think you are, too."

As his lips met hers, he got the very real sense he was the one who'd been captured.

NINETEEN

Bast figured the closed club was as good a place to meet Natalie on Monday afternoon as any other. Here, Becca and Jarrett could act as backup. They waited in Jarrett's office right now, watching on the security cameras, just in case.

Natalie's administrative leave officially turned to termination a few hours earlier. By lunch Bast had her out of her house and office and ready to get out of town, though "ready" likely wasn't the right word since she'd spent fifteen minutes sitting on a barstool, balking about going dark while Bast finalized her agreement.

The reason for her refusal, one of them anyway, hovered by the main doors to the club's dining room and eyed every employee who walked near him on their way to prep for tonight's opening and kept them far away from Natalie. Gabe MacIntosh stood six-three, maybe taller, with dark shaggy hair, a dark beard and a dark disposition. Bast had worked with him on other cases and found the man rock solid. His security company had a reputation for being the best, and that's what Natalie needed right now.

She gave Gabe the side eye before returning to glaring at Bast. "This guy? It's never going to work."

Fury vibrated in her voice. It was the one tie to the Natalie he knew before today. Gone was the pristine conservative suit and slicked-back hair. She wore jeans and her blond hair fell to her shoulders as she kept her constant vigil of looking around the room every two seconds.

Bast had never seen her as disheveled or out of control. She teetered on the verge of both now and he hated that for her. She deserved better treatment from the agency she'd devoted her life to than to fear being hounded and destroyed.

Never mind that she'd given the order for the treatment to be done to others. As far as Bast was concerned, Natalie paid penance for that when she put everything on the line for Elijah, Jarrett and Becca.

Using his best soothing lawyer voice, Bast tried again to reason with her. "You are a burnable asset, which means you need protection. Gabe is the right man for the job."

She took another look and this time the man in question glanced back and held her gaze. "He looks like he rips down redwoods with his bare hands."

Which made Gabe the perfect choice for protecting her, as far as Bast was concerned. "He might."

"I don't need a babysitter."

Gabe must have heard the word because a smile pulled at the corner of his mouth. His boots didn't make a sound as he walked over the ground he'd staked out to guard. A tattoo peeked out from under his short sleeve. Bast tried to imagine the stern woman with the hint of Southern accent spending serious time with the gun for hire. They should hate each other, yet the heated looks suggested something else might be at work. Something Bast hoped didn't get in the way of her protection.

"I have been trained to handle situations like these," she explained nice and slow as if talking to a child.

Looked like this situation called for a walk down memory lane. "We could ask Todd what he thinks but since a CIA-backed kill squad got him, that won't work."

"He died because of a gas leak and you're not funny." She slid her fingers over the glass in front of her. The ice had melted and she hadn't taken a sip.

"Not trying to be."

She swiveled on the chair and faced Bast full on, her voice dropping to a whisper. "I can go underground without help until this is worked out."

"It could be months." Bast hated to even say it. He'd walked through the possible scenarios with Becca and Elijah. Natalie could make her body a bigger target by picking the wrong hiding place. Spook the CIA into thinking she was going on the run and might be looking for a bidder for the information she possessed. No, the best thing was to keep the legal channel open, make the deal and keep her close.

"It takes you that long to write an agreement?" Her near-shout had Gabe taking a step toward them at the bar.

Bast held up a hand to keep Gabe back. Last thing he needed was two trained killers on top of him demanding answers. "It does if I want to be sure they abide by it. That they know they have something to lose."

"Which is what?"

This was the last card Bast had to play and he'd dropped the hints with Natalie's higher-ups this morning at a meeting at Langley. "Going after you tears the Jarrett agreement apart, and—"

"But it really doesn't." Natalie went from looking at Bast to studying him.

Not that the scrutiny bothered Bast. The woman sitting next to him knew how to dissect sentences and actions. He expected her to wield the same skills when dealing with him, lawyer or not.

"Jarrett and I say it does. The CIA wants the steady stream of information on foreign threats Jarrett can provide, so the option of going after you becomes less appealing."

That was the plan. Bast worked it out with Jarrett, who insisted Natalie be protected just as she had protected Becca.

"Yet you somehow make sure Jarrett holds the good stuff back."

She wasn't the only one with skills. "This is not my first day on the job."

"You're saying I'm going to have this guy hanging around for weeks." She waved a hand in Gabe's direction.

No way could he let her get away with that. She knew the timing of these things. Wanting a shorter trigger wasn't going to make it happen. "Months."

"No."

"Did something happen?"

"Other than being fired from the only job I've had since college?"

Bast knew that had to scrape her raw. She'd devoted her life to the agency, forfeited a private life. He'd read her file. She made a contribution. Made a difference. Getting tossed aside sucked.

It also showed what a mess the CIA had become, which was bad news because bad leadership meant bad decisions and a harder time in this deal. Bast already spent hours a day battling over the agreement's small print and incomprehensible wording.

"What is your issue with Gabe?" he asked, skipping the subterfuge and tact and going right for the issue.

"I don't need him."

"Did he do something?" Bast could imagine Gabe telling her to be quiet or stop complaining. Being a straightforward guy, he was there for protection. Making friends would not be on his radar.

"No."

It was the way she said it. Too strong. Too emphatic. She didn't laugh the question off as he expected. "Are you attracted to him?"

"Because I'm a woman I have to be attracted to every man who steps in front of me?" She snorted. "That's sexist. And stupid. You're better than that, Sebastian."

And that time she said too much. It was as if she abandoned all her training. Bast even saw her knee bouncing up and down. "It was a simple question."

"Your big dumb friend wants me out of town."

Dumb was dead wrong, but Bast didn't push.

"I agree with Gabe on this." Knowing Gabe, Bast guessed he picked the mountains of some nearby state as a temporary safe lodging for them.

"Out of the state."

As suspected. "Also smart."

"Of course you'd think so. You're not the one who's going to be stuck in a cabin somewhere."

A vision filled his head and Bast couldn't fight it off. "Just the two of you?"

"Don't." Her voice held a smack . . . just like the old Natalie who didn't take any shit ever. "Just because you and I slept together doesn't mean I sleep with every man I work with."

That killed Bast's amusement. "I didn't say you did."

That had been one night. With the pressure gone and deal for Becca done, they'd ordered dinner and the rest just happened. Bast didn't regret it. He admired Natalie and even buttoned-up as she was back then he found her attractive. He could tell she didn't hold it as such a great memory.

"It's what you do say that's annoying." She spun her glass around between both hands. Water sloshed over the side but she seemed not to notice. "That and the stupid grin."

The grin again. If it had anything to do with the "tell" Elijah talked about, Bast debated banning grinning altogether. "Thanks?"

"He won't even come in and sit down like a normal person."

He let the odd comment go because she was raw and ready to spike down any concerned question. "Gabe? He can guard better from a standing position in a strategic location."

Her gaze wandered back to Gabe. "Sounds like you guys are reading the same handbook."

Bast would bet he was the only one in the room who didn't have that kind of training. "I learned it from him on another case."

Her gaze switched back to Bast. "Is that person still alive?"

"Yes." Bast actually didn't know because years had passed and his access to witness protection needed to be limited, but he learned long ago a definite tone put people at ease. He threw it out whenever he could.

"No wonder you're impressed with his résumé."

"Natalie," Bast put a hand on her knee. "Trust me."

She didn't take his hand but she didn't knock it away either. "That is not one of my strengths."

"We'll stay in contact while I finish the agreement off, then you can come back and live your life." Christ, he hoped he could pull this off. "Who knows, you might grow to like Gabe."

"I haven't grown to like you yet." She shifted and looked at a spot over Bast's shoulder. "Or you."

Jarrett nodded. "Always nice to see you, Natalie."

Lost in conversation, Bast had missed Jarrett and Becca coming onto the floor, but there they were, with Jarrett right behind him and Becca looming in the doorway from the hallway. "About time you got here."

Without another word, Natalie slid off the stool and brushed the edge of her shirt down. "I expect a call soon saying this is over and telling me where to send your final check."

Becca joined the men and all three of them stared after Natalie as she walked away. She didn't stop to talk with Gabe. She breezed past him, slowing down only when he grabbed her arm and swung her behind him. Bast would swear he saw the other man smile as he opened the door and ushered Natalie out of the club.

"So," Becca made the short word last forever. "Did I overhear her say you two slept together?"

Becca had security equipment everywhere and knew the answer, so Bast refused to get sucked into that vortex. "No."

"It's good you're here." Jarrett reached over the bar and grabbed a bottle of water and held one out to Bast. "We need to talk."

He passed on the beverage. "About?"

"Let's go into my office."

Reckoning. Time had run out and he messed up. Bast knew he should come clean with Jarrett. At least give him a head's up about Kyra so he didn't hear it from Becca first. Bast had blown by her deadline, never thinking she'd spill.

As soon as they got to the office, Bast started talking. Launched right into the offensive strike. "Okay, before you say—"

"So," Becca cut him off. "We had a new member request."

"What?" Confusion blanketed Bast. This couldn't have anything to do with Kyra. "Don't you get those by the bucket load every week?"

"This one impacts you." Jarrett sat down in his big leather chair and dropped a hand behind Becca, who stood next to him.

They stood before him like a fierce wall, all tense and focused, and Bast had no idea why. He'd taken that long walk down the hall to the back rooms of the club thinking this was about Kyra. Guess not.

"I don't understand," he said.

"Your father." Jarrett delivered the bombshell.

It took a good thirty seconds for the answer to sink into Bast's mind. "Dad wants to be a member here?"

Jarrett nodded. "Lucky us."

The words still made no sense to Bast. "No fucking way."

"He seems to have forgotten he once threatened to make my life miserable." Jarrett smiled as he said it.

Becca didn't take the answer as well. "Why?"

"Because I was the piece-of-shit criminal who was ruining his son." Jarrett walked through the answer like he had it memorized. "I think the divorce was even my fault, though I can't remember how he made that leap."

Becca laughed. "No wonder you got out of the crime lord business. You were far too busy handling Bast's personal life."

Enough chitchat. Bast didn't even know if they were done when he broke in. "Okay, so when does his membership start?"

Becca and Jarrett stared at each other, then looked to Bast. Neither said anything for a few seconds. Both frowned. It was like a game of synchronized confusion.

Jarrett shook his head. "It doesn't."

"We turned down his application." Becca held out a file with a rejection sticker on it.

Without thinking, Bast looked at the file and nodded while the heaviness in his chest lifted. Their gesture meant everything. With his feelings for Kyra in constant churn status, not a lot in his personal life made sense right now. But he could count on these two.

But he couldn't let this happen. They had a business to run.

"You can't do this. I appreciate it, but let him in." They didn't want this kind of heat. No one did.

"You underestimate us." Becca looked grumpy at the thought. "I assure you, we can say no and turn down people all the time."

"You're going to tell the senior senator from the good state of Virginia that he can't join Holton Woods?" The idea made Bast laugh. He tried to remember his father ever not getting something he wanted, and couldn't come up with an example. Dad demanded exemplary treatment and caused a scene when he didn't get it. "It will cause a shitstorm."

"Let it rain." Jarrett leaned back in his chair. Looked pretty fucking satisfied doing it, too.

"Jarrett, come on."

He shrugged. "It's out of my hands. Becca already said no."

"Your father is a complete blowhard jackass, by the way." She sat down on the arm of the chair and leaned against Jarrett.

Bast had called him much worse. "That's not news."

"He went from charming to pissy then he broke into name-calling." Becca looked at Jarrett. "He has quite a range."

The cycle never stopped. His dad threw his weight around and bullied. He hid behind an office and political catchwords, but he only ran about an inch deep. Pontificating defined his style. "Was the name-calling about me or Jarrett?"

"Both." Becca smiled, as if relishing the memory of his father's diatribes. "He thinks you're blackballing him at the club. Keeping him out."

Of course he did. "Even though I didn't know he applied."

Becca put two fingers close together. "Admittedly, that's a small problem with his theory."

His dad always thought the worst of him. Never mind Lena's attempts to explain that Bast hadn't pressured her into threesomes or abandoned their marriage. Bast's father placed the blame squarely on his son and let everyone know about his disappointment. After all, the big news splash at the time didn't match with his father's family-first reelection theme. Ditching Bast, his only child, had been politically expedient.

"And he made a pass at her," Jarrett added with a thread of steel in his voice.

"What?" Not a surprise, but still.

Becca shook her head. "The many truly is a pig."

"There are two ex-wives running around the DC metro area who would agree with you." Bast didn't want to know how many other women his family-values-spouting dad ran though over the years. "But still, he will be a total pain in the ass until you relent. I don't want you going through that for me."

Becca's head dipped to the side and her long hair fell over Jarrett's shoulder. "He's cute when he's in protective mode. The glasses add to the serious look."

They didn't get it. This wasn't a game. Bast's father didn't accept the word no. "He knows powerful people. Hell, he is powerful people. Want me to list the senate committees he's on?"

Becca dropped the file and pointed to it. "I already got the alphabetical cross-reference with his résumé and bio. It's all in there, but thanks."

"And he called to remind me who he was," Jarrett said.

That piece of news stunned Bast. Actually knocked him back a step. "My father called you?"

Jarrett's deep laugh split the room. "Must have killed him to dial my number."

"I don't believe this." Bast really didn't.

"I'm sure he convinced himself he was doing me a favor by applying." Jarrett shook his head. "He started with flattery. Told me how proud he was I finally made something of myself. That I was a true American story, criminal to business owner."

Bast sat down hard in the chair across from his friends. "Jesus."

"After figuring out I wasn't changing Becca's answer, he ended by telling me he couldn't believe I was so weak as to let a woman run my business."

Becca sighed. "Like I said, a pig."

"So you both had to talk with him." Bast hated the idea of his worlds colliding and his friends getting smashed in the middle.

"For me, it was several times plus an interview, which is the normal course for an application." Becca ran a hand over Jarrett's hair. "Then I had a follow-up meeting."

Bast's mind went blank. The idea of Becca having to talk to his dad . . . the reality she didn't punch him or worse . . . none of it would register in Bast's head. "When?"

"You've been busy or I would have filled you in." Her mouth dropped into a thin line as she said it. "You're way over your deadline, by the way."

Jarrett frowned. "What does that mean?"

Kyra. This was the conversation Bast expected when he stepped in the office. But he couldn't handle it now, so they'd have to circle back. "Nothing."

"Well, point is, your dad is out." Jarrett held up both hands as if to say "end of conversation."

Bast wiped a hand over his face as he tried to find the right words to express his appreciation and let them off the hook. "Guys, I appreciate this but you can't—"

"I hate when people tell me I can't do things. Your dad tried that and I ripped up his application." Becca's flat voice said she would be happy to take on another Jameson if needed. "Well, a copy of it but it made me feel better to toss the thing."

Bast tried one last time. "You have to do what makes sense for the club."

"You are a loyal member. He is a dick." Jarrett grabbed the file off the desk and dumped it on top of the shredder to his right. "End of story."

All true, but . . . "He's not going to let it go."

"He is for now," Becca said. "I told him that given how important he is I worried some members would try to take advantage and someone might try to use him or lie about him or create a conflict of interest."

Bast felt the room tilt. "He bought that? You've got FBI and CIA guys here. Other congressmen and the guy who sits alone and looks half asleep but really runs the NSA."

Closing his eyes, Bast visually moved around last night's seating and counted four members of Congress, a cabinet member and a guy who ran a private militia and could take them all out. And those were just the obvious power players Bast knew personally.

"Your father likes a good ego stroke." Becca smiled as she said it.

Bast had the opposite reaction. His mind rebelled. "Please don't use the word 'stroke' when talking about my dad."

"Point is, we want you here," Jarrett said, cutting in. "We don't want him here."

Bast had no idea what to say or how to process any of this. His father hated Jarrett and blamed him for Bast going bad. To have life circle around to his dad asking Jarrett for a favor or any kind of approval knocked Bast back.

So did the loyalty of his friends. "You didn't have to do this for me."

Becca exhaled and the sound suggested an explosion was coming. "Now you're pissing me off."

"Bast?" Jarrett said his name quick and sharp, almost angry. "Let someone stick up for you for a change."

Bast stared at the man who started as a client and turned into a best friend. "I don't know what to say."

Becca rolled her eyes. "Since you're a lawyer, I'll bet you think of something."

"Thanks." It wasn't enough but it was heartfelt and Bast suspected Jarrett would understand that.

"Any time."

And Bast knew Jarrett meant it.

TWENTY

Kyra stood in the middle of her small apartment late Thursday night wearing her shorty pajamas and missing Bast. She regretted leaving the big bed and amazing tub, but she really hated going the whole day without even talking to him.

He'd texted that he had to work through dinner and couldn't come to the club. While impressed he'd finally figured out how to use a phone and stay in touch, not seeing him made work dull and long. So did the bore who told her all about his place in Paris and how he'd love to show her the cafés. Yeah, because that kind of line worked on her.

Feeling lonely and grumpy, she eyed up the ice cream in her freezer. If you shouldn't eat after five she wondered if it was okay to wait and eat again at two. Technically, it was morning and ice cream included dairy, so . . .

The short set of rapid knocks had her jumping. Her cell started buzzing a second later. She swiped it as she headed for the door. A glance at the screen and out the peephole confirmed both messages came from the same person. The one person she ached to see—Bast.

She opened the door with excitement jumping in her stomach. He'd come over and the gesture had her all light and floaty . . . and his frown killed her mood.

He did a quick sweep of his gaze down her body and up again. "Why are you here?"

Seemed obvious to her. "I live here."

He raised an eyebrow as he stepped past her and pushed the door shut behind them. "I meant, why aren't you at my house?"

That was where she wanted to be. On his couch, waiting for him to come home. Sharing a late snack and dragging him up the stairs. The agenda worked for her.

But she didn't want to assume and he wasn't exactly throwing open the front door and handing over a key. Hell, he still wanted their time together to be a secret. At least she thought that was true because he hadn't made a move to downgrade their status.

Sitting in the club, night after night, he treated her like a friend's sister and nothing more. Forget that he spent the later part of those evenings lodged inside her, running his tongue all over her.

She shivered at the memory and tried to pull her mind back to the present. That meant ignoring Bast's hot charcoal suit and rumpled hair, and staying focused. "I've been there since, what, Saturday? That's five days."

"And?" His frowned deepened. Who would have thought that was possible?

"I needed clothes." Okay, she knew that was lame but it was easier than asking the question she wanted to ask. She could confront him about his assy behavior and deal with his ex-wife haunting him any day of the week.

This topic was different. Asking him if he still only viewed her as a convenient sex partner crossed over to emotional danger territory. Because he could say yes.

She believed their initial deal had changed but if he said no, that they were still on a track to nowhere, then everything ended, and she could not let that happen. Not yet.

"I like what you're wearing now," he said.

"Because I'm not wearing a bra."

That got his gaze bouncing up and down again. "For the record, as I've stated several times, I prefer you without clothing."

She somehow knew he would say that. "I can only wear your tees for so many days."

He rolled back his shoulder and dropped his keys on her dresser. "Again, you resolve that by not wearing anything."

"Always the problem solver."

He folded his arms over his chest and stared her down. "Is something else going on?"

Maybe if she circled back around, she could get there. Ask without actually asking. "Saturday through Monday I was with you, then had to run back here to get work clothes."

"And Wednesday you stayed all day."

Now that they had the calendar straight . . . "I think you're missing the point."

"We don't live that far apart."

The man couldn't pick up a clue if it dropped on his feet. "It's really not a mileage issue."

"Do you want to sleep alone?"

Man, if he'd gotten there then they really were on two different pages. "No."

"Okay then." He threw up his hands. "What's the problem?"

She debated, she really did. It had been more than a week since they'd gotten together but felt like a lifetime to her. A great lifetime. One she wanted to continue, so instead of fighting and hitting the issue head-on, she parried. "Nothing."

"Of course, now that we're here." He glanced around her apartment. "And there's a bed."

"Subtle."

He unknotted his tie. "And it's late."

"Are you undressing?"

He froze in the process of taking off his jacket. "I can get inside you with the suit on, if you prefer."

Like that, fire ripped through her and worries about the status of what they were ceased to matter. Not when he stood there, looking hot, having made the trip over just to see her. Well, not just see, but he didn't have to show up and he did.

That had to mean something.

She saw the wariness in his eyes as he stood there with his arms half in the jacket and half out. "Take it all off but the glasses."

"You are consistent."

"And yet I have to keep reminding you about the glasses."

"I'll make a deal with you." He draped the coat over the chair and started on the buttons of his shirt.

"I'm listening." And watching . . . and wanting.

"You take something off, I'll take something off."

She loved when he negotiated in the bedroom. "I'm wearing less."

The tsk-tsk sound came first. Then he threw her a you-poor-thing frown. "That's not my fault."

"You're the one who told me not to wear underwear."

"My tie is off." He hitched his chin in her direction. "Remove the shirt."

"This doesn't seem equal." But she did it. Swept the material up and off, letting it float to the floor.

"My shirt for your shorts."

She ignored the part where she seemed to be taking clothes off at a faster rate than he was. "Deal."

She hooked her thumbs in the waistband and wiggled out of cotton shorts. Shifted her hips back and forth, taking a little extra time and stretching when she stood up straight again. If he wanted her naked, she'd give him naked.

He whistled. "Damn."

When he didn't say anything else, she continued to stand there. The air conditioner had cooled off the room but his heated stare kept her toasty warm.

But she was dying to touch him. If the growing bulge in his pants was any indication, he was ready, too. "You have to say what's next. This is your game, Sebastian."

"And I feel like I'm winning." Right as she started toward him, he shook his head. "Get on the bed."

Looked like her man was ready to play. Good, because she was ready to make him work for it. She sat right on the edge of the bed with her legs tight together. "Like this?"

"Turn over." He stepped closer as his shirt hit the floor. "On your stomach in the middle of the bed."

Her stomach performed a little dance. "One of your favorite positions."

"How did you know?"

"You were pretty enthusiastic last time I was in this position."

"It shows off your ass." He signaled for her to get moving. "And when I'm behind you I can squeeze your tits."

Her muscles refused to work but she somehow flipped over. Even as her rapid heartbeat threatened to kill her, she spread her fingers over the comforter. "You are a very naughty boy tonight."

The bed dipped when his knee touched the mattress. Her body rolled slightly until it leaned against his. The material of his pants scratched against her bare side.

"I'm about to get naughtier," he promised.

His blue tie came into her line of vision and the excitement pumping through her brought her to the verge of a full-body shake. "Whatcha doing?"

"Tying you to the headboard." He slid the smooth silk over her wrists in a figure eight then slipped the end around the headboard post. There was a *thwapping* sound as he pulled the knot tight. "Problem?"

Need bubbled inside her and she could barely keep her head up. "No."

"I love how you embrace your sexuality."

Fingers brushed up her legs. Then she was on her knees with her upper body against the mattress and her arms stretched out above her.

He walked around and a zipper screeched through the room. "So pretty."

She couldn't see him, but she heard the shuffle of clothes and footsteps as he moved around. Moving her head back and forth, she swiveled, trying to get a good look. "Less talk, more action."

"How about this?" His hands skimmed over her ass and down to the back of her upper thighs. "And this?" One hand traveled farther and a finger slipped inside her.

"Your hands are amazing."

"Is there any other part of me you like?" The front of his legs touched the back of hers.

She tried to say something but the outline of his erection, the way he rubbed it against her, stole her breath. All she could manage was a half-strangled sound.

He leaned over her until his stomach touched her back. "What was that?"

"All of you."

"Good answer."

The opened condom wrapper landed on the bed beside her head. She couldn't reach for it. Could barely move. Bast had her pinned to the bed with his body. The tip of his cock slid along the seam from her ass down to her slick wetness. Back and forth, teasing until her body quaked.

She pushed back against him, straining the tie until the edges dug into her skin. "Deeper."

"Oh, I don't think so." If anything he slowed the brush against her, dragging the tip through her a fraction of an inch at a time.

"Sebastian."

"The way you say my name is so hot."

When she tried to drag him in, he stopped her with a hand on her lower back. Pressing, he shifted her upper body back to her elbows and held her there with his palm.

"Please." The way he built the pressure inside her had her fighting for breath. Her insides scrambled and her mind turned to mush. She wanted hot and fast and him all over her.

But he denied her that final release.

"We're going to take our time tonight." His hand traveled up and down her back in time with the gentle rub of his cock over her.

Her palms fell open but every other part of her clenched and tightened. "I'll beg."

"Yes, you will."

"How can I make you go faster?" She couldn't drive back into him because his hand held her still. She couldn't grab him because her wrists were tied. She laid there open and vulnerable . . . and loving every minute of it.

"Not going to happen." But his breathing picked up and his voice dropped sexy deep.

Guided by his hand, his cock slipped further inside her. He filled her halfway and stopped. Not moving turned out to be a new form of sensual torture.

This time she pulled on the tie, crushing the fabric in her fists. "You're killing me."

"We can't have that." He pushed inside her then with one long thrust.

The friction sent her body bucking and her mind reeling. He slid out, steady and slow, driving her insane with the slow speed. She needed him to pick up, to do something to break through the tightening inside her.

"I'll say your name." She would make any bargain, offer anything.

He leaned down until his chest touched her back. "I want you to chant it."

When he pulled back again, she did.

TWENTY-ONE

The next night Bast grabbed Elijah out of his claustrophobic office and dragged him to the club for dinner. Eli never complained but he'd spent an unusual amount of time staring out the car window and grumbling. And now he sat in the booth with his back to the bar and the man behind hit.

A punch of guilt hit Bast. The trip gave him the opportunity to see Kyra for the first time since early that morning. See and admire. Eli, in full bodyguard mode, had little choice but to come along.

Bast glanced over at Kyra and caught a smile. Then he looked across the table and saw nothing but Elijah's dark hair. "I know you'd rather not be here."

"I have to eat." Eli never looked up from the file in front of him. He studied it as if his life depended on it.

"Eli, I get—"

"Aren't you going to say hello to your girlfriend?" Eli flipped a page. Then another. "Maybe drag her into the back for the few minutes."

After a quick look around the dining room, Bast leaned in and lowered his voice. He hoped it would blend in with the mumble of voices and clanking of silverware and dishes. "Could you maybe keep it down?"

Closing the file, Eli looked up. "It's still a secret?" His smile made it clear he knew it was.

Bast fought off the urge to fire him just because. "Yes."

Taking his time, drawing out the moment for maximum drama, Eli took a long drink from the glass in front of him. "She slept at the house all weekend and at the start of this week. Then there's last night when I got to sit in my car outside her apartment and wait for you."

"I didn't ask you to do that."

"Doesn't matter. It's the job."

This is what happened when you moved a former undercover operative into the downstairs apartment. He conducted surveillance. Bast understood the tendency but he didn't appreciate being the target. "When did you get so fucking nosy?"

Eli's frown suggested he wasn't impressed with the outburst. "I'm watching over you, which right now means I'm looking out for her, too."

Well, shit. He had a point. It was an angle Bast ignored. If someone wanted to get at him and saw her, she'd be in the firing line. And he'd be the one who put her there. That meant he had to do a full assessment of the danger to him. If it meant danger to her, he had to pull back. The one thing he absolutely did not want to do.

He'd handle that tomorrow. Right now he had another line to draw. "I appreciate that, but me being with her is not a topic for discussion."

Eli frowned. "Why?"

"Excuse me?"

"You're obviously into Kyra."

At the mention of her name, Bast had to fight off the desire to look for her in the room. "This isn't your business."

"I'm just saying, you may as well spill. Becca knows." Eli located her in the room and nodded in her direction. Then he pointed at Jarrett. "I'd say your best friend knows."

"He doesn't." Bast had no idea how Eli figured out the Becca information, but he got Jarrett wrong. The second Jarrett found out he would hunt Bast down and that hadn't happened. Bast knew it was coming and tried to figure out the best way to get there and get it over with.

"If I can decipher your tell, he can." Eli just kept drinking, as if they weren't having the most infuriating, too personal conversation ever. "Then there's the other thing."

A voice in Bast's head screamed for him to ask. "What?"

"The staring."

That wasn't true. He demanded secrecy and knew how to play his role. "I don't—"

"You don't drool, but you're right on the edge."

That hit a bit too close to the truth. "I can fire you."

Elijah shrugged. "Go ahead."

"You're not an easy man to threaten."

"Or kill." Eli emptied the glass and put it back on the table with a soft thud. "You may want to keep that in mind."

Kyra appeared at the side of the table. She wore her usual work uniform and a sunny smile. "Good evening, Mr. Jameson."

Eli scoffed. "You make her call you by your last name?"

That just made him sound like a dick, and Bast didn't like that one bit. "It's club policy."

"Makes me wonder what happens when you're alone together."

Kyra's eyes widened as she stared at Eli. "Wait, you know?"

"About you two?" Eli shot her a get-a-clue look. "I would point out I live downstairs from Bast right now."

"He knows not to talk." Bast said it more as a warning for Eli than a fact for Kyra.

And Eli immediately blew it. "Who the hell would I tell?"

"I can't even deal with this right now." Kyra glanced around then bent in a little closer. "Could I have a word with you?"

Bast couldn't think of a worse place for a so-called private chat. "How?"

"Want me to leave?" Eli was already shifting to the end of the booth to get up.

"You could go talk with Wade," she said in a singsongy voice. "Yeah, you're not the only one who knows personal things about people."

Bast bit back a smile over the way the amusement left Eli's face. "She has you there."

He swore under his breath. "Your brother is an—"

"We use the word 'difficult,'" Kyra said.

"Right. Excuse me." Eli didn't wait another minute. He slid out of the booth and headed away from the bar. In a few steps, he met up with Becca. It said something about how little he wanted to talk to Wade that he chose to go to her instead.

Kyra watched him leave. "I see what you mean. He's clearly still into Wade."

"Understatement." If anything, Bast found Elijah even more torn up about Wade lately. He went from looking sad but hopeful to shutting down completely. "What's up?"

"That was my question."

Clearly he missed a step. Bast had no idea where. "I don't get it."

"About tonight." She rolled her eyes. "You should see your face."

He guessed she saw confusion because that was the emotion bouncing around inside him. That and a healthy dose of lust. "I'm trying to figure out where you're going with this."

"Am I invited over tonight or not?" She barely opened her mouth as she asked the question.

For a second all he could do was look at her and wonder how this part of their communication kept misfiring. He thought they'd worked that out last night when he went to her place and almost ordered her into his bed. "Of course."

"You say that like it's a foregone conclusion."

Wasn't it? "I figured you'd come over after work, or I can come get you."

"Why don't we meet at the corner and I'll crawl in the trunk so no one can see us?" Her anger shot out and smacked him.

Her mood could change on a word and this time he had no idea why. "What is that supposed to mean?"

"Nothing."

A woman did not make that comment without trying to make a point. He had to be slow this evening because he couldn't ferret out what lesson he should be learning. "I'm thinking something."

"You just assumed I'd come over."

Well, yeah. "Do you not want to?"

"You're being obtuse."

Before Bast could think of an answer, Elijah stood beside Kyra. Somehow the rest of the room stayed in motion. Except for Wade who all but ignored the server in front of him in favor of watching Elijah and the unexpected party at Bast's table.

"Can I come back now?" Elijah looked down at Kyra. "Whoa. Are you okay?"

She kept her focus on Bast. "Your boss is annoying me."

"Let's not involve Eli in this."

Elijah nodded. "That would be good."

"You ask me, Bast. At the very least, you invite me." Her voice rose as the sentence continued. By the time she got to the last word, a man at the next table glanced in their direction.

"I knew I should have gone outside," Elijah mumbled as he shifted his weight from foot to foot.

Bast didn't care about the show they gave the room or Eli or anything else. Kyra seemed to be laying some new sin at his door, and he refused to accept it. "Didn't I do that when I said I was coming here for dinner?"

She shot him a you-will-pay-for-this-later glare. "You're unbelievable."

Then she was off. With a pivot, she walked off and more than one person moved out of her way as she stalked by the bar and kept going.

Bast had no idea what just happened. He knew he'd have to apologize but he'd be damned if he knew for what.

Eli took the seat across from Bast again. "I thought you were supposed to be good with women."

"I thought you liked men."

Eli stared in the direction of her heated trail. "I kind of like her, in a she-could-kick-your-ass way."

"Yeah, so do I."

"You might want to start showing it." Elijah held up a hand as if in surrender. "Just saying."

Aiming to end the conversation, Bast took an unfair shot. "How would you like it if I gave you love life advice about Wade?"

Instead of taking the bait, Eli nodded his head from side to side as if he was contemplating the question. "The way I see it neither one of us is an expert on the Royer siblings."

"You may have a point."

"But, if I can give you some advice."

"Can I stop you?" Being the boss didn't seem to do it.

"You might want to be careful because I think she's tougher than Wade."

Forget training and weapons, Bast knew that comment was correct. "No doubt."

. . .

Kyra fumed as she took a drink order and walked up to the bar to give it to Wade. She refused to look at Bast. She felt the heat of his stare, sensed him talking about her with Elijah. Since all she wanted to do was look over and flash them the finger, which had to be a club violation of some sort, she pretended they didn't exist.

She didn't want to deal with Wade either. Pretty much all males pissed her off at the moment.

She read off the order then turned to go, but he grabbed her hand and held her steady. "What's going on?"

Clueless men everywhere she looked. "I'm working."

"I'm talking about your conversation with Bast." Wade wiped off the bar then grabbed glasses to fill her order.

She couldn't exactly open up. That was part of the problem. Bast did so many things right, but when he got something wrong, it was in epic style. Insisted on secrecy. Took for granted she'd be there each night. Kept her at a distance.

She hated all of it.

Deep down she knew she was the one changing the rules. They had a deal, but not one she liked and one she always vowed to shift. From the beginning she wanted more than sex and hoped he would grow to crave something bigger, too. Part of her believed he did but then he acted like an ass and she didn't know where she stood.

Finding out the distance of the divide between what she wanted and what was scared her to death. Her, a woman raised by a two-bit criminal with an oversized ego and a desire to use her for sex to gather more resources.

She survived all that, but falling in love was killing her.

And that's what it was. If she were honest, she'd admit she'd loved him for a long time. She could push him and seduce him, but the risk of him finding out her true feelings and not returning them—or worse, not even wanting to try to return them—pounded her into the ground.

But she couldn't say any of that to the brother who sacrificed so much for her. Not yet. So, she said the obvious. "He was ordering."

Wade eyed her up as he poured. "The discussion looked pretty heated."

"When I started working here, you promised not to hover." It actually took her in combination with Jarrett and Becca to gain the promise from Wade to refrain from punching every member in the face.

He'd been adamant she work somewhere else. Anywhere else. Winning him over took time and he likely only relented because his nasty breakup with Eli had him in a weakened state.

"I stayed over here, didn't I?" Wade set a glass down a bit too hard. "I didn't barge in and cause a scene."

She glanced over and saw Bast talking with Elijah. "Gee, I wonder why."

Wade stopped shifting around behind the bar. Stopped making drinks. His big body slammed to a halt. "Meaning?"

"Elijah." They danced all around this. He told her the guy he was dating was wrong for him, then refused to discuss it again or name him. She'd pieced it all together from other people and observation.

Without moving his head, Wade gave Elijah a quick look. "What do you know about him?"

"Are you looking for an answer other than Elijah is your boyfriend and you forgot to tell me?"

"He's not my boyfriend."

Looked like her brother was in the mood for a game of verbal gymnastics. "Was."

"Still wrong." He lined up the drinks from her order. "Who told you? Becca? This sounds like Becca."

One more clueless male in a night full of them. "I have eyes, Wade. You two stare at each other like lovesick kids but what you look like you want to do to him is very grown-up."

Wade exhaled, visibly bringing his temper under control. "We were talking about whatever's going on between you and Bast."

"You want to talk about Bast. I wanted to talk about Elijah." She actually didn't want to talk about either of them. Getting lost in the monotony of work sounded better tonight. "Bottom line, you should worry about your own love life."

Wade moved as if in slow motion. His head shifted to the side and his eyes narrowed. "You're saying talking about Bast is the same thing as talking about your love life?"

Son of a bitch. Her first misstep in the secret relationship and she didn't waste it on something small. No, she went right for the sonic boom. "I was just trying to make a point."

"Really?"

"Yes."

"I'm wondering." Bast looked over at Wade again. This time the expression bordered on a glare.

Anxiety welled inside her. "What?"

"If maybe I'm the one who should be talking with Bast."

She shouted as Wade finished his sentence. "No."

"That's emphatic."

Too much. She eased back on the panic and tried to sound reasonable. "Don't mess up my job at the club."

"I won't."

Time for the more important warning. The one she feared Wade would never heed. "And leave Bast alone."

Wade scoffed. "We'll see."

TWENTY-TWO

Elijah moved around his new basement apartment, making sure he had everything just as he wanted it. With one switch he turned on the surveillance equipment, and images from around the outside of Bast's town house flickered to life in quarter squares on the two monitors set up on the kitchen table.

To be effective he should have cameras and listening devices inside the town house but Bast refused. He thought his standard-issue alarm system was sufficient. The guy knew a lot about the law but he ranked as a total amateur in the protection business.

Eli walked around the table and grabbed a beer out of the small fridge. The place measured about a thousand square feet and had been furnished and fixed up as if Bast intended to rent it out. Eli couldn't imagine that in light of how secretive the guy could be. Hell, he fit right in with the former undercover agents he hung out with.

Whatever the original plan, Eli benefitted now. The spacious one bedroom apartment qualified as the nicest place he'd ever lived, other than those months in Wade's condo. Studio dumps and half-furnished temporary safe houses filled Eli's past. This place had more than a mattress and a coffeepot. The separate rooms and obvious luxury actually made Eli twitchy. He could only be in one room at a time, so more than that struck him as unnecessary.

The doorbell to his unit rang. Two in the morning seemed like the wrong time for salesmen. That realization had him putting down the beer and grabbing for his gun as he stalked to the door.

Adrenaline pumped through him as he stood to the side of the doorframe and gave the monitors a quick peek. What he saw had him easing the grip on the weapon.

Understanding the image took another minute.

After unlocking, he opened the door. "What are you doing here?"

Wade put a hand on the side of Eli's gun and shifted the barrel away. "Put the gun down."

"Right." The weight in his hand reminded Eli he was even holding it. Until that second he'd forgotten it. Dropping his arm to the side, he used the other to usher Wade inside. "Did something happen at the club?"

"I came to talk to Bast but decided to visit you instead." Wade walked around the security setup, careful to step over stray cords. "What's all this?"

"I'm watching over Bast."

"Does he know?"

As he did ever since they broke up, Wade managed to find the comment sure to piss Eli off. His temper flared. "What kind of question is—"

"Forget it."

"I would if I knew what you were talking about."

"Just stop talking." Wade took three steps inside then turned around. His broad shoulders blocked Eli from the rest of the apartment.

Almost without thought, Eli backed up and his ass hit the door. "What's going on with you?"

"I don't want conversation." Wade slammed his palms against the wood on either side of Eli's head.

At this distance, Wade's familiar scent hit Eli. He could see the heated intensity in Wade's eyes.

Him being here. Him gathering in this close. None of it made sense. "I don't get it."

"You inside me. Fast and as filthy as you want."

Eli's mind went blank as his stomach flipped inside out. "You're offering—"

"Not a relationship. It doesn't mean we're getting back together." Wade's hand pressed against Elijah's and shoved him back against the door with a thud. "It's just sex."

Eli dreamed about this for weeks. Not in those words. Not in a suggestion that provided a release and nothing more. But it was something. Maybe a start, a step back toward the end he wanted to reach.

In any context, Wade coming here and requesting sex qualified as the ultimate fantasy. After the fighting and angry words, this scene seemed impossible as recently as this morning. But the moment waited right there at his fingertips now.

The thought of being with Wade again had Eli's brain shutting down while his body revved up for action. But he had to know this was real and not some sort of fucked-up piece of revenge.

"That's quite an offer," he said, clenching and unclenching his hands to keep from reaching for Wade too soon.

Wade didn't hold back. His fingers curled as he gathered Eli's shirt against his palm and shortened the distance between their bodies. "Take it."

The tighter grip, feeling Wade's breath against his lips, combined to send common sense into a nosedive. "It's also a pretty big change in position."

"I watched you tonight at the club. I'd forgotten how much I liked watching you." Wade's hand slipped inside Eli's shirt to touch skin. "The way you move, like you're circling prey. Those long legs eating up the floor as you walk. How you hold your body. That amazing face."

Something exploded in Eli's brain. It had always been this way.

Just thinking about stripping Wade naked and holding his thick cock in his hand set Eli's skin on fire. "And now you want to fuck."

Wade nodded. "Yes or no?"

He should have been strong and demanded more but there was no way in hell that was going to happen. Not when Wade stood there asking for it and Eli needed it so much. "Sick prick I am, I'll take what I can get."

Wade's hand went back to the wall and his body balanced there, over Eli. Unblinking, Wade stared him down. "Take your shirt off," he ordered.

"You do it." Because Eli loved the feel of Wade's strong hands running all over him.

Never breaking eye contact, Wade opened the shirt. After two buttons, his speed quickened and he ripped it right off Eli, letting if fall to the floor and leaving his chest bare. Then his hot mouth went to Eli's neck and he sucked hard.

Just as Eli caught his breath, Wade's lips moved. Down Eli's chest. Licking his nipples as his hands dipped even lower to rub over Eli's fly.

Sensations pummeled him. Hit Eli from every direction. The mix of hands and mouth brought the memories racing back to the sex they'd already shared. Ache combined with need until Eli grabbed the sides of Wade's face and dragged his mouth back up again.

The fierce kiss locked them together in a whirl of heat. Tongues, teeth—this wasn't a sweet touch. It demanded and claimed. Hands roamed and their legs tangled together in the rush to get even closer. When they broke apart they continued to hold on to each other with unbending grips.

"Where's the bedroom?" Heavy pants escaped Wade's chest as he struggled to get the words out.

The extra steps weren't needed. Eli was fine using the floor. Throwing everything off the table. "It's—"

"Just get us there."

That was all the incentive Eli needed. He took off walking and reached for his belt. After only a few steps, Wade had him up against the wall, their bodies knocking against each other as fingers touched zippers and undid buttons.

When they got to the bedroom doorway, Eli held Wade there, just as he'd fantasized about since moving in. Eli's hand dipped into the opening of Wade's dark dress pants and slipped by the elastic of his briefs. Resting his head on Wade's shoulder, Eli took out Wade's cock. Felt it grow firm and long under his hand. Marveled at the heated smoothness.

"Fuck, I need this." Wade ended the comment by fitting his mouth over Eli's and kissing him long and deep.

They somehow guided each other into the room. Their pants hung open and they caressed each other, Wade through Eli's briefs. Heat pounded off their skin. Wade's shirt was off and Eli had no idea when that happened. He was too busy pumping his hand up and down Wade's cock and watching his hips rotate in time with the thrusts. He could go on like this forever.

But the room spun. One minute Wade's arms wrapped around Eli and the next his body snaked down. Wade sat on the edge of the bed as he worked Eli's pants and underwear the rest of the way off. Then he leaned forward and his lips slipped over the end of Eli's cock with a hand at the base. Unable to move his legs or find his balance, Eli held on to Wade's broad shoulders and let him take the lead.

In and out, Eli watched his body disappear into Wade's mouth. Over and over again as the rhythm increased. His cheeks pumped in and out and he sucked. His mouth worked and a palm went to Eli's ass.

Shifting, he pulled Eli down to the mattress, at first over him, treating him to a hot kiss that threatened to blow the back of Eli's head off, then beside him on the mattress.

Eli looked up and saw Wade's determined expression floating in front of his face.

"I have condoms." Because, no matter what, Eli had stayed hopeful and kept supplied.

"Where?"

Eli lifted an arm over his head and pointed to the nightstand. "There."

"Lube?"

Shit, just the word had Elijah ready to go. "Yes."

The coolness of the room blew over Eli's bare body as Wade got up to search. Missing Wade's touch and wanting to hold on to the sensation, Eli slipped his hand up and down his cock as he waited for the man he thought of as his lover to return.

"Hey." Wade stood at the side of the bed, looking down, watching Eli's hand travel. "That's my job."

That's all Eli wanted. Strong hands and that incredible mouth. With some effort, he forced his fingers to let go and dropped his arm across the bed. "Come do it."

"After."

Eli knew what that meant. Knew how Wade liked it. Knew what turned them both on.

Sitting up, Eli moved over to make room for Wade. "Get on your back."

The big man loved being told what to do in bed. They'd spent countless hours, sometimes whole days, with Eli picking positions and seeing how much Wade could take before he begged for mercy.

He was doing a different kind of begging now. Need flared in his eyes as Wade climbed on the bed. He slumped down and the back of his hands rested against the bed. The lube and condom sat in his open palms.

"You do need this," Eli said as he crawled over Wade. Eli lay on top and let the friction of their bodies excite them as he rocked back and forth. "Fuck, who am I kidding? I need this."

Holding both of their cocks in one hand, Eli moved, bringing them together. Rubbing them against one another.

The byplay had Wade's back lifting off the bed. "Jesus, Eli. Fuck me."

"Definitely." Eli lowered his head. "But I'm going to suck you first."

"Damn." Wade threw an arm over his eyes.

It didn't take much to bring him to the edge. A sweep of the tongue over his tip. A long plunge, deep-throating him. Using the lube, Eli worked his finger into Wade's ass, stretching and readying him.

Eli wanted to take longer, to draw it out and savor, but his body rebelled. Going from constant sex with this man to nothing had Eli primed. Fitting his hips between Wade's raised legs, Eli slipped the head inside Wade. The tight push forced a groan out of both of them. The long plunge had Wade grabbing Eli's biceps.

The bed shook and the springs creaked. The thrusts shifted their bodies on the mattress. Every muscle strained and Eli fought not to come too soon. As he pumped his body, his hand went to Wade's cock. The joint pressure had him squirming on the bed.

Between the fire raging inside him and the grabbing tension in his gut, Eli felt his body reach the snapping point. He tightened his hand on Wade's cock and moved faster. His hips began to buck and Eli bit down on his bottom lip to hold off for a few more seconds.

Then the orgasm stormed through him. His body moved without a signal from his brain. He felt wetness on his hand and knew Wade got there at about the same time. Their harsh breathing matched and their body slapped together.

It was quick and hot and Eli closed his eyes and let it happen.

The daze went in and out. He drifted off. When the bed shifted again, dipped as the mattress moved, Eli opened his eyes and glanced at the alarm clock next to the bed. Two hours had passed and he'd been inside Wade a second time. They used their mouths and hands on each other. Now the small light on the desk across the room highlighted Wade's impressive ass as he tiptoed around and picked something off the floor.

Nothing like running off in the middle of the night to send the message the sex didn't matter.

The fucking coward.

Eli folded his arms behind his head and balanced his head up higher on the pillows. "I'm not asleep."

Wade spun around and a hint of guilt showed in his eyes. "I need to go."

"Okay," Eli said, because he had no idea what else to say.

"I didn't mean for this to be an all-night thing."

It meant every fucking thing in the world to Eli regardless of how long it lasted. "Right."

"I think my shirt is in the family room." Wade delivered the insight, then headed for the doorway.

Eli didn't get up. No way would he run after this man and beg. He'd already done that and lost.

Speaking of losing . . . "Will you tell Shawn about this?"

Wade froze in the middle of his mad dash.

Just like Eli hoped he would. He asked half to inflict guilt and half to put the horrible thoughts in his brain. Later, when he remembered these hours and he ached for more, the torture of knowing Wade ran from his bed to Shawn's should kill any lasting hope.

The thought that Wade could cheat without blinking hit Eli like a body blow. Nothing about that matched with the man he thought he knew.

"Maybe you guys are open about that shit. I don't know." Eli really didn't want to know but he couldn't stop talking.

"No."

"Lucky Shawn. He gets to be in the dark." Eli knew he should feel like shit for playing a role in Wade's infidelity, but Eli couldn't work up a distaste for what happened in his bed.

If Shawn and Wade had an understanding, then fine. Not that Eli understood it but he didn't know how to judge it when he benefitted from Wade's ability to stray. Eli just knew if Wade belonged to him again there was no way he'd tolerate other men in their bed.

Wade turned around then. "I mean, I didn't sleep with Shawn. We're not together."

"But I thought . . ." Eli fought off the visions of all the things he'd thought.

"I haven't been with Shawn since we broke up more than a year ago." Wade just stood there with his shirt hanging off his fingers. "I haven't been with anyone since you."

The news shot through Eli. "You let me think you went with him that night."

"Yes."

"To punish me?" Eli hadn't slept since seeing Wade with Shawn. Walked the floors and berated his actions but very little sleep. "If so, congratulations. It worked."

"I guess you're not the only one who can act like an ass."

But exhaustion was only the tip. Eli had seethed and been physically ill at the thought of Wade rolling around in his big bed—the same one Eli shared—with another man. And now this.

"Why did you bother trying to hurt me if I don't mean anything to you?" A whoosh of blood rushed through Eli. Sounds muffled and his breaths stuttered in his chest.

"Do you really think you're the only one who misses us?"

"Yes." And it slowly killed him.

Wade shook his head. "Then you're not as smart as I thought you were."

With that, Wade walked out leaving Elijah too stunned to follow.

TWENTY-THREE

Kyra had just decided not to waste the evening or, more appropriately, morning by spending it stewing over Bast's continued belief she'd be at his beck and call, since she kind of acted like she would, when Bast hit the brakes and pulled the sedan over. The streetlights highlighted the fancy street lined with expensive cars and three-story brick houses. Flowering trees gave the city neighborhood a suburban feel.

They'd parked four houses down on the other side of the street. He balanced his chest on the steering wheel and peeked out the front window in the direction of his house.

"What are we doing?" The longer she sat there, the grungier she felt. The shower moved up on her priority list. Add that to the flashbacks this scene gave her to riding with her father while he staked out houses to hit, and the old man's insistent calling over the last two days asking for a "status" on her con, and she was at the end of her patience.

Bast pointed at the house next to his. "Out front there. Isn't that Wade's car."

She read the license plate. Wade here, at this time of night.

After their conversation. That could only mean one thing. "Yeah, it is. Good for Eli . . . and Wade. And romance."

Bast groaned and not in a good way. "I hope it's sex and not a fistfight. I'm not in the mood for a visit from the police."

"If it's a battle, that means Wade came looking for it. I don't see that happening." She thought about the way Wade's gaze followed Eli around the club tonight. "No, after the looks Wade was throwing Eli tonight, I'd say this is a booty call. Which, for the record, is more than one wants to know about her big brother's evening plans."

"It's a good thing." Bast nodded. "It was never over between them. It's about time it restarted in some form."

Bast put the car in gear and coasted. The lights stayed off and the only sound came from the crunch of loose gravel against the tires.

The somewhat solemn feel had her whispering. "What are you doing?"

"Trying not to draw attention."

"I'm not an expert or anything, but this probably isn't the best way to do that." She watched the world roll by at two miles per hour. "Maybe drive like a normal person instead."

They rode until they got to the driveway. Turning, he brought them to the garage and hit the button. The whir of the door's motor had him wincing. "That's louder than I thought it would be."

"So?"

"It could draw attention, which is a problem since we need to make sure Wade doesn't see you." They pulled in and darkness fell around them as the door closed. "Just stay quiet until we get inside and we should be fine."

The one thing this was not was *fine*. "Is that a joke?"

"Wade could hear your voice on the stairs. I'm not sure how soundproof that part of the house is, so don't talk." Bast put a hand on the door handle. Looked like he was conducting some sort of mental countdown. "Ready?"

"No."

"Once we're upstairs we should be fine to talk again."

She noticed he kept up the spy talk as if she didn't speak. Even in the darkened car, she had no idea how he missed her scowl. Or the fury radiating off her.

"Let's get moving," he said. "Remember to walk quietly."

Every word he uttered made her anger rise and her cheeks flush hotter. "It will be really loud when I throw you down the stairs."

"What?"

"You're really still worried about us being detected? With everything that's going on in your life, and at work, that's the big issue?" He didn't talk about cases, but she knew he was handling something that kept him on the phone at all hours and in the office for a ridiculous amount of time each day. His schedule consisted of eating at the club, going back to work until she got off well after midnight and hunting her down.

"The quiet isn't that big of a deal. Just a suggestion."

So, she occupied a tiny part of his life? "Oh, that's okay then."

"Are you upset?"

There was no way he lagged that far behind in this conversation. "Maybe I should go."

A night at home might clear her head. Being away from his arms and his scent could provide a breath of perspective. God knew when it came to him she had almost none. She accepted too much. Feared losing him to the point she made bad decisions.

If she didn't believe the man was educable, she'd walk away. But he'd committed before. Hell, he left a bad marriage because he wanted *more* of his wife. Who did that?

"Why would you leave?" His voice hollow and halting, he sounded dumbfounded at the prospect.

"You're so worried about us being seen. I could accidentally cough and give us away."

"It would be more obvious if I pulled out of the driveway now."

Apparently he was sarcasm impaired this evening as well. "Fine."

But she had to get out of the car. Now. Sitting there raised her temperature. Much more of this and she'd bang on the walls and spill it all herself.

She opened the door and whipped it shut behind her. The bang felt way too good.

"Don't slam . . ." Bast closed his door on a soft click. His voice was a much more emphatic and harsh whisper as he came around the hood of the car to join her by the door to the house. "Could you settle down?"

She stood in front of the alarm panel with her arms crossed over her stomach. "Sure."

When he just stood there, she glared at the doorknob. He must have gotten a clue because he clicked through the code and motioned her inside. No talking, of course, because that would be a violation of his covert plan.

By the time she stepped into the kitchen and walked across to the hall, she'd whipped her temper into a frenzy. She wanted to scream and tear the walls down. Call Wade up here and let him know what had been happening. Not in detail, of course, but make him understand she was with Bast and that's where she wanted to be.

Now if only Bast would stop talking. Each word brought him closer to being tossed out a window.

She got as far as the bottom step before he called out. "Where are you going?"

"I take it the coast is clear." She had a death grip on the banister. "You know, since you're talking in a normal voice."

"Okay, wow."

Sounded like he finally picked up on the anger brewing inside her. About damn time. "I want to take a shower, or will that make too much noise?"

"I think we should talk." He said it with all the enthusiasm of *I think we should stick needles in our eyes.*

But it was interesting that now he was chatty. Figured.

She wiggled her fingers at him. "Fine. Let's go."

"Or maybe you need to cool off first." He used his best legal voice, all reasonable and calm.

She wanted to smack him. "That could take a while."

"I don't understand what's happening here."

Clearly. "And that, Bast, is the problem."

He put his hands just inches from hers on the banister and leaned. "I don't like riddles."

"No riddles. No games. No talking to other people about us. Got it. Any other rules?" Her head started to pound. Like, big-band-level pound. Too little sleep and too much grating frustration had her brain cells grinding against each other.

"Is that what this is about? The privacy part?"

It sounded prettier when he talked about privacy, but she knew the ugly truth. "I get tired of being your dirty little secret."

All the blood drained out of his face. "I've told you. You are not that."

His stunned expression had her doubting. Maybe he *really* didn't get it. "How do you figure?"

"Elijah knows. Becca. Elijah thinks Jarrett figured it out."

He proved their friends liked to gossip but that was about it.

"You think a few random people knowing pieces of what you wanted to keep hidden is the same thing as not being a secret?" she asked, phrasing it in a way he couldn't deny.

The idea Bast hadn't even told his best friend, the person he shared everything with, ate at her soul. It felt like a dismissal. A simple statement that she didn't even rate a discussion.

"By definition, yes. People knowing means it's not a secret."

She was having a discussion and he was engaging in legal

maneuvers and double talk. All the wind blew right out of her. "I guess I can't argue with that."

"I think you want to."

Her clothes stuck to her and her feet burned. "I want to go to bed. I'm tired and I need a shower."

He pushed off from the railing. "Well, I'll lock up and join you in there. After we can figure this out."

Since they'd had communication issues in the past, she made this as clear as possible. "I really just want to go to sleep."

"Sleep?" He made a face as if he'd tasted something awful.

"As in, no scx." Not tonight. She didn't view being with him as an obligation and tonight it might be. Her frustration bubbled too close to the surface for her to be able to stuff it back and enjoy him being inside her.

"Oh."

She'd expected a bigger argument than that. "Problem?"

He shook his head and held up a hand as if in surrender. "Of course not. You get to say no if you're not in the mood."

"Since I can't go home and we can't make noise, sleep seems like the best choice." Though yelling would feel pretty spectacular.

"I actually didn't say we couldn't have sex." He sounded so sincere. So giving.

He wasn't getting this at all.

"No, Bast. I did."

He'd blown it. Like, pour-gasoline-on-it-and-burn-it-all-down kind of blown it. He wasn't a complete dumbass. All the signs pointed toward her dissatisfaction. Her anger had been festering, growing over the last two days.

For some reason instead of stepping back and setting new ground rules, he fumbled his way through and messed things up even more. Which likely explained why she was on her side, turned away from him in bed.

She didn't want sex tonight and he could respect that. Kissing had been different, too. She hovered on the verge of blowing her temper but held back. His decision not to push her, not to poke around in her comments, and fix what was wrong . . . that move put them here. He gave her an out and she took it. Stupid bastard that he was.

In their short time together he'd become the king of mixed messages. He insisted on distance yet ran to her every night, wanting her by his side. She traveled back to her place and frustration ate at him until be brought her back home.

The back and forth had her on edge. Had her doubting.

I get tired of being your dirty little secret.

Her voice rang in his head. The pain in her eyes and in her tone. He'd backed her into this corner. The secrecy and the limits sucked some of the life out of her and he fucking hated himself for that.

The last time he'd felt like this about a woman, had been so sure, he walked into a marriage that turned him inside out. The list of cons for letting Kyra in stretched out long— she was too young, not ready, his background was too much for her to deal with. He sucked at commitment.

He hadn't been enough for Lena. How the hell would he be enough for a vibrant young woman who surely could find a younger, better version of him in business school?

And endings sucked. Ripped you apart, shredded the pieces that were left.

He trailed his fingers over Kyra's hair where it lay on her shoulder. Then brushed over her bare shoulder. No sex but she'd climbed into bed naked and snuggled in the covers. He wanted her to turn to him.

"It's something ridiculous like three in the morning. Why aren't you sleeping?" She flipped over on her back and stared up at the ceiling. Not at him.

"Sneaking you into the house was an asshole move." Not the admission he planned to make, but it sat on his tongue and slipped out.

She sighed. "No argument there."

"I thought I was doing it for you." He rubbed a thumb over her collarbone, loving that part of her impressive body.

"Do you still?"

"No, it was panic, pure and simple." Not the easiest admission but he made it anyway.

"And?"

That's actually all he had. For him, it was a pretty big step. "Uh."

She frowned at him. "Say you're sorry."

"I am."

This time she dropped her head back, opened her mouth and let out a huff. She may even have said "duh" but it was hard to tell through the snorting.

"Um, Kyra?"

"Do it better." She eyed him up. "The apology, I mean."

Okay, that he could handle. "Yes, ma'am."

She jabbed a finger into his chest. "And do not be sexy. You're still not getting any tonight."

He had to smile. This was the Kyra who lit his insides on fire. Smart, sexy, strong and demanding. On this level, he had a fighting chance. It was when he hurt her that his world went careening into a wall.

"I'm sorry for taking you for granted and for rushing you around tonight." He slid an arm over her stomach and pulled her tighter to his side. "I'm not sorry you're here."

"Not great but better." She linked her fingers through his. With a tug, she turned on her side away from him and brought him along with her.

"What else should I have said?"

"We're done talking. You can spoon me."

Her ass fit tight against him and he bent his legs to fit along her body from back to feet. "You know what could happen in this position."

"I'm still frustrated with you, so no."

But the anger had left her voice and he was damn grateful for that bit of news. "I deserve it."

She gathered him closer, wrapping his arm over her hip and against her waist. "I trust you to keep your word."

No way would he touch her more than he was now. He'd wait forever for her to give him the green light to move in, if that's what it took. The choice went with her.

"You can always trust me." He'd never been more serious in his life.

"I know."

That had to mean something.

The next morning, still worn out and confused, Kyra headed back to her apartment for a few more personal items. They hadn't worked out anything last night except she agreed to stay over again tonight. He insisted and even promised he wouldn't pressure her for sex. Not knowing what she needed to hear but not wanting to be away from him, she relented. Though she'd bet sex would move back onto the menu if she gave him even the slightest sign she welcomed it, which she did.

Just as she opened the front door to let herself into her place, the same one that struck her as small and a bit crappy now, Gena popped up in her doorway across the hall.

She slipped out of her place with her keys jangling on a ring around her finger. "Where have you been?"

"At Bast's house."

Gena followed Kyra inside and closed the door behind her. "That sounds serious. Like, maybe you've moved past sex and onto something bigger."

"I don't know what it is."

And that was the truth. They had something. A man didn't hold on tight enough all night to suffocate you as he whispered sweet words into your hair and not feel something. At least in sleep he wanted to keep her close.

"I need to talk with you."

"Not now." Kyra had so much on her mind. Some of it mostly good, like Bast, and some a tickling reminder of her rough past. Her father kept calling and she kept ignoring, and it was all getting to be too much.

"There's something you need to know." Usually chatty and open, Gena's body language was all closed down today. She wore a bulky sweater in summer and wrapped her arms around her as if she straddled the line between warm and freezing. Even her voice bobbled as she spoke, as if she were under the most intense pressure.

"After I've slept. Really." Kyra looked at her friend. Really looked. She had dark circles under her eyes and her skin was drawn. Gone was the laughing and trading gossip about people in the building.

Something bad had happened and she missed it. A kick of guilt settled in Kyra's belly. "Are you okay?"

"Fine."

"No offense, but you don't look it."

Gena closed her eyes for a second. "I'm serious, Kyra. Maybe you should slow down with Bast." Gena leaned against the dresser. "I mean, you guys are living together already and it's been, what, about two weeks."

As with a knee-jerk reaction, Kyra felt the need to defend and explain. "We've known each other for a very long time."

"Is that the test?"

"We're not living together." But that's what Kyra wanted. In a short time, she discovered her crush had blown into something more. Her need for him appeared never ending . . . and wasn't that a giant pain in the ass.

Gena rubbed her hands together, then through her hair. She was a ball of nerves and Kyra had no idea why.

"What do you call what you guys have?" Gena asked. "Is it dating or a boyfriend-girlfriend thing?"

"It's informal." Secretive, confusing, exhausting and exhilarating.

"So, it's sex only."

The conclusion scraped across Kyra's nerve endings. "I don't know what it is."

"Well, then it can't be that important."

"Problem is, I think it's grown to mean everything." Not think, know. And that one word change guaranteed heartache.

A deeper sadness moved into Gena's eyes. "Kyra—"

Kyra held up her hand to stop her friend's warning. "Yeah, I know. I'm screwed."

"I'm worried about you."

Kyra had to be honest. "So am I."

TWENTY-FOUR

Bast sat on a barstool at the club and experienced what could only be described as women trouble. He didn't have the patience for this today. Not any day, but *really* not today. The rocky patch with Kyra threw him. Now he had to deal with Natalie.

Good thing Becca and Jarrett hovered on the other side of the bar as reinforcements. Except for them, and Elijah and Gabe waiting on the opposite side of the room by the exit, the club was empty at this time of the day.

The people there represented a serious amount of collective firepower. Bast guessed it would take all those weapons experts plus his lawyering skills to talk some sense into Natalie. But right now she looked very unimpressed with his argument.

He tried again. "Someone broke into your house."

Sneaked in, searched everything but barely moved things around, planted a listening device and hid in the alley, planning to do God knew what. She may have found out the hard way if Gabe hadn't booby-trapped the place to tell if anyone broke in. Once he realized what happened, he stayed inside with Natalie while his brother, who was also Gabe's partner, spotted the guy in the alley and grabbed him.

Not that any of it impressed Natalie. Even now she sat next to Bast on a barstool and flipped a round silver coaster around between her fingers. "Your guard dog has a big mouth."

Bast bit back a string of profanity. "His name is Gabe and it's good he was there."

"Do you forget I am a trained field agent?" she asked with a frown that suggested everyone would be wise to remember.

"Honestly?" With a snap, Jarrett twisted off the cap to his water bottle. "It's hard to when you mention it every two seconds."

"You're not funny."

Bast had reached his limit. "And for a brilliant woman you are being pretty damn dumb."

"Oh, that's smooth." Becca sighed and shook her head and ran through a whole list of "men are idiots" gestures as she walked around the bar to Bast's side and tapped him on the shoulder. "Why don't you and your big brain switch places with me? Let me take a shot at this."

Natalie shifted on her seat, uncrossing her legs and making room for Becca to sit down. "Thank you for calling him off. All that arguing he does gives me a headache. He just keeps at it until you'll do anything to shut him up."

Becca snorted. "As if you're the only one who's ever wanted to put a bullet in those two."

"What did I do?" Jarrett held out his arms with the water bottle still in one hand.

"Quiet." Becca said without looking at the man she called the love of her life. "Look, Natalie. We're not best friends. There are times I wanted to throw you off a building—"

"Wait a second." Bast jumped in before the conversation turned into a fistfight. Maybe he talked a lot but he didn't attack. Not usually. "How is this helping?"

"I assume you know what quiet means." Becca didn't break eye contact with Natalie but aimed her comment directly at Bast. "If the two of us women got together, you guys wouldn't stand a chance."

No doubt that was true. And Bast got the strategy. Becca searched for common ground with the woman who was once her CIA contact. They'd both been in the field and wrestled with the old-boy network at the agency. If anyone could get through to Natalie, it would probably be Becca.

But Bast needed her to pick up the speed. Gabe wanted to get Natalie out and that meant fast-forwarding this process.

"You know this game. Hell, you helped create this game. No easy way out—remember telling me that when I started with Spectrum?" Becca asked, referring to the name of her last cover assignment with Elijah before they both got out. "But the reality is it can be done. You showed Bast how to beat the system for my sake, now let him work it for you."

"He thinks he gets to give the orders." Natalie glared at Bast as she talked.

Becca nodded. "Totally annoying, I get that. This one time, let him take the lead. Go spend some alone time with that bit of hotness standing with Elijah."

"I'm right here and can hear you," Jarrett said in a dry tone.

"We see you, babe." Becca winked at him then returned her gaze to Natalie. "You probably haven't taken a day off since you started working. You're overdue."

"Gabe is talking about going to a cabin." Natalie shared that bit of information with the same enthusiasm people used to describe dental surgery.

But the sharing was a problem. Even that small scrap was too much. Bast had no choice but to issue a warning before she spilled more details. "Don't say anything else."

"I know what a cover is, Bast. I'm not going to tell you where it is. Hell, I don't even know. Your boy expects me to climb in his truck and be quiet. Probably wants to blindfold me."

Becca shrugged. "Look at the guy. That could be fun."

"Nothing about this is fun."

Bast didn't want to know anything about Gabe's personal life or Natalie's sex life or if there was anything between them. He did want to make a point. Stepping out from behind the bar, he came to a stop next to Becca and focused all of his energy on Natalie. "I get that you hate this. For the record, I'm determined to finish off this negotiation and keep everyone safe, and do it as quickly as possible. You know the people I'm dealing with at the agency. They don't move fast on these things."

"You ever get tired of riding in with the white hat and saving the day?" Natalie asked.

Bast didn't think it was a real question, so he didn't treat it as one. "Who would get tired of that?"

"Fine, but get it done. Stop with your extracurricular activities—"

Bast felt his breath punch out of him. "Excuse me?"

Natalie lowered her head and stared unblinking at him. "You heard me."

Kyra. Natalie somehow knew about his relationship with Kyra. Bast didn't even know how that was possible. Unless . . . he glanced over at Becca. "What did you tell her?"

She held her hands up in mock surrender. "Hey, Natalie knows everything. Always has, but this wasn't from me. She's spooky like that."

More like nosy. Natalie gathered every bit of information and stored it away for later use. Bast knew that from experience. He didn't like his sex life being a topic she collected intel on.

He wanted to poke around but decided to breeze over the topic because now was not the time. "Your case has my full attention. Trust me."

"Make it happen." Natalie slid off the barstool. "And soon."

He was sure as hell trying. "You know the drill. No contact, no movement, no researching, no footprints."

She shot him a you've-got-to-be-kidding look. "I know what it means to go dark."

"And listen to Gabe." Bast guessed that would be a tougher sell.

Becca snorted. "I'd do more than listen to him."

Jarrett held up a hand. "Still standing right here."

Bast ignored the byplay between Becca and Jarrett and focused on getting his message through to Natalie. "You'll be back and going to Georgetown for coffee in no time."

For a second Natalie didn't say anything, then she nodded. "Right."

Before Bast could offer any other advice she'd probably ignore, she walked away. With sure steps she walked up to Gabe and Elijah, hesitating only long enough to nod and keep going. Gabe caught her in mid-exit and walked out with his body angled in front of hers.

Bast watched it all, knowing he'd picked the right man to guard Natalie. She was tough and determined but no one gave Gabe shit.

"Think it will be that easy to get this done for her?" Becca asked.

It hadn't been so far. "When did I use the word 'easy'?"

"I'll escort them out." Becca squeezed Bast's elbow. "I'm sure you and Jarrett can find something to talk about."

Jarrett balanced his hands on the edge of the bar. "Are you really going out there to get a better look at Gabe's ass?"

Becca wagged her finger at Jarrett to come closer, then she grabbed onto his tie. "I'm very happy just looking at your ass."

When they started to kiss, Bast was ready to head back to the office. "Maybe I should leave."

"Stay," Jarrett ordered before treating Becca to one last kiss and watching her walk away. He turned to Bast. "Drink?"

"Club soda." Bast didn't drink much and never during the middle of the day. Knowing Jarrett had struggled with alcohol in the past caused Bast to lose some interest in it.

"I'll make it two." Jarrett poured the drinks and slid one in front of Bast. "So, how are things really going with Natalie's negotiation?"

"I used the leverage." Bast swirled the glass, letting the ice cubes clink together. "I know it wasn't easy to agree to let an operative be a member here, and I appreciate you kicking that piece in."

That's what the CIA wanted, eyes and ears in Jarrett's club. Undercover and quiet. No raids, just for intel-collecting purposes on foreign threats and international members. The folks in charge were smart enough to know that without someone on the inside, Jarrett would turn some information over but hold a bunch back. This way, the CIA had access. But it only happened because Jarrett agreed and there was no question he would find a way to limit exposure.

"To be honest, I've always assumed the CIA had someone planted here, despite the questionable legality. If so, why not have a guy hanging out here I know about and have some control over?"

Leave it to Jarrett to spin this to his own advantage. Bast loved that about the guy. "The computer billionaire, the one who always sits by himself and is playing on that tablet, is suspect to me."

"It's more likely to be someone who blends in better, like the guy who owns the actuarial firm." Jarrett took a long sip. "He's friendly, but not too friendly. Talks with people but never offers information. Has a career not many would ask that many questions about anyway."

"Either way, thanks."

Jarrett drained the glass and set it on the bar. "I owe Natalie. She cleared the way for me to be with Becca."

"And then there's the part where you hate the people in charge at the CIA and are always happy to do something that fucks them over."

Jarrett smiled at that. "It doesn't make me sad to trap the higher-ups into letting Natalie walk away. I'm sure that pisses off more than one useless suit over there."

"From my meetings, I can assure you no one is happy." The men in charge had gone from denial, to assurances about how much they admired Natalie and her work, to claims she was a security risk.

"They threatening you?" Jarrett asked.

"The usual 'we'll lock you away and no one will know where' stuff." Bast had heard it all before. Talk of having him disbarred and how bad it would be if he ran afoul of the law and ended up in prison. If he were younger and greener, the threats might have stuck. But now he had contingencies and leverage and far more power than he had when he started this career.

"Jesus." Jarrett shook his head. "Our Constitution at work."

"Yeah, but it's garbage like this that pays my mortgage."

"Speaking of which, you doing okay?"

The question, delivered in a calm voice, put Bast on high alert. "Sure."

"Lena still hanging around?"

Bast knew his ex-wife was one of Jarrett's least favorite subjects. Him bringing it up meant he was fishing for something. Bast treaded carefully. "I know it pisses you off but she does live in the same town and we know the same people."

"I wish she'd move on and leave you alone."

Bast knew that was code for: *do not get back together with her.* "We're over."

They were long over, never to return. Lena came around, they talked and, yeah, he gave her money from time to time. None of it bothered Bast. He viewed it as the price he paid for getting out of the marriage. For not loving her the way she needed to be loved.

Since Kyra didn't seem to mind, Bast didn't have any plans to change his ways of operating. Though he wasn't about to analyze why having it be okay with Kyra made it okay in general.

"You moving on?" Jarrett refilled his glass and topped off Bast's.

"Jarrett, I swear. I'm not still in love with her."

He slammed the bottle down on the bar. "Jesus, you are going to make me ask you straight up."

"What?"

Jarrett wrapped his fingers around the edge of the bar and leaned in. "When did you start sleeping with Kyra?"

Fuck. Even though he knew this was coming, Bast didn't duck in time. He thought they'd pivoted onto Lena. Little did he know that was subterfuge for circling around to a topic on Kyra.

"How did you . . . Becca." He knew Jarrett should have heard it from him. He should have fessed up before Becca filled Jarrett in. "I knew she'd tell you."

"First, *you* should have told me." Jarrett leveled a man-to-man look at Bast. "Second, she knew for a few days before I confronted her with my suspicions about you and Kyra."

Looked like Elijah was right. Jarrett knew all along, which made not telling him even more of a shit move. Still, Bast wanted to know how. "Why were you suspicious?"

"The look." Serious, tough Jarrett made a goofy face complete with big eyes and sticking his tongue out. "The one you get."

Bast refused to believe he ever looked like that. He also vowed never to smile again. "You, too?"

"Man, it is obvious."

"Now you sound like Elijah."

Jarrett leaned in farther. "Fucking Eli knew and you didn't tell me? Explain that."

"I'm sorry. I should have told you but I didn't really know how to say it. You've known Kyra forever and think of her as a sister." Bast swallowed because the next part pricked at him. Even after the sex and being with her and wanting more time with her, this part made him wince. "That made me the sick creep who moved in on her."

"We've talked about this, the whole not wanting to be the stereotypical guys going after hot young women then casting them aside. So, what's going on? Is this just sex?"

Bast remembered the conversation and how it arose, right after his father's third divorce. His father chased younger women. If the age dropped much more, the women would be high school girls. He wasn't alone. Powerful men all over town did it.

Now Bast fell into the category and it made him sick. But what he felt for Kyra was not just lust or a drive for more sex. It started there and he'd wanted it to stay there, but the whole relationship spun out of his control and now he didn't know how to grab it back.

He exhaled, hating every minute of this topic. "No."

Jarrett's eyebrow lifted. "So, it's more than sex?"

"No . . . I don't . . ." Bast refused to minimize it. To minimize her. But it *should* only be sex. "Damn it, Jarrett. I don't know what it is."

Jarrett pushed back and stood up straight. Didn't say a word.

"What?" Bast felt a weird ache in his chest. "You think I'm a shit. You can say it."

"We've known each other a long time. I watched your marriage blow up, watched you fall apart—"

"I didn't."

"You slept on my couch for three fucking weeks." Jarrett's voice grew louder with each word. "You want me to remind you about those days. About how leaving your marriage nearly destroyed you, even though you were right to go. Hell, you waited too long to go."

"I remember those days." They dragged by and even getting off the couch had hurt.

"Then you buried it all under a bunch of nameless female bodies. Had sex, played around, lived up to the rumors about you needing to be with multiple women at one time." Jarrett stopped. It was as if all the anger blew right out of him. "And now you're with one woman . . . right?"

Bast wasn't sure what just happened or what Jarrett was trying to prove, but no way was Bast going to lie about this part. "Just Kyra. I don't want anyone else."

"Well, seems to me that says something." The seriousness cleared from Jarrett's face and the expression left behind was more than a little amused. "Maybe she really means something to you."

The dam broke. The words and thoughts poured out of Bast before he could sanitize them or word them in the "right" way. "I thought it would be quick and fun. We'd have sex a few times, her crush would disappear and we'd end it and move on."

"But?"

"One night she didn't stay at my place and I went over to fetch her. To her apartment at something insane like three in the morning. I mean, what the fuck is that? Since when do I do that shit." Bast knew he could tell Jarrett anything, but the guy didn't have to look so damn smug when hearing it. "Stop smiling."

"Sounds to me like you have it bad for her, which is weird and great at the same time."

Bast fell back on the easy argument. "She's twenty-three."

"You knew that when you slept with her the first time, so don't use it as an excuse now." Jarrett took another drink. "Besides, she'll only get older. Unfortunately, so will you."

"Shut up." Really, the guy needed to shut up.

"Piss and moan all you want but I happen to know a little about relationships."

"Because you're stupid in love with Becca?" Bast stood up because the weird spinning inside his gut had him needing to move. He didn't get far in his pacing.

"Is 'love' relevant to your situation with Kyra?"

He should say no. A flat-out denial. But the word wouldn't come. "I have no idea."

"Of course you do. You're a smart guy."

Bast rested his hands on the bar and dropped his head between his shoulders. "Don't feel like it right now."

"Wait until Wade gets done with you."

"He doesn't know." No way. He would have swooped in and demanded answers if he'd known.

"I saw him watching you and Kyra the other night. Trust me, he knows."

The words just added to the stress building inside Bast. "Shit."

"If you're so worried about people finding out, maybe you should walk away from her. Let her go find a nice grad school boy when school starts in a few weeks."

"Fuck you." Bast lifted his head and took in Jarrett's expression. "Really, man, stop smiling."

"I can't."

"Try."

"The idea of you in love again is as shocking as me being in love. But, hell, you deserve it." Jarrett's smile faded. "Seriously though, your timing stinks. This Natalie situation is dangerous, which means anyone near you is at risk."

Bast stood up again. A new wave of anxiety hit him and he reached for the stool to sit down again. "So Kyra being with me means she could be, too."

"Potentially."

"So, I should let her go." The thought made him want to heave up his breakfast. He actually had to choke back the bile rushing up his throat.

Jarrett's mouth dropped open and he shook his head. "God, you're a dumbass right now."

"Meaning?" He could move her in with Wade or . . . hell, something. Bast had no idea how to explain it all to her. She knew pieces about Becca's former life but had no idea about the danger or the CIA angle, and Natalie's case was not up for discussion.

"Figure out the best way to keep Kyra safe and do it fast." Jarrett downed the last of his glass. "And I'd be careful not to piss her off while you do it or then you'll have a huge mess on your hands. Been there."

Bast remembered Jarrett's messed-up road of getting back together with Becca and how it tore his friend up. No. Thank. You.

Reaching for his glass, Bast wished it held something more than club soda. "I'm open to any suggestion."

"Not giving you one, but watching you stumble through this will be interesting."

Bast feared "stumbling" was the exactly right word.

TWENTY-FIVE

Kyra turned the corner and stopped at Bast's office door. His space sat at the end of a private hallway with an open area for his assistant outside and a conference room on the opposite end of the floor. With the assistant at lunch, the receptionist showed Kyra back. That's when she caught a glimpse through the glass double doors down the hall of a familiar brunette standing and talking on the phone.

Bast got up when Kyra stepped inside. Stood and buttoned his coat, because that's what he did. Normally she found the automatic gesture sexy and sweet. Not today.

"Was that Lena?"

He frowned. "What are you doing here?"

The thing where he answered her questions with an unrelated one of his own made Kyra's back teeth snap together. "So we're skipping the part where I asked what *she* was doing here?"

He motioned for Kyra to sit down and slipped into his chair. "Business stuff."

Noncommittal, nonresponsive. This was starting to get old. "I'll stand."

"Is something wrong?"

Her, them, everything. She knew he viewed her role as one where she sat and waited for him to call, was ready for sex and some conversation. Nothing too taxing and all on his terms. Maybe she agreed to that at the beginning—though she refused to admit that was the case—but she wanted more now. She deserved more.

"You canceled lunch." She'd been surprised when he lay in bed last night and offered the outing today. It meant taking her in public. Making a stand.

Dumping her via telephone made her think the suggestion was a spur-of-the-moment guilt thing that he regretted first thing this morning, leading to this standoff. And that's exactly what this was.

She felt twitchy and uncomfortable. When she looked at him, she saw this stiff guy who gave her limited eye contact and mentally pushed her aside. She hated the change. Hated how easy it was for him to compartmentalize and lock her out of parts of his life.

Reality was she craved more time with him, to be a bigger part of his life. She now realized that what she wrote off as an attraction and maybe a crush had been something much deeper. She'd loved him from afar forever and now that she was with him, she needed more. But it seemed like the more she gave, the more he panicked, and she had no idea how to resolve that.

So, standoff it would be.

"I'm plowed under with work." He shifted piles of paperwork around on his desk.

The man was a machine when it came to logging long hours. That excuse would always sit between them. Despite that, she didn't resent his job or his work ethic. They were part of who he was. The emotional shutdown aspect was the one she hated.

"What's going on with you?" she asked, almost afraid to hear his answer.

He focused on her then. Stopped shuffling and moving in his chair and really looked at her. "Excuse me?"

"I hate when you use that tone."

"It's my work tone," he fired back with an even more intense version of the stern, disapproving voice.

"Are we back to that . . . or am I being punished for not ignoring your behavior last night?" That's the only thing she could think of because the man who apologized and held her all night was not this distant guy.

"I apologized for the car thing."

Thing? "Yet you're acting weird today. Is this the part where you start to push me away?"

The words stuck in her throat, but she got them out. When the time came to end it, she figured he'd give her some sort of "that was fun but it's done" speech and escort her out in a charming way that left her with good memories and an overflowing of sadness. Not that chivalrous behavior would make losing him any better.

If that was happening, she'd have to walk out to keep from breaking down. No way would she let him see her crumble.

She folded her arms over her stomach and tried to assess his mood. As she shifted her weight back and forth, a presence loomed over her shoulder. Bast glanced there and shook his head. Someone walked in. Kyra vowed if she turned around and saw Lena, there would be a diva explosion the firm's staff would be talking about a year from now.

"Sorry to interrupt." Elijah winced when Kyra glanced at him. "I'll come back."

"No, stay." This was the wrong time and wrong place for this conversation. If she was going to hash it out with Bast, let him know what he was missing by letting her go, there would be shouting, which meant they needed privacy. "I'm leaving."

"You okay?"

She studied Elijah then. The black hair and dark eyes. Something about his cheekbones. The pieces that spoke to his Asian ancestry. She thought Bast had said Eli's mother was Japanese. He was handsome and the furrowed brow suggested he was concerned for her.

No wonder Wade loved this guy, and she was pretty sure he did. Elijah might come off as removed and tough, but there was something compelling deep down. She hoped Wade could find his way back to Eli again.

"It's funny how you notice there's a problem and he can't." She hitched her thumb in Bast's direction.

Bast came around the desk to join them in the middle of his office. "There's no need to involve Elijah in this."

"Oh, right. Secrecy is the name of the game." She winked but inside she felt empty and cold. "Got it."

"I'll be in my office."

Eli took a step back and she grabbed his arm. "Do not move."

He cleared his throat. "All right."

No need for him to go. She was leaving. Running out and not looking back. Coming here had been a mistake—again. Amazing how the man who meant so much and could make her feel so loved in bed could distance himself so easily in public.

She turned to leave but Bast's voice stopped her. "I'll call you later."

"You're not coming over?" She asked even though she knew the answer—no.

He hesitated then shook his head. "I'm not sure."

"And, let me guess, you don't want me at your house tonight." That was a first. They hadn't been apart in the evenings since the beginning. The one time she tried to get some distance and find some perspective, he came hunting for her. Now he wanted space.

"Kyra." That's all. Just her name said like a warning.

Yeah, this had to be the end. "It's fine. Message received."

. . .

Bast watched her go and had to fight to stand still. The talk with Jarrett had him thinking and worrying. There wasn't an easy answer to making sure she stayed safe. Maybe increasing the distance and letting her spend more time in her normal life made sense until he finished Natalie's negotiation. It would give him a hell of an incentive to get it all resolved fast. But he hated the idea of giving her space.

When the silence wound around him, he stopped staring at the empty doorway and glanced at Elijah. "What?"

"Nothing." But his expression said something. Gone was his usual icy detachment. Eli seemed to be brimming with energy and ready to pounce.

"Say it." Not that Bast was all that sure he wanted to hear whatever thoughts ran through Eli's head at the moment.

He made a clicking sound with his tongue. And kept doing it until Bast thought his head would explode.

Eli spoke up just in time. "Pushing her away isn't the right answer."

"You're an expert on love now?" Bast couldn't believe he used the word and hoped Elijah would run right over it.

"I know when a guy is doing something dumb in order to protect someone else. I'm the king of asshole moves when it comes to men. Ask Wade."

Hiding something from Eli was not easy. For a guy everyone believed was clueless in the people relations department, Bast was amazed how often Eli's insights were dead-on. And him mentioning Wade didn't happen very often. Bast knew Eli only went there because he thought he needed to, which meant one thing: Bast had fucked up and badly.

"I'm trying to put her in a safe place." Bast moved around to his chair but didn't sit down. He rested a hand on the back and stood still.

"You think not seeing her will keep those CIA-hired goons from going after her." Elijah shook his head. "But it's way too late. They've likely had someone on you since you negotiated my deal weeks and weeks ago. They know you're sleeping with her. They know where she lives and that getting to her will kill you."

Bast's insides turned icy cold. "She's not part of this."

"Any pressure they can apply they will. You need to keep her close, not shove her away."

A wave of panic washed over the chill. "You couldn't have told me this ten minutes ago?"

"How was I supposed to know you were going to make such a big misfire?"

"I can catch her." Bast bolted around the desk, narrowly missing slamming his thigh into the corner and pushed Elijah out of the way on the way to the door.

"She was moving pretty fast."

Bast turned and pointed to the phone on his desk. "Call the lobby. Have security stop her."

There was nothing blank about Eli's expression now. Amusement played on his mouth and shone in his eyes. "That will go over well."

"I'd rather her be angry than go missing." Thinking about her being out there and vulnerable got him moving. He was down the hall before he heard Elijah's voice again.

"She's definitely going to be ticked off."

"Good." Bast reached for his cell and dialed the lobby just in case. "Angry means she cares."

"Straight people are weird."

Bast stopped. "You're admitting you're not?"

Eli waved him off. "Go rescue your woman."

Kyra got off the elevator in the lobby and made a beeline for the doors to the heated summer air outside. Three strides and she slammed to a stop. It was either that or run right over Lena and, damn, that was tempting.

But Lena stood there with her perfect brunette hair and put-together outfit of white pants, white silk blouse and long string of pearls and didn't appear ready to move. Kyra always wondered what woman could wear all that white without spilling something down her front. Now she knew.

Between her frayed nerves and the pain making her stomach roll and heave, Kyra didn't have anything left. Certainly no tact and only the thin edge of civility.

"I'm leaving. Bast is all yours." She did a two-step around Lena and aimed for those glass doors on the other side of the security station.

"Wait."

Kyra waved the other woman away. "No thanks."

"Please."

That was the one thing guaranteed to stop Kyra. She heard the pleading and then saw it mirrored in Lena's eyes. Kyra wanted to kick her own butt for sneaking a peek at Bast's ex and not just rushing past her at a heated run.

Lean wanted to talk? Fine, they would.

"I'll start," Kyra said as she prepared for more verbal battle.

Lena's eyes closed a fraction, then opened again. "Go ahead."

"I have a simple question." The same one that had been kicking around Kyra's head for months, really. "Why did you let him go if you still love him so much?"

"Can we sit?"

Kyra wanted to say no. Maybe demand the quick and painful answer she sensed coming. The last thing she wanted was a sit-down with this woman. But curiosity pulled at her. There were so many things she wanted to understand, things Bast would never share. Things he might not even know.

Kyra led Lena over to the lobby couches and sat perpendicular to her. "Go ahead."

"I loved Sebastian from the time I was a teenager." When Kyra jumped up, Lena put out a hand to stop her from bolting. "Please sit back down."

Her skin felt too tight and the banging in her head made her dizzy, but Kyra gave in and dropped into her seat. "Fine." With patience gone, she bit out the word.

"Our families knew each other and neither of us had the happiest of home lives." Lena smoothed her hands up and down her thighs. "We got swept up. People assumed we'd get married and we did. It all made sense at first but then I wanted something else."

The conversation whirled around her. Talk of love and marriage had Kyra wanting to run. Just get up and get away. To drive this home and get it over, she brought the topic around to the issue she knew ripped the marriage apart. "A different type of sex."

"The specifics don't matter. The point is Bast tried to change for me. When that didn't work, I tried to change for him. Neither ploy was successful and we were both miserable for years."

Kyra knew most of this. She'd read pieces on the Internet. Heard a bit from Bast. Listened to Jarrett grumble. But hearing the stark bleakness in Lena's voice as she talked about the disinte-gration of her marriage provided a different perspective. A solemn and devastating one.

"He left you." The urge to reach out hit Kyra and she didn't fight it. She put a hand on the armrest next to Lena's. Close enough to provide some comfort but with some space if she needed that.

"Because I couldn't do it. I was so desperate to be what he wanted and convinced I could find a way." Her voice broke off and her chest moved as she drew in a deep breath. "He figured out we were only hurting each other and filed for divorce."

These were not the words of an angry vengeful wife. If anything, Kyra heard respect and devotion. "Then why did you write the books?"

"I know it seems like I was punishing him, but that's really not it." Lena pushed her hair back, tucking it behind one ear. "I'd written the threesome handbook because I wanted to, but in hindsight I should have used a pseudonym as Bast asked me to. I was really going after my proper parents and all their lessons, but Bast got slammed in the crossfire."

On one level it made sense. On another, no. Kyra couldn't imagine attacking Bast in such a personal way. Privacy and his reputation meant everything to him and she struck at the very heart of both. "And the novel?"

"Writing that was cathartic. In fiction I could make him the monster and absolve my sins." Lena talked with her hands. They fluttered until she seemed to notice the waving and linked her fingers together. "It's a long story, but it sold and the timing was wrong and I tried to fix any reference by changing the hero and making it clear the book was not based on Bast."

"But people assumed."

"Yeah, and he got slammed again, this time even by his dad. I never wanted that. Bast knows all I tried to do behind the scenes to prevent the avalanche. How many people I called. The interviews I gave. The PR information I kept putting out absolving him. The long, awful talks with his dad." Her knuckles turned white from twisting her hands together.

This time Kyra reached the whole way out. She put her hand over Lena's. Anything to get her to calm down and breathe. "You're still connected with him."

"That's inevitable when two people share a piece of their lives." Lena offered a lopsided smile. One that didn't reach her eyes. "But I see the closeness is too much now. It didn't matter before because he hadn't really been serious with anyone, but it matters now."

"Not because of me." Letting Lena think differently appealed to Kyra. But truth was Lena got it wrong and she deserved to know that. Sharing any part of her story had to be hard. Sharing it with the woman she knew now slept with her ex was unimaginable to Kyra. She could never be that sure or that strong. "You don't understand my relationship with Bast."

"Yes, Kyra. I mean you."

"He thinks I'm too young." And that was just the first of her many sins, none of which were within her control but all of which appeared to matter to him.

Lena took Kyra's hand in her cold ones. "It's not about your age. It's about his fear."

Kyra wanted to believe but Bast's actions painted a very different picture. "You've got this all wrong."

"He did everything he could to make me happy, and in his mind he still failed. Imagine what that does to a man like Bast. A guy who can make any situation work." Lena's pleading had changed to convincing and her voice remained clear and steady now. "I've seen the way he looks at you."

"Like he wants to strangle me?"

"Like he can't live without you." Lena tapped the back of Kyra's hand then let go. "He needs a woman who's strong and determined and won't let him win all the time. I think that's you."

"How do I make him see that?" It was the wrong question to ask his former wife. Unfair and almost mean in light of how fresh her pain remained, but Lena's voice had lulled Kyra. It was so sincere. The caring in her eyes so real.

"Don't leave him." Lena stood up then, sending one last sad smile in Kyra's direction before walking away. "Think about what I said before you give up."

That's exactly what Kyra was doing, sitting there and letting the thoughts spin round and round in her head, when the security guard approached two minutes later. "Ma'am?"

The sound of the voice startled her and she glanced up as she cut off a yelp. "Yes?"

"I need you to stand up and come with me." The man reached down to tug on her arm.

"Why?" The move so shocked her that she didn't react until he had her on her feet.

"Mr. Jameson has asked that you be detained for questioning."

There was no way she heard that correctly. "What?"

The guard frowned at her. "Please don't make this difficult."

Oh, she planned to do exactly that because it struck her that yelling might be the only way for Bast to learn a lesson or two.

TWENTY-SIX

Kyra stood in the lobby, right before crossing back through security and heading outside. A guard had stopped her with a hand and still hadn't dropped it. He looked ten seconds away from frisking her.

If that happened she'd start that yelling and not stop until that weasel Bast showed his face. "He said what?"

"I've got this."

Speak of the weasel.

Bast appeared out of nowhere, sounding half out of breath. He threw up a hand and the guard moved back. The people milling around the lobby didn't go away that easily. They formed an unwanted audience, which might be convenient since she was about to give a hell of a performance.

When he reached for her, she shifted to escape his grasp. "I'm going to kick you in the balls."

"Please don't." The second time his hand connected with her arm and held her still.

The grip was firm but not painful. She could shirk out of it without trouble. She went for the threat instead and glared at his fingers. "Let go of me right now or you will lose those."

"We're going back to your place, getting a bag and you're moving in with me."

Her mouth dropped open. She felt it and couldn't stop it. Couldn't form a sentence either. It took her a full thirty seconds and several scowls at people walking by them with obvious plans on eavesdropping, to kick-start her brain again.

She leaned in and forced her scream into a rough whisper. "Are you on medication or something? I mean, if there's a reason for these personality swings, just tell me because I'm starting to get dizzy."

"Your visit came at the wrong time upstairs."

No way was she accepting that lame excuse. "Try again."

"What?" He frowned, as if her not falling at his feet and accepting his strange explanation amounted to an absolute shock to his system.

The weasel.

"You were purposely trying to piss me off up there and get me to stay away from you." Reliving the memory now had her temper spiking and a headache pulsing at her temples.

"I wasn't—"

"You have ten seconds to tell me something believable before I start screaming." She started the mental countdown as she wrestled her thumping heart rate back under control.

"The truth?"

"It better be. Between tripping over your ex, who still seems more welcome in your office than I do, and dealing with your mood swings, I'm getting very frustrated." And that was the understatement of the century. Kyra had passed frustrated and slow burn yesterday. She was headed full speed for fury territory.

His hand dropped from her arm. "Do you want out?"

"Of what?"

"Us." His voice wavered.

She thought she heard a new tone. Pain maybe. Worry definitely. "You're asking about being out. Am I even in?"

"So far in I can't see straight."

No hesitation. Simple and heartfelt, she felt the vow to her soul. He managed to rescue them from the edge of destruction in less than ten words. They'd turned a corner and she didn't even know if he realized it yet.

"Why do you want me to get a bag?" The request threw her. It was so far from any conversation they ever had. It lived up to every dream, but she dealt in reality and she needed to understand the one he currently operated in.

"I need you to move in. I can explain why later."

"Can?"

"Will." He lifted her hand and kissed her knuckles. "I promise."

That was much better. Not so clear that she should forgive and forget, but enough to get them out of the public eye and to his house. "Come on then."

"Where?"

Blowing out a shaky voice, she ignored the people watching and what the gesture meant and slid her hand under his elbow. "I'm getting the overnight bag and then you will hand me a key to your place so I don't feel like a guest when I stay there. After that you will explain to me why you keep acting like a douche."

The tension drained from his face. "I can do that."

She was betting everything on that. "Let's go."

Bast never appreciated make-up sex until right now.

He tipped his head back against the headboard and fell into the sensation of having Kyra over him, riding his cock. She lifted her body up and down as she pressed her knees tighter against his hips.

The bed thumped as she came down, sheathing him and sending his breathing into a speeding race.

"You feel so good." He pushed the words out as his muscles tensed, teetering on the edge of release.

"I love this position." Her body bucked on top of him. With each plunge, she took him deeper.

"You are not alone." Her enthusiasm made every position his favorite. But this one almost put her in a trance. Her lower body moved as if a song played in her head. She didn't hold back. She went after what she wanted and brought him right along with her.

"Move faster." He didn't beg but he stood right on the verge.

She tightened around him, clamping down until he had to grind his teeth together to keep from coming. Wanting her with him, he slid his fingers over her stomach then down. His thumb slipped over her clit, rubbing in time with their thrusts.

Fingernails dug into his shoulders and pinched his skin. Those sexy rumbling noises at the back of her throat grew louder. She was so close. He could see it in every line of her taut body and feel it in the shudder moving through her.

A hand shifted to her lower back as he guided her down, swallowing every inch of him inside her. He picked up the speed, lifting his hips and meeting her as she fell. Her breasts bounced in front of his face and he didn't waste the opportunity. Bending down, he slipped a nipple between his lips. Rolled it over his tongue.

Sucking, kissing, he licked her until she gasped and grabbed the back of his head in her palms. "Sebastian, yes."

The cries spurred him on. He brought her body down even closer to his. Not letting even a whiff of air pass between them. "Squeeze me harder."

Her head fell back as her thighs stiffened. "I can't take much more of this."

"You can." His hand brushed up and down her back, under her hair, coaxing her to lean forward and take him deeper.

"Make me come."

His heart leapt. Hearing dirty words roll off her tongue took him to a place where control failed him. "Almost there."

Leaning down, she pushed him into her again as her mouth covered his. She kissed him long and hard until he couldn't breathe. Couldn't see.

When she lifted her head, she whispered against his mouth. "I need to come."

This time he couldn't deny her. Didn't want to hold her back for one more second. "God, yes."

He slipped his hand into her hair and held her close for another kiss. Caught her soft moan with his mouth. One last time, she slipped over him then came down hard. The mix of friction with the touches and tasting set her body trembling. She clenched against him and her body pulsed.

Then she couldn't stop moving. Her chest, her legs. Those hands. He held her through the orgasm and watched her as it pummeled her. Seeing her go wild with need had to be the damn sexiest thing ever.

Now, his turn. When he came, it hit him with a knockout punch that had him wrapping his arms around her and pulling her down against his chest. With his face in her soft hair, inhaling the scent of her shampoo, he let go, pumping into her until his muscles turned weak.

Their breathing mixed and the thundering in his chest matched the pounding he heard in hers. He held on to her hips because he worried if he let go for even a second she'd come to her senses and run. The things he put her through over the last few days . . . there was no excuse.

Yeah, he could argue about keeping her safe and not wanting to hurt her. Truth was he fought an internal battle to keep her at a distance and every day he lost a little more ground. Realizing it was one thing. Living through it made him lash out, and she kept wandering directly into the firing line.

She turned her head and kissed his neck. "Okay, now explain."

The serious tone didn't match with the groaning of a second ago. "What?"

"Nice try. Having sex doesn't make me lose my memory." She sat up.

He was the one groaning then. Being inside her and feeling her all around him didn't help his concentration one bit. But he couldn't put this off another second.

Knowing that and knowing what to say turned out to be two different things. "I'm working on a case that has some danger associated with it—"

"What kind?" She snapped out the question as her hands settled on his shoulders.

"Let me finish."

She talked right over him. "You sit in a room and talk all day. How is that dangerous?"

His ego took a hit and he came out swinging. "I do a bit more than that."

He kept his voice calm and smoothed his palms over her in an effort to keep the talk from blowing into something he couldn't control. There were limits to what he could say. Things it was safer for her not to know and things his job didn't allow him to tell her.

"No, I mean that's how I need to think of it. You sitting there, all safe in your sexy suit. No danger except from being hit by falling pens."

He wanted to spend a few minutes on the "sexy suit" part but pushed ahead. Better to get it all out and analyzed. Then he could concentrate on rolling her over and taking her again. "Usually that's the case, but sometimes I deal in high-profile cases where serious secrets are involved."

She made a face as if she'd tasted something rotten. "Spy shit."

This is what happened with smart women. They cut through the crap and found the truth. In this case, hitting reality head-on only increased the danger. "Not necessarily."

Her dramatic sigh let him know she was not impressed with his verbal sparring. "I know about Becca's old job."

"How much?" Bast would bet she only knew a fraction, those things Becca could say without scaring people, which only took up a page or two of her massive CIA file.

"Enough to know she could probably kill a grown man with her pinkie."

Bast thought Becca might not need even that much pressure to take a grown man down. "You're about right."

Kyra slipped her fingers through his hair and touched the piece of his glasses that sat over his ear. "So, what's the danger?"

"I'm negotiating a deal for a person with a specific type of job."

She moved from sighing to an eye roll. "Again, spy."

"Fine. Use that word." With her tenacity and stubbornness, it was easier to let it go and move on. "And there might be some people who don't want the deal done this way."

"And you could be hurt." She skimmed her other hand over his chest.

She touched him, caressing and petting. It was as if she needed the closeness to be sure his heart still ticked. He doubted she realized how she kept touching him without breaking contact. But he knew. Knew and loved it.

"The chances are remote, but I got to thinking if someone came looking for me, they might find you." And that was the one scenario he could not tolerate. Would not allow.

She frowned. "This is one of those push-me-away-for-my-own-good type things?"

"Yes."

She shook her head. "Oh, you adorable, misguided, old-fashioned sweetheart."

Okay, not what he expected. "I liked some of those words but not others."

"Sebastian, my father is a criminal. My brother used to work as Jarrett's enforcer to collect overdue loans. I know violence. I was raised with it and it bubbles all around me."

"I don't want it to."

"I know, and that's sweet, but I'm not a naïve girl in need of constant protecting. I definitely don't want to be shielded from the truth." She shifted on his lap, easing even closer as her mouth brushed over his cheek.

He caught her hips to keep them from zooming right past talk to making love again. "I know how strong and smart you are, but the people in this case use guns and bombs."

She pulled back and stared at him. "Talk about needing protection, you're a lawyer. I don't want you involved in this."

He didn't want her scared and even now worry thrummed off her. "I don't know how much of a problem this is, but I didn't want to take the chance."

"So you tried to send me away for my own good."

There was no use denying since she absolutely understood. "Yes."

"Don't." She put a finger over his lips. "If there's danger, I want to be here, with you."

He pulled her hand away and held it in his. "I want you safe."

She skimmed her fingertips across his forehead. Picked his glasses off and gave a small throw to land them on the bedside table.

Then she turned back to him with heat in her eyes and a voice dripping with need. "I want you."

That fast heat rushed through him. It ignited and flamed over everything. Wiped out every thought of sensible conversation and security.

"Again?"

She wrapped her arms around his neck. "Still."

Not needing another hint, he took charge. Hugging her close, her rolled to the side and slipped her under him. He stared down into those sexy eyes and got lost.

In his head, the running stopped. The haze cleared and he got it. For a second, they made sense. Them together. Forget the age difference and how much easier life would be for her if she found a guy without a ton of baggage. He was falling and he wanted her right there with him during the ride down.

"This time," he stopped to kiss her. "I get to be on top."

"Also a favorite."

He laughed at how determined she looked. "Is there a position you don't like?"

"No."

TWENTY-SEVEN

The next morning Bast sat in his desk chair and prepared for a long-overdue confrontation. When he got the call, he cleared an hour off his schedule. He couldn't afford the time, but this had to happen. He owed his friend this much.

Wade didn't bother to sit down. He stood ramrod straight and perfectly still on the other side of the desk. Looking every bit of the formidable opponent and man who once kept Jarrett's clients in line through intimidation, he stared Bast down.

"How long have we known each other?" No fanfare or buildup. Wade launched right into the topic that clearly had him in its grip.

"I'm guessing this is the talk."

"She's my baby sister."

"I know." Bast didn't have siblings, but he got it. Wade spent his life protecting Kyra. Getting her out of her father's life and helping her when she'd allow it. They shared a bond and a joint life experience Bast would never understand. "Did Becca tell you?"

Wade's eyes narrowed. "She knows?"

"She figured it out early."

"I don't want to know how." Wade wiped a hand over his mouth. "What are you doing with Kyra?"

Bast couldn't spell it out. There were some things a brother didn't need to know about his sister's sex life. But her safety was a different issue. "She's staying at my house, with me, because of the Natalie situation. I wanted Kyra close to make sure she's safe."

"Hold up." Wade's voice turned deadly quiet. Filled with a vibrating fury. "She's living with you?"

That's what he got for assuming Wade had worked through all the facts. Bast wanted to kick his own ass over the fumbling delivery. "It just happened."

"This just gets better and better."

"She's there for now and for however long she needs to be." The words didn't sound right to Bast's ears. Didn't sit right inside of him. They made her sound temporary. His brain said that was the right answer but for once he wanted to turn that side of him off.

"She can move in to my place." Wade held up a hand. "Done."

"I want her with me." The truth in five simple words. Bast had tried to fight it, but there it was. "I'm not fooling around with her safety and her staying with me is not up for debate."

"I'm going to let the whole issuing-demands thing slide for a second."

Bast fought the urge to stand up. He grabbed onto the armrests and dug in for leverage. Having Wade looming right there came off as a power play. Bast guessed that's what Wade was going for and pretended not to buy into it.

"I'm not backing down on this." Keeping her close meant everything—his sanity, his happiness—and Bast would not forfeit that. Not yet. The day would come, probably too soon, where he needed to let her go and finish finding out who she was and what she wanted. He'd prepare for that day later. Not now.

Wade finally moved. Put his hands on his hips but kept his laser-like focus directed on Bast. "What's the plan here?"

"I don't a hundred percent know."

"That's not comforting."

But it was the truth and Bast didn't have anything else to offer at that moment. "I'm trying to be honest."

"Is she in love with you?" Wade kept staring, intense and still.

Bast shifted in his chair and stopped when he realized his actions bordered on squirming. The topic had anxiety welling in his chest. A churning and winding he tried to loosen with deep breaths. "You'd have to ask her."

"I'm asking you, Bast."

He had no idea how to put his feelings into words. He barely knew how to deal with any of what happened over the last two weeks, and had screwed up so much over the last few days. So he went with the one thing he knew to be fact. "This isn't a game for me and it's not casual."

"But it started out that way."

Despite what the Royer siblings thought, some things should remain private. "Do you really want to know the details of my personal relationship with your sister?"

"I want to know you're not fucking around with her." Wade's voice increased until he yelled the last two words. "Because, despite the fact I consider you a friend, I will kill you if you hurt her."

"That's fair."

"And?"

"I care about her." Bast forced his fingers to unclench from the armrests. The tension running through him tightened every muscle. "I know I'm the wrong guy for her but—"

"Why?" The expression on Wade's face matched the confusion in his voice.

"What?"

"Why are you wrong for her?"

The list spanned pages. She deserved younger, more available, less burdened. Hell, he was surprised Wade wasn't standing there reading off the cons and calling him a dirty old man.

Bast went with the most obvious. "My history."

"Come on." Wade shook his head. "Fuck, Bast. If you think that matters, spend some time in my family tree. It will scare the hell out of you."

"You and Kyra are not your father."

"Her father. I'm not blood-related to the man." Wade hesitated. He looked ready to say something but it took more than a few seconds to spit it out. "I thought you'd be worried that her background didn't match yours. That she wouldn't fit in your world."

"I don't care about that." Bast was shocked Wade thought it might. Fact was the whole "right family" bullshit never registered with Bast. Never would.

"Then what are you talking about?"

Wade sounded like his sister. They both wrote off the concerns about his reputation and his past, and Bast didn't understand why. "I keep thinking she'd be happier with some guy from business school."

"My sister tends to know what she wants. I'm not totally sure why she wants you or when that started, but trying to push her off on some random guy is just plain stupid. And, unless I'm reading the look on your face wrong, you don't want her with anyone else."

"I can't tell what you want me to do here." Bast's cell buzzed on his desk but he ignored it. This was too important. "Not that I'm going to blindly follow, because I'm not."

Wade's shoulders fell as he exhaled. "Don't hurt her and we'll be fine."

No death threats. No "find someone else" warnings. Just a normal man-to-man statement that suggested Wade gave his blessing. "That's good enough for you?"

"I don't like the idea of any guy sleeping with my sister." Wade made a hissing sound as he visibly shivered. "But at least with you I know what she's getting."

"Which is?" Bast had to ask because he honestly wasn't sure what Kyra got out of this deal other than his sometimes surly attitude and constant confusion and doubt.

"Someone I can tolerate."

"Thanks." With Wade, Bast figured that was as good as he'd ever get. It qualified as acceptance and Bast didn't downplay how important that was.

"I'll still kill you if you fuck this up."

As far as Bast could tell he'd have to stand in line behind Becca and Jarrett. "Understood."

"I'll go."

Bast waited until Wade almost reached the door. "About Eli."

"Not a topic that's on the table." But Wade turned around. Walked back to the desk. Listened without storming off.

He didn't look open to a long conversation, so Bast planted the seed fast. "So, you just wanted to try a preacher's son and move on?"

"What are you talking about?"

Just as Bast suspected. Eli didn't share. "His messed-up background. Almost makes yours seem normal."

"How do you know—"

"Natalie filled me in." Bast had seen the CIA file on Eli. The guy was such an easy mark for a clandestine organization. He had survival skills, no ties and a heap of anger that needed directing. "The guy was a minister who got kicked out of every legitimate church and took his message of hate on the road. I try to imagine Elijah living in a tent, listening to his father spout off on how gay people should be burned alive."

"That's . . . okay, awful." Wade closed his eyes for a second while he rubbed his forehead. "But at some point you grow up and put all of that bullshit aside."

"I'm a pretty smart guy and my past impacts me every single day." Bast eased back into his chair. "I can see where Eli can't shrug his off and go just be happy."

"Are you matchmaking?"

"Just laying out some facts I thought you might want to know before you fully move on." If everyone was going to mess around in *his* love life, Bast could return the favor.

"Easier said than done."

"Maybe there's a reason it's so hard."

When Bast's cell buzzed again Wade gestured toward it with a head nod. "Someone wants your attention."

"Good job getting out of the conversation." Bast first saw Eli's name on the screen. "Weird."

"What?"

"A call from Eli." And he wasn't the frantic type. If he kept calling then something was very wrong.

"Where is he?"

The facts clicked into place. The most important one flashed across Bast's brain and had him up and out of his chair. "At my house with Kyra."

"I'll drive." Wade was already headed for the door.

Kyra got to Bast's front door and entered the alarm code. Fumbling for the right key came next. Just as she got it out, she felt someone behind her. Bast would say her name. Eli would call out. No, this was someone who shouldn't be here.

Wrapping her fingers around her key, she spun around ready to attack. And scream. In this neighborhood a bone-chilling scream would stand out.

Her father's feral smile stopped her. "You've been ignoring my calls but it looks like you did very good, girl."

His presence, so out of context, threw her off stride. She held on to the doorknob for balance as she glanced up and down the street. "What are you doing here?"

"Checking out your new digs." He looked up the two stories of Bast's town house and whistled. "Fancy. Lots of money in this part of town."

'How did you know I moved in?" He couldn't know. She'd only just packed a bag.

Her father turned and pointed toward the beat-up black sedan in the street. Kyra didn't know the man leaning against the door but the face of the woman standing next to him chilled her.

"Your friend Gena." Her father nodded. "Lovely girl. Very loyal to you."

It couldn't be. They met at the apartment complex. Shared meals and talked about men. There was no way Gena worked for her dad. "I don't understand."

"She wouldn't give up any information on you." Her father's smile turned feral and sick. "And I asked so nicely, too."

Fear washed through Kyra. The thought of Gena as collateral damage had Kyra struggling to find her cell. "What did you do to her?"

"Calm down, girl." He pointed a few blocks down to where Gena stood, being held by some man. "She's fine."

Gen rushed forward and the man let her go. "Kyra, please understand. I didn't know he was following me."

"Your work is done, so shut up." Her father motioned for the man to move over and block Gena's view.

"Let her go." Kyra fought to keep the shaking out of her voice. "Right now."

"You don't issue orders, but if you let me in she can just wait out here on the sidewalk, nice and safe." Her father leaned in. "It's either that or I'll make a scene right here on your new boyfriend's front porch. We both know that will mess up your cozy setup and get you kicked out. A man like Sebastian Jameson has had enough bad press without you adding more."

Still reeling and her emotions in a whirl, Kyra could barely keep on her feet. Her world spun around her and she wanted to throw up.

But she had to get him out of there. "This isn't a setup."

"I'm not complaining. You did nice this time." Her father glanced down at the keys in her hand. "Now, open the door."

"Gena, I'll be right back." Kyra moved without thinking. Opened the door and brought the filth right into Bast's entryway. Her stomach lurched with each step but she had to focus. Had to think.

She turned around. The move put her body in front of her father's and kept him from roaming through the impressive downstairs rooms. "Bast isn't part of a scam."

"I always said if you concentrated and used some of those gifts God gave you, you'd do some fine work." Her father walked around the two-story entry and peeked up the staircase. "Look at this place."

"I'm not working with you. I'm not conning Bast." She repeated the refrain, her voice wobbling with anger.

"Calm down, girl."

The front door opened with a click. A warning sounded on the alarm, but Eli punched in the code before walking over to stand between her and her father. "Kyra, are you okay?"

"Who's this?" Her father looked Eli up and down.

She tried to block the sound of his voice and concentrate on Eli. She didn't want him in the line of fire, but she knew what he did for a living and he would help her. "I'm fine."

Eli's eyes narrowed. "That not what your friend outside said. She said you needed help in here."

"You heard my girl. You can go." Her father tilted his head, motioning toward the front door.

"I don't think so," Eli said.

"I'm her father."

Eli held his ground. If anything, he widened his stance, making his body seem even more formidable. "I know who you are."

"Is she fucking you, too?"

Eli took a threatening step forward. "What is wrong with you?"

The maneuver worked because her father moved back. The back of his leg hit a small table by the coat closet. "This is family business."

Kyra knew if she didn't put a stop to this, there would be a bloodbath and she would be at fault. She tried reasoning with the one man she knew who was totally immune. "You should go."

"Listen to her," Eli said.

Her father scoffed. Actually spit on the marble tile. "You think you're in charge?"

Eli nodded. "I am."

While she watched, he slipped a gun out of his sleeve. She had no idea he was holding it. And he looked really comfortable aiming it at her father.

The old man smiled as he patted his side. "Look at you with the gun. You think I don't have one?"

Eli didn't even blink. "You think I have only one?"

She didn't know Eli's skill level but she knew her father's ability to cheat and somehow even the playing field. "Elijah, please be careful."

"You father doesn't scare me." Eli's gaze never wavered from her father and that gun stayed steady. "Your son got away from you. Your daughter left. You're a petty criminal with a God complex."

"I don't have a son. I have a waste of a stepson. A loser homo who—"

Eli slammed her father against the wall. Put an elbow against his throat and kept pressing even after he kicked and scraped his shoes on the tile. "Stop talking. I will kill you and not feel anything."

She could see the killing hate in Eli's eyes. Feel his energy bouncing off the walls. She had no doubt he would take her father down. He'd said the wrong thing. Hurting her was bad enough. Going after Wade took Eli to the brink.

She was about to step in, try to calm the situation, when she heard Bast's firm voice. "Eli."

She rushed over to him. Threw her body in front of his, ignoring her brother standing right there and the scene in front of her. "Bast, I can explain."

"He knows the score, girl. He's gotten the goods without paying and now he will."

Bast gave her arms a squeeze as he set her aside and moved to stand right next to Eli. Bast's gaze traveled over her father with his mouth twisted in a look of disdain. "Get the fuck out of my house."

Kyra's attention bounced between the men as tension thickened the air. The standoff stretched on and Eli didn't look one inch closer to backing down. Bast looked ready to unleash his bodyguard.

"Eli, let him go." Wade didn't move from the other side of the room. Didn't have to. At the sound of his voice, Eli dropped his arm.

Her father reached for his throat as coughs doubled him over. When he stood up straight again hate poured off him. "The prodigal son returns."

"You should leave." That was all Wade said. Three words with so much anger.

Kyra had never seen him look more lethal. All dressed in black with a dark mood hovering over him. And that was nothing compared to the rage coloring Bast's cheeks and pulling down the corners of his mouth.

She saw it but her father didn't look even a little impressed with the joint fury aimed in his direction. "Nah. Not happening."

"You have two seconds to get out of my house." Bast stepped in closer, trapping her father with his back against the entry hall wall. "And then you are going to leave Kyra alone. Only talk to her if she calls you. If she feels the urge to have a father-daughter breakfast, you will show up and never talk about scams or jobs or bringing her back into the fold."

She didn't know if Bast believed she set him up. At that moment she didn't care. His deep voice fired off at her father. She'd never seen him this consumed with hate, this determined to make a point. None of it matched who she knew him to be. Now she saw the underlying steel. She got that he had a river of anger he could tap into and it made her believe he could beat her father when so many others had failed.

Her father laughed. "And you, with your prep school background and big suits, are going to make this happen?"

"Yes."

"Son, you don't know anything about the streets. My daughter has been working you and you bought into it. You let her lure you into bed."

She rushed to dispel that idea before it took hold. "That's not true." She reached for Bast but Eli blocked her path.

"You're not understanding me." Bast never broke eye contact with her father. "I don't need Eli's gun or Wade's fists. I don't even need to ask the powerful people I know to step in. Because I'll take you out myself. Don't let the house and the suit and the legal degree fool you. You come near her, you bother her, and I will make your time in prison feel like a fucking birthday party."

Her heart hammered in her ears and her chest. It beat so loud and so strong she didn't know how it didn't echo through the room. "Listen to Bast. He's not kidding."

"You won't let this guy come between us." But her father's

voice lacked conviction. This time his eyes darted and his shoes slid on the floor and he struggled to stay upright.

"Yes, she will." Wade delivered the final comment.

She thought there was only one thing to add. "Get out."

Eli shifted around, keeping his gun up as he guided her father toward the door. "If you step back on this property, I'll assume you're trying to rob the place and shoot you."

Her father looked over Eli's shoulder, directing his hate-filled spew at Wade. "This is your fault. Your fucking influence. She's fine without you around. Always was."

"That's enough." Bast opened the front door.

They were so close to ending this without violence. Kyra tried to get them there. "Listen to him."

Her father scowled. "Your so-called boyfriend."

"The man who will make your life a shitstorm if you don't slink away right now." With that, Bast tugged on the older man's arm and shoved him out the front door.

Her father turned and took one last shot. "This isn't over."

"It feels over." And for the first time, she thought it really did.

Eli waited until the smoke cleared to lower his gun. Unlocking his arms took a second, but he pushed out the rage and let his body come back down. The hit to the shoulder came out of nowhere.

"Hey." Wade stood right in front of Eli, hand out and looking for a fight. "Why didn't you tell me Kyra was living here?"

He had to be fucking kidding. "When would I have done that? You don't return texts or call me back."

Kyra stood next to them. "Guys, really. Not now. My friend is outside and needs help."

"She's fine. I locked her in my apartment and Becca is on the way to take her home." But Kyra was right about the rest. There had been enough heat and stress. Eli backed up a step and nodded. He could go downstairs and—

Wade took another step and got right back in Eli's face. "How about when I was at your house. You had no problem talking when we were in bed."

If Wade wanted a fight, Eli decided to give him one. Forget the audience. Forget their history. Eli had reached the end of his patience. "You left so damn fast after I couldn't tell you anything. Hell you didn't even put your pants on first."

"Kyra is right. This isn't the right time for this," Bast said.

"Then when?" Eli knew his boss was right but the anger erupted and Eli couldn't stop it. "Your sister is dating my boss. It's not my business."

Wade thumped a palm against his chest. "It was my business."

"Then talk to them." Eli's shout ricocheted off the chandelier.

"Everyone stop talking about me like I'm not here." Kyra put a hand on her brother's arm and one on Eli's. "Wade, enough. I am a grown woman and my sex life is not your concern. "

"That makes me want to punch Bast," Wade mumbled.

"Right now I think I could take you," Bast said almost at the same time.

"Eli saved me. He walked in here and made sure I was okay. Maybe instead of yelling and blaming and harboring whatever old grudge you have against him, you should realize you have feelings for him and work them out."

"We aren't talking about my love life." Most of the fury had left Wade's voice but he still stood frozen, as if he could go off again.

Eli understood that part. His anger hung around him like a coat, weighing down everything. The suffocation got to be too much and he headed down the hall and away from the verbal battles.

The last thing he heard was Kyra's voice. "Maybe we should be."

TWENTY-EIGHT

Kyra needed air. She stepped outside as the men talked behind her, taking turns discussing something that didn't matter right then. She was too busy standing on the front steps, watching her father's car speed down the street, narrowly missing two parked cars.

"Kyra."

She heard her name and her gaze shot to the sidewalk over to her left. Gena stood there. Kyra ran down the steps and hugged her. "I am so sorry."

"I can explain." Gena came to the bottom of the steps.

Kyra stopped her with a lift of her hand. "You don't have to. I get it. Get him."

"He showed up. I opened my door and he was there, complaining about you not calling." Gena wiped a tear away. "When he left I used the extra key and went into your apartment."

"Why?"

"To find your boyfriend's address."

"Then you headed over here to warn me." Kyra spent most of her life not trusting people and not having friends. Opening up to

Gena had been so hard and they weren't always on the same page, but they were now.

"I didn't know your father was following me."

Kyra ached for her friend. She could see the anguish on Gena's face and the hurt in her eyes. "That's who he is."

Gena twisted her hands together in front of her. "I'm so sorry."

She looked ready to cry and Kyra couldn't handle that right now. Her insides felt raw and beaten. One more hit and she'd go down. "I'm sorry you got sucked into his net."

"It wasn't your fault." Gena grabbed Kyra's hand. "I would have done anything to make sure you were okay."

Becca pulled up and got out of the car. She didn't say anything or move closer.

Humbled and exhausted, Kyra tried to flash Gena a small smile. "My friend Becca will take you home and stay with you. I'll call to check on you once I get done here."

Gena nodded. "I'll be fine. You do what you need for you."

Kyra wondered what that was, but she no longer wondered if she'd ever have friends because she clearly did.

Bast caught Kyra when she came back in and got to the bottom of the stairs. He'd asked Wade and Eli to give them some space and Wade reluctantly left. Eli stomped off. Bast had no idea where either of them was now, but they could be lurking, which made having a serious conversation with Kyra even more difficult.

Maybe he shouldn't anyway. He was way off his game.

Adrenaline still pounded him. He balled his hands into fists and walked around his entryway. Anything to burn off some of this extra energy. They were headed for a fight and if he started out yelling, she would shut down, so he had to wrestle the energy bursts and gain some control.

He could read her body language and see the showdown coming. Confronting her friend on the front porch only had her shoulders collapsing in farther. But she had to know he never wanted to see her father in his house again. Never wanted to feel the paralyzing fear of not knowing if she was okay. If he was going to be too late getting to her.

"Tell me why you kept this from me." That ate at Bast. The idea they slept together every night, talked all day on the phone, and she couldn't tell him her father had been hounding her. Bast would have stepped in and helped, but she denied him that chance until everything exploded.

"What are you talking about?"

The confused frown was a nice touch but playing stupid didn't suit her. It also sent his temper skyrocketing. "You'd been in touch with your father before today."

"Yes."

"You told me you didn't speak with him." Bast remembered fragments of a conversation about her father, but the bottom line he got was they were not in contact.

"I never said that." When Bast started to argue, she cut him off. "It doesn't matter. The point is he destroys everything he touches."

"True, but that's not good enough, Kyra." The piece she wanted to smooth over did matter and they needed to talk it through.

"He wanted me to set you up. He clearly used Gena and followed her. She could have been hurt." Kyra dropped her head into her hands.

The need to go to her, hold her, bombarded him, threatening to pull him under. But he needed the distance. One touch and they'd never get this out. It would fester. He'd let that happen with Lena and wouldn't do the same with Kyra.

He cleared his throat and tries again. "I'm asking—"

"No." She lifted her head and the devastation was so clear on her face. From the pale skin to the bleak fear in her eyes. "You don't understand how he corrupts every good thing around him. I don't want to talk about him or even think about him. Ever."

Bast went to her then. Lifted his hands to touch her. "I get that but we need closure on this."

She flinched and moved away. "That was about my life. Not about you."

The words sliced through him. Ripped and diced until he expected to see blood on the floor. "Everything about you involves me."

There wasn't a part of his life she didn't touch. Her presence took over his home. He thought about her at work. She had him rushing around during the workday instead of finishing off Natalie's case. No woman had ever distracted him from the job. Until Kyra.

She snorted at him. Made the annoying noise and waved off his words. "Since when?"

"You're living here." He couldn't think of a more obvious example.

"As a convenience. To keep me safe. For you to have an eager sex partner."

"I never said that." Jesus, this had gone upside down and sideways. He walked in wanting to protect her and now they were ripping into each other.

"You keep your distance. You come up with excuses why we can't be together." The life drained out of her. Every bit of life left her face. "You refuse to admit you feel something for me."

The accusation kicked him in the gut. He didn't have a defense, but he did have the truth. "I do."

"What? Can you name it? God knows you're hiding it well."

Eli and Wade hovered somewhere nearby and Bast's nerves still misfired from the incident with her father. Anything he said now would be wrong.

And he didn't know what to say. It was that simple. Wade could give his blessing and Jarrett could offer advice, but Bast wallowed alone in this one. The chance of being with her sat right out in front of him but there were so many reasons not to grab on to it.

He inhaled, trying to force his mind on the right topic and his brain back to reality. "We're talking about your decision to work with your father."

She sat down hard on a step. "Is that what you think this was? Me conning you."

"I didn't say that."

She threw him a wide-eyed glare. "God, how can such a smart man be so damn stupid."

"Name-calling?" He didn't accept that from anyone. "Look, you have the right to be angry."

"Gee, thanks."

"But there are limits." He tried a mental countdown. When that failed, he went back to talking. "Kyra, I am trying to hold back my temper."

"Don't."

"What?"

"Lose it." She stood up, which forced him to take a step back or be on top of her. "Let me know this is getting to you. That the idea of losing me matters even a little."

Losing her. The idea skidded across his brain and he kicked it out again. "You aren't going anywhere."

"Because you say so."

She was slowly driving him insane. She argued and challenged and didn't believe him when he told her she meant something. Maybe scaring her would have some impact. "The danger out there is still very real."

"You are going to dance around this all day, aren't you? You talk about my father and your case so you don't have to discuss the real problem."

Bast felt the conversation slip further out of his grasp. "Which is?"

"How can you not know?"

He needed her to just say it. Whatever it was, spit it out. "Don't play games. I told you I had enough of that with my first marriage."

Anger flooded her face. Her jaw clenched and her cheeks flushed. "I am not your ex. I am not the line of women you fucked after her."

Red fury swam in front of his eyes. "This is suddenly about my sexual past?"

"It's about your refusal to move into the future." She turned and headed up the steps. "When you're ready, let me know."

That fast, panic crashed over his anger, wiping it out. "You cannot leave here."

She didn't even bother to turn around. "My safety. Right. I got it."

TWENTY-NINE

Eli stared at the surveillance equipment in his apartment. He knew Kyra's father had gone and, thanks to Bast's threats and coming face-to-face with the firepower lined up to protect her, might not come back. Still, Eli wanted to be ready.

It also gave him something to concentrate on rather than the tall man looming behind him. Eli knew he should have slammed the door behind him and not let Wade get a foot inside. That would teach him to take one slow.

"I am done fighting with you and being your convenient booty call." Eli didn't look at Wade as he delivered his speech because truth was he'd give in on the latter in a second because his will-power when it came to Wade sucked. "Get out."

"I don't want either of those things."

Eli heard the door click shut and turned around to see Wade still standing there. "Then why are you here?"

Seeing him affected Eli as it always did. His mind went blank and his body got ready. He'd come to appreciate the simple things he had with Wade—watching movies and talking over dinner—but that stance, those shoulders, always put Eli at the ready.

"Why did you protect Kyra?"

"She's a human being." Seemed obvious to Eli but then Wade didn't think too highly of his former lover, so the question shouldn't have been a surprise. Still . . . "How much of a dick do you think I am?"

"Tell me why, Eli?" Wade started walking then. Getting closer as his gaze stayed steady.

"I just told you." Eli felt stalked, hunted. The small space didn't leave a lot of room for maneuvering, and Eli knew he needed distance here.

"We're not doing this dance again."

Eli had no idea what that meant but he forced his body to stop moving. This was his fucking apartment after all. Running struck him as pathetic. "You know what? You should go."

Wade stopped right in front of him, only two feet away. Close enough for the heat to pour off his body and into Eli. "I'm going to ask some questions, Eli, and you're going to answer."

"You think you're in charge?"

Wade talked right over Eli's outburst. Acted like the man in front of him wasn't two seconds away from squirming out of his skin. "Was your father really a preacher?"

Eli froze. "How do you know that?"

"I'll take that as a yes."

"Don't, because calling him that insults religious people. My father hid behind the church until the church booted him then he took his crazy preaching to these weird meetings in the middle of the woods." Memories zoomed through Eli's head. The angry people in town and getting evicted from their house. The tents hidden among the trees and the nightly prayer sessions that spun into hate-filled rages against everything and everyone.

"He knew you were gay."

There was no reason to pretend that awful day didn't happen.

Wade clearly knew something about it and wanted him to bleed, to spill it all and have nothing left. Maybe it was the final punishment.

Fine, Eli would take it then shut the door for good between them. "He walked in on me with another boy when I was a teenager and then kicked me out in a huge display in front of everyone. Happy?"

"Not even a little bit."

A pain seared across Eli's chest. He rubbed his hand over the sore spot but the burning would not go away. "Do I make sense to you now? A fucked-up kid from a fucked-up family."

"You were alone."

"You're there for Kyra. I respect that." Eli envied it. "My siblings scattered after the brain tumor took my dad and my mom ran off."

"Have you tried to contact them?"

They were believers. He was the outcast. "Being gay pretty much ended all hope of a reconciliation."

Wade's intense gaze bored into Eli. "So, you are gay?"

The word mattered so much to Wade. It once condemned Eli, ripped him apart from everything he knew, so he wasn't a fan. "I hate the label."

"Tell me what you feel."

"I . . ." No way could he go there. Exposing his background was one thing. His soul was another. "It doesn't matter."

"Elijah, please."

Eli really looked at Wade then. The pleading in his eyes and pity right there on his face. "Call me whatever you want, but yes, I'm gay. There? Are you fucking satisfied? According to my family I'm doomed, but at least I said the word for you."

Eli needed room. He pushed away from Wade and headed for the hall with no particular destination in mind. He just needed to move. "Now you can go."

"Why did you step in to help Kyra?"

Clearly Wade wanted more. Eli didn't have the energy left to fight. It drained out of him and puddled on the floor at his feet. "Your father was being a dick."

"He's my stepfather, which makes him nothing to me but a nuisance. Now answer the question." Wade closed in. "Why?"

Anxiety pummeled Eli. They stood on the edge of something and he didn't want whatever it was. "I was right there."

"Why, Eli?"

"No." He couldn't take this step. Wade would have the power and the fury and Eli would never survive it.

"I need you to say it."

The words welled up out of nowhere and spilled out of Eli before he could call them back. "For you. Okay? I did it because I love you. Jesus, do you really not know that? I love you and it makes me sick I lost you."

He tried to look away but Wade pushed him against the wall and held him there. "Look at me."

Eli couldn't do it. Couldn't open his eyes and see the smug satisfaction and know he'd failed to hold back the one piece that made him sane. "Let yourself out. I'm done with this."

In the still quiet, fingers brushed over Eli's check. The caress went right through him.

"I love you, too."

Eli's heart stopped and his eyes popped open. "What?"

"All of you. Every fucked-up inch. Every insecure bone." Wade rested his hand against Eli's chin. "From that hot body to that complex brain. Your face. Your temper. All of it."

"Why are you saying this?" This didn't make sense. Eli tried to push him away.

Wade shoved him back against the wall and anchored him there with his long legs. "You want logical and I can't give you that."

"You hate me." He'd said it and showed it every day for more than a month.

"I was furious with you because I felt betrayed. Your words only struck so deep because I gave a shit." Wade flashed a lopsided smile. "Then you were gone and I realized I'd actually been dumb enough to fall for you."

"You can't—"

Wade leaned in. "Look at my face, Elijah. You know I'm telling the truth."

Then Wade's mouth came crashing down. Eli's hand went to Wade's broad back and he grabbed fistfuls of his shirt. Anything to hold him close and have a connection, to believe if only for a second.

The kiss dragged on. A mix of rough and panting. Wade's tongue swept inside and his teeth nipped at Eli's bottom lip. It was hot and sexy and it made Eli hope when he'd long given up on that idea and when he was desperate to protect his sanity and fight the feelings off.

When they finally broke apart, Wade's hand rested against the back of Eli's head and their bodies pressed tight against each other. Eli struggled to breathe as his heart and mind raced. "So, now what?"

"We both stop fighting it." Wade kissed Eli's neck. "I want you to move back to the condo, but I think you need this place. For now. Like the job with Bast, this apartment does something for you."

They'd moved so fast Eli couldn't keep up. "This can't be happening."

'Believe." Wade's fingers went to Eli's fly and the sound of the zipper screeched across the room as Wade lowered it. "Right now I'll settle for going into your bedroom and trying to convince you."

"You want—"

Wade's hand slipped into Eli's shorts and those fingers wrapped around his cock. "To stay all night."

"Here?" Eli couldn't hold on to a single thought. The feel of

Wade's mouth against his ear and his hands all over him had his brain stuttering.

"I plan to spend most nights with you from now on." Wade's big body slipped down until he hit his knees. Tugging on Eli's pants, he had them down to his thighs and his cock free.

"I don't understand any of this."

"Let's try it this way." Wade took Eli in his mouth. Swirled his tongue around the tip of his cock, then plunged down deeper.

Eli flattened his palms against the wall behind him. "Holy shit."

"Seems appropriate after our discussion." Wade chuckled as his hand massaged Eli's balls. "We're going to go into your bedroom and then, after a lot of touching and kissing, and a round or two of me taking your cock into my mouth and sucking you off, I'm going to get on my hands and knees and you're going to push inside me."

Something shifted inside Eli. "This is more than sex. You love me."

Wade looked up as he dragged a hand higher on Eli's chest, opening buttons as he went. "And I plan on doing that forever, so it would be good if you caught up here and we got started."

The unthinkable waited in front of him. This time Eli grabbed it. He might fuck it up later, but at least he'd have this one last chance to get this right. "Any chance we could do the hands-and-knees thing first?"

"I'm happy to let you convince me."

And when Wade lowered his mouth again, Eli decided he didn't care what order they moved in so long as it was forward. "Let's go."

Bast moved around his kitchen in a trance. He listened for any noise from upstairs but the slamming of the guest room door was the last thing he heard.

"Your day sucked." Jarrett stood by the sink with his hands resting on the counter behind him.

"You didn't need to come over here to tell me that. I lived it." Bast didn't have the strength to stand. He pulled out the nearest chair and dropped into it.

"Becca is with Kyra's friend and I wanted to make sure you're okay."

Bast appreciated the check-in. He knew after texting about the run-in with Kyra's father that Jarrett would rush in. The man's friendship was the one dependable thing in Bast's life.

"I walked in and saw Kyra and Eli with a gun on her father. No, I'm not okay." Saying it now, Bast relived it. Every terrible fucking minute.

"I heard you issued a few threats of your own. Always knew a fighter lurked under that suit." Jarrett smiled as he talked.

"Something like that." Bast couldn't recall the words but he guessed Wade called in with a report, or returned to fill Jarrett in. "If Kyra hadn't been standing there I might have killed the guy."

"So, you are in love."

Bast rested an elbow on the table and rolled the empty sugar packet he found there between his fingers. Anything to keep from thinking. "That's a bit of a leap."

"Is it?" Jarrett pulled out the chair across from Bast and sat down. "You started something with her when we both know you have plenty of self-control and wouldn't have if you didn't want to. You moved her in here when you could have stored her at my place. You lost your cool when you found her in trouble."

It sounded so simple when Jarrett spelled it out. Also seemed obvious that the guy he talked about was stupid in love and unable to see straight.

"All true." Bast pressed his hand against the table to keep from fidgeting.

"And you don't think you deserve her. You with your big degrees and financial security and bone-deep decency. You think she can do better."

Didn't take long for Jarrett to drive home his point. Bast got it and knew Jarrett thought the concerns were crap, but they weren't. "She can."

"You are the only one who thinks so."

"You don't—"

"Get it? Yeah, I do." When Bast reached for the sugar packet again, Jarrett moved it out of reach. "Was I this much of a dumbass when it came to Becca?"

Thinking about those days still stunned Bast. He loved Becca with Jarrett now but that early period of reconciliation scared the hell out of him. He worried for Jarrett's sanity every minute. "You were a mess."

"Have you looked in the mirror?"

If he did he'd have to face up to the facts. They rang clear and true all of a sudden. Sitting across from his friend, trying to deny and ignore. None of it worked.

Somehow he'd fallen for Kyra. Young, sexy, bold and fierce. She'd worked her way under his skin until he couldn't think of anything else. "She thinks I believe she was in on her dad's con of me."

"Do you?"

"Of course not." Never, not even for a second. When she mentioned it, his brain had shut down.

"Go tell her that." Jarrett moved the mug and the placemat and every other thing out of Bast's reach. "And while you're at it, stop with the other shit. Drop the first-marriage baggage and take what you want with Kyra. She's good for you. Even I can see that."

Bast leaned back in the chair, ignoring the squeak of the wood joints and facing his best friend. "She's twenty-three."

"And she loves you."

Air hiccupped out of Bast's lungs and he let out something close to a gasp. "How do you know that?"

"Wade told me. Said he saw it in her eyes and now he's worried you're going to fuck this up."

He remembered her face and the way she stomped up those stairs. "I think I already did."

"Then I have two simple words for you, my friend."

"Which are?"

"Fix it." Jarrett shook his head. "Do it before she starts believing your bullshit about her needing someone else. Take it from a guy who lost it all and had to fight to get it back. You don't want that road."

Rage at the imaginary boyfriend swamped Bast. In that second, he saw her holding another guy's hand. Taking him to bed. The back of his head almost blew off. "I want her."

"Then go get her."

THIRTY

A guy couldn't have sex around here without someone pounding on the front door. Elijah mentally ticked that con on the move-in list of his new apartment as he stalked to the front of the apartment. At least in the motel no one tried to bust in. Of course, no sane person would have had sex in those beds either.

A gun in his hand and wearing nothing except an unzipped pair of jeans, he went to the door. One look on the security monitors and he opened the door without checking.

"Bast?"

He kept his head down as he walked in, clearly distracted and lost in thought. "I'm sorry to come here so late."

Wade stepped out of the bedroom. He'd found briefs and his weapon, and that was about it. "What's going on?"

Bast's head popped up and his mouth dropped open. "Oh, shit. I'm sorry."

"It's okay." It was his house, after all, and Eli and Wade had agreed their relationship wasn't a secret. They were going to try to live like normal people now. And as soon as Eli figured out what that meant, he'd do it.

Bast looked from Eli to Wade. "I didn't know you were here. Together, I mean."

"For the record, I plan to be here a lot from now on." Wade put his gun down on the kitchen table and rested a hand against Eli's lower back. "Or I will until I can convince Eli to move back into the condo with me."

This was all so new to Eli. Wade touching him in front of someone else. The comfort of hanging around the house together. The sex, which managed to get hotter each time.

But Eli wanted to walk through this part and get it right, not run. For now, he was going to stay put and live in separate places. Plus, the threat to Natalie, all of them, hadn't gone away yet, so Bast needed him here.

"Congratulations." Bast smiled through whatever was bugging him.

But Eli knew this wasn't a social call. "What's going on?"

Bast waved them off and backed his way to the front door. "It doesn't matter."

"Is my sister safe?" Wade asked as his body stiffened.

"She's fine. She's upstairs." Bast sucked in air through his front teeth. He stopped, then started forward again. "Okay, I actually wanted Eli to help me break into her apartment."

"What the fuck?" Wade's reaction didn't leave much to the imagination. He had the full protective brother going on, right down to the angry stance and yelling.

Eli tried to play it cool but the comment didn't make any sense. "Are you serious?"

There was no amusement left on Wade's face now. "I'd start explaining."

"I need to make a grand gesture to let her know how much she means to me. For that, I need something out of her closet."

Bast's explanation didn't clear up a single thing for Eli.

Wade frowned. "For her, right?"

"Don't be a jackass. Of course."

"And you thought Elijah would get you in?" Wade said the words with a hint of hesitation between each one. "You know what? I'm not even going to ask for more of an explanation."

Eli suspected that was the exact plan. "Good idea."

"I have a key to her place. Take Eli and I'll go upstairs and watch over Kyra."

Bast shook his head. "You don't have to—"

Since the conversation stayed civil and could jump the tracks at any time, Eli stepped in. Hearing Wade and Bast fight over Kyra was not how Eli wanted to spend his evening and Bast was just out of it enough to say the wrong thing and start a battle. "Your excuse for moving her in was to keep her safe. That means she shouldn't be alone. With Wade up there, she won't be."

Bast kept moving around, as if he couldn't stand still. "Fine. Can we go?"

Wade rolled his eyes. "Give me a second to find keys and pants."

He stopped on the way back to the bedroom and circled back. Before Eli knew what was happening, Wade planted a possessive kiss on his mouth. One that staked a claim and made it clear their earlier conversation was not a fluke.

Eli couldn't help but smile. Even managed to ignore Bast's exasperated move-it exhale. "Nice."

Wade winked then took off as he called over his shoulder. "I'll bring you a shirt."

"This is new," Bast said.

When Eli faced Bast again he noticed some of the daze had cleared. "We're going to try again."

Bast cuffed Eli's shoulder. "I'm happy for you."

Despite whatever weirdness was spinning around in Bast's head, Eli knew he meant it. "If I can fix my mess, maybe there's hope for you."

"What makes you think I screwed up?"

The panicked look, the crazed plan, coming to him for help. It was a pretty long list in Eli's view. "I doubt you'd be making a grand gesture otherwise."

"Let's hope it works."

Eli recognized the sound of a man worried he'd gone one step too far. He'd seen the look in the mirror for weeks. He wouldn't wish that on anyone. "For your sake, Bast. I do."

Kyra stared at her empty bag on the middle of Bast's bed and couldn't bring herself to hunt down the few things she brought over and load them in. She decided to sit down when Wade's deep voice cut through the room.

"What are you doing?"

Her insides jumped but she didn't have enough energy to move on the outside. "Packing."

Wade's footsteps thumped as he walked across the hardwood to stand next to her. "You just moved in."

Every muscle ached. She thought even her cells cried out for relief. "You were right."

"About what?"

"We're wrong for each other, me and Bast." Every word dragged out of her. Each one scraped her throat and broke her heart.

"When did I say that?"

She just realized how weird it was to find Wade in Bast's bedroom. She didn't know if Wade had ever even been in this house. "What are you doing here?"

"I was downstairs and thought I'd come up to make sure you're okay after the thing with your father."

That man ruined everything. He showed up and her life blew to hell. He stayed away and she waited and worried he'd slink out of the darkness and show up. There was no peace to be found from being his daughter.

But none of that excused her behavior. "I'm sorry I didn't tell you."

"I know there's more to this story and what's been happening, and we'll sit down and go through it, but my bigger worry right now is you."

Wade offered an emotional way out to this horrible day and she took it. She needed to explain it all, but later. Now was the time for lying.

Kyra tried to take the conversation to a safer topic. "I'll be fine. I have school starting soon and—"

"Kyra, it's me."

She glanced up, ready to ignore the pain pinging around inside her and lighten the mood. Wade's expression had her hesitating. His brow wrinkled in concern and before she could find her last store of control the words came tumbling out of her.

"I messed up and fell in love with him. Guess I am just a naïve schoolgirl." She sat on the edge of the bed and waited for the *I told you so* or something similar. When it didn't come, she looked up again. "Aren't you going to say anything?"

"Come here." When she didn't move, he opened his arms.

But she was already going. She hit his chest and his big arms wrapped around her. The hold, so secure and comfortable, made her think of all the times he'd soothed and calmed her over the years. Their relationship had morphed into something more adult but she still needed him.

Back then she would get upset, be on the verge of crying, and he would make it better. When her father told her he'd been grooming her to be part of his team, she found Wade and begged him to get her out. He didn't hesitate or ask questions. No matter what he once did for a living, he was one of the best men she knew, and through him she met Bast.

"I'm fine." She whispered the words more to convince herself than Wade.

"You said that already."

"I loved him for so long . . . I don't know how to stop."

Wade pulled back and stared down at her. No judgment, just worry in his eyes. "I had no idea before a few days ago."

"Neither did he." For a long time, neither did she. She downplayed it and thought it would go away. As she got older, it grew and when she came up with her plan to work at the club to get to him, her feelings fell into place.

Wade gave her a strangling bear hug then let go. "Tell him. The one thing I learned losing Eli and the shitty weeks since is that being stubborn and maybe even being right don't matter much when you're alone."

Speaking of which. "So, how long are you going to wallow and punish you both?"

"I said I was downstairs, didn't I?" Wade wiggled his eyebrows. "We made up."

She grabbed his hand. "That's great news."

Happiness flowed through her. She loved the idea of Wade finding love and being strong enough to grab the chance.

He eyed her with his "I'm serious here" scowl. "Now it's your turn."

If only Bast were ready and not fighting it with every ounce of strength he possessed. "It's not that easy."

"Yeah, sis. It is. The Kyra I know would make him understand."

She'd tried and she'd failed and . . . he moved her in. He flailed and stumbled but when she tried to separate from him, he held on. He could have sex with any number of women. He already had and likely stored their numbers somewhere. But when he wanted someone beside him at night, he turned to her.

Wade laughed. "Did you work it out?"

Bast had one more chance to get this right. "He's not going to know what hit him."

Bast stood in his bedroom doorway and watched her. She sat on the edge of his bed, staring at her hands and nothing else.

He had to swallow twice to make any sound come out. "Kyra."

She didn't lift her head. Didn't even twitch, making it clear she'd known he waited there. "My plan was to come back here, get my stuff and then call Becca to ask if I could go stay there."

He had to force his muscles not to move. It was either that or jump and risk scaring her. "No."

Kyra glanced up then. "You think you decide?"

"I think I communicate for a living but for some reason I'm having trouble talking with the person who matters most." He hung the clothing bag on the top of the doorframe to his closet.

She watched but didn't ask what he was doing or what he was holding. "Who?"

If she truly didn't know, he deserved the pain he had in his gut all day. "You, Kyra."

"You suck at showing it."

"I know." He walked into the room, approaching slowly and giving her time to get up and scoot away. When she didn't, he sat down next to her, letting the mattress sink and his body roll close to hers. "I never thought you tried to set me up with your father. Not even for a second."

"Seemed like it."

"I was angry because he came to you with this stupid idea and you didn't confide in me." Bast solved problems for a living, found solutions. Yet, when the person he was most desperate to keep safe ignored his skills and went it alone, it fucked him up. His anger made him question everything.

"We're just having sex. Remember?" The sadness wrapped around her voice until that's all he heard.

If anything, that sharp whack in his gut increased. He slipped his hand over hers, thinking touching her might ease the pain. "You know that's not true."

"Do I?" She angled her body so they almost faced each other. "You act like—"

"A douche. An ass. You've called me both and were accurate." He'd used harsher names on the car ride back from her apartment.

"Is this some sort of legal maneuver?"

His massaged her hand and slipped his hand over each finger. "What we have has nothing to do with work."

"You know I told myself sex would be enough. That we'd have some fun . . . but that's never what I wanted." She slipped her hand out from under his. "See, deep down I hoped you'd fall for me because I have been in love with you forever."

He almost slid right off the bed. His foot hit the floor harder than he intended and he kept blinking as his brain tried to catch up. "What?"

Her chest fell on a hard exhale as she stood up and walked over to the closet. She fingered the edge of the clothing bag he'd just hung up. "Yeah, I only recently admitted it to myself, but there you go. I love the way you look, and how you treat people. Most people, not me over the last two days, but usually."

Hope punched through his pain and his heart took off on a speed run. "Kyra—"

"But before that, in those quiet times when we were alone and you'd touch my hair or whisper my name. When you thought I was sleeping but you'd tell me all those things you liked about me. I loved those moments."

Every word she said surprised him. "You heard all that?"

"I hear everything, especially the things you hold back and don't say. The panic, your fear about loving a woman again. Your fear of failing." She squinted up at him. "Not going to deny it?"

No, he was done running. Done fighting. She loved him and he didn't understand it or even fully believe it was possible, but he refused to pretend none of this touched him. "I can't."

"Lena thinks—"

That sucked some of the growing relief right back out of him. "You talked with my ex-wife?"

"She still loves you."

"That's not true." God, he couldn't fight that battle again. His relationship with Lena was long over and he would not invite her presence into the middle of what he shared with Kyra.

"She knows you need someone other than her and she wishes she could be what you need, but she knows she can't." Kyra shrugged. "I felt sorry for her. Then I felt sorry for me."

"Why?"

"Because I don't know if I'm what you need either. She thinks I am but my past and my age scare you."

"Stop." All the arguments tangled together and got confused. She was viewing this all wrong and he had to make her understand. The adrenaline pumping through him said his happiness depended on it. "Listen to me. I don't give a shit about your past. Not at all. And your age . . ."

"I can't fix that."

"It isn't about the number. Well, it was at the beginning until I realized how sexy and smart and mature you are." Now he thought of her as younger and him as the luckiest man in DC. "Your age scares me because I know you should go to school and find a younger guy, one without baggage, who can give you a life without all the crap I drag behind me."

"Are you kidding?"

He slipped his hands over her arms and pulled her in close. "I should let you go, but call me selfish because I don't think I can."

Not, "think" at all. He knew.

Her hand went to the knot on his tie and a sexy glint shone in her eyes. "Bast, to be frank, I've had boys. You know you weren't my first. Not that we're talking numbers here because that can't lead to anything good, but you weren't even my second."

Okay, he'd be fine if they skipped this part. "So?"

"I want a man. You." She went on tiptoes and pressed a soft kiss on the top of his nose. "You with your emotional bullshit and messed-up family. You with your clingy ex-wife and need to rescue everyone. You who panics when things get emotionally close and shoves me away."

Man, she knew him cold. "I won't do that again."

"You will because you're still battling something deep inside. Because you don't think you deserve happiness and to find what you want, but you do."

His hands went to her lower back and her body slid against his. "Tell me what you want."

"I want more than now. I want a chance at forever."

Forever. Exactly what he wanted. "Let me give you that."

She pulled her head back and frowned. "You're even willing to try?"

This was it. He could pivot and use his way with words to get out of plunging straight in, but he didn't want that. He had to put it on the line and hope she'd join him.

She'd said she loved him. She took her risk. Now it was his turn.

"I know this is fast and you're unsure, but I want you to move in. For real, not just because it's safer." His gaze searched hers. "All I can think about is you. When you're not here, I want to go hunt you down and drag you back. It's this strange Neanderthal thing I've never really experienced, but I need you by my side while we work our way through this."

She bit her lower lips as her finger tightened on his tie. "And when you decide it's time to move on?"

"It's not going to happen."

She loosened the knot and pulled the tie free from his shirt. "I'm going to start school and that's going to suck because I hate school and am not good at it. Book stuff doesn't come easy to me."

His brain cells flickered off and a rush of heat pulsed through him. Through it all, he struggled to keep up. She had to know this was about more than sex and he did listen. "Why are you going?"

"Because I managed a store and I know what I really want to do is have the skills to own one." She smiled. "Jarrett helped me figure out what program made sense for me."

"Of course he did."

"He's a good guy." She unfastened one, then another button on Bast's shirt. "So are you."

"Then take a chance on me." He willed her to say yes.

"You're not that big of a risk, except that you might only ever want me for sex."

"I do want sex, but it's much deeper than that." He lifted her off her feet and groaned when she wrapped her legs around his upper thighs. "Do you really not know I'm falling for you? Can you not see it? Feel it?"

With his hands under her ass, he pulled her higher up his body. The kiss came next. A mix of hot and sweet. A promise of more to come.

Before she could say anything, he pushed ahead. "Reality is I'm half in love with you already and falling this fast scares the shit out of me."

She burst out laughing. "So romantic."

"But I want to risk it all. I was trying to do that tonight."

Her laughter faded. "What?"

"There." He turned her around and shuffled over to the clothes bag. "One of your dresses."

"I have no idea what you're talking about."

His confidence tripped. It had seemed like a good idea a half hour ago. Now he worried she'd tag him as a stalker or housebreaker. "I'm sure there are guys who can look at a woman and know her size and buy the right thing—"

"That sounds creepy to me."

"To me, too, so Wade gave me the key to your place and I went over and picked up a dress." As soon as the words were out Bast knew he had fumbled that like he had so much else.

Her eyebrow lifted. "Not creepy at all."

"Point is I wanted you to wear it when we went out on our first official date tomorrow." He pressed her back against the wall. Balanced her there as his hand traveled over her shirt to cup her breast and smile over the feel of her.

"Out with me in public?"

"You want me, you get all of me."

She unbuttoned the rest of her shirt and slipped a hand over his chest. "I can handle that."

"Yeah, well. Wait until you meet my dad."

"He's going to think I'm too young for you."

"Actually, he'll think you're too young for me but the perfect age for him." Bast almost lost his train of thought when her fingers went to his belt. "Dad's an expert on families, having had three of them so far."

Before he could say anything else, she put a hand against his cheek and forced him to stop talking. "I love you."

Three words that scared the hell out of him a few weeks ago now set him free. "And I love you."

"That doesn't sound like a guy who's just falling."

"Wait until I say it a few weeks from now." With every day it would grow and take hold. He already hated being away from her. He couldn't imagine how strong those feelings would be in a month, or even a year. And he planned to stick around and find out.

"I can give you the time you need to be ready for us."

He loved her even more for saying that.

"I don't want time or distance. I want you." He kissed her, long enough to send a message. Short enough to leave room for so much more. "My one and only."

"That's an offer that will make me stay." Her fingers slipped past his waistband and into his briefs. "But you should know that once I dig in, I'm not going to let you go. No divorce, no pushing me away. You get me, only me, forever."

Marriage. A concept he'd pushed aside and decided would never be for him again. Now he wondered. With her, he might be willing to try again.

"Deal." His lips went to her neck and he inhaled the warm scent that lingered there.

"So, this dinner is tomorrow and not tonight, right?" She wrapped her fingers around his cock and moved her hand up and down.

"Yes." It was the only word he could force out.

"Then you know what time it is?"

"I'm hoping you say time for make-up sex." He got her shirt undone and debated the benefits of carrying her to the bed versus taking her against the wall.

She rubbed her thumb over the tip of his cock. When he treated her to a sharp inhale, she did it a second time. "Once again we're on the same wavelength."

Against the wall won. "See, we're perfect for each other."

Her mouth lingered over his. "I'll give you all night to prove it."

And he did.

ABOUT THE AUTHOR

Bestselling and award-winning author **HelenKay Dimon** spent twelve years in the most unromantic career ever—divorce lawyer. After dedicating all that time and effort to helping people terminate relationships, she is thrilled to write romance novels full time. Her books have been featured at *E! Online* and in the *Chicago Tribune*, and she has had two of her books named "Red-Hot Reads" in *Cosmopolitan* magazine. When not writing, she teaches fiction and romance writing at MiraCosta College and UCSD and generally wastes a lot of time watching bad Syfy channel movies.

HelenKay loves to talk with her readers and can be reached through her website, helenkaydimon.com, or her Facebook page, facebook.com/HelenKayDimon.